A Gray Eye Or So
— Complete

by

Frank Frankfort Moore

A Gray Eye Or So — Complete
by Frank Frankfort Moore

ISBN: 978-93-69072-39-2

Published by

DOUBLE 9 BOOKS
2/13-B, Ansari Road
Daryaganj, New Delhi – 110002
info@double9books.com
www.double9books.com
Tel. 011-40042856

ABOUT THE AUTHOR

Frank Frankfort Moore (1855-1931) was an Irish novelist, playwright, and poet. He was a unionist and a Protestant from Belfast, yet his historical fiction during the Home Rule agitation did not shy away from themes of Irish-Catholic dispossession. Moore was born in Limerick but raised in Belfast, where he recalls seeing dragoons, sabres drawn, rushing sectarian riots in the street below his nursery window as his earliest recollection. Moore's father was a successful clockmaker and goldsmith, and the family was well-educated (French and German were both spoken). The elder Moore, however, as a member of the ultra-puritan Open Brethren group, wanted to limit his children's reading to religious and didactic publications. Michael Paget Baxter, the evangelist who recognized Emperor Napoleon III as the Beast in the Book of Revelation, was a frequent visitor. Moore attended the Royal Belfast Academical Institution, where he swiftly learned to reject his father's ideas. He remembered the spread of certain slanderous lyrics titled "Mr. Baxter and The Beast," which "proved" that Baxter himself was the Antichrist. Moore praised Irish scientist John Tyndall's statement of scientific materialism at a British Science Association conference in Belfast in 1874, mocking the angry reaction of local Presbyterian ministers.

CONTENTS

VOLUME 1

CHAPTER I
ON CERTAIN ABSTRACTIONS

I WAS talking about woman in the abstract," said Harold.

The other, whose name was Edmund—his worst enemies had never abbreviated it—smiled, lifted his eyes unto the hills as if in search of something, frowned as if he failed to find it, smiled a cat's-paw of a smile—a momentary crinkle in the region of the eyes—twice his lips parted as if he were about to speak; then he gave a laugh—the laugh of a man who finds that for which he has been searching.

"Woman in the abstract?" said he. "Woman in the abstract? My dear Harold, there is no such thing as woman in the abstract. When you talk about Woman enthusiastically, you are talking about the woman you love; when you talk about Woman cynically, you are talking about the woman who won't love you."

"Maybe your honours never heard tell of Larry O'Leary?" said the Third—for there was a Third, and his name was Brian; his duty was to row the boat, and this duty he interpreted by making now and again an elaborate pretence of rowing, which deceived no one.

"That sounds well," said Harold; "but do you want it to be applied? Do you want a test case of the operation of your epigram—if it is an epigram?"

"A test case?"

"Yes; I have heard you talk cynically about woman upon occasions. Does that mean that you have been unloved by many?"

Again the man called Edmund looked inquiringly up the purple slope of the hill.

"You're a wonderful clever gentleman," said Brian, as if communing with himself, "a wonderful gentleman entirely! Isn't he after casting his eyes at the very spot where old Larry kept his still?"

"No," said Edmund; "I have never spoken cynically of women. To do so would be to speak against my convictions. I have great hope of Woman."

"Yes; our mothers and sisters are women," said Harold. "That makes us hopeful of women. Now we are back in the wholesome regions of the abstract once more, so that we have talked in a circle and are precisely where we started, only that I have heard for the first time that you are hopeful of Woman."

"That's enough for one day," said Edmund.

"Quite," said Harold.

"You must know that in the old days the Excise police looked after the potheen—the Royal Irish does it now," said the Third. "Well, as I say, in the old days there was a reward of five pounds given by the Excisemen for the discovery of a private still. Now Larry had been a regular hero at transforming the innocent smiling pratie into the drink that's the curse of the country, God bless it! But he was too wary a lad for the police, and he rolled keg after keg down the side of Slieve Gorm. At last the worm of his still got worn out—they do wear out after a dozen years or so of stiff work—and people noticed that Larry was wearing out too, just through thinking of where he'd get the three pound ten to buy the new machinery. They tried to cheer him up, and the decent boys was so anxious to give him heart that there wasn't such a thing as a sober man to be found in all the country side. But though the brave fellows did what they could for him, it was no use. He never got within three pound five of the three pound ten that he needed. But just as things was at their worst, they mended. Larry was his old self again, and the word went round that the boys might get sober by degrees.

"Now what did our friend Larry do, if you please, but take his old worn-out still and hide it among the heather of the hill fornenst us—Slieve Glas is its name—and then he goes the same night to the Excise officer, in the queer secret way.

"'I'm in a bad way for money, or it's not me that would be after turning informer,' says he, when he had told the officer that he knew where the still was concealed.

"'That's the worst of you all,' says the officer. 'You'll not inform on principle, but only because you're in need of money.'

"'More's the pity, sir,' says Larry.

"'Where's the still?' says the officer.

"'If I bring you to it,' says Larry, 'it must be kept a dead secret, for the owner is the best friend I have in the world.'

"'You're a nice chap to inform on your best friend,' says the officer.

"'I'll never be able to look at him straight in the face after, and that's the truth,' says Larry.

"Well, your honours, didn't Larry lead the officer and a couple of the Excisemen up the hill in the dark of the early morning, and sure enough they came upon the old still, hid among the heather. It was captured, and Larry got the five pound reward, and was able to buy a brand-new still with the money, besides having thirty shillings to the good in his pocket. After that, was it any wonder that he became one of the greatest informers in the country? By the Powers, he made a neat thing out of the business of leading the officers to his own stills and pocketing the reward. He was thirty shillings to the good every time. Ah, Larry was a boy!"

"So I judge," said the man called Edmund, with an unaffected laugh— he had studied the art of being unaffected. "But you see, it was not of the Man but of the Woman we were talking."

"That's why I thought that the change would be good for your honours," remarked Brian. "When gentlemen that I've out in this boat with me, begin to talk together in a way that has got no sense in it at all, I know that they're talking about a woman, and I tell them the story of Larry O'Leary."

Neither the man called Edmund, nor the man called Harold, talked any more that day upon Woman as a topic.

CHAPTER II
ON A GREAT HOPE

I THINK you remarked that you had great hope of Woman," said Harold, the next day. The boat had drifted once again into the centre of the same scene, and there seemed to be a likelihood of at least two of the boat's company drifting back to the topic of the previous afternoon.

"Yes, you certainly admitted that you had great hope of Woman."

"And so I have. Woman felt, long ago; she is beginning to feel again."

"You don't think that feeling is being educated out of her? I certainly have occasional suspicions that this process is going on. Why, just think of the Stafford girl. She can tell you at a moment's notice the exact difference between an atheist, an infidel, an agnostic, a freethinker, and the Honest Doubter."

"She has been reading modern fiction—that's all. No, I don't think that what is called education makes much difference to a woman. After all, what does this thing called education mean? It simply means that a girl can read all the objectionable passages of the ancient poets without the need of a translation. I have hope of Woman because she is frequently so intensely feminine."

"Maybe you never heard tell of how the Widdy MacDermott's cabin came to be a ruin," said the Third.

"Feeling and femininity will, shall I say, transform woman into our ideal?" said Harold.

"Transform is too strong a word," said Edmund. "And as for our ideal, well, every woman is the ideal of some man for a time."

"And that truth shows not only how lowly is the ideal of some men, but also how unwise it is to attempt to speak of woman in the abstract. I begin to think that what you said yesterday had a grain of truth in it, though it was an epigram."

"The Widdy MacDermott—oh, the Widdy Mac-Dermott," said the Third, as though repeating the burden of a ballad. "They made a pome about her in Irish, that was near as full of nonsense as if it had been in the English. You see when Tim, her husband, went to glory he left the cow behind him, taking thought for the need of his widdy, though she hadn't been a widdy when he was acquainted with her. Well, your honours, the byre was a trifle too near the edge of the bog hole, so that when one end fell out, there wasn't much of the mud walls that stood. Then one blessed morning the childer came running into the cabin to tell their mother that the cow was sitting among the ruins of its home."

"A Marius of the farmyard," remarked Edmund.

"Likely enough, sir. Anyhow, there she sat as melancholy as if she was a Christian. Of course, as the winter was well for'ard it wouldn't do to risk her life by leaving her to wander about the bogs, so they drove her into the cabin—it was a tight fit for her, passing through the door—she could just get in and nothing to spare; but when she was inside it was warm and comfortable that the same cow made the cabin, and the childer were wondering at the end of a month how they could have been such fools as to shiver through the winter while the cow was outside.

"In another month some fine spring days came, and the cabin was a bit close and stuffy with the cow inside, and the widdy herself turned the animal's head to the door and went to drive her out for exercise and ventilation. But the way the beast had been fed and petted told upon her, and by the Powers, if she didn't stick fast in the doorway.

"They leathered her in the cabin and they coaxed her from outside, but it was all of no use. The craythur stood jammed in the door, while the childer crawled in and out of the cabin among her hind legs—the fore legs was half a cow's length outside. That was the situation in the middle of the day, and all the neighbours was standing round giving advice, and calling in to the widdy herself—who, of course, was a prisoner in the cabin—not to lose heart.

"'It's not heart I'm afeard of losing—it's the cow,' says she.

"Well, your honours, the evening was coming on, but no change in the situation of affairs took place, and the people of the country-side was getting used to the appearance of the half cow projecting beyond the door of the cabin, and to think that maybe, after all, it was nothing outside the ordinary course of events, when Barney M'Bratney, who does the carpentering at the Castle, came up the road.

"He took in the situation with the glance of the perfessional man, and says he, 'By the Powers, its a case of the cow or the cabin. Which would ye rather be after losing, Widdy?'

"'The cabin by all means,' says she.

"'You're right, my good woman,' says he. 'Come outside with you.'

"Well, your honours, the kindly neighbours hauled the widdy outside over the back of the cow, and then with a crowbar Barney attacked the walls on both sides of the door. In ten minutes the cow was free, but the cabin was a wreck.

"Of course his lardship built it up again stronger than it ever was, but as he wouldn't make the door wide enough to accommodate the cow—he offered to build a byre for her, but that wasn't the same—he has never been so respected as he was before in the neighbourhood of Ballyboreen."

"That's all very well as a story," said Edmund; "but you see we were talking on the subject of the advantages of the higher education of woman."

"True for you, sir," said Brian. "And if the Widdy MacDermott had been born with eddication would she have let her childer to sleep with the cow?"

"Harold," said Edmund, "there are many side lights upon the general question of the advantages of culture in women."

"And the story of the Widdy MacDermott is one of them?" said Harold.

"When I notice that gentlemen that come out in the boat with me begin to talk on contentious topics, I tell them the story of how the Widdy MacDermott's cabin was wrecked," said Brian.

CHAPTER III
ON HONESTY AND THE WORKING MAN

DON'T you think," remarked Edmund, the next day, as the boat drifted under the great cliffs, and Brian was discharging with great ability his normal duty of resting on his oars. "Don't you think that you should come to business without further delay?"

"Come to business?" said Harold.

"Yes. Two days ago you lured me out in this coracle to make a communication to me that I judged would have some bearing upon your future course of life. You began talking of Woman with a touch of fervour in your voice. You assured me that you were referring only to woman in the abstract, and when I convinced you—I trust I convinced you—that woman in the abstract has no existence, you got frightened—as frightened as a child would be, if the thing that it has always regarded as a doll were to wink suddenly, suggesting that it had an individuality, if not a distinction of its own—that it should no longer be included among the vague generalities of rags and bran. Yesterday you began rather more boldly. The effects of education upon the development of woman, the probability that feeling would survive an intimate acquaintance with Plato in the original. Why not take another onward step today? In short, who is she?"

Harold laughed—perhaps uneasily.

"I'm not without ambition," said he.

"I know that. What form does your ambition take? A colonial judgeship, after ten years of idleness at the bar? A success in literature that shall compensate you for the favourable criticisms of double that period? The ownership of the Derby winner? An American heiress, moving in the best society in Monte Carlo? A co-respondency in brackets with a Countess? All these are the legitimate aspirations of the modern man."

"Co-respondency as a career has, no doubt, much to recommend it to some tastes," said Harold. "It appears to me, however, that it would be easy for an indiscreet advocate to over-estimate its practical value."

"You haven't been thinking about it?"

"You see, I haven't yet met the countess."

"What, then, in heaven's name do you hope for?"

"Well, I would say Parliament, if I could be sure that that came within the rather narrow restrictions which you assigned to my reply. You said 'in heaven's name.'"

"Parliament! Parliament! Great Powers! is it so bad as that with you?"

"I don't say that it is. I may be able to get over this ambition as I've got over others—the stroke oar in the Eight, for instance, the soul of Sarasate, the heart of Miss Polly Floss of the Music Halls. Up to the present, however, I have shown no sign of parting with the surviving ambition of many ambitions."

"I don't say that you're a fool," said the man called Edmund. He did not speak until the long pause, filled up by the great moan of the Atlantic in the distance and the hollow fitful plunge of the waters upon the rocks of the Irish shore, had become awkwardly long. "I can't say that you're a fool."

"That's very good of you, old chap."

"No; I can't conscientiously say that you're a fool."

"Again? This is becoming cloying. If I don't mistake, you yourself do a little in the line I suggest."

"What would be wisdom—comparative wisdom—on my part, might be idiotcy—"

"Comparative idiotcy?"

"Sheer idiotcy, on yours. I have several thousands a year, and I can almost—not quite—but I affirm, almost, afford to talk honestly to the Working man. No candidate for Parliament can quite afford to be honest to the Working man."

"And the Working man returns the compliment, only he works it off on the general public," said Harold.

The other man smiled pityingly upon him—the smile of the professor of anatomy upon the student who identifies a thigh bone—the smile which the *savant* allows himself when brought in contact with a discerner of the obvious.

"No woman is quite frank in her prayers—no politician is quite honest with the Working man."

"Well. I am prepared to be not quite honest with him too."

"You may believe yourself equal even to that; but it's not so easy as it sounds. There is an art in not being quite honest. However, that's a detail."

"I humbly venture so to judge it."

"The main thing is to get returned."

"The main thing is, as you say, to get the money."

"The money?"

"Perhaps I should have said the woman."

"The woman? the money? Ah, that brings us round again in the same circle that we traversed yesterday, and the day before. I begin to perceive."

"I had hope that you would—in time."

"I shouldn't wonder if we heard the Banshee after dark," said the Third.

"You are facing things boldly, my dear Harold," said Edmund.

"What's the use of doing anything else?" inquired Harold. "You know how I am situated."

"I know your father."

"That is enough. He writes to me that he finds it impossible to continue my allowance on its present scale. His expenses are daily increasing, he says. I believe him."

"Too many people believe in him," said Edmund. "I have never been among them."

"But you can easily believe that his expenses are daily increasing."

"Oh, yes, I am easily credulous on that point. Does he go the length of assigning any reason for the increase?"

"It's perfectly preposterous—he has no notion of the responsibilities of fatherhood—of the propriety of its limitations so far as an exchange of confidences is concerned. Why, if it were the other way—if I were to write to tell him that I was in love, I would feel a trifle awkward—I would think it almost indecent to quote poetry—Swinburne—something about crimson mouths."

"I dare say; but your father—"

"He writes to tell me that he is in love."

"In love?"

"Yes, with some—well, some woman."

"Some woman? I wonder if I know her husband." There was a considerable pause.

Brian pointed a ridiculous, hooked forefinger toward a hollow that from beneath resembled a cave, half-way up the precipitous wall of cliffs.

"That's where she comes on certain nights of the year. She stands at the entrance to that cave, and cries for her lover as she cried that night when she came only to find his dead body," said Brian, neutralizing the suggested tragedy in his narrative by keeping exhibited that comical crook in his index finger. "Ay, your honours, it's a quare story of pity." Both his auditors looked first at his face, then at the crook in his finger, and laughed. They declined to believe in the pity of it.

"It is preposterous," said Harold. "He writes to me that he never quite knew before what it was to love. He knows it now, he says, and as it's more expensive than he ever imagined it could be, he's reluctantly compelled to cut down my allowance. Then it is that he begins to talk of the crimson mouth—I fancy it's followed by something about the passion of the fervid South—so like my father, but like no other man in the world. He adds that perhaps one day I may also know 'what'tis to love.'"

"At present, however, he insists on your looking at that form of happiness through another man's eyes? Your father loves, and you are to learn—approximately—what it costs, and pay the expenses."

"That's the situation of the present hour. What am I to do?"

"Marry Helen Craven."

"That's brutally frank, at any rate."

"You see, you're not a working man with a vote. I can afford to be frank with you. Of course, that question which you have asked me is the one that was on your mind two days ago, when you began to talk about what you called 'woman in the abstract.'"

"I dare say it was. We have had two stories from Brian in the meantime."

"My dear Harold, your case is far from being unique. Some of its elements may present new features, but, taken as a whole, it is commonplace. You have ambition, but you have also a father."

"So far I am in line with the commonplace."

"You cannot hope to realize your aims without money, and the only way by which a man can acquire a large amount of money suddenly, is by a deal on the Stock Exchange or at Monte Carlo, or by matrimony. The last is the safest."

"There's no doubt about that. But—"

"Yes, I know what's in your mind. I've read the scene between Captain Absolute and his father in 'The Rivals'—I read countless fictions up to the point where the writers artlessly introduce the same scene, then I throw away the books. With the examples we have all had of the success of the *mariage de convenance* and of the failure of the *mariage d'amour* it is absurd to find fault with the Johnsonian dictum about marriages made by the Lord Chancellor."

"I suppose not," said Harold. "Only I don't quite see why, if Dr. Johnson didn't believe that marriages were made in heaven, there was any necessity for him to run off to the other extreme."

"He merely said, I fancy, that a marriage arranged by the Lord Chancellor was as likely to turn out happily as one that was—well, made in heaven, if you insist on the phrase. Heaven, as a match-maker, has much to learn."

"Then it's settled," said Harold, with an affectation of cynicism that amused his friend and puzzled Brian, who had ears. "I'll have to sacrifice one ambition in order to secure the other."

"I think that you're right," said Edmund. "You're not in love just now—so much is certain."

"Nothing could be more certain," acquiesced Harold, with a laugh. "And now I suppose it is equally certain that I never shall be."

"Nothing of the sort. That cynicism which delights to suggest that marriage is fatal to love, is as false as it is pointless. Let any man keep his eyes open and he will see that marriage is the surest guarantee that exists of the permanence of love."

"Just as an I O U is a guarantee—it's a legal form. The money can be legally demanded."

"You are a trifle obscure in your parallel," remarked Edmund.

"I merely suggested that the marriage ceremony is an I O U for the debt which is love. Oh, this sort of beating about a question and making it the subject of phrases can lead nowhere. Never mind. I believe that, on the whole, the grain of advice which I have acquired out of your bushel of talk, is good, and is destined to bear good fruit. I'll have my career in the world, that my father may learn 'what'tis to love.' My mind is made up. Come, Brian, to the shore!"

"Not till I tell your honour the story of the lovely young Princess Fither," said the boatman, assuming a sentimental expression that was extremely comical.

"Brian, Prince of Storytellers, let it be brief," said Edmund.

"It's to his honour I'm telling this story, not to your honour, Mr. Airey," said Brian. "You've a way of wrinkling up your eyes, I notice, when you speak that word 'love,' and if you don't put your tongue in your cheek when anyone else comes across that word accidental-like, you put your tongue in your cheek when you're alone, and when you think over what has been said."

"Why, you're a student of men as well as an observer of nature, O Prince," laughed Edmund.

"No, I've only eyes and ears," said Brian, in a deprecating tone.

"And a certain skill in narrative," said Harold. "What about the beauteous Princess Fither? What dynasty did she belong to?"

"She belonged to Cashelderg," replied Brian. "A few stones of the ruin may still be seen, if you've any imagination, on the brink of the cliff that's called Carrigorm—you can just perceive its shape above the cove where his lordship's boathouse is built."

"Yes; I see the cliff—just where a castle might at one time have been built. And that's the dynasty that she belonged to?" said Harold.

"The same, sir. And on our side you may still see—always supposing that you have the imagination—"

"Of course, nothing imaginary can be seen without the aid of the imagination."

"You may see the ruins of what might have been Cashel-na-Mara, where the Macnamara held his court—Mac na Mara means Son of the Waves, you must know."

"It's a matter of notoriety," said Edmund.

"The Macnamaras and the Casheldergs were the deadliest of enemies, and hardly a day passed for years—maybe centuries—without some one of the clan getting the better of the other. Maybe that was how the surplus population was kept down in these parts. Anyhow there was no talk, so far as I've heard, of congested districts in them days. Well, sir, it so happened that the Prince of the Macnamaras was a fine, handsome, and brave young fellow, and the Princess Fither of Cashelderg was the most beautiful of Irish women, and that's saying a good deal. As luck would have it, the young people came together. Her boat was lost in a fog one night and drifting upon the sharp rocks beyond the headland. The cries of the poor girl were heard on both sides of the Lough—the blessed Lough where we're now floating— but no one was brave enough to put out to the rescue of the Princess—no one, did I say? Who is it that makes a quick leap off the cliffs into the rolling waters beneath? He fights his way, strong swimmer that he is! through the surge, and, unseen by any eye by reason of the fog, he reaches the Princess's boat. Her cries cease. And a keen arises along the cliffs of Carrigorm, for her friends think that she has been swallowed up in the cruel waves. The keen goes on, but it's sudden changed into a shout of joy; for a noble young figure appears as if by magic on the cliff head, and places the precious burden of her lovely daughter in the arms of her weeping mother, and then vanishes."

"And so the feud was healed, and if they didn't live happy, we may," said Edmund.

"That's all you know about the spirit of an ancient Irish family quarrel," said Brian pityingly. "No, sir. The brave deed of the young Prince only made the quarrel the bitterer. But the young people had fallen in love with each other, and they met in secret in that cave that you see there just above us—the Banshee's Cave, it's called to this day. The lovely Princess put off in her boat night after night, and climbed the cliff face—there was no path in them days—to where her lover was waiting for her in the cave. But at last some wretch unworthy of the name of a man got to learn the secret and told it to the Princess's father. With half-a-dozen of the clan he lay in wait for the young Prince in the cave, and they stabbed him in twelve places with their daggers. And even while they were doing the murder, the song of the Princess was heard, telling her lover that she was coming. She climbed the face of the cliff and with a laugh ran into the trysting-place. She stumbled over the body of her lover. Her father stole out of the darkness of the cave and grasped her by the wrist. Then there rang out over the waters the cry, which still sounds on some nights from a cave—the cry of the girl when she learned the truth—the cry of the girl as, with a superhuman effort, she released herself from her father's iron grasp, and sprang from the head of the cliff you see there above, into the depths of the waters where we're now floating."

There was a pause before Edmund remarked, "Your story of the Montague-Macnamaras and the Capulet-Casheldergs is a sad one, Brian. And you have heard the cry of the young Princess with your own ears, I dare say?"

"That I have, your honour. And it's the story of the young Princess Fither and her lover that I tell to gentlemen that put their tongues in their cheeks when they're alone, and thinking of the way the less knowing ones talk of love and the heart of a woman."

Both Edmund and Harold began to think that perhaps the Irish boatman was a shrewder and a more careful listener than they had given him.

CHAPTER IV
ON FABLES

VERY amusing indeed was Edmund's parody of the boatman's wildly-romantic story. The travesty was composed for the benefit of Miss Craven, and the time of its communication was between the courses of the very excellent dinner which Lord Innisfail had provided for his numerous guests at his picturesque Castle overlooking Lough Suangorm—that magnificent fjord on the West Coast of Ireland. Lord Innisfail was a true Irishman. When he was away from Ireland he was ever longing to be back in it, and when he was in Ireland he was ever trying to get away from it. The result of his patriotism was a residence of a month in Connaught in the autumn, and the rest of the year in Connaught Square or Monte Carlo. He was accustomed to declare—in England—that Ireland and the Irish were magnificent. If this was his conviction, his self-abnegation, displayed by carefully avoiding both, except during a month every year, was all the greater.

And yet no one ever gave him credit for possessing the virtue of self-abnegation.

He declared—in England—that the Irish race was the finest on the face of the earth, and he invariably filled his Castle with Englishmen.

He was idolized by his Irish tenantry, and they occasionally left a few birds for his guests to shoot on his moors during the latter days of August.

Lord Innisfail was a man of about fifty years of age. His wife was forty and looked twenty-five: their daughter was eighteen and looked twenty-four.

Edmund Airey, who was trying to amuse Miss Craven by burlesquing the romance of the Princess Fither, was the representative in Parlament of an English constituency. His father had been in business—some people said on the Stock Exchange, which would be just the opposite. He had, however, died leaving his son a considerable fortune extremely well invested—a fact which tended strongly against the Stock Exchange theory. His son showed no desire to go on the turf or to live within reach to the European gaming-table. If there was any truth in the Stock Exchange theory, this fact tended to weaken the doctrine of heredity.

He had never blustered on the subject of his independence of thought or action. He had attached himself unobtrusively to the Government party on entering Parlament, and he had never occasioned the Whips a moment's anxiety during the three years that had elapsed since the date of his return. He was always found in the Government Lobby in a division, and he was thus regarded by the Ministers as an extremely conscientious man. This is only another way of saying that he was regarded by the Opposition as an extremely unscrupulous man.

His speeches were brief, but each of them contained a phrase which told against the Opposition. He was wise enough to refrain from introducing into any speech so doubtful an auxiliary as argument, in his attempts to convince the Opposition that they were in the wrong. He had the good sense to perceive early in his career that argument goes for nothing in the House of Commons, but that trusted Governments have been turned out of office by a phrase. This power of perception induced him to cultivate the art of phrase-making. His dexterity in this direction had now and again made the Opposition feel uncomfortable; and as making the Opposition feel uncomfortable embodies the whole science of successful party-government in England, it was generally assumed that, if the Opposition could only be kept out of power after the General Election, Edmund Airey would be rewarded by an Under-Secretaryship.

He was a year or two under forty, tall, slender, and so distinguished-looking that some people—they were not his friends—were accustomed to say that it was impossible that he could ever attain to political distinction.

He assured Miss Craven that, sitting in the stern sheets of the boat, idly rocking on the smooth swell that rolled through the Lough from the Atlantic, was by far the most profitable way of spending two hours of the afternoon. Miss Craven doubted if this was a fact. "Where did the profit come in except to the boatman?" she inquired.

Mr. Airey, who knew that Miss Craven was anxious to know if Harold had been of the profitable boating-party, had no idea of allowing his powers of travesty to be concealed by the account, for which the young woman was longing, of Harold and the topics upon which he had conversed. He assured her that it was eminently profitable for anyone interested in comparative mythology, to be made acquainted with the Irish equivalent to the Mantuan fable.

"Fable!" almost shrieked Miss Craven. "Mantuan fable! Do you mean to suggest that there never was a Romeo and Juliet?"

"On the contrary, I mean to say that there have been several," said Mr. Airey. "They exist in all languages. I have come unexpectedly upon them in India, then in Japan, afterwards they turned up, with some delicate Maori variations, in New Zealand when I was there. I might have been prepared for them at such a place as this You know how the modern melodramas are made, Miss Craven?"

"I have read somewhere, but I forget. And you sat alone in the boat smoking, while the boatman droned out his stories?" remarked the young woman, refusing a cold *entrée*.

"I will tell you how the melodramas are made," said Mr. Airey, refusing to be led up to Harold as a topic. "The artist paints several effective pictures of scenery and then one of the collaborateurs—the man who can't write, for want of the grammar, but who knows how far to go with the public—invents the situation to work in with the scenery. Last of all, the man who has grammar—some grammar—fills in the details of the story."

"Really! How interesting! And that's how Shakespeare wrote 'Romeo and Juliet'? What a fund of knowledge you have, Mr. Airey!"

Mr. Airey, by the method of his disclaimer, laid claim to a much larger fund than any that Miss Craven had attributed to him.

"I only meant to suggest that traditional romance is evolved on the same lines," said he, when his deprecatory head-shakes had ceased. "Given the scenic effects of 'Romeo and Juliet,' the romance on the lines of 'Romeo and Juliet' will be forthcoming, if you only wait long enough. When you pay a visit to any romantic glen with a torrent—an amateurish copy of an unknown Salvator Rosa—ask for the 'Lover's Leap' and it will be shown to you."

"I'll try to remember."

"Given, as scenic details, the ruin of a Castle on one side of the Lough, the ruin of a Castle on the other, and the names of the hereditary enemies, the story comes naturally—quite as naturally—not to say overmuch about it—as the story of the melodrama follows the sketch of the scenic effects in the theatre. The transition from Montague to Macnamara—from Capulet to Cashelderg is easy, and there you are."

"And here we are," laughed Miss Craven. "How delightful it is to be able to work out a legend in that way, is it not, Mr. Durdan?" and she turned to a man sitting at her left.

"It's quite delightful, I'm sure," said Mr. Durdan. "But Airey is only adapting the creed of his party to matters of everyday life. What people say about his party is that they make a phrase first and then look out for a policy to hang upon it. Government by phrase is what the country is compelled to submit to."

Mr. Durdan was a prominent member of the Opposition.

CHAPTER V
ON A PERILOUS CAUSEWAY

MISS CRAVEN laughed and watched Mr. Airey searching for a reply beneath the frill of a Neapolitan ice. She did not mean that he should find one. Her aim was that he should talk about Harold Wynne. The dinner had reached its pianissimo passages, so to speak. It was dwindling away into the *marrons glacés* and *fondants* stage, so she had not much time left to her to find out if it was indeed with his friend Edmund Airey that Harold had disappeared every afternoon.

Edmund Airey knew what her aim was. He was a clever man, and he endeavoured to frustrate it. Ten minutes afterwards he was amazed to find that he had told her all that she wanted to know, and something over, for he had told her that Harold was at present greatly interested in the question of the advisability of a man's entering public life by the perilous causeway—the phrase was Edmund Airey's—of matrimony.

As he chose a cigar for himself—for there was a choice even among Lord Innisfail's cigars—he was actually amazed to find that the girl's purpose had been too strong for his resolution. He actually felt as if he had betrayed his friend to the enemy—he actually put the matter in this way in his moment of self-reproach.

Before his cigar was well alight, however, he had become more reasonable in his censorship of his own weakness. An enemy? Why, the young woman was the best friend that Harold Wynne could possibly have. She was young—that is, young enough—she was clever—had she not got the better of Edmund Airey?—and, best of all, she was an heiress.

"The perilous causeway of matrimony"—that was the phrase which had come suddenly into his mind, and, in order to introduce it, he had sent the girl away feeling that she was cleverer than he was.

"The perilous causeway of matrimony," he repeated. "With a handrail of ten thousand a year—there is safety in that."

He looked down the long dining-hall, glistening with silver, to where Harold stood facing the great window, the square of which framed a dim picture of a mountain slope, purple with heather, that had snared the last light of the sunken sun. The sea horizon cut upon the slope not far from its summit, and in that infinity of Western distance there was a dash of drifting crimson.

Harold Wynne stood watching that picture of the mountain with the Atlantic beyond, and Edmund watched him.

There was a good deal of conversation flying about the room. The smokers of cigarettes talked on a topic which they would probably have called Art. The smokers of pipes explained in a circumstantial way, that carried suspicion with it to the ears of all listeners, their splendid failures to secure certain big fish during the day. The smokers of cigars talked of the Horse and the House—mostly of the Horse. There was a rather florid judge present—he had talked himself crimson to the appreciative woman who had sat beside him at dinner, on the subject of the previous racing-season, and now he was talking himself purple on the subject of the future season. He had been at Castle Innisfail for three days, and he had steadily refused to entertain the idea of talking on any other subject than the Horse from the standpoint of a possible backer.

This was the judge, who, during the hearing of a celebrated case a few months before—a case that had involved a reference to an event known as the City and Suburban, inquired if that was the name of a Railway Company. Hearing that it was a race, he asked if it was a horse race or a dog race.

Harold remained on his feet in front of the window, and Edmund remained watching him until the streak of crimson had dwindled to a flaming Rahab thread. The servants entered the room with coffee, and brought out many subtle gleams from the old oak by lighting the candles in the silver sconces.

Every time that the door was opened, the sound of a human voice (female) trying, but with indifferent success, to scale the heights of a song that had been saleable by reason of its suggestions of passion—drawing-room passion—saleable passion—fought its way through the tobacco smoke of the dining-hall. Hearing it fitfully, such men as might have felt inclined to leave half-smoked cigars for the sake of the purer atmosphere of the drawingroom, became resigned to their immediate surroundings.

A whisper had gone round the table while dinner was in progress, that Miss Stafford had promised—some people said threatened—to recite something in the course of the evening. Miss Stafford was a highly-educated young woman. She spoke French, German, Italian and Spanish. This is only another way of saying that she could be uninteresting in four languages. In addition to the ordinary disqualifications of such young women, she recited a little—mostly poems about early childhood, involving a lisp and a pinafore. She wished to do duty as an object lesson of the possibility of combining with an exhaustive knowledge of mathematical formulæ, the strongest instincts of femininity. Mathematics and motherhood were not necessarily opposed to one another, her teachers had assured the world, through the medium of magazine articles. Formulæ and femininity went hand in hand, they endeavoured to prove, through the medium of Miss Stafford's recitations; so she acquired the imaginary lisp of early childhood, and tore a pinafore to shreds in the course of fifteen stanzas.

It was generally understood among men that one of these recitations amply repaid a listener for a careful avoidance of the apartment where it took place.

The threat that had been whispered round the dinner-table formed an excuse for long tarrying in front of the coffee cups and Bénédictine.

"Boys," at length said Lord Innisfail, endeavouring to put on an effective Irish brogue—he thought it was only due to Ireland to put on a month's brogue. "Boys, we'll face it like men. Shall it be said in the days to come that we ran away from a lisp and a pinafore?" Then suddenly remembering that Miss Stafford was his guest, he became grave. "Her father was my friend," he said. "He rode straight. What's the matter with the girl? If she does know all about the binomial-theorem and German philosophy, has she not some redeeming qualities? You needn't tell me that there's not some good in a young woman who commits to memory such stuff as that—that what's its name—the little boy that's run over by a 'bus or something or other and that lisps in consequence about his pap-pa. No, you needn't argue with me. It's extremely kind of her to offer to recite, and I will stand up for her, confound her! And if anyone wants to come round with the Judge and me to the stables while she's reciting, now's the time. Will you take another glass of claret, Wynne?"

"No, thank you," said Harold. "I'm off to the drawing-room."

He followed the men who were straggling into the great square hall where a billiard table occupied an insignificant space. The skeleton of an ancient Irish elk formed a rather more conspicuous object in the hall, and was occasionally found handy for the disposal of hats, rugs, and overcoats.

"She is greatly interested in the Romeo and Juliet story," remarked Edmund, strolling up to him.

"She—who?" asked Harold.

"The girl—the necessary girl. The—let us say, alternative. The—the handrail."

"The handrail?"

"Yes. Oh, I forgot: you were not within hearing. There was something said about the perilous causeway of matrimony."

"And that suggested the handrail idea to you? No better idea ever occurred even to you, O man of many ideas, and of still more numerous phrases."

"She is responsive—she is also clever—she is uncommonly clever—she got the better of me."

"Say no more about her cleverness."

"I will say no more about it. A man cannot go a better way about checking an incipient passion for a young woman than by insisting on her cleverness. We do not take to the clever ones. Our ideal does not include a power of repartee."

"Incipient passion!"

There was a suspicion of bitterness in Harold's voice, as he repeated the words of his friend.

"Incipient passion! I think we had better go into the drawing-room."

They went into the drawing-room.

CHAPTER VI
ON THE INFLUENCE OF AN OCEAN

MISS CRAVEN was sitting on a distant sofa listening, or pretending to listen, which is precisely the same thing, with great earnestness to the discourse of Mr. Durdan, who, besides being an active politician, had a theory upon the question of what Ibsen meant by his "Master Builder."

Harold said a few words to Miss Innisfail, who was trying to damp her mother's hope of getting up a dance in the hall, but Lady Innisfail declined to be suppressed even by her daughter, and had received promises of support for her enterprise in influential quarters. Finding that her mother was likely to succeed, the girl hastened away to entreat one of her friends to play a "piece" on the pianoforte.

She knew that she might safely depend upon the person to whom she applied for this favour, to put a stop to her mother's negotiations. The lady performed in the old style. Under her hands the one instrument discharged the office of several. The volume of sound suggested that produced by the steam orchestra of a switchback railway.

Harold glanced across the room and perceived that, while the performer was tearing notes by the handful and flinging them about the place—up in the air, against the walls—while her hands were worrying the bass notes one moment like rival terrier puppies over a bone, and at other times tickling the treble rather too roughly to be good fun—Miss Craven's companion had not abandoned the hope of making himself audible if not intelligible. He had clearly accepted the challenge thrown down by the performer.

Harold perceived that a man behind him had furtively unlatched one of the windows leading to the terrace, and was escaping by that means, and not alone. From outside came the hearty laughter of the judge telling an open-air story to his host. People looked anxiously toward the window. Harold shook his head as though suggesting that that sort of interruption must be put a stop to at once, and that he was the man to do it.

He went resolutely out through the window.

"'Which was immediately suppressed by the officers of the court,'" said Edmund, in the ear of Lady Innisfail.

He spoke too soon. The judge's laugh rolled along like the breaking of a tidal wave. It was plain that Harold had not gone to remonstrate with the judge.

He had not. He had merely strolled round the terrace to the entrance hall. Here he picked up one of the many caps which were hanging there, and putting it on his head, walked idly away from the castle, hearing only the floating eulogy uttered by the judge of a certain well-known jockey who was, he said, the kindliest and most honourable soul that had ever pulled the favourite.

A longing had come to him to hurry as far as he could from the Castle and its company—they were hateful to him just at that instant. The shocking performance of the woman at the pianoforte, the chatter of his fellow-guests, the delicate way in which his friend Edmund Airey made the most indelicate allusions, the *nisi prius* jocularity of the judge—he turned away from all with a feeling of repulsion.

And yet Lord Innisfail's cook was beyond reproach as an artist.

Harold Wynne had accepted the invitation of Lady Innisfail in cold blood. She had asked him to go to Castle Innisfail for a few weeks in August, adding, "Helen Craven has promised to be among our party. You like her, don't you?"

"Immensely," he had replied.

"I knew it," she had cried, with an enthusiasm that would have shocked her daughter. "I don't want a discordant note at our gathering. If you look coldly on Helen Craven I shall wish that I hadn't asked you; but if you look on her in—well, in the other way, we shall all be happy."

He knew exactly what Lady Innisfail meant to convey. It had been hinted to him before that, as he was presumably desirous of marrying a girl with a considerable amount of money, he could not do better than ask Miss Craven to be his wife. He had then laughed and assured Lady Innisfail that if their happiness depended upon the way he looked upon Miss Craven, it would be his aim to look upon her in any way that Lady Innisfail might suggest.

Well, he had come to Castle Innisfail, and for a week he had given himself up to the vastness of the Western Cliffs—of the Atlantic waves—of the billowy mountains—of the mysterious sunsets. It was impossible to escape from the overwhelming influence of the Atlantic in the region of Castle Innisfail. Its sound seemed to go out to all the ends of the earth. At the Castle there was no speech or language where its voice was not heard. It was a sort of background of sound that had to be arranged for by anyone desirous of expressing any thought or emotion in that region. Even the judge had to take it into consideration upon occasions. He never took into consideration anything less important than an ocean.

For a week the influence of the Atlantic had overwhelmed Harold. He had given himself up to it. He had looked at Miss Craven neither coldly nor in the other way—whatever it was—to which Lady Innisfail had referred as desirable to be adopted by him. Miss Craven had simply not been in his thoughts. Face to face with the Infinite one hesitates to give up one's attention to a question of an income that may be indicated by five figures only.

But at the end of a week, he received a letter from his father, who was Lord Fotheringay, and this letter rang many changes upon the five-figure-income question. The question was more than all the Infinities to Lord Fotheringay, and he suggested as much in writing to his son.

"Miss Craven is all that is desirable," the letter had said. "Of course she is not an American; but one cannot expect everything in this imperfect world. Her money is, I understand, well invested—not in land, thank heaven! She is, in fact, a CERTAINTY, and certainties are becoming rarer every day."

Here the letter went on to refer to some abstract questions of the opera in Italy—it was to the opera in Italy that Lord Fotheringay w as, for the time being, attached. The progress made by one of its ornaments—gifted with a singularly flexible soprano—interested him greatly, and Harold had invariably found that in proportion to the interest taken by his father in the exponents of certain arts—singing, dancing, and the drama—his own allowance was reduced. He knew that his father was not a rich man, for a peer. His income was only a trifle over twelve thousand a year; but he also knew that only for his father's weaknesses, this sum should be sufficient for him to live on with some degree of comfort. The weaknesses, however, were there, and they had to be calculated on. Harold calculated on them;

and after doing the sum in simple subtraction with the sound of the infinite ocean around him, he had asked his friend Edmund Airey to pass a few hours in the boat with him. Edmund had complied for three consecutive afternoons, with the result that, with three ridiculous stories from the Irish boatman, Harold had acquired a certain amount of sound advice from the friend who was in his confidence.

He had made up his mind that, if Miss Craven would marry him, he would endeavour to make her the wife of a distinguished man.

That included everything, did it not?

He felt that he might realize the brilliant future predicted for him by his friends when he was the leader of the party of the hour at Oxford. The theory of the party was—like everything that comes from Oxford—eminently practical. The Regeneration of Humanity by means of Natural Scenery was its foundation. Its advocates proved to their own satisfaction that, in every question of morality and the still more important question of artistic feeling, heredity was not the dominant influence, but natural scenery.

By the party Harold was regarded as the long-looked-for Man—what the world wanted was a Man, they declared, and he was destined to be the Man.

He had travelled a good deal on leaving the University, and in a year he had forgotten that he had ever pretended that he held any theory. A theory he had come to believe to be the paper fortress of the Immature. But the Man—that was a different thing. He hoped that he might yet prove himself to be a man, so that, after all, his friends—they had also ceased to theorize— might not have predicted in vain.

Like many young men without experience, he believed that Parliament was a great power. If anyone had told him that the art of gerrymandering is greater than the art of governing, he would not have known what his informant meant.

His aspirations took the direction of a seat in the House of Commons. In spite of the fact of his being the son of Lord Fotheringay, he believed that he might make his mark in that Assembly. The well-known love of the Voter for social purity—not necessarily in Beer—and his intolerance of idleness—excepting, of course, when it is paid for by an employer—had, he knew, to be counted on. Lord Fotheringay was not, he felt, the ideal of the Working man, but he hoped he might be able to convince the Working man—the Voter—that Lord Fotheringay's most noted characteristics had not descended to his son.

From his concern on this point it will be readily understood how striking a figure was the Voter, in his estimation.

It is not so easy to understand how, with that ideal Voter—that stern unbending moralist—before his eyes, he should feel that there was a great need for him to be possessed of money before offering himself to any constituency. The fact remained, however, that everyone to whom he had confided his Parliamentary aspirations, had assured him at the outset that money had to be secured before a constituency could be reckoned on. His friend Edmund Airey had still further impressed upon him this fact; and now he had made up his mind that his aspirations should not be discouraged through the lack of money.

He would ask Helen Craven that very night if she would have the goodness to marry him.

CHAPTER VII
ON THE ADVANTAGES OF A FULL MOON

WHY the fact of his having made up his mind to ask Miss Craven who, without being an American, still possessed many qualities which are generally accepted as tending to married happiness, should cause him to feel a great longing to leave Castle Innisfail, its occupants, and its occupations behind him for evermore, it is difficult to explain on any rational grounds. That feeling was, however, upon him, and he strode away across the billowy moorland in the direction of the cliffs of the fjord known as Lough Suangorm.

The moon was at its full. It had arisen some little way up the sky and was showering its red gold down the slopes of the two cone-shaped mountains that guard the pass of Lamdhu; the deep glen was flooded with moonlight— Harold could perceive in its hollows such objects as were scarcely visible on the ordinary gray days of the West of Ireland. Then he walked until he was on the brink of the great cliffs overhanging the lough. From the high point on which he stood he could follow all the curves of the lough out to the headlands at its entrance seven miles away. Beyond those headlands the great expanse of sea was glittering splendidly in the moonlight, though the moon had not risen high enough to touch the restless waters at the base of the cl iffs on which he stood. The waters were black as they struggled within their narrow limits and were strangled in the channel. Only a white thread of surf marked the breaking place of the waves upon the cliffs.

He went down the little track, made among the rocks of the steep slope, until he reached the natural cavern that bore the name of the Banshee's Cave.

It was scarcely half-way up the face of the cliff. From that hollow in the rocks the descent to the waters of the lough was sheer; but the cave was easily accessible by a zig-zag path leading up from a small ledge of rocks which, being protected by a reef that started up abruptly half a dozen yards out in the narrow channel, served as a landing place for the fishing boats, of which there were several owned in the tiny village of Carrigorm.

He stood at the entrance to the cavern, thinking, not upon the scene which, according to the boatman's story, had been enacted at the place several hundreds—perhaps thousands (the chronology of Irish legends is vague)—of years before, but upon his own prospects.

"It is done," he said, looking the opposite cliffs straight in the face, as though they were Voters—(candidates usually look at the Voters straight in the face the first time they address them). "It is done; I cast it to the winds—to the seas, that are as indifferent to man's affairs as the winds. I must be content to live without it. The career—that is enough!"

What it was that he meant to cast to the indifference of the seas and the winds was nothing more than a sentiment—a vague feeling that he could not previously get rid of—a feeling that man's life without woman's love was something incomplete and unsatisfactory.

He had had his theory on this subject as well as on others long ago—he had gone the length of embodying it in sonnets.

Was it now to go the way of the other impracticable theories?

He had cherished it for long. If it had not been dear to him he would not have subjected himself to the restriction of the sonnet in writing about it. He would have adopted the commonplace and facile stanza. But a sonnet is a shrine.

He had felt that whatever might happen to him, however disappointed he might become with the world and the things of the world, that great and splendid love was before him, and he felt that to realize it would be to forget all disappointments—to forget all the pangs which the heart of man knows when its hour of disillusion comes.

Love was the reward of the struggle—the deep, sweet draught that refreshes the heart of the toiler, he felt. In whatever direction illusion may lie, love was not in that direction.

That had been his firm belief all his life, and now he was standing at the entrance to the cavern—the cavern that was associated with a story of love stronger than death—and he had just assured himself that he had flung to the seas and the winds all his hopes of that love which had been in his dreams.

"It is gone—it is gone!" he cried, looking down at that narrow part of the lough where the boat had been tumbling during the afternoon.

What had that adviser of his said? He remembered something of his words—something about marriage being a guarantee of love.

Harold laughed grimly as he recalled the words. He knew better. The love that he had looked for was not such as was referred to by his friend Mr. Airey. It was——

But what on earth was the good of trying to recall what it was? The diamonds that Queen Guinevere flung into the river, made just the same splash as common stones would have done under the same circumstances: and the love which he had cherished was, when cast to the winds, no more worthy of being thought precious than the many other ideas which he had happily rid himself of in the course of his walk through the world.

This was how he repressed the thought of his conversation with his friend; and after a while the recollections that he wished to suppress yielded to his methods.

Once more the influences of the place—the spectacle of the infinite mountains, the voice of the infinite sea—asserted themselves as they had done during the first week of his arrival at the Castle. The story of the legendary Prince and Princess came back to him as though it were the embodiment of the influences of the region of romance in the midst of which he was standing.

What had Brian the boatman said? The beautiful girl had crossed the narrow channel of the lough night after night and had climbed the face of the cliffs to her lover at their dizzy trysting-place—the place where he was now standing.

Even while he thought upon the details, as carefully narrated by the boatman, the moon rose high enough to send her rays sweeping over the full length of the lough. For a quarter of an hour a single thin crag of the Slieve Gorm mountains had stood between the moon and the narrowing of the lough. The orb rose over the last thin peak of the crag. The lough through all its sinuous length flashed beneath his eyes like a Malayan crease, and in the waters just below the cliffs which a moment before had been black, he saw a small boat being rowed by a white figure.

"That is the lovely Princess of the story," said he. "She is in white—of course they are all in white, these princesses. It's marvellous what a glint of moonlight can do. It throws a glamour over the essentially commonplace, the same way that—well, that that fancy known as love does upon occasions, otherwise the plain features of a woman would perish from the earth and not be perpetuated. The lumpy daughter of the village who exists simply to show what an artist was Jean François Millet, appears down there to float through the moonlight like the restless spirit of a princess. Is she coming to meet the spirit of her lover at their old trysting-place? Ah, no, she is probably about to convey a pannikin of worms for bait to one of the fishing boats."

CHAPTER VIII
ON THE ZIG-ZAG TRACK

HAROLD WYNNE was in one of those moods which struggle for expression through the medium of bitter phrases. He felt that he did well to be cynical. Had he not outlived his belief in love as a necessity of life?

He watched with some degree of interest the progress of the tiny boat rowed by the white figure. He had tried to bring himself to believe that the figure was that of a rough fisher-girl—the fisher-girls are not rough, however, on that part of the coast, and he knew it, only his mood tended to roughness. He tried to make himself believe that a coarse jest shrieked through the moonlight to reach the ears of an appreciatively coarse fisherman, would not be inconsistent with the appearance of that white figure. He felt quite equal to the act of looking beneath the glory and the glamour of the moonlight and of seeing there only the commonplace. He was, he believed, in a mood to revel in the disillusion of a man.

And yet he watched the progress of the boat through the glittering waters, without removing his eyes from it.

The white figure in the boat was so white as to seem the centre of the light that flashed along the ripples and silvered the faces of the cliffs—so much was apparent to him in spite of his mood. As the boat approached the landing-place at the ledge of rock a hundred feet below him, he also perceived that the rower handled her oars in a scientific way unknown to the fisher-girls; and the next thing that he noticed was that she wore a straw hat and a blouse of a pattern that the fisher-girls were powerless to imitate, though the skill was easily available to the Mary Anns and the Matilda Janes who steer (indifferently) perambulators through the London parks. He was so interested in what he saw, that he had not sufficient presence of mind to resume his cynical mutterings, or to inquire if it was possible that the fashion of the year as regards sailor hats and blouses, was a repetition of that of the period of the Princess Fither.

He was more than interested—he was puzzled—as the boat was skilfully run alongside the narrow landing ledge at the foot of the cliffs, and when the girl—the figure was clearly that of a girl—landed—-she wore yachting shoes—carrying with her the boat's painter, which she made fast in a business-like way to one of the iron rings that had been sunk in the face of the cliff for the mooring of the fishing boats, he was more puzzled still. In another moment the girl was toiling up the little zig-zag track that led to the summit of the cliffs.

The track passed within a yard or two of the entrance to the cavern. He thought it advisable to step hack out of the moonlight, so that the girl should not see him. She was doubtless, he thought, on her way to the summit of the cliffs, and she would probably be startled if he were to appear suddenly before her eyes. He took a step or two back into the friendly shadow of the cavern, and waited to hear her footsteps on the track above him.

He waited in vain. She did not take that zigzag track that led to the cliffs above the cave. He heard her jump—it was almost a feat—from the track by which she had ascended, on to a flat rock not a yard from the entrance to the cavern. He shrunk still further back into the darkness, and then there came before the entrance the most entrancing figure of a girl that he had ever seen.

She stood there delightfully out of breath, with the moonlight bringing out every gracious curve in her shape. So he had seen the limelight reveal the graces of a breathless *danseuse*, when taking her "call."

"My dear Prince," said the girl, with many a gasp. "You have treated me very badly. It's a pull—undeniably a pull—up those rocks, and for the third time I have kept my tryst with you, only to be disappointed."

She laughed, and putting a shapely foot—she was by no means careful to conceal her stocking above the ankle—upon a stone, she quietly and in a matter-of-fact way, tied the lace of her yachting shoe.

The stooping was not good for her—he felt that, together with a few other matters incidental to her situation. He waited for the long breath he knew she would draw on straightening herself.

It came. He hoped that her other shoe needed tying; but it did not.

He watched her as she stood there with her back to him. She was sending her eyes out to the Western headlands.

"No, my Prince; on the whole I'm not disappointed," she said. "That picture repays me for my toil by sea and land. What a picture! But what would it be to be here with—with—love!"

That was all she said.

He thought it was quite enough.

She stood there like a statue of white marble set among the black rocks. She was absolutely motionless for some minutes; and then the sigh that fluttered from her lips was, he knew, a different expression altogether from that which had come from her when she had straightened herself on fastening her shoe.

His father was a connoisseur in sighs; Harold did not profess to have the same amount of knowledge on the subject, but still he knew something. He could distinguish roughly on some points incidental to the sigh as a medium of expression.

After that little gasp which was not quite a gasp, she was again silent; then she whispered, but by no means gently, the one word "Idiot!" and in another second she had sent her voice into the still night in a wild musical cry—such a cry as anyone gifted with that imaginative power which Brian had declared to be so necessary for archæological research, might attribute to the Banshee—the White Lady of Irish legends.

She repeated the cry an octave higher and then she executed what is technically known as a "scale" but ended with that same weird cry of the Banshee.

Once again she was breathless. Her blouse was turbulent just below her throat.

"If Brian does not cross himself until he feels more fatigue than he would after a pretence at rowing, I'll never play Banshee again," said the girl. "*Ta, ta, mon Prince; a rivederci.*"

He watched her poise herself for the leap from the rock where she was standing, to the track—her grace was exquisite—it suggested that of the lithe antelope. The leap took her beyond his sight, and he did not venture immediately to a point whence he could regain possession of her with his eyes. But when he heard the sound of her voice singing a snatch of song—it was actually "*L'amour est un oiseau rebelle*"—the Habanera from "Carmen"—he judged that she had reached the second angle of the zig-zag downward, and he took a step into the moonlight.

There she went, lilting the song and keeping time with her feet, until she reached the ledge where the boat was moored. She unfastened the painter, hauled the boat close, and he heard the sound of the plunge of the bows as she jumped on one of the beams, the force of her jump sending the boat far from shore.

She sat for some minutes on the beam amidship, listlessly allowing the boat to drift away from the rocks, then she put out her hands for the oars. Her right hand grasped one, but there was none for the left to grasp. Harold perceived that one of the oars had disappeared.

There was the boat twenty yards from the rock drifting away beyond the control of the girl.

CHAPTER IX
ON THE HELPLESSNESS OF WOMAN

THE girl had shown so much adroitness in the management of the little craft previously, he felt—with deep regret—that she would be quite equal to her present emergency. He was mistaken. She had reached the end of her resources in navigation when she had run the boat alongside the landing place. He saw—with great satisfaction—that with only one oar she was helpless.

What should he do?

That was what he asked himself when he saw her dip her remaining oar into the water and paddle a few strokes, making the boat describe an awkward circle and bringing it perilously close to a jagged point of the reef that did duty as a natural breakwater for the mooring place of the boats. He came to the conclusion that if he allowed her to continue that sort of paddling, she would run the boat on the reef, and he would be morally responsible for the disaster and its consequences, whatever they might be. He had never felt more conscientious than at that moment.

He ran down the track to the landing ledge, but before he had reached the latter, the girl had ceased her efforts and was staring at him, her hands still resting on the oar.

He had an uneasy feeling that he was scarcely so picturesquely breathless as she had been, and this consciousness did not tend to make him fluent as he stood upon the rocky shelf not a foot above the ridges of the silver ripples.

He found himself staring at her, just as she was staring at him.

Quite a minute had passed before he found words to ask her if he could be of any help to her.

"I don't know," she replied, in a tone very different from that in which she had spoken at the entrance to the cavern. "I don't really know. One of the oars must have gone overboard while the boat was moored. I scarcely know what I am to do."

"I'm afraid you're in a bad way!" said he, shaking his head. The change in the girl's tone was very amusing to him. She had become quite demure; but previously, demureness had been in the background. "Yes, I'm afraid your case is a very bad one."

"So bad as that?" she asked.

"Well, perhaps not quite, but still bad enough," said he. "What do you want to do?"

"To get home as soon as possible," she replied, without the pause of a second.

Her tone was expressive. It conveyed to him the notion that she had just asked if he thought that she was an idiot. What could she want to do if not to go home?

"In that case," said he, "I should advise you to take the oar to the sculling place in the centre of the stern. The boat is a stout one and will scull well."

"But I don't know how to scull," said she, in a tone of real distress; "and I don't think I can begin to learn just now."

"There's something in that," said he. "If I were only aboard I could teach you in a short time."

"But—"

She had begun her reply without the delay of a second, but she did not get beyond the one word. He felt that she did not need to do so: it was a sentence by itself.

"Yes," said he, "as you say, I'm not aboard. Shall I get aboard?"

"How could you?" she inquired, brightening up.

"I can swim," he replied.

She laughed.

"The situation is not so desperate as that," she cried.

He also laughed.

They both laughed together.

She stopped suddenly and looked up the cliffs to the Banshee's Cave.

Was she wondering if he had been within hearing when she had been—and not in silence—at the entrance to the cave?

He felt that he had never seen so beautiful a girl. Even making a liberal allowance for that glamour of the moonlight, which he had tried to assure himself was as deceptive as the glamour of love, she was, he felt, the most beautiful girl he had ever seen.

He crushed down every suggestion that came to him as to the best way of helping her out of her difficulty. It was his opportunity.

Then she turned her eyes from the cliff and looked at him again.

There was something imploring in her look.

"Keep up your heart," said he. "Whose boat is that, may I ask?"

"It belongs to a man named Brian—Brian something or other—perhaps O'Donal."

"In that case I think it almost certain that you will find a fishing line in the locker astern—a fishing line and a tin bailer—the line will help you out of the difficulty."

Before he had quite done speaking she was in the stern sheets, groping with one hand in the little locker.

She brought out, first, a small jar of whiskey, secondly, a small pannikin that served a man's purpose when he wished to drink the whiskey in unusually small quantities, and was also handy in bailing out the boat, and, thirdly, a fishing line-wound about a square frame.

She held up the last-named so that Harold might see it.

"I thought it would be there," said he. "Now if you can only cast one end of that line ashore, I will catch it and the boat will be alongside the landing-place in a few minutes. Can you throw?"

She was silent. She examined the hooks on the whale-bone cross-cast.

He laughed again, for he perceived that she was reluctant to boast of the possession of a skill which was denied to all womankind.

"I'll explain to you what you must do," he said. "Cut away the cast of hooks."

"But I have no knife."

"Then I'll throw mine into the bottom of your boat. Look out."

Being a man, he was able to make the knife alight within reasonable distance of the spot at which he aimed. He saw her face brighten as she picked up the implement and, opening it, quickly cut away the cast of hooks.

"Now make fast the leaden sinker to the end of the fishing line, unwind it all from the frame, and then whirl the weight round and sling it ashore— anywhere ashore."

She followed his instructions implicitly, and the leaden weight fled through the air, with the sound of a shell from a mortar.

"Well thrown!" he cried, as it soared above his head; and it was well thrown—so well that it carried overboard every inch of the line and the frame to which it was attached.

"How stupid of me!" she said.

"Of me, you mean," said he. "I should have told you to make it fast. However, no harm is done. I'll recover the weight and send it back to you."

He had no trouble in effecting his purpose. He threw the weight as gently as possible into the bow of the boat, she picked it up, and the line was in her hands as he took in the slack and hauled the boat alongside the shelf of rock.

It cannot have escaped notice that the system of hauling which he adopted had the result of bringing their hands together. They scarcely touched, however.

"Thank you," said she, with profound coldness, when the boat was alongside.

"Your case was not so desperate, after all," he remarked, with just a trifle less frigidity in his tone, though he now knew that she was the most beautiful girl he had ever seen. He had talked of the glamour of moonlight. How could he have been so ridiculous?

"No, my case was not so very desperate," she said. "Thank you so much."

Did she mean to suggest that he should now walk away?

"I can't go, you know, until I am satisfied that your *contretemps* is at an end," said he. "My name is Wynne—Harold Wynne. I am a guest of Lord Innisfail's. I dare say you know him."

"No," she replied. "I know nobody."

"Nobody?"

"Nobody here. Of course I daily hear something about Lord Innisfail and his guests."

"You know Brian—he is somebody—the historian of the region. Did you ever hear the story of the Banshee?"

She looked at him, but he flattered himself that his face told her nothing of what she seemed anxious to know.

"Yes," she said, after a pause. "I do believe that I heard the story of the Banshee—a princess, was she not—a sort of princess—an Irish princess?"

"Strictly Irish. It is said that the cry of the White Lady is sometimes heard even on these nights among the cliffs down which the Princess flung herself."

"Really?" said she, turning her eyes to the sea. "How strange!"

"Strange? well—perhaps. But Brian declares that he has heard the cry with his own ears. I have a friend who says, very coarsely, that if lies were landed property Brian would be the largest holder of real estate in the world."

"Your friend does not understand Brian." There was more than a trace of indignation in her voice. "Brian has imagination—so have all the people about here. I must get home as soon as possible. I thank you very much for your trouble. Goodnight."

"I have had no trouble. Good-night."

He took off his cap, and moved away—to the extent of a single step. She was still standing in the boat.

"By the way," he said, as if the thought had just occurred to him; "do you intend going overland?"

The glamour of the moonlight failed to conceal the troubled look that came to her eyes. He regained the step that he had taken away from her, and remarked, "If you will be good enough to allow me, I will scull you with the one oar to any part of the coast that you may wish to reach. It would be a pleasure to me. I have nothing whatever to do. As a matter of fact, I don't see that you have any choice in the matter."

"I have not," she said gravely. "I was a fool—such a fool! But—the story of the Princess—"

"Pray don't make any confession to me," said he. "If I had not heard the story of the Princess, should I be here either?"

"My name," said she, "is Beatrice Avon. My father's name you may have heard—most people have heard his name, though I'm afraid that not so many have read his books."

"But I have met your father," said he. "If he is Julius Anthony Avon, I met him some years ago. He breakfasted with my tutor at Oxford. I have read all his hooks."

"Oh, come into the boat," she cried with a laugh. "I feel that we have been introduced."

"And so we have," said he, stepping upon the gunwale so as to push off the boat. "Now, where is your best landing place?"

She pointed out to him a white cottage at the entrance to a glen on the opposite coast of the lough, just below the ruins—they could be seen by the imaginative eye—of the Castle of Carrigorm. The cottage was glistening in the moonlight.

"That is where we have been living—my father and I—for the past month," said she. "He is engaged on a new work—a History of Irish Patriotism, and he has begun by compiling a biographical dictionary of Irish Informers. He is making capital progress with it. He has already got to the end of the seventh volume and he has very nearly reached the letter C—oh, yes, he is making rapid progress."

"But why is he at this place? Is he working up the Irish legends as well?"

"It seems that the French landed here some time or other, and that was the beginning of a new era of rebellions. My father is dealing with the period, and means to have his topography strictly accurate."

"Yes," said Harold, "if he carefully avoids everything that he is told in Ireland his book may tend to accuracy."

CHAPTER X
ON SCIENCE AND ART

A BOAT being urged onwards—not very rapidly—by a single oar resting in a hollow in the centre of the stern, and worked from side to side by a man in evening dress, is not a sight of daily occurrence. This may have suggested itself to the girl who was seated on the midship beam; but if she was inclined to laugh, she succeeded in controlling her impulses.

He found that he was more adroit at the science of marine propulsion than he had fancied he was. The boat was making quite too rapid progress for his desires, across the lough.

He asked the girl if she did not think it well that she should become acquainted with at least the scientific principle which formed the basis of the marine propeller. It was extremely unlikely that such an emergency as that which had lately arisen should ever again make a demand upon her resources, but if such were ever to present itself, it might be well for her to be armed to overcome it.

Yes, she said, it was extremely unlikely that she should ever again be so foolish, and she hoped that her father would not be uneasy at her failure to return at the hour at which she had told him to expect her.

He stopped rocking the oar from side to side in order to assure her that she could not possibly be delayed more than a quarter of an hour through the loss of the oar.

She said that she was very glad, and that she really thought that the boat was making more rapid progress with his one oar than it had done in the opposite direction with her two oars.

He began to perceive that his opportunities of making her acquainted with the science of the screw propeller were dwindling. He faced the oar boldly, however, and he felt that he had at least succeeded in showing her how effective was the application of a scientific law to the achievement of his end—assuming that that end was the driving of the boat through the waters.

He was not a fool. He knew very well that there is nothing which so appeals to the interest of a woman as seeing a man do something that she cannot do.

When, after five minutes' work, he turned his head to steer the boat, he found that she was watching him.

She had previously been watching the white glistening cottage, with the light in one window only.

The result of his observation was extremely satisfactory to him. He resumed his toil without a word.

And this was how it happened that the boat made so excellent a passage across the lough.

It was not until the keel grated upon the sand that the girl spoke. She made a splendid leap from the bows, and, turning, asked him if he would care to pay a visit to her father.

He replied that he feared that he might jeopardize the biography of some interesting informer whose name might occur at the close of the letter B. He hoped that he would be allowed to borrow the boat for his return to the cliffs, and to row it back the next day to where it was at the moment he was speaking.

His earnest sculling of the boat had not made all thought for the morrow impracticable. He had been reflecting through the silence, how he might make the chance of meeting once more this girl whose face he had seen for the first time half an hour before.

She had already given him an absurd amount of trouble, she said. The boat was one that she had borrowed from Brian, and Brian could easily row it across next morning.

But he happened to know that Brian was to be in attendance on Mr. Durdan all the next day. Mr. Durdan had come to the West solely for the purpose of studying the Irish question on the spot. He had, consequently, spent all his time, deep-sea fishing.

"So you perceive that there's nothing for it but for me to bring back the boat, Miss Avon," said he.

"You do it so well," she said, with a tone of enthusiasm in her voice. "I never admired anything so much—your sculling, I mean. And perhaps I may learn something about—was it the scientific principle that you were kind enough to offer to teach me?"

"The scientific principle," said he, with an uneasy feeling that the girl had seen through his artifice to prolong the crossing of the lough. "Yes, you certainly should know all about the scientific principle."

"I feel so, indeed. Good-night."

"Good-night," said he, preparing to push the boat off the sand where it had grounded. "Goodnight. By the way, it was only when we were out with Brian in the afternoon that he told us the story of the Princess and her lover. He added that the cry of the White Lady would probably be heard when night came."

"Perhaps you may hear it yet," said she. "Goodnight."

She had run up the sandy beach, before he had pushed off the boat, and she never looked round.

He stood with one foot on the gunwale of the boat in act to push into deep water, thinking that perhaps she might at the last moment look round.

She did not.

He caught another glimpse of her beyond the furze that crowned a ridge of rocks. But she had her face steadfastly set toward the white cottage.

He threw all his weight upon the oar which he was using as a pole, and out the boat shot into the deep water.

"Great heavens!" said Edmund Airey. "Where have you been for the past couple of hours?"

"Where?" repeated Miss Craven in a tone of voice that should only be assumed when the eyes, of the speaker are sparkling. But Miss Craven's eyes were not sparkling. Their strong point was not in that direction. "I'm afraid you must give an account of yourself, Mr. Wynne," she continued. She was standing by the side of Edmund Airey, within the embrace of the mighty antlers of the ancient elk in the hall. The sound of dance music was in the air, and Miss Craven's face was flushed.

"To give an account of myself would be to place myself on a level of dulness with the autobiographers whose reminiscences we yawn over."

"Then give us a chance of yawning," cried Miss Craven.

"You do not need one," said he. "Have you not been for some time by the side of a Member of Parliament?"

"He has been over the cliffs," suggested the Member of Parliament. He was looking at Harold's shoes, which bore tokens of having been ill-treated beyond the usual ill-treatment of shoes with bows of ribbon above the toes.

"Yes," said Harold. "Over the cliffs."

"At the Banshee's Cave, I'm certain," said Miss Craven.

"Yes, at the Banshee's Cave."

"How lovely! And you saw the White Lady?" she continued.

"Yes, I saw the White Lady."

"And you heard her cry at the entrance to the cave?"

"Yes, I heard her cry at the entrance to the cave."

"Nonsense!" said she.

"Utter nonsense!" said he. "I must ask Lady Innisfail to dance."

He crossed the hall to where Lady Innisfail was seated. She was fanning herself and making sparkling replies to the inanities of Mr. Durdan, who stood beside her. She had been engaged in every dance, Harold knew, from the extra gravity of her daughter.

"What does he mean?" Miss Craven asked of Edmund Airey in a low—almost an anxious, tone.

"Mean? Why, to dance with Lady Innisfail. He is a man of determination."

"What does he mean by that nonsense about the Banshee's Cave?"

"Is it nonsense?"

"Of course it is. Does anyone suppose that the legend of the White Lady is anything but nonsense? Didn't you ridicule it at dinner?"

"At dinner; oh, yes: but then you must remember that no one is altogether discreet at dinner. That cold *entrée*—the Russian salad—"

"A good many people are discreet neither at dinner nor after it."

"Our friend Harold, for instance? Oh, I have every confidence in him. I know his mood. I have experienced it myself. I, too, have stood in a sculpturesque attitude and attire, on a rock overhanging a deep sea, and I have been at the point of dressing again without taking the plunge that I meant to take."

"You mean that he—that he—oh, I don't know what you mean."

"I mean that if he had been so fortunate as to come upon you suddenly at the Banshee's Cave or wherever he was to-night, he would have—well, he would have taken the plunge."

He saw the girl's face become slightly roseate in spite of the fact of her being the most self-controlled person whom he had ever met. He perceived that she appreciated his meaning to a shade.

He liked that. A man who is gifted with the power of expressing his ideas in various shades, likes to feel that his power is appreciated. He knew that there are some people who fancy that every question is susceptible of being answered by yea or nay. He hated such people.

"The plunge?" said Miss Craven, with an ingenuousness that confirmed his high estimate of her powers of appreciation. "The plunge? But the Banshee's Cave is a hundred feet above the water."

"But men have taken headers—"

"They have," said she, "and therefore we should finish our waltz."

They did finish their waltz.

CHAPTER XI
ON HEAVEN AND THE LORD CHANCELLOR

MR. DURDAN was explaining something—he usually was explaining something. When he had been a member of the late Government his process of explaining something was generally regarded as a fine effort at mystification. In private his explanations were sometimes intelligible. As Harold entered the room where a straggling breakfast was proceeding— everything except dinner had a tendency to be straggling at Castle Innisfail— Mr. Dur dan was explaining how Brian had been bewildered.

It was a profitable theme, especially for a man who fondly believed that he had the power of reproducing what he imagined to be the Irish brogue of the boatman.

Harold gathered that Mr. Durdan had already had a couple of hours of deep-sea fishing in the boat with Brian—the servants were all the morning carrying into the dining-room plates of fish of his catching (audibly sneered at by the fly-fishers, who considered their supreme failures superior to the hugest successes of the deep-sea fishers).

But the fishing was not to the point. What Mr. Durdan believed to be very much to the point were the "begorras," the "acushlas," the "arrahs" which he tried to make his auditors believe the boatman had uttered in telling him how he had been awakened early in the night by hearing the cry of the Banshee.

Every phrase supposed to have been employed by the boatman was reproduced by the narrator; and his auditors glanced meaningly at one another. It would have required a great deal of convincing to make them fancy for a moment that the language of Brian consisted of an imaginary Irish exclamation preceding a purely Cockney—occasionally Yorkshire— idiom. But the narrator continued his story, and seemed convinced that his voice was an exact reproduction of Brian's brogue.

Harold thought that he would try a little of something that was not fish—he scarcely minded what he had, provided it was not fish, he told the servant. And as there was apparently some little-difficulty in procuring such a comestible, Harold drank some coffee and listened to Mr. Durdan's story—he recommenced it for everyone who entered the breakfast-room.

Yes, Brian had distinctly heard the cry of the Banshee, he said; but a greater marvel had happened, for he found one of his boats that had been made fast on the opposite shore of the lough in the early part of the night, moored at the landing-ledge at the base of the cliffs beneath the Banshee's Cave. By the aid of many a gratuitous "begorra," Mr. Durdan indicated the condition of perplexity in which the boatman had been all the time he was baiting the lines. He explained that the man had attributed to "herself"— meaning, of course, the White Lady—the removal of the boat from the one side of the lough to the other. It was plain that the ghost of the Princess was a good oarswoman, too, for a single paddle only was found in the boat. It was so like a ghost, he had confided to Mr. Durdan, to make a cruise in a way that was contrary—the accent on the second syllable—to nature.

"He has put another oar aboard and is now rowing the boat back to its original quarters," said Mr. Durdan, in conclusion. "But he declares that, be the Powers!"—here the narrator assumed once more the hybrid brogue—"if the boat was meddled with by 'herself' again he would call the priest to bless the craft, and where would 'herself' be then?"

"Where indeed?" said Lord Innisfail.

Harold said nothing. He was aware that Edmund was looking at him intently. Did he suspect anything, Harold wondered.

He gave no indication of being more interested in the story than anyone present, and no one present seemed struck with it—no one, except perhaps, Miss Craven, who had entered the room late, and was thus fortunate enough to obtain the general drift of what Mr. Durdan was talking about, without having her attention diverted by his loving repetition of the phrases of local colour.

Miss Craven heard the story, laughed, glanced at her plate, and remarked with some slyness that Mr. Durdan was clearly making strides in his acquaintance with the Irish question. She then glanced—confidentially— at Edmund Airey, and finally—rather less confidentially—at Harold.

He was eating of that which was not fish, and giving a good deal of attention to it.

Miss Craven thought he was giving quite too much attention to it. She suspected that he knew more about the boat incident than he cared to express, or why should he be giving so much attention to his plate?

As for Harold himself, he was feeling that it would be something of a gratification to him if a fatal accident were to happen to Brian.

He inwardly called him a meddlesome fool. Why should he take it upon him to row the boat across the lough, when he, Harold, had been looking forward during the sleepless hours of the night, to that exercise? When he had awakened from an early morning slumber, it was with the joyous feeling that nothing could deprive him of that row across the lough.

And yet he had been deprived of it, therefore he felt some regret that, the morning being a calm one, Brian's chances of disaster when crossing the lough were insignificant.

All the time that the judge was explaining in that lucid style which was the envy of his brethren on the Bench, how impossible it would be for the Son of Porcupine to purge himself of the contempt which was heaped upon him owing to his unseemly behaviour at a recent race meeting—the case of the son of so excellent a father as Porcupine turning out badly was jeopardizing the future of Evolution as a doctrine—Harold was trying to devise some plan that should make him independent of the interference of the boatman. He did not insist on the plan being legitimate or even reasonable; all that he felt was that he must cross the lough.

He thought of the girl whom he had seen in that atmosphere of moonlight; and somehow he came to think of her as responsible for her exquisite surroundings. There was nothing commonplace about her—that was what he felt most strongly as he noticed the excellent appetites of the young women around him. Even Miss Stafford, who hoped to be accepted as an Intellect embodied in a mere film of flesh—she went to the extreme length of cultivating a Brow—tickled her trout with the point of her fork much less tenderly than the fisherman who told her the story—with an impromptu bravura passage or two—of its capture, had done.

But the girl whom he had seen in the moonlight—whom he was yearning to see in the sunlight—was as refined as a star. "As refined as a star," he actually murmured, when he found himself with an unlighted cigar between his fingers on that part of the terrace which afforded a fine view of the lough—the narrow part as well—his eyes were directed to the narrow part. "As refined as a star—a—"

He turned himself round with a jerk. "A star?"

His father's letter was still in his pocket. It contained in the course of its operatic clauses some references to a Star—a Star, who, alas! was not refined—who, on the contrary, was expensive.

He struck a match very viciously and lit his cigar.

Miss Craven had just appeared on the terrace.

He dropped his still flaming match on the hard gravel walk and put his foot upon it.

"A star!"

He was very vicious.

"She is not a particularly good talker, but she is a most fascinating listener," said Edmund Airey, who strolled up.

"I have noticed so much—when you have been the talker," said Harold. "It is only to the brilliant talker that the fascinating listener appeals. By the way, how does 'fascinated listener' sound as a phrase? Haven't I read somewhere that the speeches of an eminent politician were modelled on the principle of catching birds by night? You flash a lamp upon them and they may be captured by the score. The speeches were compared to the lantern and the public to the birds."

"Gulls," said Edmund. "My dear Harold, I did not come out here to exchange opinions with you on the vexed question of vote-catching or gulls—it will be time enough to do so when you have found a constituency."

"Quite. And meantime I am to think of Miss Craven as a fascinating listener? That's what you have come to impress upon me."

"I mean that you should give yourself a fair chance of becoming acquainted with her powers as a listener—I mean that you should talk to her on an interesting topic."

"Would to heaven that I had your capacity of being interesting on all topics."

"The dullest man on earth when talking to a woman on love as a topic, is infinitely more interesting to her than the most brilliant man when talking to her on any other topic."

"You suggest a perilous way to the dull man of becoming momentarily interesting."

"Of course I know the phrase which, in spite of being the composition of a French philosopher, is not altogether devoid of truth—yes, '*Qui parle d'amour fait l'amour*'."

"Only that love is born, not made."

"Great heavens! have you learned that—that, with your father's letter next your heart?"

Harold laughed.

"Do you fancy that I have forgotten your conversation in the boat yesterday?" said he. "Heaven on one side and the Lord Chancellor on the other."

"And you have come to the conclusion that you are on the side of heaven? You are in a perilous way."

"Your logic is a trifle shaky, friend. Besides, you have no right to assume that I am on the side of heaven."

"There is a suggestion of indignation in your voice that gives me hope that you are not in so evil a case as I may have suspected. Do you think that another afternoon in the boat—"

"Would make me on the side of the Lord Chancellor? I doubt it. But that is not equivalent to saying that I doubt the excellence of your advice."

"Yesterday afternoon I flattered myself that I had given you such advice as commended itself to you, and yet now you tell me that love is born, not made. The man who believes that is past being advised. It is, I say, the end of wisdom. What has happened since yesterday afternoon?"

"Nothing has happened to shake my confidence in the soundness of your advice," said Harold, but not until a pause had occurred—a pause of sufficient duration to tell his observant friend that something had happened.

"If nothing has happened—Miss Craven is going to sketch the Round Tower at noon," said Edmund—the Round Tower was some distance through the romantic Pass of Lamdhu.

"The Round Tower will not suffer; Miss Craven is not one of the landscape libellers," remarked Harold.

Just then Miss Innisfail hurried up with a face lined with anxiety.

Miss Innisfail was the sort of girl who always, says, "It is I."

"Oh, Mr. Airey," she cried, "I have come to entreat of you to do your best to dissuade mamma from her wild notion—the wildest she has ever had. You may have some restraining influence upon her. She is trying to get up an Irish jig in the hall after dinner—she has set her heart on it."

"I can promise you that if Lady Innisfail asks me to be one of the performers I shall decline," said Edmund.

"Oh, she has set her heart on bringing native dancers for the purpose," cried the girl.

"That sounds serious," said Edmund. "Native dances are usually very terrible visitations. I saw one at Samoa."

"I knew it—yes, I suspected as much," murmured the girl, shaking her head. "Oh, we must put a stop to it. You will help me, Mr. Airey?"

"I am always on the side of law and order," said Mr. Airey. "A mother is a great responsibility, Miss Innisfail."

Miss Innisfail smiled sadly, shook her head again, and fled to find another supporter against the latest frivolity of her mother.

When Edmund turned about from watching her, he saw that his friend Harold Wynne had gone off with some of the yachtsmen—for every day a yachting party as well as deep-sea-fishing, and salmon-fishing parties— shooting parties and even archæological parties were in the habit of setting-out from Castle Innisfail.

Was it possible that Harold intended spending the day aboard the cutter, Edmund asked himself.

Harold's mood of the previous evening had been quite intelligible to him—he had confessed to Miss Craven that he understood and even sympathized with him. He was the man who was putting off the plunge as long as possible, he felt.

But he knew that that attitude, if prolonged, not only becomes ridiculous, but positively verges on the indecent. It is one thing to pause for a minute on the brink of the deep water, and quite another to remain shivering on the rock for half a day.

Harold Wynne wanted money in order to realize a legitimate ambition. But it so happened that he could not obtain that money unless by marrying Miss Craven—that was the situation of the moment. But instead of asking Miss Craven if she would have the goodness to marry him, he was wandering about the coast in an aimless way.

Lady Innisfail was the most finished artist in matchmaking that Edmund had ever met. So finished an artist was she that no one had ever ventured to suggest that she was a match-maker. As a matter of fact, her reputation lay in just the opposite direction. She was generally looked upon as a marrer of matches. This was how she had achieved some of her most brilliant successes. She was herself so fascinating that she attracted the nicest men to her side; but, somehow, instead of making love to her as they meant to do, they found themselves making love to the nice girls with whom she surrounded herself. When running upon the love-making track with her, she switched them on, so to speak, to the nice eligible girls, and they became engaged before they quite knew what had happened.

This was her art, Edmund knew, and he appreciated it as it deserved.

She appreciated him as he deserved, he also acknowledged; for she had never tried to switch him on to any of her girls. By never making love to her he had proved himself to be no fit subject for the exercise of her art.

If a man truly loves a woman he will marry anyone whom she asks him to marry.

This, he knew, was the precept that Lady Innisfail inculcated upon the young men—they were mostly very young men—who assured her that they adored her. It rarely failed to bring them to their senses, she had admitted to Edmund in the course of a confidential lapse.

By bringing them to their senses she meant inducing them to ask the right girls to marry them.

Edmund felt that it was rather a pity that his friend Harold had never adored Lady Innisfail. Harold had always liked her too well to make love to her. This was rather a pity, Edmund felt. It practically disarmed Lady Innisfail, otherwise she would have taken care that he made straightforward love to Miss Craven.

As for Harold, he strolled off with the yachtsmen, giving them to understand that he intended sailing with them. The cutter was at her moorings in the lough about a mile from the Castle, and there was a narrow natural dock between the cliffs into which the dingey ran to carry the party out to the yacht.

It was at this point that Harold separated himself from the yachtsmen—not without some mutterings on their part and the delivery of a few reproaches with a fresh maritime flavour about them.

"What was he up to at all?" they asked of one another.

He could scarcely have told these earnest inquirers what he was up to. But his mood would have been quite intelligible to them had they known that he had, within the past half hour made up his mind to let nothing interfere with his asking Helen Craven if she would be good enough to marry him.

CHAPTER XII
ON THE MYSTERY OF MAN

HE meant to ask her at night. He had felt convinced, on returning after his adventure in his dinner dress, that nothing could induce him to think of Miss Craven as a possible wife. While sitting at breakfast, he had felt even more confident on this point; and yet now his mind was made up to ask her to marry him.

It must be admitted that his mood was a singular one, especially as, with his mind full of his resolution to ask Miss Craven to marry him, he was wandering around the rugged coastway, wondering by what means he could bring himself by the side of the girl with whom he had crossed the lough on the previous night.

His mood will be intelligible to such persons as have had friends who occasionally have found it necessary to their well-being to become teetotallers. It is well known that the fascination of the prospect of teetotalism is so great for such persons that the very thought of it compels them to rush off in the opposite direction. They indulge in an outburst of imbibing that makes even their best friends stand aghast, and then they 'take the pledge' with the cheerfulness of a child.

Harold Wynne felt inclined to allow his feelings an outburst, previous to entering upon a condition in which he meant his feelings to be kept in subjection.

To engage himself to marry Miss Craven was, he believed, equivalent to taking the pledge of the teetotaller so far as his feelings were concerned.

Meantime, however, he remained unpledged and with an unbounded sense of freedom.

And this was why he laughed loud and long when he saw in the course of his stroll around the cliffs, a small oar jammed in a crevice of the rocks a hundred feet below where he was walking.

He laughed again when he had gone—not so cautiously as he might have done—down to the crevice and released the oar.

It was, he knew, the one that had gone adrift from the boat the previous night.

He climbed the cliff to the Banshee's Cave and deposited the piece of timber in the recesses of that place. Then he lay down on the coarse herbage at the summit of the cliff until it was time to drift to the Castle for lunch. Life at the Castle involved a good deal of drifting. The guests drifted out in many directions after breakfast and occasionally drifted back to lunch, after which they drifted about until the dinner hour.

While taking lunch he was in such good spirits as made Lady Innisfail almost hopeless of him.

Edmund Airey had told her the previous night that Harold intended asking Miss Craven to marry him. Now, however, perceiving how excellent were his spirits, she looked reproachfully across the table at Edmund.

She was mutely asking him—and he knew it—how it was possible to reconcile Harold's good spirits with his resolution to ask Helen Craven to marry him? She knew—and so did Edmund—that high spirits and the Resolution are rarely found in association.

An hour after lunch the girl with the Brow entreated Harold's critical opinion on the subject of a gesture in the delivery of a certain poem, and the discussion of the whole question occupied another hour. The afternoon was thus pretty far advanced before he found himself seated alone in the boat which had been at the disposal of himself and Edmund during the two previous afternoons. The oar that he had picked up was lying at his feet along the timbers of the boat.

The sun was within an hour of setting when Brian appeared at the Castle bearing a letter for Lady Innisfail. It had been entrusted to him for delivery to her ladyship by Mr. Wynne, he said. Where was Mr. Wynne? That Brian would not take upon him to say; only he was at the opposite side of the lough. Maybe he was with Father Conn, who was the best of good company, or it wasn't a bit unlikely that it was the District Inspector of the Constabulary he was with. Anyhow it was sure that the gentleman had took a great fancy to the queer places along the coast, for hadn't he been to the thrubble to give a look in at the Banshee's Cave, the previous night, just because he was sthruck with admiration of the story of the Princess that he, Brian, had told him and Mr. Airey in the boat?

The letter that Lady Innisfail received and glanced at while drinking tea on one of the garden seats outside the Castle, begged her ladyship to pardon the writer's not appearing at dinner that night, the fact being that he had unexpectedly found an old friend who had taken possession of him.

"It was very nice of him to write, wasn't it, my dear?" Lady Innisfail remarked to her friend Miss Craven, who was filtering a novel by a popular French author for the benefit of Lady Innisfail. "It was very nice of him to write. Of course that about the friend is rubbish. The charm of this neighbourhood is that no old friend ever turns up."

"You don't think that—that—perhaps—" suggested Miss Craven with the infinite delicacy of one who has been employed in the filtration of Paul Bourget.

"Not at all—not at all," said Lady Innisfail, shaking her head. "If it was his father it would be quite another matter."

"Oh!"

"Lord Fotheringay is too great a responsibility even for me, and I don't as a rule shirk such things," said Lady Innisfail. "But Harold is—well, I'll let you into a secret, though it is against myself: he has never made love even to me."

"That is inexcusable," remarked Miss Craven, with a little movement of the eyebrows. She did not altogether appreciate Lady Innisfail's systems. She had not a sufficient knowledge of dynamics and the transference of energy to be able to understand the beauty of the "switch" principle. "But if he is not with a friend—or—or—the other—"

"The enemy—our enemy?"

"Where can he be—where can he have been?"

"Heaven knows! There are some things that are too wonderful for me. I fancied long ago that I knew Man. My dear Helen, I was a fool. Man is a mystery. What could that boy mean by going to the Banshee's Cave last night, when he might have been dancing with me—or you?"

"Romance?"

"Romance and rubbish mean the same thing to such men as Harold Wynne, Helen—you should know so much," said Lady Innisfail. "That is, of course, romance in the abstract. The flutter of a human white frock would produce more impression on a man than a whole army of Banshees."

"And yet the boatman said that Mr. Wynne had spent some time last night at the Cave," said Miss Craven. "Was there a white dress in the question, do you fancy?"

Lady Innisfail turned her large and luminous eyes upon her companion. So she was accustomed to turn those orbs upon such young men as declared that they adored her. The movement was supposed to be indicative of infinite surprise, with abundant sympathy, and a trace of pity.

Helen Craven met the luminous gaze with a smile, that broadened as she murmured, "Dearest Lilian, we are quite alone. It is extremely unlikely that your expression can be noticed by any of the men. It is practically wasted."

"It is the natural and reasonable expression of the surprise I feel at the wisdom of the—the—"

"Serpent?"

"Not quite. Let us say, the young matron, lurking beneath the harmlessness of the—the—let us say the *ingenue*. A white dress! Pray go on with '*Un Cour de Femme*'."

Miss Craven picked up the novel which had been on the ground, flattened out in a position of oriental prostration and humility before the wisdom of the women.

CHAPTER XIII
ON THE ART OF COLOURING

THE people of the village of Ballycruiskeen showed themselves quite ready to enter into the plans of their pastor in the profitable enterprise of making entertainment for Lady Innisfail and her guests. The good pastor had both enterprise and imagination. Lady Innisfail had told him confidentially that day that she wished to impress her English visitors with the local colour of the region round about. Local colour was a phrase that she was as fond of as if she had been an art critic; but it so happened that the pastor had never heard the phrase before; he promptly assured her, however, that he sympathized most heartily with her ladyship's aspirations in this direction. Yes, it was absolutely necessary that they should be impressed with the local colour, and if, with this impression, there came an appreciation of the requirements of the chapel in the way of a new roof, it would please him greatly.

The roof would certainly be put on before the winter, even if the work had to be carried out at the expense of his Lordship, Lady Innisfail said with enthusiasm; and if Father Constantine could only get up a wake or a dance or some other festivity for the visitors, just to show them how picturesque and sincere were the Irish race in the West, she would take care that the work on the roof was begun without delay.

Father Constantine—he hardly knew himself by that name, having invariably been called Father Conn by his flock—began to have a comprehensive knowledge of what was meant by the phrase "local colour." Did her ladyship insist on a wake, he inquired.

Her ladyship said she had no foolish prejudices in the matter. She was quite willing to leave the whole question of the entertainment in the hands of his reverence. He knew the people best and he would be able to say in what direction their abilities could be exhibited to the greatest advantage. She had always had an idea, she confessed, that it was at a wake they shone; but, of course, if Father Constantine thought differently she would make no objection, but she would dearly like a wake.

The priest did not even smile for more than a minute; but he could not keep that twinkle out of his eyes even if the chapel walls in addition to the roof depended on his self-control.

He assured her ladyship that she was perfectly right in her ideas. He agreed with her that the wake was the one festivity that was calculated to bring into prominence the varied talents of his flock. But the unfortunate thing about it was its variableness. A wake was something that could not be arranged for beforehand—at least not without involving a certain liability to criminal prosecution. The elements of a wake were simple enough, to be sure, but simple and all as they were, they were not always forthcoming.

Lady Innisfail thought this very provoking. Of course, expense was no consideration—she hoped that the pastor understood so much. She hoped he understood that if he could arrange for a wake that night she would bear the expense.

The priest shook his head.

Well, then, if a wake was absolutely out of the question—she didn't see why it should be, but, of course, he knew best—why should he not get up an eviction? She thought that on the whole the guests had latterly heard more about Irish evictions than Irish wakes. There was plenty of local colour in an eviction, and so far as she could gather from the pictures she had seen in the illustrated papers, it was extremely picturesque—yes, when the girls were barefooted, and when there was active resistance. Hadn't she heard something about boiling water?

The twinkle had left the priest's eyes as she prattled away. He had an impulse to tell her that it was the class to which her ladyship belonged and not that to which he belonged, who had most practice in that form of entertainment known as the eviction. But thinking of the chapel roof, he restrained himself. After all, Lord Innisfail had never evicted a family on his Irish estate. He had evicted several families on his English property, however; but no one ever makes a fuss about English evictions. If people fail to pay their rent in England they know that they must go. They have not the imagination of the Irish.

"I'll tell your ladyship what it is," said Father Conn, before she had quite come to the end of her prattle: "if the ladies and gentlemen who have the honour to be your ladyship's guests will take the trouble to walk or drive round the coast to the Curragh of Lamdhu after supper—I mean dinner—to-night, I'll get up a celebration of the Cruiskeen for you all."

"How delightful!" exclaimed her ladyship. "And what might a celebration of the Cruiskeen be?"

It was at this point that the imagination of the good father came to his assistance. He explained, with a volubility that comes to the Celt only when he is romancing, that the celebration of the Cruiskeen was a prehistoric rite associated with the village of Ballycruiskeen. Cruiskeen was, as perhaps her ladyship had heard, the Irish for a vessel known to common people as a jug—it was, he explained, a useful vessel for drinking out of—when it held a sufficient quantity.

Of course Lady Innisfail had heard of a jug—she had even heard of a song called "The Cruiskeen Lawn"—did that mean some sort of jug?

It meant the little full jug, his reverence assured her. Anyhow, the celebration of the Cruiskeen of Ballycruiskeen had taken place for hundreds—most likely thousands—of years at the Curragh of Lamdhu—Lamdhu meaning the Black Hand—and it was perhaps the most interesting of Irish customs. Was it more interesting than a wake? Why, a wake couldn't hold a candle to a Cruiskeen, and the display of candles was, as probably her ladyship knew, a distinctive feature of a wake.

Father Conn, finding how much imaginary archæology Lady Innisfail would stand without a protest, then allowed his imagination to revel in the details of harpers—who were much more genteel than fiddlers, he thought, though his flock preferred the fiddle—of native dances and of the recitals of genuine Irish poems—probably prehistoric. All these were associated with a Cruiskeen, he declared, and a Cruiskeen her ladyship and her ladyship's guests should have that night, if there was any public spirit left in Ballycruiskeen, and he rather thought that there was a good deal still left, thank God!

Lady Innisfail was delighted. Local colour! Why, this entertainment was a regular Winsor and Newton Cabinet.

It included everything that people in England were accustomed to associate with the Irish, and this was just what the guests would relish. It was infinitely more promising than the simple national dance for which she had been trying to arrange.

She shook Father Conn heartily by the hand, but stared at him when he made some remark about the chapel roof—she had already forgotten all about the roof.

The priest had not.

"God forgive me for my romancing!" he murmured, when her ladyship had departed and he stood wiping his forehead. "God forgive me! If it wasn't for the sake of the slate or two, the ne'er a word but the blessed truth would have been forced from me. A Cruiskeen! How was it that the notion seized me at all?"

He hurried off to an ingenious friend and confidential adviser of his, whose name was O'Flaherty, and who did a little in the horse-dealing line—a profession that tends to develop the ingenuity of those associated with it either as buyers or sellers—and Mr. O'Flaherty, after hearing Father Conn's story, sat down on the side of one of the ditches, which are such a distinctive feature of Ballycruiskeen and the neighbourhood, and roared with laughter.

"Ye've done it this time, and no mistake, Father Conn," he cried, when he had partially recovered from his hilarity. "I always said you'd do it some day, and ye've done it now. A Cruiskeen! Mother of Moses! A Cruiskeen! Oh, but it's yourself has the quare head, Father Conn!"

"Give over your fun, and tell us what's to be done—that's what you're to do if there's any good in you at all," said the priest.

"Oh, by my soul, ye'll have to carry out the enterprise in your own way, my brave Father Conn," said Mr. O'Flaherty. "A Cruiskeen! A——"

"Phinny O'Flaherty," said the priest solemnly, "if ye don't want to have the curse of the Holy Church flung at that red head of yours, ye'll rise and put me on the way of getting up at least a jig or two on the Curragh this night."

After due consideration Mr. O'Flaherty came to the conclusion that it would be unwise on his part to put in motion the terrible machinery of the Papal Interdict—if the forces of the Vatican were to be concentrated upon him he might never again be able to dispose of a "roarer" as merely a "whistler" to someone whose suspicions were susceptible of being lulled by a brogue. Mr. Phineas O'Flaherty consequently assured Father Conn that he would help his reverence, even if the act should jeopardize his prospects of future happiness in another world.

CHAPTER XIV
ON AN IRISH DANCE

LADY INNISFAIL'S guests—especially those who had been wandering over the mountains with guns all day—found her rather too indefatigable in her search for new methods of entertaining them. The notion of an after-dinner stroll of a few miles to the village of Ballycruiskeen for the sake of witnessing an entertainment, the details of which Lady Innisfail was unable to do more than suggest, and the attractions of which were rather more than doubtful, was not largely relished at the Castle.

Lord Innisfail announced his intention of remaining where he had dined; but he was one of the few men who could afford to brave Lady Innisfail's disdain and to decline to be chilled by her cold glances. The other men who did not want to be entertained on the principles formulated by Lady Innisfail, meanly kept out of her way after dinner. They hoped that they might have a chance of declaring solemnly afterwards, that they had been anxious to go, but had waited in vain for information as to the hour of departure, the costume to be worn, and the password—if a password were needed—to admit them to the historic rites of the Cruiskeen.

One of the women declined to go, on the ground that, so far as she could gather, the rite was not evangelical. Her views were evangelical.

One of the men—he was an Orangeman from Ulster—boldly refused to attend what was so plainly a device planned by the Jesuits for the capture of the souls—he assumed that they had souls—of the Innisfail family and their guests.

Miss Craven professed so ardently to be looking forward to the entertainment, that Mr. Airey, with his accustomed observance of the distribution of high lights in demeanour as well as in conversation. felt certain that she meant to stay at the Castle.

His accuracy of observation was proved when the party were ready to set out for Ballycruiskeen. MIss Craven's maid earned that lady's affectionate regards to her hostess; she had been foolish enough to sit in the sun during the afternoon with that fascinating novel, and as she feared it would, her indiscretion had given her a headache accompanied by dizziness. She would thus be unable to go with the general party to the village, but if she possibly could, she would follow them in an hour—perhaps less.

Edmund Airey smiled the smile of the prophet who lives to see his prediction realized—most of the prophets died violent deaths before they could have that gratification.

"Yes, it was undoubtedly an indiscretion," he murmured.

"Sitting in the sun?" said Lady Innisfail.

"Reading Paul Bourget," said he.

"Of course," said Lady Innisfail. "Talking of indiscretions, has anyone seen—ah, never mind."

"It is quite possible that the old friend whom you say he wrote about, may be a person of primitive habits—he may be inclined to retire early," said Mr. Airey.

Lady Innisfail gave a little puzzled glance at him—the puzzled expression vanished in a moment, however, before the ingenuousness of his smile.

"What a fool I am becoming!" she whispered. "I really never thought of that."

"That was because you never turned your attention properly to the mystery of the headache," said he.

Then they set off in the early moonlight for their walk along the cliff path that, in the course of a mile or so, trended downward and through the Pass of Lamdhu, with its dark pines growing half-way up the slope on one side. The lower branches of the trees stretched fantastic arms over the heads of the party walking on the road through the Pass. In the moonlight these fantastic arms seemed draped. The trees seemed attitudinizing to one another in a strange pantomime of their own.

The village of Ballycruiskeen lay just beyond the romantic defile, so that occasionally the inhabitants failed to hear the sound of the Atlantic hoarsely roaring as it was being strangled in the narrow part of the lough. They were therefore sometimes merry with a merriment impossible to dwellers nearer the coast.

It did not appear to their visitors that this was one of their merry nights. The natives were commanded by their good priest to be merry for "the quality," under penalties with which they were well acquainted. But merriment under a penalty is no more successful than the smile which is manufactured in a photographer's studio.

Father Conn made the mistake of insisting on all the members of his flock washing their faces. They had washed all the picturesqueness out of them, Mr. Airey suggested.

The Curragh of Ballycruiskeen was a somewhat wild moorland that became demoralized into a bog at one extremity. There was, however, a sufficiently settled portion to form a dancing green, and at one side of this patch the shocking incongruity of chairs—of a certain sort—and even a sofa—it was somewhat less certain—met the eyes of the visitors.

"Mind this, ye divils," the priest was saying in an affectionate way to the members of his flock, as the party from the Castle approached. "Mind this, it's dancing a new roof on the chapel that ye are. Every step ye take means a slate, so it does."

This was clearly the peroration of the pastor's speech.

The speech of Mr. Phineas O'Flaherty, who was a sort of unceremonious master of the ceremonies, had been previously delivered, fortunately when the guests were out of hearing.

At first the entertainment seemed to be a very mournful one. It was too like examination day at a village school to convey an idea of spontaneous mirth. The "quality" sat severely on the incongruous chairs—no one was brave enough to try the sofa—and some of the "quality" used double eye-glasses with handles, for the better inspection of the performers. This was chilling to the performers.

In spite of the efforts of Father Conn and his stage manager, Mr. O'Flaherty, the members of the cast for the entertainment assumed a huddled appearance that did themselves great injustice. They declined to group themselves effectively, but suggested to Mr. Durdan—who was not silent on the subject—one of the illustrations to Foxe's Book of Martyrs—a scene in which about a score of persons about to be martyred are shown to be awaiting, with an aspect of cheerful resignation that deceived no one, their "turn" at the hands of the executioner.

The merry Irish jig had a depressing effect at first. The priest was well-meaning, but he had not the soul of an artist. When a man has devoted all his spare moments for several years to the repression of unseemly mirth, he is unwise to undertake, at a moment's notice, the duties of stimulating such mirth. Under the priest's eye the jig was robbed of its jiguity, so to speak. It was the jig of the dancing class.

Mr. O'Flaherty threatened to scandalize Father Conn by a few exclamations about the display of fetlocks—the priest had so little experience of the "quality" that he fancied a suggestion of slang would be offensive to their ears. He did not know that the hero of the "quality" in England is the costermonger, and that a few years ago the hero was the cowboy. But Edmund Airey, perceiving with his accustomed shrewdness, how matters stood, managed to draw the priest away from the halfhearted exponents of the dance, and so questioned him on the statistics of the parish—for Father Conn was as hospitable with his statistics as he was with his whiskey punch upon occasions—that half an hour had passed before they returned together to the scene of the dance, the priest with a five-pound note of Mr. Airey's pressed against his heart.

"Murder alive! what's this at all at all?" cried Father Conn, becoming aware of the utterance of whoop after whoop by the dancers.

"It's the jig they're dancin' at last, an' more power to thim!" cried Phineas O'Flaherty, clapping his hands and giving an encouraging whoop or two.

He was right. The half dozen couples artistically dishevelled, and rapidly losing the baleful recollections of having been recently tidied up to meet the "quality"—rapidly losing every recollection of the critical gaze of the "quality"—of the power of speech possessed by the priest—of everything, clerical and lay, except the strains of the fiddle which occupied an intermediate position between things lay and clerical, being wholly demoniac—these half dozen couples were dancing the jig with a breadth and feeling that suggested the youth of the world and the reign of Bacchus.

Black hair flowing in heavy flakes over shoulders unevenly bare—shapely arms flung over heads in an attitude of supreme self-abandonment—a passionate advance, a fervent retreat, then an exchange of musical cries like wild gasps for breath, and ever, ever, ever the demoniac music of the fiddle, and ever, ever, ever the flashing and flying from the ground like the feet of the winged Hermes—flashing and flashing with the moonlight over all, and the fantastic arms of the hill-side pines stretched out like the fringed arms of a grotesque Pierrot—this was the scene to which the priest returned with Edmund Airey.

He threw up his hands and was about to rush upon the half-frenzied dancers, when Edmund grasped him by the arm, and pointed mutely to the attitude of the "quality."

Lady Innisfail and her friends were no longer sitting frigidly on their chairs—the double eye-glasses were dropped, and those who had held them were actually joining in the whoops of the dancers. Her ladyship was actually clapping her hands in the style of encouragement adopted by Mr. O'Flaherty.

The priest stood in the attitude in which he had been arrested by the artful Edmund Airey. His eyes and his mouth were open, and his right hand was pressed against the five-pound note that he had just received. There was a good deal of slate-purchasing potentialities in a five-pound note. If her ladyship and her guests were shocked—as the priest, never having heard of the skirt dance and its popularity in the drawing-room—believed they should be, they were not displaying their indignation in a usual way. They were almost as excited as the performers.

Father Conn seated himself without a word of protest, in one of the chairs vacated by the Castle party. He felt that if her ladyship liked that form of entertainment, the chapel roof was safe. The amount of injury that would be done to the Foul Fiend by the complete re-roofing of the chapel should certainly be sufficient to counteract whatever sin might be involved in the wild orgy that was being carried on beneath the light of the moon. This was the consolation that the priest had as he heard whoop after whoop coming from the dancers.

Six couples remained on the green dancing-space. The fiddler was a wizened, deformed man with small gleaming eyes. He stood on a stool and kept time with one foot. He increased the time of the dance so gradually as to lead the dancers imperceptibly on until, without being aware of it, they had reached a frenzied pitch that could not be maintained for many minutes. But still the six couples continued wildly dancing, the moonlight striking them aslant and sending six black quivering shadows far over the ground. Suddenly a man dropped out of the line and lay gasping on the grass. Then a girl flung herself with a cry into the arms of a woman who was standing among the onlookers. Faster still and faster went the grotesquely long arms of the dwarf fiddler—his shadow cast by the moonlight was full of horrible suggestions—and every now and again a falsetto whoop came from him, his teeth suddenly gleaming as his lips parted in uttering the cry.

The two couples, who now remained facing one another, changing feet with a rapidity that caused them to appear constantly off the ground, were encouraged by the shouts and applause of their friends. The air was full of cries, in which the spectators from the Castle joined. Faster still the demoniac music went, every strident note being clearly heard above the shouts. But when one of the two couples staggered wildly and fell with outstretched arms upon the grass, the shriek of the fiddle sounded but faintly above the cries.

The priest could restrain himself no longer. He sprang to his feet and kicked the stool from under the fiddler, sending the misshapen man sprawling in one direction and his instrument with an unearthly shriek in another.

Silence followed that shriek. It lasted but a few seconds, however. The figure of a man—a stranger—appeared running across the open space between the village and the Curragh, where the dance was being held.

He held up his right hand in so significant a way, that the priest's foot was arrested in the act of implanting another kick upon the stool, and the fiddler sat up on the ground and forgot to look for his instrument through surprise at the apparition.

"It's dancin' at the brink of the grave, ye are," gasped the man, as he approached the group that had become suddenly congested in anticipation of the priest's wrath.

"Why, it's only Brian the boatman, after all," said Lady Innisfail. "Great heavens! I had such a curious thought as he appeared. Oh, that dancing! He did not seem to be a man."

"This is no doubt part of the prehistoric rite," said Mr. Airey.

"How simply lovely!" cried Miss Stafford.

"In God's name, man, tell us what you mean," said the priest.

"It's herself," gasped Brian. "It's the one that's nameless. Her wail is heard over all the lough—I heard it with my ears and hurried here for your reverence. Don't we know that she never cries except for a death?"

"He means the Banshee," said Lady Innisfail.

"The people, I've heard, think it unlucky to utter her name."

"So lovely! Just like savages!" said Miss Stafford.

"I dare say the whole thing is only part of the ceremony of the Cruiskeen," said Mr. Durdan.

"Brian O'Donal," said the priest; "have you come here to try and terrify the country side with your romancin'?"

"By the sacred Powers, your reverence, I heard the cry of her myself, as I came by the bend of the lough. If it's not the truth that I'm after speaking, may I be the one that she's come for."

"Doesn't he play the part splendidly?" said Lady Innisfail. "I'd almost think that he was in earnest. Look how the people are crossing themselves."

Miss Stafford looked at them through her double eye-glasses with the long handle.

"How lovely!" she murmured. "The Cruiskeen is the Oberammergau of Connaught."

Edmund Airey laughed.

"God forgive us all for this night!" said the priest. "Sure, didn't I think that the good that would come of getting on the chapel roof would cover the shame of this night! Go to your cabins, my children. You were not to blame. It was me and me only. My Lady"—he turned to the Innisfail party—"this entertainment is over. God knows I meant it for the best."

"But we haven't yet heard the harper," cried Lady Innisfail.

"And the native bards," said Miss Stafford. "I should so much like to hear a bard. I might even recite a native poem under his tuition."

Miss Stafford saw a great future for native Irish poetry in English drawing-rooms. It might be the success of a season.

"The entertainment's over," said the priest.

"It's that romancer Brian, that's done it all," cried Phineas O'Flaherty.

"Mr. O'Flaherty, if it's not the truth may I—oh, didn't I hear her voice, like the wail of a girl in distress?" cried Brian.

"Like what?" said Mr. Airey.

"Oh, you don't believe anything—we all know that, sir," said Brian.

"A girl in distress—I believe in that, at any rate," said Edmund.

"Now!" said Miss Stafford, "don't you think that I might recite something to these poor people?" She turned to Lady Innisfail. "Poor people! They may never have heard a real recitation—'The Dove Cote,' 'Peter's Blue Bell'—something simple."

There was a movement among her group.

"The sooner we get back to the Castle the better it will be for all of us," said Lady Innisfail. "Yes, Father Constantine, we distinctly looked for a native bard, and we are greatly disappointed. Who ever heard of a genuine Cruiskeen without a native bard? Why, the thing's absurd!"

"A Connaught Oberammergau without a native bard! *Oh, Padre mio— Padre mio!*" said Miss Stafford, daintily shaking her double eye-glasses at the priest.

"My lady," said he, "you heard what the man said. How would it be possible for us to continue this scene while that warning voice is in the air?"

"If you give us a chance of hearing the warning voice, we'll forgive you everything, and say that the Cruiskeen is a great success," cried Lady Innisfail.

"If your ladyship takes the short way to the bend of the lough you may still hear her," said Brian.

"God forbid," said the priest.

"Take us there, and if we hear her, I'll give you half a sovereign," cried her ladyship, enthusiastically.

"If harm comes of it don't blame me," said Brian. "Step out this way, my lady."

"We may still be repaid for our trouble in coming so far," said one of the party. "If we do actually hear the Banshee, I, for one, will feel more than satisfied."

Miss Stafford, as she hurried away with the party led by Brian, wondered if it might not be possible to find a market for a Banshee's cry in a London drawing-room. A new emotion was, she understood, eagerly awaited. The serpentine dance and the costermonger's lyre had waned. It was extremely unlikely that they should survive another season. If she were to be first in the field with the Banshee's cry, introduced with a few dainty steps of the jig incidental to a poem with a refrain of "Asthore" or "Mavourneen," she might yet make a name for herself.

CHAPTER XV
ON THE SHRIEK

IN a space of time that was very brief, owing to the resolution with which Lady Innisfail declined to accept the suggestion of short cuts by Brian, the whole party found themselves standing breathless at the beginning of the line of cliffs. A mist saturated with moonlight had drifted into the lough from the Atlantic. It billowed below their eyes along the surface of the water, and crawled along the seared faces of the cliffs, but no cold fingers of the many-fingered mist clasped the higher ridges. The sound of the crashing of the unseen waves about the bases of the cliffs filled the air, but there was no other sound.

"Impostor!" said Edmund Airy, turning upon Brian. "You heard no White Lady to-night. You have jeopardized our physical and your spiritual health by your falsehood."

"You shall get no half sovereign from me," said Lady Innisfail.

"Is it me that's accountable for her coming and going?" cried Brian, with as much indignation as he could afford. Even an Irishman cannot afford the luxury of being indignant with people who are in the habit of paying him well, and an Irishman is ready to sacrifice much to sentiment. "It's glad we should all be this night not to hear the voice of herself."

Lady Innisfail looked at him. She could afford to be indignant, and she meant to express her indignation; but when it came to the point she found that it was too profound to be susceptible of expression.

"Oh, come away," she said, after looking severely at Brian for nearly a minute.

"Dear Lady Innisfail," said Mr. Durdan, "I know that you feel indignant, fancying that we have been disappointed. Pray do not let such an idea have weight with you for a moment."

"Oh, no, no," said Miss Stafford, who liked speaking in public quite as well as Mr. Durdan. "Oh, no, no; you have done your best, dear Lady Innisfail. The dance was lovely; and though, of course, we should have liked to hear a native bard or two, as well as the Banshee—"

"Yet bards and Banshees we know to be beyond human control," said Mr. Airey.

"We know that if it rested with you, we should hear the Banshee every night," said Mr. Durdan.

"Yes, we all know your kindness of heart, dear Lady Innisfail," resumed Miss Stafford.

"Indeed you should hear it, and the bard as well," cried Lady Innisfail. "But as Mr. Airey says—and he knows all about bard and Banshees and such like things Great heaven! We are not disappointed after all, thank heaven!"

Lady Innisfail's exclamation was uttered after there floated to the cliffs where she and her friends were standing, from the rolling white mist that lay below, the sound of a long wail. It was repeated, only fainter, when she had uttered her thanksgiving, and it was followed by a more robust shout.

"Isn't it lovely?" whispered Lady Innisfail.

"I don't like it," said Miss Stafford, with a shudder. "Let us go away— oh, let us go away at once."

Miss Stafford liked simulated horrors only. The uncanny in verse was dear to her; but when, for the first time, she was brought face to face with what would have formed the subject of a thrilling romance with a suggestion of the supernatural, she shuddered.

"Hush," said Lady Innisfail; "if we remain quiet we may hear it again."

"I don't want to hear it again," cried Miss Stafford. "Look at the man. He knows all about it. He is one of the natives."

She pointed to Brian, who was on his knees on the rock muttering petitions for the protection of all the party.

He knew, however, that his half sovereign was safe, whatever might happen. Miss Stafford's remark was reasonable. Brian should know all about the Banshee and its potentialities of mischief.

"Get up, you fool!" said Edmund Airey, catching the native by the shoulder. "Don't you know as well as I do that a boat with someone aboard is adrift in the mist?"

"Oh, I know that you don't believe in anything." said Brian.

"I believe in your unlimited laziness and superstition," said Edmund. "I'm very sorry, my dear Lady Innisfail, to interfere with your entertainment, but it's perfectly clear to me that someone is in distress at the foot of the cliffs."

"How can you be so horrid—so commonplace?" said Lady Innisfail.

"He is one of the modern iconoclasts," said another of the group. "He would fling down our most cherished beliefs. He told me that he considered Madame Blavatsky a swindler."

"Dear Mr. Airey," said Miss Stafford, who was becoming less timid as the wail from the sea had not been repeated. "Dear Mr. Airey, let us entreat of you to leave us our Banshee whatever you may take from us."

"There are some things in heaven and earth that refuse to be governed by a phrase," sneered Mr. Durdan.

"Mules and the members of the Opposition are among them," said Edmund, preparing to descend the cliffs by the zig-zag track.

He had scarcely disappeared in the mist when there was a shriek from Miss Stafford, and pointing down the track with a gesture, which for expressiveness, she had never surpassed in the most powerful of her recitations, she flung herself into Lady Innisfail's arms.

"Great heavens!" cried Lady Innisfail. "It is the White Lady herself'!"

"We're all lost, and the half sovereign's nothing here or there," said Brian, in a tone of complete resignation.

Out of the mist there seemed to float a white figure of a girl. She stood for some moments with the faint mist around her, and while the group on the cliff watched her—some of them found it necessary to cling together— another white figure floated through the mist to the side of the first, and then came another figure—that of a man—only he did not float.

"I wish you would not cling quite so close to me, my dear; I can't see anything of what's going on," said Lady Innisfail to Miss Stafford, whose head was certainly an inconvenience to Lady Innisfail.

With a sudden, determined movement she shifted the head from her bosom to her shoulder, and the instant that this feat was accomplished she cried out, "Helen Craven!"

"Helen Craven?" said Miss Stafford, recovering the use of her head in a moment.

"Yes, it's Helen Craven or her ghost that's standing there," said Lady Innisfail.

"And Harold Wynne is with her. Are you there, Wynne?" sang out Mr. Durdan.

"Hallo?" came the voice of Harold from below. "Who is there?"

"Why, we're all here," cried Edmund, emerging from the mist at his side. "How on earth did you get here?—and Miss Craven—and—he looked at the third figure—he had never seen the third figure before.

"Oh, it's a long story," laughed Harold. "Will you give a hand to Miss Craven?"

Mr. Airey said it would please him greatly to do so, and by his kindly aid Miss Craven was, in the course of a few minutes, placed by the side of Lady Innisfail.

She took the place just vacated by Miss Stafford on Lady Innisfail's bosom, and was even more embarrassing to Lady Innisfail than the other had been. Helen Craven was heavier, to start with.

But it was rather by reason of her earnest desire to see the strange face, that Lady Innisfail found Helen's head greatly in her way.

"Lady Innisfail, when Miss Craven is quite finished with you, I shall present to you Miss Avon," said Harold.

"I should be delighted," said Lady Innisfail. "Dearest Helen, can you not spare me for a moment?"

Helen raised her head.

It was then that everyone perceived how great was the devastation done by the mist to the graceful little curled fringes of her forehead. Her hair was lank, showing that she had as massive a brow as Miss Stafford's, if she wished to display it.

"It is a great pleasure to me to meet you, Miss Avon; I'm sure that I have often heard of you from Mr. Wynne and—oh, yes, many other people," said Lady Innisfail. "But just now—well, you can understand that we are all bewildered."

"Yes, we are all bewildered," said Miss Avon. "You see, we heard the cry of the White Lady—"

"Of course," said Harold; "we heard it too. The White Lady was Miss Craven. She was in one of the boats, and the mist coming on so suddenly, she could not find her way back to the landing place. Luckily we were able to take her boat in tow before it got knocked to pieces. I hope Miss Craven did not over-exert herself."

"I hope not," said Lady Innisfail. "What on earth induced you to go out in a boat alone, Helen—and suffering from so severe a headache into the bargain?"

"I felt confident that the cool air would do me good," said Miss Craven. somewhat dolefully.

Lady Innisfail looked at her in silence for some moments, then she laughed.

No one else seemed to perceive any reason for laughter.

Lady Innisfail then turned her eyes upon Miss Avon. The result of her observation was precisely the same as the result of Harold's first sight of that face had been. Lady Innisfail felt that she had never seen so beautiful a girl.

Then Lady Innisfail laughed again.

Finally she looked at Harold and laughed for the third time. The space of a minute nearly was occupied by her observations and her laughter.

"I think that on the whole we should hasten on to the Castle," said she at length. "Miss Craven is pretty certain to be fatigued—we are, at any rate. Of course you will come with us, Miss Avon."

The group on the cliff ceased to be a group when she had spoken; but Miss Avon did not move with the others. Harold also remained by her side.

"I don't know what I should do," said Miss Avon. "The boat is at the foot of the cliff."

"It would be impossible for you to find your course so long as the mist continues," said Harold. "Miss Avon and her father—he is an old friend of mine—we breakfasted together at my college—are living in the White House—you may have heard its name—on the opposite shore—only a mile by sea, but six by land," he added, turning to Lady Innisfail.

"Returning to-night is out of the question," said Lady Innisfail. "You must come with us to the Castle for to-night. I shall explain all to your father to-morrow, if any explanation is needed." Miss Avon shook her head, and murmured a recognition of Lady Innisfail's kindness.

"There is Brian," said Harold. "He will confront your father in the morning with the whole story."

"Yes, with the whole story," said Lady Innisfail, with an amusing emphasis on the words. "I already owe Brian half a sovereign."

"Oh, Brian will carry the message all for love," cried the girl.

Lady Innisfail did her best to imitate the captivating freshness of the girl's words.

"All for love—all for love!" she cried.

Harold smiled. He remembered having had brought under his notice a toy nightingale that imitated the song of the nightingale so closely that the Jew dealer, who wanted to sell the thing, declared that no one on earth could tell the difference between the two.

The volubility of Brian in declaring that he would do anything out of love for Miss Avon was amazing. He went down the cliff face to bring the boats round to the regular moorings, promising to be at the Castle in half an hour to receive Miss Avon's letter to be put into her father's hand at his hour of rising.

By the time Miss Avon and Harold had walked to the Castle with Lady Innisfail, they had acquainted her with a few of the incidents of the evening—how they also had been caught by the mist while in their boat, and had with considerable trouble succeeded in reaching the craft in which Miss Craven was helplessly drifting. They had heard Miss Craven's cry for help, they said, and Harold had replied to it. But still they had some trouble picking up her boat.

Lady Innisfail heard all the story, and ventured to assert that all was well that ended well.

"And this is the end," she cried, as she pointed to the shining hall seen through the open doors.

"Yes, this is the end of all—a pleasant end to the story," said the girl.

Harold followed them as they entered.

He wondered if this was the end of the story, or only the beginning.

CHAPTER XVI
ON THE VALUE OF A BAD CHARACTER

IT was said by some people that the judge, during his vacation, had solved the problem set by the philosopher to his horse. He had learned to live on a straw a day, only there was something perpetually at the end of his straw—something with a preposterous American name in a tumbler to match.

He had the tumbler and the straw on a small table by his side while he watched, with great unsteadiness, the strokes of the billiard players.

From an hour after dinner he was in a condition of perpetual dozing. This was his condition also from an hour after the opening of a case in court, which required the closest attention to enable even the most delicately appreciative mind to grasp even its simplest elements.

He had, he said, been the most widely awake of counsel for thirty years, so that he rather thought he was entitled to a few years dozing as a judge.

Other people—they were his admirers—said that his dozing represented an alertness far beyond that of the most conscientiously wakeful and watchful of the judicial establishment in England.

It is easy to resemble Homer—in nodding—and in this special Homeric quality the judge excelled; but it was generally understood that it would not be wise to count upon his nodding himself into a condition of unobservance. He had already delivered judgment on the character of the fine cannons of one of the players in the hall, and upon the hazards of the other. He had declined to mark the game, however, and he had thereby shown his knowledge of human nature. There had already been four disputes as to the accuracy of the marking. (It was being done by a younger man).

"How can a man expect to make his favourite break after some hours on a diabolical Irish jaunting car?" one of the players was asking, as he bent over the table.

The words were uttered at the moment of Harold's entrance, close behind Lady Innisfail and Miss Avon.

Hearing the words he stood motionless before he had taken half-a-dozen steps into the hall.

Lady Innisfail also stopped at the same instant, and looked over her shoulder at Harold.

Through the silence there came the little click of the billiard balls.

The speaker gave the instinctive twist of the practised billiard player toward the pocket that he wished the ball to approach. Then he took a breath and straightened himself in a way that would have made any close observer aware of the fact that he was no longer a young man.

There was, however, more than a suggestion of juvenility in his manner of greeting Lady Innisfail. He was as effusive as is consistent with the modern spirit of indifference to the claims of hostesses and all other persons.

He was not so effusive when he turned to Harold; but that was only to be expected, because Harold was his son.

"No, my boy," said Lord Fotheringay, "I didn't fancy that you would expect to see me here to-night—I feel surprised to find myself here. It seems like a dream to me—a charming dream-vista with Lady Innisfail at the end of the vista. Innisfail always ruins his chances of winning a game by attempting a screw back into the pocket. He leaves everything on. You'll see what my game is now."

He chalked his cue and bent over the table once more.

Harold watched him make the stroke. "You'll see what my game is," said Lord Fotheringay, as he settled himself down to a long break.

Harold questioned it greatly. His father's games were rarely transparent.

"What on earth can have brought him?—oh, he takes one's breath away," whispered Lady Innisfail to Harold, with a pretty fair imitation of a smile lingering about some parts of her face.

Harold shook his head. There was not even the imitation of a smile about his face.

Lady Innisfail gave a laugh, and turned quickly to Miss Avon.

"My husband will be delighted to meet you, my dear," said she. "He is certain to know your father."

Harold watched Lord Innisfail shaking hands with Miss Avon at the side of the billiard table, while his father bent down to make another stroke. When the stroke was played he saw his father straighten himself and look toward Miss Avon.

The look was a long one and an interested one. Then the girl disappeared with Lady Innisfail, and the look that Lord Fotheringay cast at his son was a short one, but it was quite as intelligible to that soft as the long look at Miss Avon had been to him.

Harold went slowly and in a singularly contemplative mood to his bedroom, whence he emerged in a space, wearing a smoking-jacket and carrying a pipe and tobacco pouch.

The smoking-jackets that glowed through the hall towards the last hour of the day at Castle Innisfail were a dream of beauty.

Lady Innisfail had given orders to have a variety of sandwiches and other delicacies brought to the hall for those of her guests who had attended the festivities at Ballycruiskeen; and when Harold found his way downstairs, he perceived in a moment that only a few of the feeble ones of the house-party—the fishermen who had touches of rheumatism and the young women who cherished their complexions—were absent from the hall.

He also noticed that his father was seated by the side of Beatrice Avon and that he was succeeding in making himself interesting to her.

He knew that his father generally succeeded in making himself interesting to women.

In another part of the hall Lady Innisfail was succeeding in making herself interesting to some of the men. She also was accustomed to meet with success in this direction. She was describing to such as had contrived to escape the walk to Ballycruiskeen, the inexhaustibly romantic charm of the scene on the Curragh while the natives were dancing, and the descriptions certainly were not deficient in colour.

The men listened to her with such an aspect of being enthralled, she felt certain that they were full of regret that they had failed to witness the dance. It so happened, however, that the result of her account of the scene was to lead those of her audience who had remained at the Castle, to congratulate themselves upon a lucky escape.

And all this time, Harold noticed that his father was making himself interesting to Beatrice Avon.

The best way for any man to make himself interesting to a woman is to show himself interested in her. He knew that his father was well aware of this fact, and that he was getting Beatrice Avon to tell him all about herself.

But when Lady Innisfail reached the final situation in her dramatic account of the dance, and hurried her listeners to the brink of the cliff—

when she reproduced in a soprano that was still vibratory, the cry that had sounded through the mist—when she pointed to Miss Avon in telling of the white figure that had emerged from the mist—(Lady Innisfail did not think it necessary to allude to Helen Craven, who had gone to bed)—the auditors' interest was real and not simulated. They looked at the white figure as Lady Innisfail pointed to her, and their interest was genuine.

They could at least appreciate this element of the evening's entertainment, and as they glanced at Harold, who was eating a number of sandwiches in a self-satisfied way, they thought that they might safely assume that he was the luckiest of the *dramatis personae* of the comedy—or was it a tragedy?—described by Lady Innisfail.

And all this time Harold was noticing that his father, by increasing his interest in Beatrice, was making himself additionally interesting to her.

But the judge had also—at the intervals between his Homeric nods—been noticing the living things around him. He put aside his glass and its straw—he had been toying with it all the evening, though the liquid that mounted by capillary attraction up the tube was something noisome, without a trace of alcohol—and seated himself on the other side of the girl.

He assured her that he had known her father. Lord Fotheringay did not believe him; but this was not to the point, and he knew it. What was to the point was the fact that the judge understood the elements of the art of interesting a girl almost as fully as Lord Fotheringay did, without having quite made it the serious business of his life. The result was that Miss Avon was soon telling the judge all about herself—this was what the judge professed to be the most anxious to hear—and Lord Fotheringay lit a cigar.

He felt somewhat bitterly on the subject of the judge's intrusion. But the feeling did not last for long. He reflected upon the circumstance that Miss Avon could never have heard that he himself was a very wicked man.

He knew that the interest that attaches to a man with a reputation for being very wicked is such as need fear no rival. He felt that should his power to interest a young woman ever be jeopardized, he could still fall back upon his bad character and be certain to attract her.

CHAPTER XVII
ON PROVIDENCE AS A MATCH-MAKER

OF course," said Lady Innisfail to Edmund Airey the next day. "Of course, if Harold alone had rescued Helen from her danger last night, all would have been well. You know as well as I do that when a man rescues a young woman from a position of great danger, he can scarcely do less than ask her to marry him."

"Of course," replied Edmund. "I really can't see how, if he has any dramatic appreciation whatever, he could avoid asking her to marry him."

"It is beyond a question," said Lady Innisfail. "So that if Harold had been alone in the boat all would have been well. The fact of Miss Avon's being also in the boat must, however, be faced. It complicates matters exceedingly."

Edmund shook his head gravely.

"I knew that you would see the force of it," resumed Lady Innisfail. "And then there is his father—his father must be taken into account."

"It might be as well, though I know that Lord Fotheringay's views are the same as yours."

"I am sure that they are; but why, then, does he come here to sit by the side of the other girl and interest her as he did last evening?"

"Lord Fotheringay can never be otherwise than interesting, even to people who do not know how entirely devoid of scruple he is."

"Of course I know all that; but why should he come here and sit beside so very pretty a girl as this Miss Avon?"

"There is no accounting for tastes, Lady Innisfail.

"You are very stupid, Mr. Airey. What I mean is, why should Lord Fotheringay behave in such a way as must force his son's attention to be turned in a direction that—that—in short, it should not be turned in? Heaven knows that I want to do the best for Harold—I like him so well that I could almost wish him to remain unmarried. But you know as well as I do, that it is absolutely necessary for him to marry a girl with a considerable amount of money."

"That is as certain as anything can be. I gave him the best advice in my power on this subject, and he announced his intention of asking Miss Craven to marry him."

"But instead of asking her he strolled round the coast to that wretched cave, and there met, by accident, the other girl—oh, these other girls are always appearing on the scene at the wrong moment."

"The world would go on beautifully if it were not for the Other Girl." said Edmund. "If you think of it, there is not an event in history that has not turned upon the opportune or inopportune appearance of the Other Girl. Nothing worth speaking of has taken place, unless by the agency of the Other Girl."

"And yet Lord Fotheringay comes here and sits by the side of this charming girl, and his son watches him making himself interesting to her as, alas! he can do but too easily. Mr. Airey, I should not be surprised if Harold were to ask Miss Avon to-day to marry him—I should not, indeed."

"Oh, I think you take too pessimistic a view of the matter altogether, Lady Innisfail. Anyhow, I don't see that we can do more than we have already done. I think I should feel greatly inclined to let Providence and Lord Fotheringay fight out the matter between them."

"Like the archangel and the Other over the body of Moses?"

"Well, something like that."

"No, Mr. Airey; I don't believe in Providence as a match-maker."

Mr. Airey gave a laugh. He wondered if it was possible that Harold had mentioned to her that he, Edmund, had expressed the belief that Providence as a match-maker had much to learn.

"I don't see how we can interfere," said he. "I like Harold Wynne greatly. He means to do something in the world, and I believe he will do it. He affords a convincing example of the collapse of heredity as a principle. I like him if only for that."

Lady Innisfail looked at him in silence for a few moments.

"Yes," she said, slowly. "Harold does seem to differ greatly from his father. I wonder if it is the decree of Providence that has kept him without money."

"Do you suggest that the absence of money—?"

"No, no; I suggest nothing. If a man must be wicked he'll be wicked without money almost as readily as with it. Only I wonder, if Harold had come in for the title and the property—such as it was—at the same age as his father was when he inherited all, would he be so ready as you say he is to do useful work on the side of the government of his country?"

"That is a question for the philosophers," said Edmund.

In this unsatisfactory way the conversation between Lady Innisfail and Mr. Airey on the morning after Lord Fotheringay's arrival at the Castle, came to an end. No conversation that ends in referring the question under consideration to the philosophers, can by any possibility be thought satisfactory. But the conversation could not well be continued when Miss Craven, by the side of Miss Avon, was seen to be approaching.

Edmund Airey turned his eyes upon the two girls, then they rested upon the face of Beatrice.

As she came closer his glance rested upon the eyes of Beatrice. The result of his observation was to convince him that he had never before seen such beautiful eyes.

They were certainly gray; and they were as full of expression as gray eyes can be. They were large, and to look into them seemed like looking into the transparent depths of an unfathomed sea—into the transparent heights of an inexhaustible heaven.

A glimpse of heaven suggests the bliss of the beatified. A glimpse of the ocean suggests shipwreck.

He knew this perfectly well as he looked at her eyes; but only for an instant did it occur to him that they conveyed some message to him.

Before he had time to think whether the message promised the bliss of the dwellers in the highest heaven, or the disaster of those who go down into the depths of the deepest sea, he was inquiring from Helen Craven if the chill of which she had complained on the previous night, had developed into a cold.

Miss Craven assured him that, so far from experiencing any ill effects from her adventure, she had never felt better in all her life.

"But had it not been for Miss Avon's hearing my cries of despair, goodness knows where I should have been in another ten minutes," she added, putting her arm round Miss Avon's waist, and looking, as Edmund had done, into the mysterious depths of Miss Avon's gray eyes.

"Nonsense!" said Miss Avon. "To tell you the plain truth, I did not hear your cries. It was Mr. Wynne who said he heard the White Lady wailing for her lover."

"How could he translate the cry so accurately?" said Edmund. "Do you suppose that he had heard the Banshee's cry at the same place?"

He kept his eyes upon Miss Avon's face, and he saw in a moment that she was wondering how much he knew of the movements of Harold Wynne during the previous two nights.

Helen Craven looked at him also pretty narrowly. She was wondering if he had told anyone that he had suggested to her the possibility of Harold's being in the neighbourhood of the Banshee's Cave during the previous evening.

Both girls laughed in another moment, and then Edmund Airey laughed also—in a sort of way. Lady Innisfail was the last to join in the laugh. But what she laughed at was the way in which Edmund had laughed.

And while this group of four were upon the northern terrace, Harold was seated the side of his father on one of the chairs that faced the south. Lord Fotheringay was partial to a southern aspect. His life might be said to be a life of southern aspects. He meant that it should never be out of the sun, not because some of the incidents that seemed to him to make life worth preserving were such as could best stand the searching light of the sun, but simply because his was the nature of the butterfly. He was a butterfly of fifty-seven—a butterfly that found it necessary to touch up with artificial powders the ravages of years upon the delicate, downy bloom of youth—a butterfly whose wings had now and again been singed by contact with a harmful flame—whose still shapely body was now and again bent with rheumatism. Surely the rheumatic butterfly is the most wretched of insects!

He had fluttered away from a fresh singeing, he was assuring his son. Yes, he had scarcely strength left in his wings to carry him out of the sphere of influence of the flame. He had, he said in a mournful tone, been very badly treated. She had treated him very badly. The Italian nature was essentially false—he might have known it—and when an Italian nature is developed with a high soprano, very shrill in its upper register, the result was—well, the result was that the flame had singed the wings of the elderly insect who was Harold's father.

"Talk of money!" he cried, with so sudden an expression of emotion that a few caked scraps of sickly, roseate powder fluttered from the crinkled lines of his forehead—Talk of money! It was not a matter of hundreds—

he was quite prepared for that—but when the bill ran up to thousands— thousands—thousands—oh, the whole affair was sickening. (Harold cordially agreed with him, though he did not express himself to this effect). Was it not enough to shake one's confidence in woman—in human nature— in human art (operatic)—in the world?

Yes, it was the Husband.

The Husband, Lord Fotheringay was disposed to regard in pretty much the same light as Mr. Airey regarded the Other Girl. The Husband was not exactly the obstacle, but the inconvenience. He had a habit of turning up, and it appeared that in the latest of Lord Fotheringay's experiences his turning up had been more than usually inopportune.

"That is why I followed so close upon the heels of my letter to you," said the father. "The crash came in a moment—it was literally a crash too, now that I think upon it, for that hot-blooded ruffian, her husband, caught one corner of the table cloth—we were at supper—and swept everything that was on the table into a corner of the room. Yes, the bill is in my portmanteau. And she took his part. Heavens above! She actually took his part. I was the scoundrel—*briccone!*—the coarse Italian is still ringing in my ears. It was anything but a charming duetto. He sang a basso—her upper register was terribly shrill—I had never heard it more so. Artistically the scene was a failure; but I had to run for all that. Humiliating, is it not, to be overcome by something that would, if subjected to the recognized canons of criticism, be pronounced a failure? And he swore that he would follow me and have my life. Enough. You got my letter. Fortune is on your side, my boy. You saved her life last night."

"Whose life did I save?" asked the son. "Whose life? Heavens above! Have you been saving more than one life?"

"Not more than one—a good deal less than one. Don't let us get into a sentimental strain, pater. You are the chartered—ah, the chartered sentimentalist of the family. Don't try and drag me into your strain. I'm not old enough. A man cannot pose as a sentimentalist nowadays until he is approaching sixty."

"Really? Then I shall have to pause for a year or two still. Let us put that question aside for a moment. Should I be exceeding my privileges if I were to tell you that I am ruined?—Financially ruined, I mean, of course; thank heaven, I am physically as strong as I was—ah, three years ago."

"You said something about my allowance, I think."

"If I did not I failed in my duty as a father, and I don't often do that, my boy—thank God, I don't often do that."

"No," said Harold. "If the whole duty of a father is comprised in acquainting his son with the various reductions that he says he finds it necessary to make in his allowance, you are the most exemplary of fathers, pater."

"There is a suspicion of sarcasm—or what is worse, epigram in that phrase," said the father. "Never mind, you cannot epigram away the stern fact that I have now barely a sufficient income to keep body and soul together. I wish you could."

"So do I," said Harold. "But yours is a *ménage à trois*. It is not merely body and soul with your but body, soul, and sentiment—it is the third element that is the expensive one."

"I dare say you are right. Anyhow, I grieve for your position, my boy. If it had pleased Heaven to make me a rich man, I would see that your allowance was a handsome one."

"But since it has pleased the other Power to make you a poor one—"

"You must marry Miss Craven—that's the end of the whole matter, and an end that most people would be disposed to regard as a very happy one, too. She is a virtuous young woman, and what is better, she dresses extremely well. What is best of all, she has several thousands a year."

There was a suggestion of the eighteenth century phraseology in Lord Fotheringay's speech, that made him seem at least a hundred years old. Surely people did not turn up their eyes and talk of virtue since the eighteenth century, Harold thought. The word had gone out. There was no more need for it. The quality is taken for granted in the nineteenth century.

"You are a trifle over-vehement," said he.

"Have I ever refused to ask Miss Craven to marry me?"

"Have you ever asked her—that's the matter before us?"

"Never. But what does that mean? Why, simply that I have before me instead of behind me a most interesting quarter of an hour—I suppose a penniless man can ask a wealthy woman inside a quarter of an hour, to marry him. The proposition doesn't take longer in such a case than an honourable one would."

"You are speaking in a way that is not becoming in a son addressing his father," said Lord Fotheringay. "You almost make me ashamed of you."

"You have had no reason to be ashamed of me yet," said Harold. "So long as I refrain from doing what you command me to do, I give you no cause to be ashamed of me."

"That is a pretty thing for a son to say," cried the father, indignantly.

"For heaven's sake don't let us begin a family broil under the windows of a house where we are guests," said the son, rising quickly from the chair. "We are on the border of a genuine family bickering. For God's sake let us stop in time."

"I did not come here to bicker," said the father. "Heavens above! Am I not entitled to some show of gratitude at least for having come more than a thousand miles—a hundred of them in an Irish train and ten of them on an Irish jolting car—simply to see that you are comfortably settled for life?"

"Yes," said the son, "I suppose I should feel grateful to you for coming so far to tell me that you are ruined and that I am a partner in your ruin." He had not seated himself, and now he turned his back upon his father and walked round to the west side of the Castle where some of the girls were strolling. They were waiting to see how the day would develop—if they should put on oilskins and sou'westers or gauzes and gossamer—the weather on the confines of the ocean knows only the extremes of winter or summer.

The furthest of the watchers were, he perceived, Edmund Airey and Miss Avon. He walked toward them, and pronounced in a somewhat irresponsible way an opinion upon the weather.

Before the topic had been adequately discussed, Mr. Durdan and another man came up to remind Mr. Airey that he had given them his word to be of their party in the fishing boat, where they were accustomed to study the Irish question for some hours daily.

Mr. Airey protested that his promise had been wholly a conditional one. It had not been made on the assumption that the lough should be moaning like a Wagnerian trombone, and it could not be denied that such notes were being produced by the great rollers beneath the influence of a westerly wind.

Harold gave a little shrug to suggest to Beatrice that the matter was not one that concerned her or himself in the least, and that it might be as well if Mr. Airey and his friends were left to discuss it by themselves.

The shrug scarcely suggested all that he meant it to suggest, but in the course of a minute he was by the side of the girl a dozen yards away from the three men.

"I wonder if you chanced to tell Mr. Airey of the queer way you and I met," she said in a moment.

"How could I have told any human being of that incident?" he cried. "Why do you ask me such a question?"

"He knows all about it—so much is certain," said she. "Oh, yes, he gave me to understand so much—not with brutal directness, of course."

"No, I should say not—brutal directness is not in his line," said Harold.

"But the result is just the same as if he had been as direct as—as a girl."

"As a girl?"

"Yes. He said something about Miss Craven's voice having suggested something supernatural to Brian, and then he asked me all at once if there had been any mist on the previous evening when I had rowed across the lough. Now I should like to know how he guessed that I had crossed the lough on the previous night."

"He is clever—diabolically clever," said Harold after a pause. "He was with Miss Craven in the hall—they had been dancing—when I returned—I noticed the way he looked at me. Was there anything in my face to tell him that—that I had met you?"

She looked at his face and laughed.

"Your face," she said. "Your face—what could there have been apparent on your face for Mr. Airey to read?"

"What—what?" his voice was low. He was now looking into her gray eyes. "What was there upon my face? I cannot tell. Was it a sense of doom? God knows. Now that I look upon your face—even now I cannot tell whether I feel the peace of God which passes understanding, or the doom of those who go down to the sea and are lost."

"I do not like to hear you speak in that way," said she. "It would be better for me to die than to mean anything except what is peaceful and comforting to all of God's creatures."

"It would be better for you to die," said he. He took his eyes away from hers. They stood side by side in silence for some moments, before he turned suddenly to her and said in quite a different strain. "I shall row you across the lough when you are ready. Will you go after lunch?"

"I don't think that I shall be going quite so soon," said she. "The fact is that Lady Innisfail was good enough to send Brian with another letter to my father—a letter from herself, asking my father to come to the Castle for a day or two, but, whether he comes or not, to allow me to remain for some days."

Again some moments passed before Harold spoke.

"I want you to promise to let me know where you go when you leave Ireland," said he. "I don't want to lose sight of you. The world is large. I wandered about in it for nearly thirty years before meeting you."

She was silent. It seemed as if she was considering whether or not his last sentence should be regarded as a positive proof of the magnitude of the world.

She appeared to come to the conclusion that it would be unwise to discuss the question—after all, it was only a question of statistics.

"If you wish it," said she, "I shall let you know our next halting-place. I fancy that my poor father is less enthusiastic than he was some years ago on the subject of Irish patriotism. At any rate, I think that he has worked out all the battles fought in this region."

"Only let me know where you go," said he. "I do not want to lose sight of you. What did you say just now—peace and comfort to God's creatures? No, I do not want to lose sight of you."

CHAPTER XVIII
ON THE PROFESSIONAL MORALIST

THE people—Edmund Airey was one of them—who were accustomed to point to Harold Wynne as an example of the insecurity of formulating any definite theory of heredity, had no chance of being made aware of the nature of the conversations in which he had taken part, or they might not have been quite so ready to question the truth of that theory.

His father had made it plain to him, both by letter and word of mouth, that the proper course for him to pursue was one that involved asking Helen Craven to marry him—the adoption of any other course, even a prosaic one, would practically mean ruin to him; and yet he had gone straight from the side of his father, not to the side of Miss Craven, but to the side of Miss Avon. And not only had he done this, but he had looked into the gray eyes of Beatrice when he should have been gazing with ardour—or simulated ardour—into the rather lustreless orbs of Helen.

To do precisely the thing which he ought not to have done was certainly a trait which he had inherited from his father.

But he had not merely looked into the eyes of the one girl when he should have been looking into those of the other girl, he had spoken into her ears such words as would, if spoken into the ears of the other girl, have made her happy. The chances were that the words which he had spoken would lead to unhappiness. To speak such words had been his father's weakness all his life, so that it seemed that Harold had inherited this weakness also.

Perhaps for a moment or two, after Edmund Airey had sauntered up, having got the better of the argument with Mr. Durdan—he flattered himself that he had invariably got the better of him in the House of Commons— Harold felt that he was as rebellious against the excellent counsels of his father as his father had ever been against the excellent precepts which society has laid down for its own protection. He knew that the circumstance of his father's having never accepted the good advice which had been offered to him as freely as advice, good and bad, is usually offered to people who are almost certain not to follow it, did not diminish from the wisdom of the course which his father had urged upon him to pursue. He had acknowledged to Edmund Airey some days before, that the substance of the advice was good, and had expressed his intention of following it—nay, he felt even when he had walked straight from his father's side to indulge in that earnest look into the eyes of Beatrice, that it was almost inevitable that he should take the advice of his father; for however distasteful it may be, the advice of a father is sometimes acted on by a son. But still the act of rebellion had been pleasant to him—as pleasant to him as his father's acts of the same character had been to his father.

And all this time Helen Craven was making her usual elaborate preparations for finishing her sketch of some local scene, and everyone knew that she could not seek that scene unless accompanied by someone to carry her umbrella and stool.

Lord Fotheringay perceived this in a moment from his seat facing the south. He saw that Providence was on the side of art, so to speak—assuming that a water-colour sketch of a natural landscape by an amateur is art, and assuming that Providence meant simply an opportunity for his son to ask Miss Craven to marry him.

Lord Fotheringay saw how Miss Craven lingered with her colour-box in one hand and her stool in the other. What was she waiting for? He did not venture to think that she was waiting for Harold to saunter up and take possession of her apparatus, but he felt certain that if Harold were to saunter up, Miss Craven's eyes would brighten—so far as such eyes as hers could brighten. His teeth met with a snap that threatened the gold springs when he saw some other man stroll up and express the hope that Miss Craven would permit him to carry her stool and umbrella, for her sketching umbrella was brought from the hall by a servant.

Lord Fotheringay's indignation against his son was great afterwards. He made an excellent attempt to express to Edmund Airey what he felt on the subject of Harold's conduct, and Edmund shook his head most sympathetically.

What was to be done, Lord Fotheringay inquired. What was to be done in order to make Harold act in accordance with the dictates not merely of prudence but of necessity as well?

Mr. Airey could not see that any positive action could be taken in order to compel Harold to adopt the course which every sensible person would admit was the right course—in fact the only course open to him under the circumstances. He added that only two days ago Harold had admitted that he meant to ask Miss Craven to marry him.

"Heavens above!" cried Lord Fotheringay. "He never admitted so much to me. Then what has occurred to change him within a few days?"

"In such a case as this it is as well not to ask *what* but *who*," remarked Edmund.

Lord Fotheringay looked at him eagerly. "Who—who—you don't mean another girl?"

"Why should I not mean another girl?" said Edmund. "You may have some elementary acquaintance with woman, Lord Fotheringay."

"I have—yes, elementary," admitted Lord Fotheringay.

"Then surely you must have perceived that a man's attention is turned away from one woman only by the appearance of another woman," said Edmund.

"You mean that—by heavens, that notion occurred to me the moment that I saw her. She is a lovely creature, Airey."

"'A gray eye or so!' said Airey."

"A gray eye or so!" cried Lord Fotheringay, who had not given sufficient attention to the works of Shakespeare to recognize a quotation. "A gray—Oh, you were always a cold-blooded fellow. Such eyes, Airey, are so uncommon as—ah, the eyes are not to the point. They only lend colour to your belief that she is the other girl. Yes, that notion occurred to me the moment she entered the hall."

"I believe that but for her inopportune appearance Harold would now be engaged to Miss Craven," said Edmund.

"There's not the shadow of a doubt about the matter," cried Lord Fotheringay—both men seemed to regard Miss Craven's acquiescence in the scheme which they had in their minds, as outside the discussion altogether. "Now what on earth did Lady Innisfail mean by asking a girl with such eyes to stay here? A girl with such eyes has no business appearing among people like us who have to settle our mundane affairs to the best advantage. Those eyes are a disturbing influence, Airey. They should never be seen while matters are in an unsettled condition. And Lady Innisfail professes to be Harold's friend."

"And so she is," said Edmund. "But the delight that Lady Innisfail finds in capturing a strange face—especially when that face is beautiful—overcomes all other considerations with her. That is why, although anxious—she was anxious yesterday, though that is not saying she is anxious today—to hear of Harold's proposing to Miss Craven, yet she is much more anxious to see the effect produced by the appearance of Miss Avon among her guests."

"And this is a Christian country!" said Lord Fotheringay solemnly, after a pause of considerable duration.

"Nominally," said Mr. Airey,

"What is society coming to, Airey, when a woman occupying the position of Lady Innisfail, does not hesitate to throw all considerations of friendship to the winds solely for the sake of a momentary sensation?"

Lord Fotheringay was now so solemn that his words and his method of delivering them suggested the earnestness of an evangelist—zeal is always expected from an evangelist, though unbecoming in an ordained clergyman. He held one finger out and raised it and lowered it with the inflections of his voice with the skill of a professional moralist.

He had scarcely spoken before Miss Avon, by the side of the judge and Miss Innisfail, appeared on the terrace.

The judge—he said he had known her father—was beaming on her. Professing to know her father he probably considered sufficient justification for beaming on her.

Lord Fotheringay and his companion watched the girl in silence until she and her companions had descended to the path leading to the cliffs.

"Airey," said Lord Fotheringay at length. "Airey, that boy of mine must be prevented from making a fool of himself—he must be prevented from making a fool of that girl. I would not like to see such a girl as that—I think you said you noticed her eyes—made a fool of."

"It would be very sad," said Edmund. "But what means do you propose to adopt to prevent the increase by two of the many fools already in the world?"

"I mean to marry the girl myself," cried Lord Fotheringay, rising to his feet—not without some little difficulty, for rheumatism had for years been his greatest enemy.

CHAPTER XIX
ON MODERN SOCIETY

EDMUND AIREY had the most perfect command of his features under all circumstances. While the members of the Front Opposition Benches were endeavouring to sneer him into their lobby, upon the occasion of a division on some question on which it was rumoured he differed from the Government, he never moved a muscle. The flaunts and gibes may have stung him, but he had never yet given an indication of feeling the sting; so that if Lord Fotheringay looked for any of those twitches about the corners of Mr. Airey's mouth, which the sudden announcement of his determination would possibly have brought around the mouth of an ordinary man, he must have had little experience of his companion's powers.

But that Lord Fotheringay felt on the whole greatly flattered by the impassiveness of Edmund Airey's face after his announcement, Edmund Airey did not for a moment doubt. When a man of fifty-seven gravely announces his intention to another man of marrying a girl of, perhaps, twenty, and with eyes of remarkable lustre, and when the man takes such an announcement as the merest matter of course, the man who makes it has some reason for feeling flattered.

The chances are, however, that he succeeds in proving to his own satisfaction that he has no reason for feeling flattered; for the man of fifty-seven who is fool enough to entertain the notion of marrying a girl of twenty with lustrous eyes, is certainly fool enough to believe that the announcement of his intention in this respect is in no way out of the common.

Thus, when, after a glance concentrated upon the corners of Edmund Airey's mouth, Lord Fotheringay resumed his seat and began to give serious reasons for taking the step that he had declared himself ready to take—reasons beyond the mere natural desire to prevent Miss Avon from being made a fool of—he gave no indication of feeling in the least flattered by the impassiveness of the face of his companion.

Yes, he explained to Mr. Airey, he had been so badly treated by the world that he had almost made up his mind to retire from the world—the exact words in which he expressed that resolution were "to let the world go to the devil in its own way."

Now, as the belief was general that Lord Fotheringay's presence in the world had materially accelerated its speed in the direction which he had indicated, the announcement of his intention to allow it to proceed without his assistance was not absurd.

Yes, he had been badly treated by the world, he said. The world was very wicked. He felt sad when he thought of the vast amount of wickedness there was in the world, and the small amount of it that he had already enjoyed. To be sure, it could not be said that he had quite lived the life of the ideal anchorite: he admitted—and smacked his lips as he did so—that he had now and again had a good time (Mr. Airey did not assume that the word "good" was to be accepted in its Sunday-school sense) but on the whole the result was disappointing.

"As saith the Preacher," remarked Mr. Airey, when Lord Fotheringay paused and shook his head so that another little scrap of caked powder escaped from the depths of one of the wrinkles of his forehead.

"The Preacher—what Preacher?" he asked.

"The Preacher who cried *Vanitas Vanitatum*," said Edmund.

"He had gone on a tour with an Italian opera company," said Lord Fotheringay, "and he had fallen foul of the basso. Airey, my boy, whatever you do, steer clear of a prima donna with a high soprano. It means thousands—thousands, and a precipitate flight at the last. You needn't try a gift of paste—the finest productions of the Ormuz Gem Company—'a Tiara for Thirty Shillings'—you know their advertisement—no, I've tried that. It was no use. The real thing she would have—Heavens above! Two thousand pounds for a trinket, and nothing to show for it, but a smashing of supper plates and a hurried flight. Ah, Airey, is it any wonder that I should make up my mind to live a quiet life with—I quite forget who was in my mind when I commenced this interesting conversation?"

"It makes no difference," said Mr. Airey. "The principle is precisely the same. There is Miss Innisfail looking for someone, I must go to her."

"A desperately proper girl," said Lord Fotheringay. "As desperately proper as if she had once been desperately naughty. These proper girls know a vast deal. She scarcely speaks to me. Yes, she must know a lot."

His remarks were lost upon Mr. Airey, for he had politely hurried to Miss Innisfail and was asking her if he could be of any assistance to her.

But when Miss Innisfail replied that she was merely waiting for Brian, the boatman, who should have returned long ago from the other side of the lough, Mr. Airey did not return to Lord Fotheringay.

He had had enough of Lord Fotheringay for one afternoon, and he hoped that Lord Fotheringay would understand so much. He had long ago ceased to be amusing. As an addition to the house-party at the Castle he was unprofitable. He knew that Lady Innisfail was of this opinion, and he was well aware also that Lady Innisfail had not given him more than a general and very vague invitation to the Castle. He had simply come to the Castle in order to avoid the possibly disagreeable consequences of buying some thousands of pounds' worth of diamonds—perhaps it would be more correct to say, diamonds costing some thousands of pounds, leaving worth out of the question—for a woman with a husband.

Airey knew that the philosophy of Lord Fotheringay was the philosophy of the maker of omelettes. No one has yet solved the problem of how to make omelettes without breaking eggs. Lord Fotheringay had broken a good many eggs in his day, and occasionally the result was that his share of the transaction was not the omelette but the broken shells. Occasionally, too, Edmund Airey was well aware, Lord Fotheringay had suffered more inconvenience than was involved in the mere fact of his being deprived of the comestible. His latest adventure. Airey thought, might be included among such experiences. He had fled to the brink of the ocean in order to avoid the vengeance of the Husband. "Here the pursuer can pursue no more," was the line that was in Edmund Airey's mind as he listened to the fragmentary account of the latest *contretemps* of the rheumatic butterfly.

Yes, he had had quite enough of Lord Fotheringay's company. The announcement of his intention to marry Miss Avon had not made him more interesting in the eyes of Edmund Airey, though it might have done so in other people's eyes—for a man who makes himself supremely ridiculous makes himself supremely interesting as well, in certain circles.

The announcement made by Lord Fotheringay had caused him to seem ridiculous, though of course Edmund had made no sign to this effect: had he made any sign he would not have heard the particulars of Lord Fotheringay's latest fiasco, and he was desirous of learning those particulars. Having become acquainted with them, however, he found that he had had quite enough of his company.

But in the course of the afternoon Mr. Airey perceived that, though in his eyes there was something ridiculous in the notion of Lord Fotheringay's expression of a determination to marry Beatrice Avon, the idea might not seem quite so ridiculous to other people—Miss Avon's father, for instance.

In another moment he had come to the conclusion that the idea might not seem altogether absurd to Miss Avon herself.

Young women of twenty—even when they have been endowed by heaven with lustrous eyes (assuming that the lustre of a young woman's eyes is a gift from heaven, and not acquired to work the purposes of a very different power)—have been known to entertain without repugnance the idea of marrying impecunious peers of fifty-seven; and upon this circumstance Edmund pondered.

Standing on the brink of a cliff at the base of which the great rollers were crouching like huge white-maned lions, Mr. Airey reflected as he had never previously done, upon the debased condition of modern society, in which such incidents are of constant occurrence. But, however deplorable such incidents are, he knew perfectly well that there never had existed a society in the world where they had not been quite as frequent as they are in modern society in England.

Yes, it was quite as likely as not that Lord Fotheringay would be able to carry out the intention which he had announced to his confidant of the moment.

But when Mr. Airey thought of the lustrous eyes of Beatrice Avon, recalling the next moment the rheumatic movements of Lord Fotheringay and the falling of the scrap of caked powder from his forehead, he felt quixotic enough to be equal to the attempt to prevent the realization of Lord Fotheringay's intention.

It was then that the thought occurred to him—Why should not Harold, who was clearly ready to fall in love with the liquid eyes of Beatrice Avon, ask her to marry him instead of his father?

The result of his consideration of this question was to convince him that such an occurrence as it suggested should be averted at all hazards.

Only the worst enemy that Harold Wynne could have—the worst enemy that the girl could have—would like to see them married.

It would be different if the hot-blooded Italian husband were to pursue the enemy of his household to the brink of the Atlantic cliffs and then push him over the cliffs into the depths of the Atlantic Ocean. But the hot-blooded Italian was not yet in sight, and Edmund knew very well that so long as Lord Fotheringay lived, Harold was dependent on him for his daily bread.

If Harold were to marry Miss Avon, it would lie in his father's power to make him a pauper, or, worse, the professional director with the honorary prefix of "Honourable" to his name, dear to the company promoter.

On the death of Lord Fotheringay Harold would inherit whatever property still remained out of the hands of the mortgagees; but Edmund was well aware of the longevity of that species of butterfly which is susceptible of rheumatic attacks; so that for, perhaps, fifteen years Harold might remain dependent upon the good-will of his father for his daily bread.

It thus appeared to Mr. Airey that the problem of how to frustrate the intentions of Lord Fotheringay, was not an easy one to solve.

He knew the world too well to entertain for a moment the possibility of defeating Lord Fotheringay's avowed purpose by informing either the girl or her father of the evil reputation of Lord Fotheringay. The evil deeds of a duke have occasionally permitted his wife to obtain a divorce; but they have never prevented him from obtaining another wife.

All this Mr. Edmund Airey knew, having lived in the world and observed the ways of its inhabitants for several years.

VOLUME 2

CHAPTER XX
ON AN OAK SETTEE

HE was still pondering over the many aspects of the question which, to his mind, needed solution, when he returned to the Castle, to find Lord Fotheringay in a chair by the side of a gaunt old man who, at one period of his life, had probably been tall, but who was now stooped in a remarkable way. The stranger seemed very old, so that beside him Lord Fotheringay looked comparatively youthful. Of this fact no one was better aware than Lord Fotheringay.

Edmund Airey had seen portraits of the new guest, and did not require to be told that he was Julius Anthony Avon, the historian of certain periods.

The first thought that occurred to him when he saw the two men side by side, was that Lord Fotheringay would not appear ridiculous merely as the son-in-law of Mr. Avon. To the casual observer at any rate he might have posed as the son of Mr. Avon.

He himself seemed to be under the impression that he might pass as Mr. Avon's grandson, for he was extremely sportive in his presence, attitudinizing on his settee in a way that Edmund knew must have been agonizing to his rheumatic joints. Edmund smiled. He felt that he was watching the beginning of a comedy.

He learned that Mr. Avon had yielded to the persuasion of Lady Innisfail and had consented to join his daughter at the Castle for a few days. He was not fond of going into society; but it so happened that Castle Innisfail had been the centre of an Irish conspiracy at the early part of the century, and this fact made the acceptance by him of Lady Innisfail's invitation a matter of business.

Hearing the nature of the work at which he was engaged, Lord Fotheringay had lost no time in expounding to him, in that airy style which he had at his command, the various mistakes that had been made by several generations of statesmen in dealing with the Irish question. The fundamental error which they had all committed was taking the Irish and their rebellions and conspiracies too seriously.

This theory he expounded to the man who was writing a biographical dictionary of Irish informers, and was about to publish his seventh volume, concluding the letter B.

Mr. Avon listened, gaunt and grim, while Lord Fotheringay gracefully waved away statesman after statesman who had failed signally, by reason of taking Ireland and the Irish seriously.

There was something grim also in Edmund Airey's smile as he glanced at this beginning of the comedy.

That night Miss Stafford added originality to the ordinary terrors of her recital. She explained that hitherto she had merely interpreted the verses of others: now, however, she would draw upon her store of original poems.

Of course, Edmund Airey was outside the drawingroom while this was going on. So were many of his fellow-guests, including Helen Craven. Edmund found her beside him in a secluded part of the hall. He was rather startled by her sudden appearance. He forgot to greet her with one of the clever things that he reserved for her and other appreciative young women—for he still found a few, as any man with a large income may, if he only keeps his eyes open. "What a fool you must think me," were the words with which Miss Craven greeted him, so soon as he became aware of her presence.

Strange to say, he had a definite idea that she had said something clever—at any rate something that impressed him more strongly than ever with the idea that she was a clever girl.

And yet she had assumed that he must think her a fool.

"A fool?" said he, "To think you so would be to write myself down one, Miss Craven."

"Mr Airey," said she, "I am a woman. Long ago I was a girl. You will thus believe me when I tell you that I never was frank in all my life. I want to begin now."

"Ah, now I know the drift of your remark," said he. "A fool. Yes, you made a good beginning: but supposing that I were to be frank, where would you be then?"

"I want you to begin also, Mr Airey," said she.

"To begin? Oh, I made my start years ago—when I entered Parliament," said he. "I was perfectly frank with the Opposition when I pointed out their mistakes. I have never yet been frank with a friend, however. That is why I still have a few left."

"You must be frank with me now; if you won't it doesn't matter: I'll be so to you. I admit that I behaved like an idiot; but you were responsible for it—yes, largely."

"That is a capital beginning. Now tell me what you have done or left undone—above all, tell me where my responsibility comes in."

"You like Harold Wynne?"

"You suggest that a mere liking involves a certain responsibility?"

"I love him."

"Great heavens!"

"Why should you be startled at the confession when you have been aware of the fact for some time?"

"I never met a frank woman before. It is very terrible. Perhaps I shall get used to it."

"Why will you not drop that tone?" she said, almost piteously. "Cannot you see how serious the thing is to me?"

"It is quite as serious to me," he replied. "Men have confided in me— mostly fools—a woman never. Pray do not continue in that strain."

"Then find words for me—be frank."

"I will. You mean to say, Miss Craven, that I think you a fool because, acting on the hint which I somewhat vaguely, but really in good faith, dropped, you tried to impersonate the figure of the legend at that ridiculous cave. Is not that what you would say if you had the courage to be thoroughly frank?"

"Thank you," said she, in a still weaker voice. "It is not so easy being frank all in a moment."

"No, not if one has accustomed oneself to—let us say good manners," he added.

"When I started for the boats after you had all left for that nonsense at the village, I felt certain that you were my friend as well as Harold Wynne's, and that you had good reason for believing that he would be about the cave shortly after our hour of dining. I'm not very romantic."

"Pardon me," said he. "You are not quite frank. If you were you would say that, while secretly romantic, you follow the example of most young women nowadays in ridiculing romance."

"Quite right," she said. "I admitted just now that I found it difficult to be frank all in a moment. Anyhow I believed that if I were to play the part of the Wraith of the Cave within sight of Harold Wynne, he might—oh, how could I have been such a fool? But you—you, I say, were largely responsible for it, Mr. Airey." She was now speaking not merely reproachfully but fiercely. "Why should you drop those hints—they were much more than hints—about his being so deeply impressed with the romance—about his having gone to the cave on the previous evening, if you did not mean me to act upon them?"

"I did mean you to act upon them," said he. "I meant that you and he should come together last night, and I know that if you had come together, he would have asked you to marry him. I meant all that, because I like him and I like you too—yes, in spite of your frankness."

"Thank you," said she, giving him her hand. "You forgive me for being angry just now?"

"The woman who is angry with a man without cause pays him the greatest compliment in her power," he remarked. "Fate was against us."

"You think that she is so very—very pretty?" said Miss Craven.

"She?—fate?—I'll tell you what I think. I think that Harold Wynne has met with the greatest misfortune of his life."

"If you believe that, I know that I have met with the greatest of my life."

The corner of the hall was almost wholly in shadow. The settee upon which Mr. Airey and Miss Craven were sitting, was cut off from the rest of the place by the thigh hone of the great skeleton elk. Between the ribs of the creature, however, some rays of light passed from one of the lamps; and, as Mr. Airey looked sympathetically into the face of his companion, he saw the gleam of a tear upon her cheek.

He was deeply impressed—so deeply that some moments had passed before he found himself wondering what she would say next. For a moment he forgot to be on his guard, though if anyone had described the details of a similar scene to him, he would probably have smiled while remarking that when the lamplight gleams upon a tear upon the cheek of a young woman of large experience, is just when a man needs most to be on his guard, He felt in another moment, however, that something was coming.

He waited for it in silence.

It seemed to him in that pause that he was seated by the side of someone whom he had never met before. The girl who was beside him seemed to have nothing in common with Helen Craven. So greatly does a young woman change when she becomes frank.

This is why so many husbands declare—when they are also frank—that the young women whom they marry are in every respect different from the young women who promise to be their wives.

"What is going to happen?" Helen asked him in a steady voice.

"God knows," said he.

"I saw them together just after they left you this morning," said she. "I was at one of the windows of the Castle, they were far along the terrace; but I'm sure that he said something to her about her eyes."

"I should not be surprised if he did," said Edmund. "Her eyes invite comment."

"I believe that in spite of her eyes she is much the same as any other girl."

"Is that to the point?" he asked. He was a trifle disappointed in her last sentence. It seemed to show him that, whatever Beatrice might be, Helen was much the same as other girls.

"It is very much to the point," said she. "If she is like other girls she will hesitate before marrying a penniless man."

"I agree with you," said he. "But if she is like other girls she will not hesitate to love a penniless man."

"Possibly—if, like me, she can afford to do so. But I happen to know that she cannot afford it. This brings me up to what has been on my mind all day. You are, I know, my friend; you are Harold Wynne's also. Now, if you want to enable him to gratify his reasonable ambition—if you want to make him happy—to make me happy—you will prevent him from ever asking Beatrice Avon to marry him."

"And I am prepared to do so much for him—for you—for her. But how can I do it?"

"You can take her away from him. You know how such things are done. You know that if a distinguished man such as you are, with a large income such as you possess, gives a girl to understand that he is, let us say, greatly interested in her, she will soon cease to be interested in any undistinguished and penniless son of a reprobate peer who may be before her eyes."

"I have seen such a social phenomenon," said he. "Does your proposition suggest that I should marry the young woman with 'a gray eye or so'?"

"You may marry her if you please—that's entirely a matter for yourself. I don't see any need for you to go that length. Have I not kept my promise to be frank?"

"You have," said he.

She had risen from the settee. She laid her hand on one of his that rested on a projection of the old oak carving, and in another instant she was laughing in front of Norah Innisfail, who was rendered even more proper than usual through having become acquainted with Miss Stafford's notions of originality in verse-making.

CHAPTER XXI
ON THE ELEMENTS OF PARTY POLITICS

MR. AIREY was actually startled by the suggestion which Miss Craven had made with, on the whole, considerable tact as well as inconceivable frankness.

He had been considering all the afternoon the possibility of carrying out the idea which it seemed Helen Craven had on her mind as well; but it had never occurred to him that his purpose might be achieved through the means suggested by the young woman who had just gone from his side.

His first impression was that the proposal made to him was the cruellest that had ever come from one girl in respect of another girl. He had never previously had an idea that a girl could be so heartless as to make such a suggestion as that which had come from Helen Craven; but in the course of a short space of time, he found it expedient to revise his first judgment on this matter. Helen Craven meant to marry Harold—so much could scarcely be doubted—and her marrying him would be the best thing that could happen to him. She was anxious to prevent his marrying Miss Avon; and surely this was a laudable aim, considering that marrying Miss Avon would be the worst thing that could happen to him—and to Miss Avon as well.

It might possibly be regarded as cruel by some third censors for Miss Craven to suggest that he, Edmund, after leading the other girl to believe that he was desirous of marrying her—or at least to believe that she might have a chance of marrying him—might stop short. To be sure, Miss Craven had not, with all her frankness, said that her idea was that he should refrain from asking the other girl to marry him, but only that the question was one that concerned himself alone.

He thought over this point for some time, and the conclusion he came to was that, after all, whether or not the cynical indifference of the suggestion amounted to absolute cruelty, the question concerned himself alone. Even if he were not to ask her to marry him after leading her to suppose that he intended doing so, he would at any rate have prevented her from the misery of marrying Harold; and that was something for which she might be thankful to him. He would also have saved her from the degradation of receiving a proposal of marriage from Lord Fotheringay; and that was also something for which she might be thankful to him.

Being a strictly party politician, he regarded expediency as the greatest of all considerations. He was not devoid of certain scruples now and again; but he was capable of weighing the probable advantages of yielding to these scruples against the certain advantages of—well, of throwing them to the winds.

For some minutes after Helen Craven had left him he subjected his scruples to the balancing process, and the result was that he found they were as nothing compared with the expediency of proceeding as Helen had told him that it was advisable for him to proceed.

He made up his mind that he would save the girl—that was how he put it to himself—and he would take extremely good care that he saved himself as well. Marriage would not suit him. Of this he was certain. People around him were beginning to be certain of it also. The mothers in Philistia had practically come to regard him as a *quantité négligeable*. The young women did not trouble themselves about him, after a while. It would not suit him to marry a young woman with lustrous eyes, he said to himself as he left his settee; but it would suit him to defeat the machinations of Lord Fotheringay, and to induce his friend Harold Wynne to pursue a sensible course.

He found himself by the side of Beatrice Avon before five minutes had passed, and he kept her thoroughly amused for close upon an hour—he kept her altogether to himself also, though many chances of leaving his side were afforded the girl by considerate youths, and by one smiling person who had passed the first bloom of youth and had reached that which is applied by the cautious hare's foot in the hand of a valet.

Before the hour of brandy-and-sodas and resplendent smoking-jackets had come, the fact of his having kept Beatrice Avon so long entertained had attracted some attention.

It had attracted the attention of Miss Craven, who commented upon it with a confidential smile at Harold. It attracted the attention of Harold's father, who commented upon it with a leer and a sneer. It attracted the attention of Lady Innisfail, who commented upon it with a smile that caused the dainty dimple in her chin to assume the shape of the dot in a well-made note of interrogation.

It also attracted the attention of quite a number of other persons, but they reserved their comments, which was a wise thing for them to do.

As she said good-night to him, she seemed, Edmund Airey thought, to be a trifle fascinated as well as fascinating. He felt that he had had a delightful hour—it was far more delightful than the half hour which he had passed on the settee at the rear of the skeleton elk.

His feeling in this matter simply meant that it was far more agreeable to him to see a young woman admiring his cleverness than it was to admire the cleverness of another young woman.

He enjoyed his smoke by the side of the judge; for when a man is absorbed in the thoughts of his own cleverness he can still get a considerable amount of passive enjoyment out of the story of How the Odds fell from Thirteen to Five to Six to Four against Porcupine for some prehistoric Grand National.

Harold Wynne now and again glanced across the hall at the man who professed to be his best friend. He could perceive without much trouble that Edmund Airey was particularly well pleased with himself.

This meant, he thought, that Edmund had been particularly well pleased with Beatrice Avon.

Lord Fotheringay was too deeply absorbed in giving point to a story, founded upon personal experience, which he was telling to his host, to give a moment's attention to Edmund Airey, or to make an attempt to interpret his aspect.

It was only when his valet was putting him carefully to bed—he required very careful handling—that he recollected the effective way in which Airey had snubbed him, when he had made an honest attempt to reach Miss Avon conversationally.

He now found time to wonder what Airey meant by preventing the girl from being entertained—Lord Fotheringay assumed, as a matter of course, that the girl had not been entertained—all the evening. He had no head, however, for considering such a question in all its aspects. He only resolved that in future he would take precious good care that when there was any snubbing in the air, he would be the dispenser of it, not the recipient.

Lord Fotheringay was not a man of genius, but upon occasions he could be quite as disagreeable as if he were. He had studied the art of administering snubs, and though he had never quite succeeded in snubbing a member of Parliament of the same standing as Mr. Airey, yet he felt quite equal to the duty, should he find it necessary to make an effort in this direction.

He was sleeping the sleep of the reprobate, long before his son had succeeded in sleeping the sleep of the virtuous. Harold had more to think about, as well as more capacity of thinking, than his father. He was puzzled at the attitude of his friend and counsellor, Edmund Airey. What on earth could he have meant by appropriating Beatrice Avon, Harold wondered. He assumed that Airey had some object in doing what he had done. He knew that his friend was not the man to do anything without having an object in view. Previously he had been discreet to an extraordinary degree in his attitude toward women. He had never even made love to those matrons to whom it is discreet to make love. If he had ever done so Harold knew that he would have heard of it; for there is no fascination in making love to other men's wives, unless it is well known in the world that you are doing so. The school-boy does not smoke his cigarette in private. The fascination of the sin lies in his committing it so that it gets talked about.

Yes, Airey had ever been discreet, Harold knew, and he quite failed to account for his lapse—assuming that it was indiscreet to appropriate Beatrice Avon for an hour, and to keep her amused all that time.

Harold himself had his own ideas of what was discreet in regard to young women, and he had acted up to them. He did not consider that, so far as the majority of young women were concerned, he should be accredited with much self-sacrifice for his discretion.

Had a great temperance movement been set on foot in Italy in the days of Cæsar Borgia, the total abstainers would not have earned commendation for their self-sacrifice. Harold Wynne had been discreet in regard to most women simply because he was afraid of them. He was afraid that he might some day be led to ask one of them to marry him—one of them whom he would regard as worse than a Borgia poison ever after.

The caution that he had displayed in respect of Helen Craven showed how discreet he had accustomed himself to be.

He reflected, however, that in respect of Beatrice Avon he had thrown discretion to the winds From the moment that he had drawn her hands to his by the fishing line, he had given himself up to her. He had been without the power to resist.

Might it not, then, be the same with Edmund Airey? Might not Edmund, who had invariably been so guarded as to be wholly free from reproach so far as women were concerned, have found it impossible to maintain that attitude in the presence of Beatrice?

And if this was so, what would be the result?

This was the thought which kept Harold Wynne awake and uncomfortable for several hours during that night.

CHAPTER XXII
ON THE WISDOM OF THE MATRONS

LADY INNISFAIL made a confession to one of her guests—a certain Mrs. Burgoyne—who was always delighted to play the *rôle* of receiver of confessions. The date at which Lady Innisfail's confession was made was three days after the arrival of Beatrice Avon at the Castle, and its subject was her own over-eagerness to secure a strange face for the entertainment of her guests.

"I thought that the romantic charm which would attach to that girl, who seemed to float up to us out of the mist—leaving her wonderful eyes out of the question altogether—would interest all my guests," said she.

"And so it did, if I may speak for the guests," said Mrs. Burgoyne. "Yes, we were all delighted for nearly an entire day."

"I am glad that my aims were not wholly frustrated," said Lady Innisfail. "But you see the condition we are all in at present."

"I cannot deny it," replied Mrs. Burgoyne, with a sigh. "My dear, a new face is almost as fascinating as a new religion."

"More so to some people—generally men," said Lady Innisfail. "But who could have imagined that a young thing like that—she has never been presented, she tells me—should turn us all topsy turvy?"

"She has a good deal in her favour," remarked Mrs. Burgoyne. "She is fresh, her face is strange, she neither plays, sings, nor recites, and she is a marvellously patient listener."

"That last comes through being the daughter of a literary man," said Lady Innisfail. "The wives and daughters of poets and historians and the like are compelled to be patient listeners. They are allowed to do nothing else."

"I dare say. Anyhow that girl has made the most of her time since she came among us."

"She has. The worst of it is that no one could call her a flirt."

"I suppose not. But what do you call a girl who is attractive to all men, and who makes all the men grumpy, except the one she is talking to?"

"I call her a—a clever girl," replied Lady Innisfail. "Don't we all aim at that sort of thing?"

"Perhaps we did—once," said Mrs. Burgoyne, who was a year or two younger than her hostess. "I should hope that our aims are different now. We are too old, are we not?—you and I—for any man to insult us by making love to us."

"A woman is never too old to be insulted, thank God," said Lady Innisfail; and Mrs. Burgoyne's laugh was not the laugh of a matron who is shocked.

"All the same," added Lady Innisfail, "our pleasant party threatens to become a fiasco, simply because I was over-anxious to annex a new face. I had set my heart upon bringing Harold Wynne and Helen Craven together; but now they have become hopelessly good friends."

"She is very kind to him."

"Yes, that's the worst of it; she is kind and he is indifferent—he treats her as if she were his favourite sister."

"Are matters so bad as that?"

"Quite. But when the other girl is listening to what another man is saying to her, Harold Wynne's face is a study. He is as clearly in love with the other girl as anything can be. That, old reprobate—his father—has his aims too—horrid old creature! Mr. Durdan has ceased to study the Irish question with a deep-sea cast of hooks in his hand: he spends some hours every morning devising plans for spending as many minutes by the side of Beatrice. I do believe that my dear husband would have fallen a victim too, if I did not keep dinning into his ears that Beatrice is the loveliest creature of our acquaintance. I lured him on to deny it, and now we quarrel about it every night."

"I believe Lord Innisfail rather dislikes her," said Mrs. Burgoyne.

"I'm convinced of it," said Lady Innisfail. "But what annoys me most is the attitude of Mr. Airey. He professed to be Harold's friend as well as Helen's, and yet he insists on being so much with Beatrice that Harold will certainly be led on to the love-making point—"

"If he has not passed it already," suggested Mrs. Burgoyne.

"If he has not passed it already; for I need scarcely tell you, my dear Phil, that a man does not make love to a girl for herself alone, but simply because other men make love to her."

"Of course."

"So that it is only natural that Harold should want to make love to Beatrice when he is led to believe that Edmund Airey wants to marry her."

"The young fool! Why could he not restrain his desire until Mr. Airey has married her? But do you really think that Mr. Airey does want to marry her?"

"I believe that Harold Wynne believes so—that is enough for the present. Oh, no. You'll not find me quite so anxious to annex a strange face another time."

From the report of this confidential duologue it may possibly be perceived, first, that Lady Innisfail was a much better judge of the motives and impulses of men than Miss Craven was; and, secondly, that the presence of Beatrice at the Castle had produced a marked impression upon the company beneath its roof.

It was on the evening of the day after the confidential duologue just reported that there was an entertainment in the hall of the Castle. It took the form of *tableaux* arranged after well-known pictures, and there was certainly no lack of actors and actresses for the figures.

Mary Queen of Scots was, of course, led to execution, and Marie Antoinette, equally as a matter of course, appeared in her prison. Then Miss Stafford did her best to realize the rapt young woman in Mr. Sant's "The Soul's Awaking"—Miss Stafford was very wide awake indeed, some scoffer suggested; and Miss Innisfail looked extremely pretty—a hostess's daughter invariably looks pretty—as "The Peacemaker" in Mr. Marcus Stone's picture.

Beatrice Avon took no part in the *tableaux*—the other girls had not absolutely insisted on her appearing beside them on the stage that had been fitted up; they had an + informal council together, Miss Craven being stage-manager, and they had come to the conclusion that they could get along very nicely without her assistance.

Some of them said that Beatrice preferred flirting with the men. However this may have been, the fact remained that Harold, when he had washed the paint off his face—he had been the ill-tempered lover, Miss Craven being the young woman with whom he was supposed to have quarrelled, requiring the interposition of a sweet Peacemaker in the person of Miss Innisfail—went round by a corridor to the back of the hall, and stood for a few minutes behind a 'portiere that took the place of a door at one of the entrances. The hall was, of course, dimly lighted to make the contrast with the stage the greater, so that he could not see the features of the man who was sitting on the chair at the end of the row nearest the *portiere*; but the applause that greeted a reproduction of the picture of a monk shaving himself, having previously used no other soap than was supplied by a particular maker, had scarcely died away before Harold heard the voice of Edmund Airey say, in a low and earnest tone, to someone who was seated beside him, "I do hope that before you go away, you will let me know where you will next pitch your tent. I don't want to lose sight of you."

"If you wish I shall let you know when I learn it from my father," was the reply that Harold heard, clearly spoken in the voice of Beatrice Avon.

Harold went back into the billowy folds of the tapestry curtain, and then into the corridor. The words that he had overheard had startled him. Not merely were the words spoken by Edmund Airey the same as he himself had employed a few days before to Beatrice, but her reply was practically the same as the reply which she had made to him.

When the last of the figurantes had disappeared from the stage, and when the buzz of congratulations was sounding through the hall, now fully lighted, Harold was nowhere to be seen.

Only a few of the most earnest of the smokers were still in the hall when, long past midnight, he appeared at the door leading to the outer hall or porch. His shoes were muddy and his shirt front was pulpy, for the night was a wet one.

He explained to his astonished friends that it was invariably the case that putting paint and other auxiliaries to "making up" on his face, brought on a headache, which he had learned by experience could only be banished by a long walk in the open air.

Well, he had just had such a walk.

He did not expect that his explanation would carry any weight with it; and the way he was looked at by his friends made him aware of the fact that, in giving them credit for more sense than to believe him, he was doing them no more than the merest justice.

No one who was present on his return placed the smallest amount of credence in his story. What many of them did believe was of no consequence.

CHAPTER XXIII
ON THE ATLANTIC

THE boats were scattered like milestones—as was stated by Brian—through the sinuous length of Lough Suangorm. The cutter yacht *Acushla* was leading the fleet out to the Atlantic, with two reefs in her mainsail, and although she towed a large punt, and was by no means a fast boat, she had no difficulty in maintaining her place, the fact being that the half-dozen boats that lumbered after her were mainly fishing craft hailing from the village of Cairndhu, and, as all the world knows, these are not built for speed but endurance. They are half-decked and each carries a lug sail. One of the legends of the coast is that when a lug sail is new its colour is brown, and as a new sail is never seen at Cairndhu there are no means of finding out if the story is true or false. The sails, as they exist, are kaleidoscopic in their patchwork. It is understood that anything will serve as a patch for a lug sail. Sometimes the centre-piece of an old coat has been used for this purpose; but if so, it is only fair to state that it is on record that the centre-piece of an old sail has been shaped into a jacket for the ordinary wearing of a lad.

The lug sail may yet find its way into a drawing room in Belgravia and repose side by side with the workhouse sheeting which occupies an honoured place in that apartment.

On through the even waves that roll from between the headlands at the entrance, to the little strand of pebbles at the end of the lough, the boats lumbered. The sea and sky were equally gray, but now and again a sudden gleam of sunshine would come from some unsuspected rift in the motionless clouds, and fly along the crests of the waves, revealing a green transparency for an instant, and then, flashing upon the sails, make apparent every patch in their expanse, just as a flash of lightning on a dark night reveals for a second every feature of a broad landscape.

As the first vessel of the little fleet, pursuing an almost direct course in spite of the curving of the shores of the Irish fjord, approached one coast and then the other, the great rocks that appeared snow-white, with only a dab of black here and there, became suddenly all dark, and the air was filled with what seemed like snow flakes. The cries of the innumerable sea birds, that whirled about the disturbing boat before they settled and the rocks became gradually white once more, had a remarkable effect when heard against that monotonous background, so to speak, of rolling waves.

The narrow lough was a gigantic organ pipe through which the mighty bass of the Atlantic roared everlastingly.

But when the headlands at the entrance were reached, the company who sat on the weather side of the cutter *Acushla* became aware of a commingling of sounds. The organ voice of the lough only filled up the intervals between the tremendous roar of the lion-throated waves that sprang with an appalling force half way up the black faces of the sheer cliffs, and broke in mid-air. All day long and all night long those inexhaustible billows come rushing upon that coast; and watching them and listening to them one feels how mean are contemporary politics as well as other things.

"That's the Irish question," remarked Lord Innisfail, who was steering his own cutter.

He nodded in the direction of the waves that were clambering up the headlands. What he meant exactly he might have had difficulty in explaining.

"Very true, very true," said Mr. Durdan, sagaciously, hoping to provoke Mr. Airey to reply, and thinking it likely that he would learn from Mr. Airey's reply what was Lord Innisfail's meaning.

But Mr. Airey, who had long ago become acquainted with Mr. Durdan's political methods, did not feel it incumbent on him to make the attempt to grapple with the question—if it was a question—suggested by Lord Innisfail.

The metaphor of a host should not, he knew, be considered too curiously. Like the wit of a police-court magistrate, it should be accepted with effusion.

"Stand by that foresheet," said Lord Innisfail to one of the yacht's hands. "We'll heave to until the other craft come up."

In a few moments the cutter had all way off her, and was simply tumbling about among the waves in a way that made some of the ship's company hold their breath and think longingly of pale brandy.

The cruise of the *Acushla* and the appearance of the fleet of boats upon the lough were due to the untiring energy of Lady Innisfail and to the fact that at last Brian, the boatman, had, by the help of Father Conn, come to grasp something of the force of the phrase "local colour".

Lady Innisfail was anxious that her guests should carry away certain definite impressions of their sojourn at the Connaught castle beyond those that may be acquired at any country-house, which everyone knows may be comprised in a very few words. A big shoot, and an incipient scandal usually constitute the record of a country-house entertainment. Now, it was not that Lady Innisfail objected to a big shoot or an incipient scandal—she admitted that both were excellent in their own way—but she hoped to do a great deal better for her guests. She hoped to impart to their visit some local colour.

She had hung on to the wake and the eviction, as has already been told, with pertinacity. The *fête* which she believed was known to the Irish peasantry as the Cruiskeen, had certainly some distinctive features; though just as she fancied that the Banshee was within her grasp, it had vanished into something substantial—this was the way she described the scene on the cliffs. Although her guests said they were very well satisfied with what they had seen and heard, adding that they had come to the conclusion that if the Irish had only a touch of humour they would be true to the pictures that had been drawn of them, still Lady Innisfail was not satisfied.

Of course if Mr. Airey were to ask Miss Avon to marry him, her house-party would be talked about during the winter. But she knew that it is the marriages which do not come off that are talked about most; and, after all, there is no local colour in marrying or giving in marriage, and she yearned for local colour. Brian, after a time, came to understand something of her ladyship's yearnings. Like the priest and the other inhabitants, he did not at first know what she wanted.

It is difficult to impress upon Fuzzy-wuzzy that he would be regarded as a person of distinction in the Strand and as an idol in Belgravia. At his home in the Soudan he is a very commonplace sort of person. So in the region of Lough Suangorm, but a casual interest attaches to the caubeen, which in Piccadilly would be followed by admiring crowds, and would possibly be dealt with in Evening Editions.

But, as has just been said, Brian and his friends in due time came to perceive the spectacular value to her ladyship's guests of the most commonplace things of the country; and it was this fact that induced Brian to tell three stories of a very high colour to Mr. Airey and Mr. Wynne.

It was also his appreciation of her ladyship's wants that caused him to suggest to her the possibility of a seal-hunt constituting an element of

CHAPTER XXIV
ON THE CHANCE

WHEN the fishing boats came within half a cable's length of the cutter, Lord Innisfail gave up the tiller to Brian, who was well qualified to be the organizer of the expedition, having the reputation of being familiar with the haunts and habits of the seals that may be found—by such as know as much about them as Brian—among the great caves that pierce for several miles the steep cliffs of the coast.

The responsibility of steering a boat under the headlands, either North or South, was not sought by Lord Innisfail. For perhaps three hundred and fifty days in every year it would be impossible to approach the cliffs in any craft; but as Brian took the tiller he gave a knowing glance around the coast and assured his lordship that it was a jewel of a day for a seal-hunt, and added that it was well that he had brought only the largest of the fishing boats, for anything smaller would sink with the weight of the catch of seals.

He took in the slack of the main sheet and sent the cutter flying direct to the Northern headland, the luggers following in her wake, though scarcely preserving stations or distances with that rigorous naval precision which occasionally sends an ironclad to the bottom.

The man-of-war may run upon a reef, and the country may be called on to pay half a million for the damage; but it can never be said that she fails to maintain her station prescribed by the etiquette of the Royal Navy in following the flagship, which shows that the British sailor, wearing epaulettes, is as true as the steel that his ship is made of, and a good deal truer than that of some of the guns which he is asked to fire.

In a short time the boats had cleared the headland, and it seemed to some of the cutter's company as if they were given an opportunity of looking along the whole west coast of Ireland in a moment. Northward and southward, like a study in perspective, the lines of indented cliffs stretched until they dwindled away into the gray sky. The foam line that was curved

"Now, my lard," said Brian, who seemed at last to realize his responsibilities, "all we've got to do is to grab the craythurs; but that same's a caution. We'll be at least an hour-and-a-half in the caves, and as it will be cold work, and maybe wet work, maybe some of their honours wouldn't mind standing by the cutter."

The suggestion was heartily approved of by some of the yacht's company. Lady Innisfail said she was perfectly satisfied with such local colour as was available without leaving the yacht, and it was understood that Miss Avon would remain by her side. Mr. Airey said he thought he could face with cheerfulness a scheme of existence that did not include sitting with varying degrees of uneasiness in a small boat while other men speared an inoffensive seal.

"Such explanations are not for the Atlantic Ocean," said Harold, getting over the side of the yacht into the punt that Brian had hauled close—Lord Innisfail was already in the bow.

In a short time, by the skilful admiralship of Brian, the other boats, which were brought up from the luggers, were manned, and their stations were assigned to them, one being sent to explore a cave a short distance off, while another was to remain at the entrance to pick up any seals that might escape. The same plan was adopted in regard to the great cave, the entrance to which was close to where the yacht was moored. Brian arranged that his boat should enter the cave, while another, fully manned, should stand by the rocks to capture the refugees.

All the boats then started for their stations—all except the punt with Brian at the yoke lines, Harold and Mr. Durdan in the stern sheets, one of the hands at the paddles, and Lord Innisfail in the bows; for when this craft was about to push off, Brian gave an exclamation of discontent.

"What's the matter now?" asked Lord Innisfail.

"Plenty's the matter, my lard," said Brian. "The sorra a bit of luck we'll have this day if we leave the ladies behind us."

"Then we must put up with bad luck," said Lord Innisfail. "Go down on your knees to her ladyship and ask her to come with us if you think that will do any good."

"Oh, her ladyship would come without prayers if she meant to," said Brian. "But it's Miss Avon that's open to entreaty. For the love of heaven and the encouragement of sport, step into the boat, Sheila, and you'll have something to talk about for the rest of your life."

Beatrice shook her head at the appeal, but that wouldn't do for Brian. "Look, my lady, look at her eyes, aren't they just jumping out of her head like young trout in a stream in May?" he cried to Lady Innisfail. "Isn't she waiting for you to say the word to let her come, an' not a word does any gentleman in the boat speak on her behalf."

The gentlemen remained dumb, but Lady Innisfail declared that if Miss Avon was not afraid of a wetting and cared to go in the boat, there was no reason why she should not do so.

In another moment Beatrice had stepped into the punt and it had pushed off with a cheer from Brian. The men in the other boats, now in the distance, hearing the cheer, but without knowing why it arose, sent back an answer that aroused the thousand echoes of the cliffs and the ten thousand sea birds that arose in a cloud from every crevice of the rocks. Thus it was that the approach of the boat to the great cave did not take place in silence.

Harold had not uttered a word. He had not even looked at Edmund Airey's face to see what expression it wore when Beatrice stepped into the boat.

"Did you ever hear anything like Airey's roundabout phrase about a scheme of existence?" said Mr. Durdan.

"It is his way of putting a simple matter," said Harold. "You heard of the man who, in order to soften down the fact that a girl had what are colloquially known as beetle-crushers, wrote that her feet tended to increase the mortality among coleoptera?"

"I'm afraid that the days of the present government are numbered," said Mr. Durdan, who seemed to think that the remark was in logical sequence with Harold's story.

Beatrice looked wonderingly at the speaker; it was some moments before she found an echo in the expression on Harold's face to what she felt.

The man who could think of such things as the breaking up of a government, when floating in thirty fathoms of green sea, beneath the shadow of such cliffs as the boat was approaching, was a mystery to the girl, though she was the daughter of one of the nineteenth century historians, to whom nothing is a mystery.

The boat entered the great cave without a word being spoken by any one aboard, and in a few minutes it was being poled along in semi-darkness. The lapping of the swell from the entrance against the sides of the cave sounded on through the distance of the interior, and from those mysterious depths came strange sounds of splashing water, of dropping stalactites, and now and again a mighty sob of waves choked within a narrow vent.

Silently the boat was forced onward, and soon all light from the entrance was obscured. Through total darkness the little craft crept for nearly half a mile.

Suddenly a blaze of light shot up with startling effect in the bows of the boat. It only came from a candle that Brian had lit: but its gleam was reflected in millions of stalactites into what seemed an interminable distance—millions of stalactites on the roof and the walls, and millions of ripples beneath gave back the gleam, until the boat appeared to be the centre of a vast illumination.

The dark shadows of the men who were using the oars as poles, danced about the brilliant roof and floor of the cave, adding to the fantastic charm of the scene.

"Now," said Brian, in a whisper, "these craythurs don't understand anything that's said to them unless by a human being, so we'll need to be silent enough. We'll be at the first ledge soon, and there maybe you'll wait with the lady, Mr. Wynne—you're heavier than Mr. Durdan, and every inch of water that the boat draws is worth thinking about. I'll leave a candle with you, but not a word must you speak."

"All right," said Harold. "You're the manager of the expedition; we must obey you; but I don't exactly see where my share in the sport comes in."

"I'd explain it all if I could trust myself to speak," said Brian. "The craythurs has ears." The ledge referred to by him was reached in silence. It was perhaps six inches above the water, and in an emergency it might have afforded standing room for three persons. So much Harold saw by the light of the candle that the boatman placed in a niche of rock four feet above the water.

At a sign from Brian, Harold got upon the ledge and helped Beatrice out of the boat.

The light of the candle that was in the bow of the boat gleamed upon the figure of a man naked from the waist up, and wearing a hard round hat with a candle fastened to the brim.

Harold knew that this was the costume of the seal-hunter of the Western caves, for he had had a talk with Brian on the subject, and had learned that only by swimming with a lighted candle on his forehead for a quarter of a mile, the hunter could reach the sealing ground at the termination of the cave.

Without a word being spoken, the boat went on, and its light soon glimmered mysteriously in the distance.

Harold and Beatrice stood side by side on the narrow ledge of rock and watched the dwindling of the light. The candle that was on the niche of rock almost beside them seemed dwindling also. It had become the merest spark. Harold saw that Brian had inadvertently placed it so that the dripping of the water from the roof sent flecks of damp upon the wick.

He stretched out his hand to shift it to another place, but before he could touch it, a large stalactite dropped upon it, and not only extinguished it, but sent it into the water with a splash.

The little cry that came from the girl as the blackness of darkness closed upon them, sounded to his ears as a reproach.

"I had not touched it," said he. "Something dropped from the roof upon it. You don't mind the darkness?"

"Oh, no—no," said she, doubtfully. "But we were commanded to be dumb."

"That command was given on the assumption that the candle would continue burning—now the conditions are changed," said he, with a sophistry that would have done credit to a cabinet minister.

"Oh," said she.

There was a considerable pause before she asked him how long he thought it would be before the boat would return.

He declined to bind himself to any expression of opinion on the subject.

Then there was another pause, filled up only by the splash of something falling from the roof—by the wash of the water against the smooth rock.

"I wonder how it has come about that I am given a chance of speaking to you at last?" said he.

"At last?" said she, repeating his words in the same tone of inquiry.

"I say at last, because I have been waiting for such an opportunity for some time, but it did not come. I don't suppose I was clever enough to make my opportunity, but now it has come, thank God."

Again there was silence. He seemed to think that he had said something requiring a reply from her, but she did not speak.

"I wonder if you would believe me when I say that I love you," he remarked.

"Yes," she replied, as naturally as though he had asked her what she thought of the weather. "Yes, I think I would believe you. If you did not love me—if I was not sure that you loved me, I should be the most miserable girl in all the world."

"Great God!" he cried. "You do not mean to say that you love me, Beatrice?"

"If you could only see my face now, you would know it," said she. "My eyes would tell you all—no, not all—that is in my heart."

He caught her hands, after first grasping a few handfuls of clammy rock, for the hands of the truest lovers do not meet mechanically.

"I see them," he whispered—"I see your eyes through the darkness. My love, my love!"

He did not kiss her. His soul revolted from the idea of the commonplace kiss in the friendly secrecy of the darkness.

There are opportunities and opportunities. He believed that if he had kissed her then she would never have forgiven him, and he was right. "What a fool I was!" he cried. "Two nights ago, when I overheard a man tell you, as I had told you long ago—so long ago—more than a week ago—that he did not want you to pass out of his sight—when I heard you make the same promise to him as you had made to me, I felt as if there was nothing left for me in the world. I went out into the darkness, and as I stood at the place when I first saw you, I thought that I should be doing well if I were to throw myself headlong down those rocks into the sea that the rain was beating upon. Beatrice, God only knows if it would be better or worse for you if I had thrown myself down—if I were to leave you standing alone here now."

"Do not say those words—they are like the words I asked you before not to say. Even then your words meant everything to me. They mean everything to me still."

He gave a little laugh. Triumph rang through it. He did not seem to think that his laughter might sound incongruous to her.

"This is my hour," he said. "Whatever fate may have in store for me it cannot make me unlive this hour. And to think that I had got no idea that such an hour should ever come to me—that you should ever come to me, my beloved! But you came to me. You came to me when I had tried to bring myself to feel that there was something worth living for in the world apart from love."

"And now?"

"And now—and now—now I know that there is nothing but love that is worth living for. What is your thought, Beatrice—tell me all that is in your heart?"

"All—all?" She now gave the same little laugh that he had given. She felt that her turn had come.

She gave just the same laugh when his feeling of triumph had given place to a very different feeling—when he had told her that he was a pauper—that he had no position in the world—that he was dependent upon his father for every penny that he had to spend, with the exception of a few hundred pounds a year, which he inherited from his mother—that it was an act of baseness on his part to tell her that he loved her.

He had plenty of time for telling her all this, and for explaining his position thoroughly, for nearly an hour had passed before a gleam of light and a hail from the furthest recesses of the cave, made them aware of the fact that other interests than theirs existed in the world.

And yet when he had told her all that he had to tell to his disadvantage, she gave that little laugh of triumph. He would have given a good deal to be able to see the expression which he knew was in those wonderful eyes of hers, as that laugh came from her.

Not being able to do so, however, he could only crush her hands against his lips and reply to the boat's hail.

Brian, on hearing of the mishap to the candle, delivered a torrent of execration against himself. It took Harold some minutes to bring himself up to the point of Lord Innisfail's enthusiasm on the subject of seal-fishing. Five excellent specimens were in the bottom of the boat, and the men who had swum after them were there also. A strong odour of whiskey was about them; and the general idea that prevailed was that they would not suffer from a chill, though they had been in the water for three quarters of an hour.

As the other boats only succeeded in capturing three seals among them all, Brian had statistics to bear out his contention that the presence of Beatrice had brought luck to his boat.

He pocketed two sovereigns which Harold handed him when the boats returned to the mooring-place, and he was more profuse than ever in his abuse of his own stupidity in placing the candle so as to be affected by the damp from the roof.

His eyes twinkled all the time in a way that made Harold's cheeks red.

The judge found Miss Avon somewhat *distraite* after dinner that night. He became pensive in consequence. He wondered if she thought him elderly.

He did not mind in the least growing old, but the idea of being thought elderly was abhorrent to him.

The next day Beatrice and her father returned to their cottage at the other side of the lough.

CHAPTER XXV
ON THE SOCIAL VALUE OF THE REPROBATE

SOMETHING remarkable had occurred. Lord Fotheringay had been for a fortnight under one roof without disgracing himself.

The charitable people said he was reforming.

The others said he was aging rapidly.

The fact remained the same, however: he had been a fortnight at the Castle and he had not yet disgraced himself.

Mrs. Burgoyne congratulated Lady Innisfail upon this remarkable occurrence, and Lady Innisfail began to hope that it might get talked about. If her autumn party at Castle Innisfail were to be talked about in connection with the reform of Lord Fotheringay, much more interest would be attached to the party and the Castle than would be the result of the publication of the statistics of a gigantic shoot. Gigantic shoots did undoubtedly take place on the Innisfail Irish property, but they invariably took place before the arrival of Lord Innisfail and his guests, and the statistics were, for obvious reasons, not published. They only leaked out now and again.

The most commonplace people might enjoy the reputation attaching to the careful preservation and the indiscriminate slaughter of game; but Lady Innisfail knew that the distinction accruing from a connection with a social scandal of a really high order, or with a great social reform—either as regards a hardened reprobate or an afternoon toilet—was something much greater.

Of course, she understood perfectly well that in England the Divorce Court is the natural and legitimate medium for attaining distinction in the form of a Special Edition and a pen and ink portrait; but she had seen great things accomplished by the rumour of an unfair game of cards, as well as by a very daring skirt dance.

Next to a high-class scandal, the discovery of a new religion was a means of reaching eminence, she knew. With the exact social value attaching to the Reform of a Hardened Reprobate, she was as yet unacquainted, the fact being that she had never had any experience of such an incident—it was certainly very rare in the society in which she moved, so that it is not surprising that she was not prepared to say at a moment how much it would count in the estimation of the world.

But if the Reform of a Reprobate—especially a reprobate with a title—was so rare as to be uncatalogued, so to speak, surely it should be of exceptional value as a social incident. Should it not partake of the prestige which attaches to a rare occurrence?

This was the way that Mrs. Burgoyne put the matter to her friend and hostess, and her friend and hostess was clever enough to appreciate the force of her phrases. She began to perceive that although Lord Fotheringay had come to the Castle on the slenderest of invitations, and simply because it suited his purpose—although she had been greatly annoyed at his sudden appearance at the Castle, still good might come of it.

She did not venture to estimate from the standpoint of the moralist, the advantages accruing to the Reformed Reprobate himself from the incident of his reform, she merely looked at the matter from the standpoint of the woman of society—which is something quite different—desirous of attaining a certain social distinction.

Thus it was that Lady Innisfail took to herself the credit of the Reform of the Reprobate, and petted the reprobate accordingly, giving no attention whatever to the affairs of his son. These affairs, interesting though they had been to her some time before, now became insignificant compared with the Great Reform.

She even went the length of submitting to be confided in by Lord Fotheringay; and she heard, with genuine interest, from his own lips that he considered the world in general to be hollow. He had found it so. He had sounded the depths of its hollowness. He had found that in all grades of society there was much evil. The working classes—he had studied the question of the working man not as a parliamentary candidate, consequently honestly—drank too much beer. They sought happiness through the agency of beer; but all the beer produced by all the brewers in the House of Lords would not bring happiness to the working classes. As for the higher grades of society—the people who were guilty of partaking of unearned increment—well, they were wrong too. He thought it unnecessary to give the particulars of the avenues through which they sought happiness. But they were all wrong. The domestic life—there, and there only, might one find the elements of true happiness. He knew this because he had endeavoured to reach happiness by every other avenue and had failed in his endeavours. He now meant to supply his omission, and he regretted that it had never occurred to him to do so before. Yes, some poet or other had written something or other on the subject of the great charm of a life of domesticity, and Lord Fotheringay assured Lady Innisfail in confidence that that poet was right.

Lady Innisfail sighed and said that the Home—the English Home— with its simple pleasures and innocent mirth, was where the Heart—the English Heart—was born. What happiness was within the reach of all if they would only be content with the Home! Society might be all very well in its way. There were duties to be discharged—every rank in life carried its duties with it; but how sweet it was, after one had discharged one's social obligations, to find a solace in the retirement of Home.

Lord Fotheringay lifted up his hands and said "Ah—ah," in different cadences.

Lady Innisfail folded her hands and shook her head with some degree of solemnity. She felt confident that if Lord Fotheringay was in earnest, her autumn party would be talked about with an enthusiasm surpassing that which would attach to the comments on any of the big shoots in Scotland, or in Yorkshire, or in Wales.

But when Lord Fotheringay had an opportunity of conversing alone with Mr. Airey, he did not think it necessary to dwell upon the delights which he had begun to perceive might be found in a life of pure domesticity. He took the liberty of reminding Mr. Airey of the conversation they had on the morning after Miss Avon's arrival at the Castle.

"Had we a conversation then, Lord Fotheringay?" said Mr. Airey, in a tone that gave Lord Fotheringay to understand that if any contentious point was about to be discussed, it would rest with him to prove everything.

"Yes, we had a conversation," said Lord Fotheringay. "I was foolish enough to make a confidant of you."

"If you did so, you certainly were foolish," said Edmund, quietly.

"I have been keeping my eyes open and my ears open as well, during the past ten days," said Lord Fotheringay, with a leer that was meant to be significant. Edmund Airey, however, only took it to signify that Lord Fotheringay could easily be put into a very bad temper. He said nothing, but allowed Lord Fotheringay to continue. "Yes, let me tell you that when I keep both eyes and ears open not much escapes me. I have seen and heard a good deal. You are a clever sort of person, friend Airey; but you don't know the world as I know it."

"No, no—as you know it—ah, no," remarked Mr. Airey.

Lord Fotheringay was a trifle put out by the irritating way in which the words were spoken. Still, the pause he made was not of long duration.

"You have your game to play, like other people, I suppose," he resumed, after the little pause.

"You are at liberty to suppose anything you please, my dear Lord Fotheringay," said Mr. Airey, with a smile.

"Come," said Lord Fotheringay, adopting quite another tone. "Come, Airey, speaking as man to man, wasn't it a confoundedly shabby trick for you to play upon me—getting me to tell you that I meant to marry that young thing—to save her from unhappiness, Airey?"

"Well?" said Airey.

"Well?" said Lord Fotheringay.

"You didn't complete your sentence. Was the shabby trick accepting your confidence?"

"The shabby trick was trying to win the affection of the young woman after I had declared to you my intention."

"That was the shabby trick, was it?"

"I have no hesitation in saying that it was."

"Very well. I hope that you have nothing more to confide in me beside this—your confidences have so far been singularly uninteresting."

Lord Fotheringay got really angry.

"Let me tell you—" he began, but he was stopped by Airey.

"No, I decline to let you tell me anything," said he. "You accused me just now of being so foolish as to listen to your confidences. I, perhaps, deserved the reproach. But I should be a fool if I were to give you another chance of levelling the same accusation against me. You will have to force your confidences on someone else in future, unless such as concern your liver. You confided in me that your liver wasn't quite the thing. How is it to-day?"

"I understand your tactics," said Lord Fotheringay, with a snap. "And I'll take good care to make others acquainted with them also," he added. "Oh, no, Mr. Airey; I wasn't born yesterday."

"To that fact every Peerage in the kingdom bears testimony," said Mr. Airey.

Lord Fotheringay had neglected his cigar. It had gone out. He now took three or four violent puffs at it; he snapped it from between his teeth, looked at the end, and then dropped it on the ground and stamped on it.

"It was your own fault," said Airey. "Try one of mine, and don't bother yourself with other matters."

"I'll bother myself with what I please," said Lord Fotheringay with a snarl.

But he took Mr. Airey's cigar, and smoked it to the end. He knew that Mr. Airey smoked Carolinas.

This little scene took place outside the Castle before lunch on the second day after the departure of Mr. Avon and his daughter; and, after lunch, Lord Fotheringay put on a yachting jacket and cap, and announced his intention of having a stroll along the cliffs. His doctor had long ago assured him, he said, that he did not take sufficient exercise nor did he breathe enough fresh air. He meant in future to put himself on a strict regimen in this respect, and would begin at once.

He was allowed to carry out his intention alone—indeed he did not hint that his medical adviser had suggested company as essential to the success of any scheme of open air exercise.

The day was a breezy one, and the full force of the wind was felt at the summit of the cliff coast; but like many other gentlemen who dread being thought elderly, he was glad to seize every opportunity of showing that he was as athletic as the best of the young fellows; so he strode along, gasping and blowing with quite as much fresh air in his face as the most exacting physician could possibly have prescribed for a single dose.

He made his way to the mooring-place of the boats, and he found Brian in the boat-house engaged in making everything snug.

He was very civil to Brian, and after a transfer of coin, inquired about the weather.

There was a bit of a draught of wind in the lough, Brian said, but it was a fine day for a sail. Would his lardship have a mind for a bit of a sail? The *Acushla* was cruising, but the *Mavourneen*, a neat little craft that sailed like a swallow, was at his lardship's service.

After some little consideration, Lord Fotheringay said that though he had no idea of sailing when he left the Castle, yet he never could resist the temptation of a fine breeze—it was nothing stronger than a breeze that was blowing, was it?

"A draught—just a bit of a draught," said the man.

"In that case," said Lord Fotheringay, "I think I may venture. In fact, now that I come to think of it, I should like to visit the opposite shore. There is a Castle or something, is there not, on the opposite shore?"

"Is it a Castle?" said Brian. "Oh, there's a power of Castles scattered along the other shore, my lard. It's thrippin' over them your lardship will be after doin.'"

"Then we'll not lose a moment in starting," said Lord Fotheringay.

CHAPTER XXVI
ON FRANKNESS AND FRIENDSHIP

BRIAN took care that no moment was lost. In the course of a very few minutes Lord Fotheringay was seated on the windward thwarts of the boat, his hands grasping the gunwale to right and left, and his head bowed to mitigate in some measure the force of the shower of sea-water that flashed over the boat as her hows neatly clipped the crest off every wave.

Lord Fotheringay held on grimly. He hated the sea and all connected with it; though he hated the House of Lords to almost as great an extent, yet he had offered the promoter of the Channel Tunnel to attend in the House and lend the moral weight of his name to the support of the scheme. It was only the breadth and spontaneousness of Brian's assurance that the breeze was no more than a draught, that had induced him to carry out his cherished idea of crossing the lough.

"Didn't I tell your lardship that the boat could sail with the best of them?" said the man, as he hauled in the sheet a trifle, and brought the boat closer to the wind—a manouvre that did not tend to lessen the cascade that deluged his passenger.

Lord Fotheringay said not a word. He kept his head bowed to every flap of the waves beneath the bows. His attitude would have commended itself to any painter anxious to produce a type of Submission to the Will of Heaven.

He was aging quickly—so much Brian perceived, and dwelt upon—with excellent effect—in his subsequent narrative of the voyage to some of the servants at the Castle. The cosmetic that will withstand the constant application of sea-water has yet to be invented, so that in half an hour Lord Fotheringay would not have been recognized except by his valet. Brian had taken aboard a well-preserved gentleman with a rosy complexion and a moustache almost too black for nature. The person who disembarked at the opposite side of the lough was a stooped old man with lank streaky cheeks and a wisp of gray hair on each side of his upper lip.

"And it's a fine sailor your lardship is entirely," remarked the boatman, as he lent his tottering, dazed passenger a helping hand up the beach of pebbles. "And it's raal enjoyment your lardship will be after having among the Castles of the ould quality, after your lardship's sail."

Not a word did Lord Fotheringay utter. He felt utterly broken down in spirit, and it was not until he had got behind a rock and had taken out a pocket-comb and a pocket-glass, and had by these auxiliaries, and the application of a grain or two of roseate powder without which he never ventured a mile from his base of supplies, repaired some of the ravages of his voyage, that he ventured to make his way to the picturesque white cottage, which Miss Avon had once pointed out to him as the temporary residence of her father and herself.

It was a five-roomed cottage that had been built and furnished by an enthusiastic English fisherman for his accommodation during his annual residence in Ireland. One, more glance did Lord Fotheringay give to his pocket-mirror before knocking at the door.

He would have had time to renew his youth, had he had his pigments handy, before the door was opened by an old woman with a shawl over her shoulders and a cap, that had possibly once been white, on her straggling hairs.

She made the stage courtesy of an old woman in front of Lord Fotheringay, and explained that she was a little hard of hearing—she was even obliging enough to give a circumstantial account of the accident that was responsible for her infirmity.

"Miss Avon?" said the old woman, when Lord Fotheringay had repeated his original request in a louder tone. "Miss Avon? no, she's not here now—not even her father, who was a jewel of a gentleman, though a bit queer. God bless them both now that they have gone back to England, maybe never to return."

"Back to England. When?" shouted Lord Fotheringay.

"Why, since early in the morning. The Blessed Virgin keep the young lady from harm, for she's swater than honey, and the Saints preserve her father, for he was—"

Lord Fotheringay did not wait to hear the position of the historian defined by the old woman. He turned away from the door with such words as caused her infirmity to be a blessing in disguise.

When Brian greeted his return with a few well-chosen phrases bearing upon the architecture of the early Celtic nobles, Lord Fotheringay swore at him; but the boatman, who did a little in that way himself when under extreme provocation, only smiled as Lord Fotheringay took his seat in the boat once more, and prepared for the ordeal of his passage.

There was a good deal in Brian's smile.

The wind had changed most unaccountably, he explained, so that it would, he feared, be absolutely necessary to tack out almost to the entrance of the lough in order to reach the mooring-place. For the next hour he became the exponent of every system of sailing known to modern navigators. After something over an hour of this manoeuvring, he had compassion upon his victim, and ran the boat before the wind—he might have done so at first if Lord Fotheringay had not shown such a poor knowledge of men as to swear at him—to the mooring-place.

"If it's not making too free with your lardship, I'd offer your lardship a hand up the track," said Brian. "It's myself that has to go up to the Castle anyway, with a letter to her ladyship from Miss Avon. Didn't the young lady give it to me in the morning before she started with his honour her father on the car?"

"And you knew all this time that Miss Avon and her father had left the neighbourhood?" said Lord Fotheringay, through his store teeth.

"Tubbe sure I did," said Brian. "But Miss Avon didn't live in one of the Castles of the ould quality that your lardship was so particular ready to explore."

Lord Fotheringay felt that his knowledge of the world and the dwellers therein had its limits.

It was at Lord Fotheringay's bedside that Harold said his farewell to his father the next day. Lord Fotheringay's incipient rheumatism had been acutely developed by his drenching of the previous afternoon, and he thought it prudent to remain in bed.

"You're going, are you?" snarled the Father.

"Yes, I'm going," replied the Son. "Lord and Lady Innisfail leave to-morrow."

"Have you asked Miss Craven to marry you?" inquired the Father.

"No," said Harold.

"Why not—tell me that?"

"I haven't made up my mind on the subject of marrying."

"Then the sooner you make it up the better it will be for yourself. I've been watching you pretty closely for some days—I did not fail to notice a certain jaunty indifference to what was going on around you on the night of your return from that tomfoolery in the boats—seal-hunting, I think they called it. I saw the way you looked at Helen Craven that night. Contempt, or something akin to contempt, was in every glance. Now you know that she is to be at Ella's in October. You have thus six weeks to make up your mind to marry her. If you make up your mind to marry anyone else, you may make up your mind to live upon the three hundred a year that your mother left you. Not a penny you will get from me. I've stinted myself hitherto to secure you your allowance. By heavens, I'll not do so any longer. You will only receive your allowance from me for another year, and then only by signing a declaration at my lawyer's to the effect that you are not married. I've heard of secret marriages before now, but you needn't think of that little game. That's all I've to say to you."

"And it is enough," said Harold. "Good-bye." He left the room and then he left the Castle, Lady Innisfail only shaking her head and whispering, "You have disappointed me," as he made his adieux.

The next day all the guests had departed—all, with the exception of Lord Fotheringay, who was still too ill to move. In the course of some days, however, the doctor thought that he might without risk—except, of course, such as was incidental to the conveyance itself—face a drive on an outside car, to the nearest railway-station.

Before leaving him, as she was compelled to do owing to her own engagements, Lady Innisfail had another interesting conversation—it almost amounted to a consultation—with her friend Mrs. Burgoyne on the subject of the Reform of the Hardened Reprobate. And the result of their further consideration of the subject from every standpoint, was to induce them to believe that, with such a powerful incentive to the Higher Life as an acute rheumatic attack, Lord Fotheringay's reform might safely be counted on. It might, at any rate, be freely discussed during the winter. If, subsequently, he should become a backslider, it would not matter. His reform would have gone the way of all topics.

Helen Craven and Edmund Airey had also a consultation together on the subject upon which they had previously talked more than once.

Each of them showed such an anxiety to give prominence to the circumstance that they were actuated solely for Harold's benefit in putting into practice the plan which one of them had suggested, it was pretty clear that they had an uneasy feeling that they required some justification for the course which they had thought well to pursue.

Yes, they agreed that Harold should be placed beyond the power of his father. Mr. Airey said he had never met a more contemptible person than Lord Fotheringay, and for the sake of making Harold independent of such a father, he would, he declared, do again all that he had done during the week of Miss Avon's sojourn at the Castle.

It was, indeed, sad, Miss Craven felt, that Harold should have such a father.

"Perhaps it was because I felt this so strongly that I—I—well, I began to ask myself if there might not be some way of escape for him," said she, in a pensive tone that was quite different from the tone of the frank communication that she had made to Mr. Airey some time before.

"I can quite understand that," said Edmund. "Well, though Harold hasn't shown himself to be wise—that is—"

"We both know what that means," said she, anticipating his definition of wisdom so far as Harold was concerned.

"We do," said Edmund. "If he has not shown himself to be wise in this way, he has not shown himself to be a fool in another way."

"I suppose he has not," said she, thoughtfully.

"Great heavens! you don't mean to think that—"

"That he has told Beatrice Avon that he loves her? No, I don't fancy that he has, still—"

"Still?"

"Well, I thought that, on their return from that awful seal-hunt, I saw a change in both of them. It seemed to me that—that—well, I don't quite know how I should express it. Haven't you seen a thirsty look on a man's face?"

"A thirsty look? I believe I have seen it on a woman's face."

"It may be the same. Well, Harold Wynne's face wore such an expression for days before the seal-hunt—I can't say that I noticed it on Beatrice Avon's face at the same time; but so soon as they returned from the boats on that evening, I noticed the change on Harold's—perhaps it was only fancy."

"I am inclined to believe that it was fancy. In my belief none of us was quite the same after that wild cruise. I was beside Miss Avon all the time that we were sailing out to the caves, and though she and Harold were in the boat together, yet Lord Innisfail and Durdan were in the same boat also. I can't see how they could have had any time for an understanding while they were engaged in looking after the seals."

Miss Craven shook her head doubtfully. It was clear that she was a believer in the making of opportunities in such matters as those which they were discussing.

"Anyhow, we have done all that we could reasonably be expected to do," said she.

"And perhaps a trifle over," said he. "If it were not that I like Harold so much—and you, too, my dear"—this seemed an afterthought—"I would not have done all that I have done. It is quite unlikely that Miss Avon and I shall be under the same roof again, but if we should be, I shall, you may be certain, find out from her whether or not an understanding exists between her and Harold. But what understanding could it be?"

Miss Craven smiled. Was this the man who had made such a reputation for cleverness, she asked herself—a man who placed a limit on the opportunities of lovers, and then inquired what possible understanding could be come to between a penniless man and a girl with "a gray eye or so."

"What understanding?" said she. "Why, he may have unfolded to her a scheme for becoming Lord High Chancellor after two year's hard work at the bar, with a garden-party now and again; or for being made a Bishop in the same time; and their understanding may be to wait for one another until the arrival of either event. Never mind. We have done our best for him."

"For them," said Edmund.

Yes, he tried to bring himself to believe that all that he had done was for the benefit of his friend Harold and for his friend Beatrice—to say nothing of his friend Helen as well. After a time he did almost force himself to believe that there was nothing that was not strictly honourable in the endeavour that he had made, at Helen's suggestion, to induce Beatrice Avon to perceive the possibility of her obtaining a proposal of marriage from a rich and distinguished man, if she were only to decline to afford the impecunious son of a dissolute peer an opportunity of telling her that he loved her.

Now and again, however, he had an uneasy twinge, as the thought occurred to him that if some man, understanding the exact circumstances of the case, were to be as frank with him as Helen Craven had been (once), that man might perhaps be led to say that he had been making a fool of Beatrice for the sake of gratifying his own vanity.

It was just possible, and he knew it, that that frank friend—assuming that frankness and friendship may exist together—might be disposed to give prominence in this matter to the impulses of vanity, to the exclusion of the impulses of friendship, and a desire to set the crooked straight.

Even the fortnight which he spent in Norway with one of the heads of the Government party—a gentleman who would probably have shortly at his disposal an important Under-Secretaryship—failed quite to abate these little twinges that he had when he reflected upon the direction that might be taken by a frank friend, in considering the question of the responsibility involved in his attitude toward Miss Avon.

It was just a week after Lord Fotheringay had left Castle Innisfail that a stranger appeared in the neighbourhood—a strange gentleman with the darkest hair and the fiercest eyes ever seen, even in that region of dark hair and eyes. He inquired who were the guests at the Castle, and when he learned that the last of them—a distinguished peer named Lord Fotheringay—had gone some time, and that it was extremely unlikely that the Castle would be open for another ten months, his eyes became fiercer than ever. He made use of words in a strange tongue, which Brian declared, if not oaths, would do duty for oaths without anyone being the wiser.

The stranger departed as mysteriously as he had come.

CHAPTER XXVII
ON CIRCUMVENTING A STAG

IF Edmund Airey had a good deal to think about in Norway, Harold Wynne was certainly not without a subject for thought in Scotland.

It was with a feeling of exultation that he had sat in the bows of the cutter *Acushla* on her return to her moorings after that seal-hunt which everyone agreed had been an extraordinary success. Had this expression of exultation been noticed by Lady Innisfail, it would, naturally, have been attributed by her to the fact that he had been in the boat that had made the largest catch of seals. To be sure, Miss Craven, who had observed at least a change in the expression upon his face, did not attribute it to his gratification on having slaughtered some seals, but then Miss Craven was more acute than an ordinary observer.

He felt that he did well to be exultant, as he looked at Beatrice Avon standing by the side of Lord Innisfail at the tiller. The wind that filled the mainsail came upon her face and held her garments against her body, revealing every gracious curve of her shape, and suggesting to his eyes a fine piece of sculpture with flying drapery.

And she was his.

It seemed to him when he had begun to speak to her in the solemn darkness of the seal-cave, that it was impossible that he could receive any answer from her that would satisfy him. How was it possible that she could love him, he had asked himself at some agonizing moments during the week. He thought that she might possibly have come to love him in time, if she had not been with him in the boat during that night of mist, when the voice of Helen Craven had wailed round the cliffs. Her arrival at the Castle could not but have revealed to her the fact that she might obtain an offer of marriage from someone who was socially far above him; and thus he had almost lost all hope of her.

And yet she was his.

The course adopted by his friend Edmund Airey had astonished him. He could not believe that Airey had fallen in love with her. It was not consistent with Airey's nature to fall in love with anyone, he believed. But he knew that in the matter of falling in love, people do not always act consistently with their character; so that, after all, Airey might be only waiting an opportunity to tell her that he had fallen in love with her.

The words that he had overheard Airey speak to her upon the night of the *tableaux* in the hall—words that had driven him out into the night of rain and storm to walk madly along the cliffs, and to wonder if he were to throw himself into the waves beneath, would he be strong enough to let himself sink into their depths or weak enough to make a struggle for life—those words had cleared away whatever doubts he had entertained as to Edmund's intentions.

And yet she was his.

She had answered his question so simply and clearly—with such earnestness and tenderness as startled him. It seemed that they had come to love each other, as he had read of lovers doing, from the first moment that they had met. It seemed that her love had, like his, only increased through their being kept apart from each other—mainly by the clever device of Miss Craven and the co-operation of Edmund Airey, though, of course, Harold did not know this.

His reflections upon this marvel—the increase of their love, though they had few opportunities of being together and alone—would have been instructive even to persons so astute and so ready to undertake the general control of events as Mr. Airey and Miss Craven. Unfortunately, however, they were as ignorant of what had taken place to induce these reflections as he was of the conspiracy between them to keep him apart from Beatrice to secure his happiness and the happiness of Beatrice.

The fact that Beatrice loved him and had confessed her love for him, though they had had so few opportunities of being together, seemed to him the greatest of all the marvels that he had recently experienced.

As he gave a farewell glance at the lough and recollected how, a fortnight before, he had walked along the cliffs and had cast to the winds all his cherished ideas of love, he could not help feeling that he had been surrounded with marvels. He had had a narrow escape—he actually regarded a goodlooking young woman with several thousands of pounds of an income, as a narrow escape.

This was the last of the reflections that came to him with the sound of the green seas choked in the narrows of the lough.

The necessity of preserving himself from sudden death—the Irish outside car on which he was driving was the worst specimen he had yet seen—absorbed all his thoughts when he had passed through the village of Ballycruiskeen; and by the time he had got out of the train that carried him to the East Coast—a matter of six hours travelling—and aboard the steamer that bore him to Glasgow, the exultation that he had felt on leaving Castle Innisfail, and on reflecting upon the great happiness that had come to him, was considerably chastened.

He was due at two houses in Scotland. At the first he meant to do a little shooting. The place was not inaccessible. After a day's travelling he found himself at a railway station fifteen miles from his destination. He eventually reached the place, however, and he had some shooting, which, though indifferent, was far better than it was possible to obtain on Lord Innisfail's mountains—at least for Lord Innisfail's guests to obtain.

The second place was still further north—it was now and again alluded to as the North Pole by some visitors who had succeeded in finding their way to it, in spite of the directions given to them by the various authorities on the topography of the Highlands. Several theories existed as to the best way of reaching this place, and Harold, who knew sufficient Scotch to be able to take in the general meaning of the inhabitants without the aid of an interpreter, was made aware while at the shooting lodge, of these theories. Hearing, however, that some persons had actually been known to find the place, he felt certain that they had struck out an independent course for themselves. It was incredible to him that any of them had reached it by following the directions they had received on the subject. He determined to follow their example; and he had reached the place—eventually.

It was when he had been for three days following a stag, that he began to think of his own matters in a dispassioned way. Crawling on one's stomach along a mile or two of boggy land and then wriggling through narrow spaces among the rocks—sitting for five or six hours on gigantic sponges (damp) of heather, with one's chin on one's knees for strategical purposes, which the gillies pretend they understand, but which they keep a dead secret—shivering as the Scotch mist clothes one as with a wet blanket, then being told suddenly that there is a stag thirty yards to windward—getting a glimpse of it, missing it, and then hearing the gillies exchanging remarks in a perfectly intelligible Gaelic regarding one's capacity—these incidents constitute an environment that tends to make one look dispassionately upon such marvels as Harold had been considering in a very different spirit while the Irish lough was yet within hearing.

On the third day that he had been trying to circumvent the stag, Harold felt despondent—not about the stag, for he had long ago ceased to take any interest in the brute—but about his own future.

It is to be regretted (sometimes) that an exchange of sentiments on the subject of love between lovers does not bring with it a change of circumstances, making possible the realization of a scheme of life in which those sentiments shall play an active part—or at least as active a part as sentiments can play. This was Harold's great regret. Since he had found that he loved Beatrice and that Beatrice loved him, the world naturally appeared lovelier also. But it was with the loveliness of a picture that hangs in a public gallery, not as an individual possession.

His material circumstances, so far from having improved since he had confessed to Edmund Airey that it was necessary for him to marry a woman with money, had become worse; and yet he had given no thought to the young woman with the money, but a great many thoughts to the young woman who had, practically, none. He felt that no more unsatisfactory state of matters could be imagined. And yet he felt that it would be impossible to take any steps with a view of bringing about a change.

He had received several letters from Beatrice, and he had written several to her; but though in more than one he had told her in that plain strain which one adopts when one does not desire to be in any way convincing, that it was a most unfortunate day for her when she met him, still he did not suggest that their correspondence should cease.

What was to be the end of their love?

It was the constant attempt to answer this question that gave the stag his chance of life when, on the afternoon of the third day, Harold was commanded by his masters the gillies to fire into that thickening in the mist which he was given to understand by an unmistakable pantomime, was the stag.

While the gillies were exchanging their remarks in Gaelic, flavouring them with very smoky whiskey, he was thinking, not of the escape of the stag, but of what possible end there could be to the love that existed between Beatrice and himself.

It was the renewed thinking upon this question that brought about the death of that particular stag and two others before the next evening, for he had arrived at a point when he felt that he must shoot either a stag or himself. He had arrived at a condition of despair that made pretty severe demands upon him.

The slaughter of the stags saved him. When he saw their bodies stretched before him he felt exultant once more. He felt that he had overcome his fate; and it was the next morning before he realized the fact that he had done nothing of the sort—that the possibility of his ever being able to marry Beatrice Avon was as remote as it had been when he had fired blindly into the mist, and his masters, who had carried the guns, exhausted (he believed) the resources, of Gaelic sarcasm in comment.

CHAPTER XXVIII
ON ENJOYING A RESPITE

IT was the first week in October when Harold Wynne found himself in London. He had got a letter from Beatrice in which she told him that she and her father would return to London from Holland that week. Mr. Avon had conscientiously followed the track of an Irish informer in whom he was greatly interested, and who had, at the beginning of the century, found his way to Holland, where he was looked upon as a poor exile from Erin. He had betrayed about a dozen of his fellow-countrymen to their enemies, and had then returned to Ireland to live to an honoured old age on the proceeds of the bargain he had made for their heads.

The result of Harold's consideration of the position that he occupied in regard to Beatrice, was this visit to London. He made up his mind that he should see her and tell her that, like Mrs. Browning's hero, he loved her so well that he only could leave her.

He could bring himself to do it, he felt. He believed that he was equal to an act of heroic self-sacrifice for the sake of the girl—that was how he put the matter to himself when being soaked on the Scotch mountain. Yes, he would go to her and tell her that the conclusion to which he had come was that they must forget one another—that only unhappiness could result from the relationship that existed between them. He knew that there is no more unsatisfactory relationship between a man and a woman than that which has love for a basis, but with no prospect of marriage; and he knew that so long as his father lived and continued selfish—and only death could divide him from his selfishness—marriage with Beatrice was out of the question.

It was with this resolution upon him that he drove to the address in the neighbourhood of the British Museum, where Beatrice said she was to be found with her father.

It was one of those mansions which at some period in the early part of the century had been almost splendid; now it was simply large. It was not the house that Harold would have cared to occupy, even rent free—and this was a consideration to him. But for a scholar who had a large library of his own, and who found it necessary to be frequently in the neighbourhood of the larger Library at the Museum, the house must undoubtedly have had its advantages.

She was not at home. The elderly butler said that Mr. Avon had found it necessary to visit Brussels for a few days, and he had thus been delayed on the Continent beyond the date he had appointed for his return. He would probably be in England by the end of the week—the day was Wednesday.

Harold left the gloom of Bloomsbury behind him, feeling a curious satisfaction at having failed to see Beatrice—the satisfaction of a respite. Some days must elapse before he could make known his resolution to her.

He strolled westward to a club of which he was a member—the Bedouin, and was about to order dinner, when someone came behind him and laid a hand, by no means gently, on his shoulder. Some of the Bedouins thought it *de rigueur* to play such pranks upon each other; and, to do them justice, it was only rarely that they dislocated a friend's shoulder or gave a nervous friend a fit. People said one never knew what was coming from the moment they entered the Bedouin Club, and the prominent Bedouins accepted this statement as embodying one of the most agreeable of its many distinctive features.

Harold was always prepared for the worst in this place, so when the force of the blow swung him round and he saw an extremely plain arrangement of features, distorted by a smile of extraordinary breadth, beneath a closely-cropped crown of bright red hair, he merely said, "Hallo, Archie, you here? I thought you were in South Africa lion-hunting or something."

The smile that had previously distorted the features of the young man, was of such fulness that it might reasonably have been taken for granted that it could not be increased; the possessor showed, however, that that smile was not the result of a supreme effort. So soon as Harold had spoken he gave a wink, and that wink seemed to release the mechanical system by which his features were contorted, for in an instant his face became one mouth. In plain words, this mouth of the young man had swallowed up his other features. All that could be seen of his face was that enormous mouth flanked by a pair of enormous ears, like plantain leaves growing on each side of the crater of a volcano.

Harold looked at him and laughed, then picked up a *menu* card and studied it until he calculated that the young man whom he had addressed as Archie should have thrown off so much of his smile as would enable him to speak.

He gave him plenty of time, and when he looked round he saw that some of the young man's features had succeeded in struggling to the surface, as it were, beneath the circular mat of red hair that lay between his ears.

"No South Africa for me, tarty chip," said Archie. ("Tarty chip" was the popular term of address that year among young men about town. Its philological significance was never discovered.)

"No South Africa for me; I went one better than that," continued the young man.

"I doubt it," said Harold. "I've had my eye on you until lately. You have usually gone one worse. Have you any money left—tell the truth?"

"Money? I asked the tarty chips that look after that sort of thing for me how I stood the other day," said Archie, "and I'm ashamed to say that I've been spending less than my income—that is until a couple of months ago. I've still about three million. What does that mean?"

"That you've got rid of about a million inside two years," said Harold.

"You're going it blind," said Archie. "It only means that I've spent fifty decimals in eighteen months. I can spare that, tarty chip." (It may possibly be remembered that in the slang of the year a decimal signified a thousand pounds.) "That means that you've squandered a fortune, Archie," said Harold, thinking what fifty thousand pounds would mean to him.

"There's not much of a squander in the deal when I got value for it," said Archie. "I got plenty of value. I've got to know all about this world."

"And you'll soon get to know all about the next, if you go on at this rate," said Harold.

"Not me; I've got my money in sound places. You heard about my show."

"Your show? I've heard about nothing for the past year but your shows. What's the latest? I want something to eat."

"Oh, come with me to my private trough," cried the young man. "Don't lay down a mosaic pavement in your inside in this hole. Come along, tarty chip; I've got a *chef* named Achille—he knows what suits us—also some '84 Heidsieck. Come along with me, and I'll tell you all about the show. We'll go there together later on. We'll take supper with her."

"Oh! with her?"

"To be sure. You don't mean to say that you haven't heard that I've taken the Legitimate Theatre for Mrs. Mowbray? Where on God's footstool have you been for the past month?"

"Not further than the extreme North of Scotland. It was far enough. I saw a paragraph stating that Mrs. Mowbray, after being a failure in a number of places, had taken the Legitimate. What has that got to say to you?"

"Not much, but I've got a good deal to say to it. Oh, come along, and I'll tell you all about it. I'm building a monument for myself. I've got the Legitimate and I mean to make Irving and the rest of them sit up."

CHAPTER XXIX
ON THE ADVANTAGES OF READY MONEY

ARCHIE BROWN was the only son of Mr. John Brown, the eminent contractor. Mr. John Brown had been a man of simple habits and no tastes. When a working navvy he had acquired a liking for oatmeal porridge, and up to the day of his death, when he had some twenty thousand persons in his employment, each of them earning money for him, he never rose above this comestible. He lived a thoroughly happy life, taking no thought about money, and having no idea, beyond the building of drinking fountains in his native town, how to spend the profits realized on his enormous transactions.

Now, as the building of even the most complete system of drinking fountains, in a small town in Scotland, does not produce much impression upon the financial position of a man with some millions of pounds in cash, and making business profits to the extent of two hundred thousand a year, it was inevitable that, when a brick one afternoon fell on Mr. John Brown's head and fractured his skull so severely as to cause his death, his only son should be left very well provided for.

Archie Brown was left provided with some millions in cash, and with property that yielded him about one hundred pounds a day.

Up to the day of his father's death he had never had more than five hundred a year to spend as pocket-money—he had saved even out of this modest sum, for he had scarcely any more expensive tastes than his father, though he had ever regarded *sole à la Normande* as more palatable than oatmeal porridge as a breakfast dish.

He had never caused his father a moment's uneasiness; but as soon as he was given a bird's eye view, so to speak, of his income, he began to ask himself if there might not be something in the world more palatable even than *sole à la Normande*.

In the course of a year or two he had learned a good deal on the subject of what was palatable and what was not; for from the earliest records it is understood that the knowledge of good and the knowledge of evil may be found on the one tree.

He began to be talked about, and that is always worth paying money for—some excellent judges say that it is the only thing worth paying money for. Occasionally he paid a trifle over the market price for this commodity. But then he knew that he generally paid more than the market price for everything that he bought, from his collars, which were unusually high, down to his boots, which were of glazed kid, so that he did not complain.

He found that, after a while, the tradespeople, seeing that he paid them cash, treated him fairly, and that the person who supplied him with cigars was actually generous when he bought them by the thousand.

People who at first had fancied that Mr. Archibald Brown was a plunger—that is, a swindler whom they could swindle out of his thousands—had reason to modify their views on the subject after some time. For six months he had been imposed upon in many directions. But with all the other things which had to be paid for, the fruit of the Tree of Knowledge of Good and Evil should, he knew, be included. Imported in a fresh condition this was, he knew, expensive; but he had a sufficient acquaintance with the elements of fruit-culture to be well aware of the fact that in this condition it is worth very much more than the canned article.

He bought his knowledge of good and evil fresh.

He was no fool, some people said, exultantly.

These were the people whose friends had tried to impose on him but had not succeeded.

He was no fool, some people said regretfully.

These were the people who had tried to impose on him but had not succeeded.

Harold had always liked Archie Brown, and he had offered him much advice—vegetarian banquets of the canned fruit of the Tree of Knowledge. The shrewd outbursts of confidence in which Archie indulged now and again, showed Harold that he was fast coming to understand his position in society—his friends and his enemies.

Harold, after some further persuasion, got into the hansom which Archie had hailed, and was soon driving down Piccadilly to the spacious rooms of the latter—rooms furnished in a wonderful fashion. As a panorama of styles the sitting-room, which was about thirty feet square, with a greenhouse in the rear, would have been worth much to a lecturer on the progress or decadence of art—any average lecturer could make the furniture bear out his views, whether they took one direction or the other.

Two cabinets which had belonged to Louis XV were the finest specimens known in the world. They contained Sèvres porcelain and briar-root pipes.

A third cabinet was in the purest style of boarding house art. A small gilt sofa was covered with old French tapestry which would have brought five pounds the square inch at an auction. Beside it was the famous Four-guinea Tottenham Armchair in best Utrecht velvet—three-nine-six in cretonne, carriage paid to any railway-station in the United Kingdom.

A chair, the frame of which was wholly of ivory, carved in Italy, in the seventeenth century, by the greatest artist that ever lived, apparently had its uses in Archie Brown's *entourage*, for it sustained in an upright position a half-empty soda-water bottle—the bottle would not have stood upright but for the high relief in the carving of the flowing hair of the figure of Atalanta at one part of the frame. Near it was an interesting old oak chair that was for some time believed to have once belonged to King Henry VIII.

In achieving this striking contrast to the carved ivory, Mr. Brown thought that he had proved his capacity to appreciate an important element in artistic arrangement. He pointed it out to Harold without delay. He had pointed it out to every other person who had visited his rooms.

He also pointed out a picture by one Rembrandt which he had picked up at an auction for forty shillings. A dealer had subsequently assured him that if he wanted a companion picture by the same painter he would not guarantee to procure it for him at a lower figure than twenty-five guineas— perhaps it might even cost him as high as thirty; therefore—the logic was Archie's—the Rembrandt had been a dead bargain.

Harold looked at this Burgomaster's Daughter in eighteenth century costume, and said that undoubtedly the painter knew what he was about.

"And so does Archie, tarty chip," said his host, leading him to one of the bedrooms.

"Now it's half past seven," said Archie, leaving him, "and dinner will be served at a quarter to eight. I've never been late but once, and Achille was so hurt that he gave me notice. I promised that it should never occur again, and it hasn't. He doesn't insist on my dressing for dinner, though he says he should like it."

"Make my apologies to Achille," said Harold.

"Oh, that won't be necessary," said Archie seriously—"at least I think it won't."

Harold had never been in these rooms before—he wondered how it had chanced that he came to them at all. But before he had partaken of more than one of the *hors d'ouvres*—there were four of them—he knew that he had done well to come. Achille was an artist, the Sauterne was Chateau Coutet of 1861, and the champagne was, as Archie had promised it should be, Heidsieck of 1884. The electric light was artfully toned down, and the middle-aged butler understood his business.

"This is the family trough," said Archie. "I say, Harry, isn't it one better than the oatmeal porridge of our dads—I mean of my dad; yours, I know, was always one of us; my dad wasn't, God bless him! If he had been we shouldn't be here now. He'd have died a pauper."

Harold so far forgot himself as to say, "Doesn't Carlyle remark somewhere that it's the fathers who work that the sons—ah, never mind."

"Carlyle? What Carlyle was that? Do I know him?" asked Archie.

"No," said Harold, shaking his head.

"He isn't a tarty chip, eh?"

"Tart, not tarty."

"Oh. Don't neglect this jelly. It's the best thing that Achille does. It's the only thing that he ever repeats himself in. He came to me boasting that he could give me three hundred and sixty-five different dinners in the year. 'That's all very well,' said I, 'but what about Leap Year?' I showed him there that his bluff wouldn't do. 'Pass' said I, and he passed. But we understand one another now. I will say that he has never repeated himself except in this jelly. I make him give it to me once a week."

"You're right," said Harold. "It is something to think about."

"Yes, while you're in front of it, but never after," said Archie. "That's what Achille says. 'The true dinner,' says he, 'is the one that makes you think while you're at it, but that never causes you a thought afterwards.'"

"Achille is more than an artist, he is a philosopher," said Harold. "What does he call this?" he glanced at the menu card. "'*Glace à la chagrin d'Achille*' What does he mean by that? 'The chagrin of Achilles'? Where does the chagrin come in?"

"Oh, he has some story about a namesake of his," said Archie. "He was cut up about something, and he wouldn't come out of the marquee."

"The tent," cried Harold. "Achilles sulked in his tent. Of course, that's the '*chagrin d'Achille.*'"

"Oh, you heard of it too? Then the story has managed to leak out somehow. They always do. There's nothing in it. Now I'll tell you all about the show. Try one of these figs."

Harold helped himself to a green fig, the elderly butler placed a decanter of claret on the table, and disappeared with the noiselessness of a shadow.

CHAPTER XXX
ON THE LEGITIMATE IN ART

WHEN the history of the drama in England during the last twenty years of the nineteenth century comes to be written, the episode of the management of the Legitimate Theatre by Mrs. Mowbray will doubtless be amply treated from the standpoint of art, and the historian will, it may be confidently expected, lament the want of appreciation on the part of the public for the Shakespearian drama, to which the closing of the Legitimate Theatre was due.

There were a considerable number of persons, however, who showed a readiness to assert that the management of the Legitimate by Mrs. Mowbray should be looked upon as a purely—only purely was not the word they used—social incident, having no basis whatever in art. It failed, they said, not because the people of England had ceased to love Shakespeare, but because Mr. Archie Brown had ceased to love Mrs. Mowbray.

However this may be, there were also people who said that the Legitimate Theatre under the management of Mrs. Mowbray could not have been so great a financial failure, after all; for Mrs. Mowbray, when her season came to an end, wore as expensive dresses as ever, and drove as expensive horses as ever; and as everyone who had been associated with the enterprise had been paid—some people said overpaid—the natural assumption was that Shakespeare on the stage was not so abhorrent to the people of England as was generally supposed.

The people who took this view of the matter were people who had never heard the name of Mr. Archie Brown—people who regarded Mrs. Mowbray as a self-sacrificing lady who had so enthusiastic a desire to make the public acquainted with the beauties of Shakespeare, that she was quite content to spend her own fortune (wherever that came from) in producing "Cymbeline" and other masterpieces at the Legitimate.

There were other people who said that Archie Brown was a young ass.

There were others who said that Mrs. Mowbray was a harpy.

There were others still—they were mostly men—who said that Mrs. Mowbray was the handsomest woman in England.

The bitterest—they were mostly women—said that she was both handsome and a harpy.

The truth regarding the difficult question of the Legitimate Theatre was gathered by Harold Wynne, as he swallowed his claret and ate his olives at the dining table at Archie Birown's rooms in Piccadilly.

He perceived from what Archie told him, that Archie had a genuine enthusiasm in the cause of Shakespeare. How he had acquired it, he might have had considerable difficulty in explaining. He also gathered that Mrs. Mowbray cared very little for Shakespeare except as a medium for impressing upon the public the fact—she believed it to be a fact—that Mrs. Mowbray was the most beautiful woman in England.

"Cymbeline" had, she considered, been written in the prophetic instinct, which the author so frequently manifested, that one day a woman with such shapely limbs as Mrs. Mowbray undoubtedly possessed, might desire to exhibit them to the public of this grand old England of Shakespeare's and ours.

Mrs. Mowbray was probably the most expensive taste that any man in England could entertain.

All this Harold gathered from the account of the theatrical enterprise, as communicated to him by Archie after dinner.

And the best of it all was, Archie assured him, that no human being could say a word against the character of Mrs. Mowbray.

"I never heard a word against the character of her frocks," said Harold.

"It's a big thing, the management of the Legitimate," said Archie, gravely.

"No doubt; even when it's managed, shall we say, legitimately?" said Harold.

"I feel the responsibility, I can tell you," said Archie. "Shakespeare has never been given a proper chance in England; and although she's a year or two older than me, yet on the box seat of my coach she doesn't look a day over twenty-two—just when a woman is at her best, Harry. What I want to know is, shall it be said of us that Shakespeare—the immortal Shakespeare, mind you—Stratford upon Avon, you know—"

"I believe I have his late address," said Harold.

"That's all right. But what I want to know is, shall it be said that we are willing to throw our Shakespeare overboard? In the scene in the front of the cave she is particularly fine."

In an instant Harold's thoughts were carried back to a certain scene in front of a cave on a moonlight night; and for him the roar of life through Piccadilly was changed to the roar of the Atlantic. His thoughts remained far away while Archie talked gravely of building himself a monument by his revival of "Cymbeline", with which the Legitimate had been opened by Mrs. Mowbray. Of course, the thing hadn't begun to pay yet, he explained. Everyone knew that the Bicycle had ruined theatrical business in London; but the Legitimate could fight even the Bicycle, and when the public had the beauty of Mrs. Mowbray properly impressed upon them, Shakespeare would certainly obtain that recognition which he deserves from England. Were Englishmen proud of Shakespeare, or were they not? that was what Archie wished very much to know. If the people of your so-called British Islands wish to throw Shakespeare overboard, just let them say so. But if they threw him over, the responsibility would rest with them; Mrs. Mowbray would still be the handsomest woman in England. At any rate, "Cymbeline" at the Legitimate would be a monument.

"As a lighthouse is a monument," said Harold, coming back from the Irish lough to Piccadilly.

"I knew you'd agree with me," said Archie. "You know that I've always had a great respect for your opinion, Harry. I don't object so much as some tarty chips to your dad. I wish he'd see Mrs. Mowbray. There's no vet. whose opinion I'd sooner take on the subject than his. He'd find her all right."

Harold looked at the young man whose plain features—visible when he did not smile too broadly—displayed the enthusiasm that possessed him when he was fancying that his devotion to the beauty of Mrs. Mowbray was a true devotion to Shakespeare. Archie Brown, he was well aware, was very imperfectly educated.

He was not, however, much worse than the general run of people. Like them he knew only enough of Shakespeare to be able to misquote him now and again; and, like them, he believed that. Darwinism meant nothing more than that men had once been monkeys.

Harold looked at Archie, and felt that Mrs. Mowbray was a fortunate woman in having met with him. The monument was being raised, Harold felt; and he was right. The management of the Legitimate-Theatre was a memorial to Vanity working heart, and soul with Ignorance to the praise and glory of Shakespeare.

CHAPTER XXXI
ON A BLACK SHEEP

BEFORE Archie had completed his confidences, a visitor was announced.

"Oh, it's only old Playdell," said Archie. "You know old Playdell, of course."

"I'm not so certain that I do," said Harold.

"Oh, he's a good old soul who was kicked out of the Church by the bishop for doing something or other. He's useful to me—keeps my correspondence in order—spots the chaps that write the begging letters, and sees that they don't get anything out of me, while he takes care that all the genuine ones get all that they deserve. He's an Oxford man."

"Playdell—Playdell," said Harold. "Surely he can't be the fellow that got run out for marrying people without a licence?"

"That's his speciality," said Archie. "Come along, chippie Chaplain. Chip in, and have a glass of something."

A middle-aged man, wearing the coat and the tie of a cleric, entered the room with a smile and a bow to Harold.

"You've heard of Mr. Wynne, Play?" said Archie. "The Honourable Harold Wynne. He's heard of you—yes, you bet your hoofs on that."

"I dare say you've heard of me, Mr. Wynne," said the man. "It's the black sheep in a flock that obtain notoriety; the colourless ones escape notice. I'm a black sheep."

"You're about as black as they make them, old Play," remarked Archie, with a prompt and kindly acquiescence. "But your blackness doesn't go deeper than the wool."

"You say that because you are always disposed to be charitable, Archie," said Mr. Playdell. "Even with you I'm afraid that another notorious character is not so black as he's painted."

"Neither he is," said Archie. "You know as well as I do that the devil is not so black as he used to be—he's turning gray in his old age."

"They treated me worse than they treated the Fiend himself, Mr. Wynne," said Playdell. "They turned me out of the Church, but the Church still retains the Prince of Darkness. He is still the most powerful auxiliary that the Church knows."

"If you expressed that sentiment when in orders," said Harold, "I can quite easily understand how you find yourself outside the Church."

"I was quite orthodox when in the Church, Mr. Wynne. I couldn't afford to be otherwise," said Playdell. "I wasn't even an Honest Doubter. I felt that if I had begun to doubt I might become a Dissenter before I knew what I was about. It is only since I left the Church that I've indulged in the luxury of being unorthodox."

"Take a glass of wine for your stomach's sake," said Archie.

"That lad is the son of a Scotch Nonconformist," said Mr. Playdell to Harold; "hence the text. Would it be unorthodox to say that an inscrutable Providence did not see fit to preserve the reply of Timothy to that advice? For my own part I cannot doubt for a moment that Timothy inquired for what other reason his correspondent fancied he might take the wine. I like my young patron's La Rose. It must have been something very different from this that the person alluded to when he said 'my love is better than wine.' Yes, I've always thought that the truth of the statement was largely dependent on the wine."

"I'll take my oath that isn't orthodox," said Archie. "You'd better mind what you're about, chippie Chaplain, or I'll treat you as the bishop did. This is an orthodox household, let me tell you."

"I feel like Balaam's ass sometimes, Mr. Wynne, in this situation," said Mr. Playdell. "In endeavouring to avoid the angel with the sword on one hand—that is the threatening orthodoxy of the Church—I make myself liable to a blow from the staff of the prophet—our young friend is the prophet."

"I will say this for you, chippie Chaplain," said Archie, "you've kept me straight. Not that I ever did take kindly to the flowing bowl; but we all know what temptations there are." He looked into his glass and spoke solemnly, shaking his head. "Yes, Harry, I've never drunk a thimbleful more than I should since old Play here lectured me."

"If I could only persuade you—"commenced Mr. Playdell.

"But I'm not such an ass," cried Archie, interrupting him. Then he turned to Harold, saying, "The chippie Chaplain wants to marry me to some one whose name we never mention. That has always been his weakness—marrying tarty chips that he had no right to marry."

"If I don't mistake, Mr. Playdell, it was this little weakness that brought you to grief," said Harold.

"It was the only point that the bishop could lay hold of, Mr. Wynne," said Playdell. "I held, and I still hold, that the ceremony of marriage may be performed by any person who has been ordained—that the question of a licence is not one that should come forward upon any occasion. Those who hold other opinions are those who would degrade the ordinance into a mere civil act."

"And you married without question every couple who came to you, I believe?" said Harold.

"I did, Mr. Wynne. And I will be happy to marry any other couples who come to me for that purpose now."

"But, you are no longer in the Church, and such marriages would be no marriages in the eyes of the law."

"Nothing can be more certain, Mr. Wynne. But I know that there are many persons in this country who hold, with me, that the ordinance is not one that should be made the subject of a licence bought from a bishop—who hold that the very act of purchase is a gross degradation of the ordinance of God."

"I say, chippie Chaplain, haven't we had enough of that?" said Archie. "You've pegged away at that marriage business with me for a good many months. Now, I say, pass the marriage business. Let us have a fresh deal."

"Mr. Wynne, I merely wished to explain my position to you," said Playdell. "I'm on the side of the angels in this question, as a great statesman but a poor scientist said of another question."

"Pass the statesman as well," cried Archie.

"What do tarty chips like us care for politics or other fads? He told me the other day, Harry, that instead of introducing a bill for the admission of ladies as members of Parliament, it would soon be necessary to introduce a bill for the admission of gentlemen as members—yes, you said that. You can't deny it."

"I don't," said Mr. Playdell. "The result of the last General Election—"

"Pass the General Election," shouted Archie. "Mr. Wynne hates that sort of thing. Now give an account of yourself. What have you done to earn your screw since morning?"

"This is what I have come to, Mr. Wynne," said Playdell. "Think of it; a clergyman and M.A. Oxon, forced to give an account of his stewardship to a young cub like that!" He laughed after a moment of seriousness.

"You don't seem to feel deeply the degradation," remarked Harold.

"It's nothing to the depths to which I have fallen," said Mr. Playdell. "I was never more than a curate, but in spite of the drawback of being privileged to preach the Gospel twice a week, the curacy was a comfortable one. I published two volumes of my sermons, Mr. Wynne. They sold poorly in England, but I believe that in America they made the fortune of the publishers that pirated them. It is perfectly well known that my sermons achieved a great and good purpose in the States. They were practical. I will say that for them. The leader of the corner in hogs who ran the prices up last autumn, sold out of the business, I understand, after reading my sermon on the text, 'The husks that the swine do eat.' Several judges also resigned, admitting that they were converted. It was freely stated that even a Congressman had been reformed by one sermon of mine, while another was known to have brought tears to the eyes of a reporter on the *New York Herald*. And yet, with all these gratifying results, I never got a penny out of the American edition. Just think what would happen on this side of the Atlantic if, let us say, a Royal Academician were to find grace through a sermon, or—to assume an extreme case—a member of the Stock Exchange? Why, the writer would be a made man. I had thoughts of going to America, Mr. Wynne. At any rate, I'm going to deal with the publishers there directly. A firm in Boston is at present about to boom a Bowdlerized edition of the Bible which I have prepared for family reading in the States—not a word in it that the purest-minded young woman in all Boston might not see. It should sell, Mr. Wynne. I'm also translating into English a volume of American humour."

"I'll give you a chance of going to America, before you sleep if you don't dry up about your sermons and suchlike skittles," said Archie. "The decanter's beside you. Fill your glass. Mr. Wynne is coming to my show to-night."

Mr. Playdell passed the decanter without filling his glass. "You know that I never take more than one glass of La Rose," said he. "I have found out all about your house painter who fell off the ladder and broke all his ribs—he is the same as your Clergyman's Orphan, and he lives in the same house as your Widow of a Naval Officer whose little all was invested in a fraudulent building society—he is also 'First Thessalonians seven and ten. P.O.O. or stamps'."

"Great Godfrey!" cried Archie; "and I had already written out a cheque for twenty pounds to send to that swindler! Do you mean to tell me, Play, that all those you've mentioned are impostors?"

"All? Why, there's only one impostor among the lot," said Mr. Playdell. "He is 'First Thessalonians,' and he has at least a dozen branch establishments."

"It's enough to make a tarty chip disgusted with God's footstool," said Archie. "Before old Play took me in hand I used to fling decimals about right and left, without inquiry."

"He was the sole support of several of the most notorious swindlers in the country," said Mr. Playdell. "I've managed to whittle them down considerably. Shakespeare is at present the only impostor that has defied my efforts," he added, in a whisper to Harold.

Harold laughed. He was beginning to feel some remorse at having previously looked on Archie Brown as a good-natured fool. He now felt that, in spite of Mrs. Mowbray, he would not wreck his life.

CHAPTER XXXII
ON SHAKESPEARE AND SUPPER

CARRIAGES by the score were waiting at the fine Corinthian entrance to the Legitimate, when Harold and Archie reached the theatre in their hansom. The *façade* of the Legitimate Theatre is so severely Corinthian that foreign visitors invariably ask what church it is.

It was probably the classical columns supporting the pediment of the entrance that caused Archie to abate his frivolous conversation with his friend in the hansom—Archie had been expressing the opinion that it was exhilarating—only exhilarating was not the word he used—to swear at a man who had once been a clergyman and who still wore the dress of a cleric. "A chap feels that his turn has come," he had said. "No matter how wrong they are you can't swear at them and tell them to come down out of that, when they're in their own pulpits—they'd have you up for brawling. That's why I like to take it out of old Playdell. He tells me, however, that there's no dean in the Church that gathers in the decimals as he does in my shop. But, bless you! he saves me his screw three times over."

But now that the classical front of the Legitimate came in view, Archie became solemn.

He possibly appreciated the feelings of a conscientious clergyman when about to enter his Church.

Shakespeare was a great responsibility.

So was Mrs. Mowbray.

The performance was not quite over; but before Archie had paid the hansomeer, the audience was streaming out from every door.

"Stand here and listen to what the people are saying." whispered Archie. "I often do it. It is only in this way that you can learn how much appreciation for Shakespeare still remains in England."

He took up his position with Harold at the foot of the splendid staircase of the theatre, where the people chatted together while waiting for their carriages.

With scarcely an exception, the remarks had a hearing upon the performance of "Cymbeline." Only two ladies confined their criticisms to their respective medical advisers.

Of the others, one man said that Mrs. Mowbray bore a striking resemblance to her photographs.

A second said that she was the most beautiful woman in England.

A third said that she knocked sparks out of Polly Floss in the same line of business. (Polly Floss was the leading exponent of burlesque).

One woman said that Mrs. Mowbray was most picturesquely dressed.

A second said that she was most picturesquely undressed.

A third wondered if Liberty had got the exact tint of the robe that Mrs. Mowbray had worn in the second act.

"And yet some people say that there's no appreciation of Shakespeare in England!" said Archie, as he led Harold round the stalls, over which the attendants were spreading covers, and on to Mrs. Mowbray's private rooms.

"From the crowds that went out by every door, I judge that the theatre is making money, at any rate; and I suppose that's the most practical test of appreciation," said Harold.

"Oh, they don't all pay," said Archie. "That's a feature of theatrical management that it takes an outsider some time to understand. Mrs. Mowbray should understand it pretty well by this time, so should her business manager. I'm just getting to understand it."

"You mean to say that the people are allowed to come in without paying?"

"It amounts to that in the long run—literally the long run—of the piece, I believe. Upon my soul, there are some people who fancy that a chap runs a show as a sort of free entertainment for the public. The dramatic critics seem to fancy that a chap produces a play, simply in order to give them an opportunity of showing off their own cleverness in slating it. It seems that a writer-chap can't show his cleverness in praising a piece, but only in slanging it."

"I think that I'd try and make people pay for their seats."

"I used always to pay for mine in the old days—but then, I was always squandering my money."

"I have always paid for mine."

"The manager says that if you asked people to pay, they'd be mortally offended and never enter the theatre again, and where would you be then?"

"Where, indeed?" said Harold. "I expect your manager must know his business thoroughly."

"He does. It requires tact to get people to come to see Shakespeare," said Archie. "But a chap can't build a monument for himself without paying for it."

"It would be ridiculous to expect it," said Harold.

Pushing aside a magnificent piece of heavy drapery, Archie brought his friend into a passage illuminated by the electric light; and knocking at a door at the farther end, he was admitted by Mrs. Mowbray's maid, into a prettily-furnished sitting-room and into the presence of Mrs. Mowbray, who was sitting robed in something very exquisite and cloud-like—not exactly a peignoir but something that suggested a peignoir.

She was like a picture by Romney. If one could imagine all the charm of all the pictures of Emma Hamilton (*née* Lyon) which Romney painted, meeting harmoniously in another creature, one would come within reasonable distance of seeing Mrs. Mowbray, as Harold saw her when he entered the room.

Even with the disadvantage of the exaggerated colour and the over-emphasized eye-lashes necessary for the searching illumination of the footlights, she was very lovely, Harold acknowledged.

But all the loveliness of Mrs. Mowbray produced but a trifling effect compared to that produced by her charm of manner. She was the most natural woman ever known.

The position of the natural man has been defined by an eminent authority. But who shall define the position of the natural woman?

It was Mrs. Mowbray's perfect simplicity, especially when talking to men—as a matter of fact she preferred talking to men rather than to women—that made her seem so lovely—nay, that made a man feel that it was good for him to be in her presence. She was devoid of the smallest trace of affectation. She seemed the embodiment of truth. She never smiled for the sake of conventionality. But when she did smile, just as Harold entered the room, her head turning round so that her face was looking over her shoulder, she had all the spiritual beauty of the loveliest picture ever painted by Greuze, consequently the loveliest picture ever painted by the hand of man.

And yet she was so very human.

An Algy and an Eddy were already in the room—the first was a Marquis, the second was the eldest son of a duke. Both were handsome lads, of quiet manners, and both were in the Household Cavalry. Mrs. Mowbray liked to be surrounded by the youngest of men.

Harold had been acquainted with her long before she had become an actress. He had not had an opportunity of meeting her since; but he found that she remembered him very well.

She had heard of his father, she said, looking at him in a way that did not in the least suggest a picture by Greuze.

When people referred to his father they did not usually assume a look of innocence. Most of them would have had difficulty in assuming such a look under any circumstances.

"My father is frequently heard of," said Harold.

"And your father's son also," said Mrs. Mowbray. "What a freak of Lady Innisfail's! She lured you all across to Ireland. I heard so much. And what came of it, after all?"

"Acute admiration for the allurements of Lady Innisfail in my case, and a touch of acute rheumatism in my father's case," said Harold.

"Neither will be fatal to the sufferers," said Mrs. Mowbray—"or to Lady Innisfail, for that matter," she added.

"I should say not," remarked Algy. "We all admire Lady Innisfail."

"Few cases of acute admiration of Lady Innisfail have proved fatal, so far as I can hear, Lord Brackenthorpe," said Mrs. Mowbray. "Young mem have suffered from it and have become exemplary husbands and parents."

"And if they don't live happy, that we may," said Archie.

"That's the end of the whole matter," said. Harold.

"That's the end of the orthodox fairy tale," said Mrs. Mowbray. "Was your visit to Ireland a fairy story, Mr. Wynne?"

Harold wondered how much this woman knew of the details of his visit to Ireland. Before he-could think of an answer in the same strain, Mrs. Mowbray had risen from the little gilt sofa, and had taken a step or two toward her dressing-room. The look she tossed to Harold, when she turned round with her fingers on the handle of the door, was a marvellous one.

Had it been attempted by any other woman, it would have provoked derision on the part of the average man—certainly on the part of Harold

Wynne. But, coming from Mrs. Mowbray, it conveyed—well, all that she meant it to convey. It was not merely fascinating, it was fascination itself.

It was such a look as this, he felt—but nearly a year had passed before he had thought of the parallel—that Venus had cast at Paris upon a momentous occasion. It was the glance of Venus Victrix. It made a man think—a year or so afterwards—of Ahola and Aholibah, of Ashtoreth, of Cleopatra, of Faustina, of Iseult, of Rosamond.

And yet the momentary expression of her features was as simple and as natural as that worn by one of Greuze's girls.

"She'll not be more than ten minutes," said

Archie. "I don't know how she manages to dress herself in the time."

He did not exaggerate. Mrs. Mowbray returned in ten minutes, with no trace of paint upon her face, wearing a robe that seemed to surround her with fleecy clouds. The garment was not much more than an atmosphere—it was a good deal less substantial than the atmosphere of London in December or that of Sheffield in June.

"We shall have the pleasantest of suppers," she said, "and the pleasantest of chats. I understand that Mr. Wynne has solved the Irish problem."

"And what is the solution, Mrs. Mowbray?" said Lord Brackenthorpe.

"The solution—ah—'a gray eye or so'," said Mrs. Mowbray.

The little Mercutio swagger with which she gave point to the words, was better than anything she had done on the stage.

"And now, Mr. Wynne, you must lead the way with me to our little supper-room," said she, before the laugh, in which everyone joined, at the pretty bit of comedy, had ceased.

Harold gave her his arm.

When at the point of entering the room—it was daintily furnished with old English oak and old English silver—Mrs. Mowbray said, in the most casual way possible, "I hope you will tell me all that may be told about that charming White Lady of the Cave. How amusing it must have been to watch the chagrin of Lord Fotheringay, when Mr. Airey gave him to understand that he meant to make love to that young person with the wonderful eyes."

"It was intensely amusing, indeed," said Harold, who had become prepared for anything that Mrs. Mowbray might say.

"Yes, you must have been amused; for, of course, you knew that Mr. Airey was not in earnest—that he had simply been told off by Miss Craven to amuse himself with the young person, in order to induce her to take her beautiful eyes off—off—someone else, and to turn them admiringly upon Mr. Airey."

"That was the most amusing part of the comedy, of course," said Harold.

"What fools some girls are!" laughed Mrs. Mowbray. It was well known that she disliked the society of women.

"It's a wise provision of nature that the fools should be the girls."

"Oh, I have known a fool or two among men," said Mrs. Mowbray, with another laugh.

"Have known—did you say *have known?*" said Harold.

"Any girl who has lived in this world of ours for a quarter of a century, should have seen enough to make her aware of the fact that the best way to set about increasing the passion of, let us say, the average man—"

"No, the average man is passionless."

"Well, the passion of whatever man you please—for a young woman whom he loves, or fancies he loves—it's all the same in the end—is to induce him to believe that several other men are also in love with her."

"That is one of the rudiments of a science of which you are the leading exponent," said Harold.

"And yet Miss Craven was foolish enough to fancy that the man of whom she was thinking, would give himself up to think of her so soon as he believed that Mr. Airey was in love with her rival! Ah, here are our lentils and pulse. How good it is of you to imperil your digestions by taking supper with me, when only a few hours can have passed since you dined."

"Digestion is not an immortal soul," said Harold, "and I believe that immortal souls have been imperilled before now, for the sake of taking supper with the most beautiful woman in the world."

"Have you ever heard a woman say that I am beautiful?" she asked.

"Never," said Harold. "That is the one sin which a woman never pardons in another."

"You do not know women—" with a little pitying smile. "A woman will forgive a woman for being more beautiful than herself—for being less virtuous than herself, but never for being better-dressed than herself."

"For how many of the three sins do you ask forgiveness of woman—two or three?" said Harold, gently.

But instead of making an answer, Mrs. Mowbray said something about the necessity of cherishing a digestion. It was disgraceful, she said, that bread-and-butter and arithmetic should be forced upon a school boy—that such magnificent powers of digestion as he possessed should not be utilized ta the uttermost.

Lord Brackenthorpe said he knew a clever artist chap, who had drawn a sketch of about a thousand people crowding over one another, in an American hotel, in order to see a boy, who had been overheard asking his mother what was the meaning of the word dyspepsia.

Mrs. Mowbray wondered if the melancholy of Hamlet was due to a weak digestion.

Harold said he thought it should rather be accepted as evidence that there was a Schleswig-Holstein question even in Hamlet's day.

Meantime, the pheasants and sparkling red Burgundy were affording compensation for the absence of any brilliant talk.

Then the young men lit their cigarettes. Mrs. Mowbray had never been known to risk her reputation (for femininity) by letting a cigarette between her lips; but her femininity was in no way jeopardized—rather was it accentuated—by her liking to be in the neighbourhood of where cigarettes were being smoked—that is, when the cigarettes were good and when the smokers were pleasant young men with titles, or even unpleasant young men with thousands.

After the lapse of an hour, a message came regarding Mrs. Mowbray's brougham. Her guests rose and she looked about for her wrap.

While Harold Wynne was laying it on her lovely shoulders, she kept her eyes fixed upon his. Hers were full of intelligence. When he had carefully fastened the gold clasp just beneath the hollow of her throat—it required very careful handling—she poised her head to the extent of perhaps a quarter of an inch to one side, and laughed; then she moved away from him, but turned her head so that her face was once more over her shoulder, like the face of the Greuze girl from whom she had learnt the trick.

He knew that she wanted him to ask her from whom she had heard the stories regarding Castle Innisfail and its guests.

He also knew that the reason she wanted him to ask her this question, was in order that she might have the delight of refusing to answer him, while keeping him in the expectancy of receiving an answer.

Such a delight would, of course, be a malicious one. But he knew that it would be a thoroughly womanly one, and he knew that Mrs. Mowbray was a thorough woman.

Therefore he laughed back at her and did not ask her anything—not even to take his arm out to her brougham.

Archie Brown did, and she took his arm, still looking over her shoulder at Harold.

It only needed that the lovely, wicked look should vanish in a sentence.

And it did.

The full lips parted, and the poise of the head was increased by perhaps the eighth part of an inch.

"'A gray eye or so,'" she murmured.

Her laughter rang down the corridor.

"And the best of it all is, that no one can say a word against her character," said Archie.

This was the conclusion of his rhapsody in the hansom, in which he and Harold were driving down Piccadilly—a rhapsody upon the beauty, the genius, and the expensiveness of Mrs. Mowbray.

Harold was silent. The truth was that he was thinking about something far apart from Mrs. Mowbray, her beauty, her doubtful genius, and her undoubted power of spending money.

"What do you say?" said Archie. "Great Godfrey! you don't mean to say that you've heard a word breathed against her character?"

"On the contrary," said Harold, "I've always heard it asserted that Mrs. Mowbray is the best dressed woman in London."

"Give me your hand, old chap; I knew that I could trust you to do her justice," cried Archie.

CHAPTER XXXIII
ON BLESSING OR DOOM

EVEN before he slept, Harold Wynne found that he had a good many matters to think about, in addition to the exquisitely natural poises of Mrs. Mowbray's shapely head.

It was apparent to him that Mrs. Mowbray had somehow obtained a circumstantial account of the appearance of Beatrice Avon at the Irish Castle, and of the effect that had been produced, in more than one direction, by her appearance.

But the most important information that he had derived from Mrs. Mowbray was that which had reference to the attitude of Edmund Airey toward Beatrice.

Undoubtedly, Mrs. Mowbray had, by some means, come to be possessed of the truth regarding the apparent fascination which Beatrice had for Edmund Airey. It was a trick—it was the result of a conspiracy between Helen Craven and Edmund, in order that he, Harold, should be prevented from even telling Beatrice that he loved her. Helen had felt certain that Beatrice, when she fancied—poor girl!—that she had produced so extraordinary an impression upon the wealthy and distinguished man, would be likely to treat the poor and undistinguished man, whose name was Harold Wynne, in such a way as would prevent him from ever telling her that he loved her!

And Edmund had not hesitated to play the part which Helen had assigned to him! For more than a moment did Harold feel that his friend had behaved in a grossly dishonourable way. But he knew that his friend, if taxed with behaving dishonourably, would be ready to prove—if he thought it necessary—that, so far from acting dishonourably, he had shown himself to be Harold's best friend, by doing his best to prevent Harold from asking a penniless girl to be his wife. Oh, yes, Mr. Edmund Airey would have no trouble in showing, to the satisfaction of a considerable number of people—perhaps, even to his own satisfaction—that he was acting the part of a truly conscientious; and, perhaps, a self-sacrificing friend, by adopting Helen Craven's suggestion.

Harold felt very bitter toward his friend Edmund Airey; though it was unreasonable for him to do so; for had not he come to precisely the same conclusion as his friend in respect of Beatrice, this conclusion being, of course, that nothing but unhappiness could be the result of his loving Beatrice, and of his asking Beatrice to love him?

If Edmund Airey had succeeded in preventing him from carrying out his designs, Harold would be saved from the necessity of having with Beatrice that melancholy interview to which he was looking forward; therefore it was unreasonable for him to entertain any feeling of bitterness toward Edmund.

But for all that, he felt very bitterly toward Edmund—a fact which shows that, in some men as well as in all women, logic is subordinate to feeling.

It was also far from logical on his part to begin to think, only after he had accused his friend of dishonourable conduct, of the source whence the evidence upon which he had founded his accusation, was derived.

How had Mrs. Mowbray come to hear how Edmund Airey had plotted with Helen Craven, he asked himself. He began to wonder how she could have heard about the gray eyes of Beatrice, to which she had alluded more than once, with such excellent effect from the standpoint of art. From whom could she have heard so much?

She certainly did not hear it from Mr. Durdan, even if she was acquainted with him, which was doubtful; for Mr. Durdan was discreet. Besides, Mr. Durdan was rarely eloquent on any social subject. He was the sort of man who makes a tour on the Continent and returns to tell you of nothing except a flea at Bellaggio.

Was it possible that some of the fishing men had been taking notes unknown to any of their fellow guests, for the benefit of Mrs. Mowbray?

Harold did not think so.

After some time he ceased to trouble himself with these vain speculations. The fact—he believed it to be a fact—remained the same: someone who had been at Castle Innisfail had given Mrs. Mowbray a highly circumstantial account of certain occurrences in the neighbourhood of the Castle; and if Mrs. Mowbray had received such an account, why might not anyone else be equally favoured?

Thus it was that he strayed into new regions of speculation, where he could not possibly find any profit. What did it matter to him if everyone in London knew that Edmund Airey had plotted with Helen Craven, to prevent an impecunious man from marrying a penniless girl? All that remained for him to do was to go to the girl, and tell her that he had made a mistake—that he would be asking her to make too great a sacrifice, were he to hold her to her promise to love him and him only.

It was somewhat curious that his resolution in this matter should be strengthened by the fact of his having learned that Edmund Airey had not been in earnest, in what was generally regarded at Castle Innisfail as an attitude of serious, and not merely autumn, love-making, in respect of Beatrice.

He did not feel at all annoyed to learn that, if he were to withdraw from the side of Beatrice, his place would not be taken by that wealthy and distinguished man, Edmund Airey. When he had at first made up his mind to go to Beatrice and ask her to forget that he had ever told her that he loved her, he had had an uneasy feeling that his friend might show even a greater interest than he had done on the evening of the *tableaux* at the Castle, in the future movements of Beatrice.

At that time his resolution had not been overwhelming in its force. But now that Mrs. Mowbray had made that strange communication—it almost amounted to a revelation—to him, he felt almost impatient at the delay that he knew there must be before he could see the girl and make his confession to her.

He had two more days to think over his resolution, in addition to his sleepless night after receiving Mrs. Mowbray's confidences; and the result of keeping his thoughts in the one direction was, that at last he had almost convinced himself that he was glad that the opportunity had arrived for him to present himself to the girl, in order to tell her that he would no longer stand in the way of her loving someone else.

When he found himself in her presence, however, his convictions on this particular point were scarcely so strong as they might have been.

She was sitting in front of the fire in the great drawing-room that retained all the original decorations of the Brothers Adam, and she was wearing something beautifully simple—something creamy, with old lace. The furniture of the room also belonged to the period of the Adams, and on the walls were a number of coloured engravings by Bartolozzi after Cipriani and Angelica Kauffmann.

She was in his arms in a moment. She gave herself to him as naturally and as artlessly as though she were a child; and he held her close to him, looking down upon her face without uttering a word—kissing her mouth conscientiously, her shell-pink cheeks earnestly, her forehead scrupulously, and her chin playfully.

This was how he opened the interview which he had arranged to part them for ever.

Then they both drew a long breath simultaneously, and both laughed in unison.

Then he held her away from him for a few seconds, looking upon her exquisite face. Again he kissed her—but this time solemnly and with something of the father about the action.

"At last—at last," he said.

"At last," she murmured in reply.

"It seems to me that I have never seen you before," said he. "You seem to be a different person altogether. I do not remember anything of your face, except your eyes—no, by heavens! your eyes are different also."

"It was dark as midnight in the depths of that seal-cave," she whispered.

"You mean that—ah, yes, my beloved! If I could have seen your eyes at that moment I know I should have found them full of the light that I now see in their depths. You remember what I said to you on the morning after your arrival at the Castle? Your eyes meant everything to me then—I knew it—beatitude or doom."

"And you know now what they meant?"

He looked at her earnestly and passionately for some moments. Then his hands dropped suddenly as though they were the hands of a man who had died in a moment—his hands dropped, he turned away his face.

"God knows, God knows," he said, with what seemed like a moan.

"Yes," she said; "God knows, and you know as well as God that in my heart there is nothing that does not mean love for you. Does love mean blessing or doom?"

"God knows," said he again. "Your love should mean to me the most blessed thing on earth."

"And your love makes me most blessed among women," said she.

This exchange of thought could scarcely be said to make easier the task which he had set himself to do before nightfall.

He seemed to become aware of this, for he went to the high mantelpiece, and stood with his hands upon it, earnestly examining the carved marble frieze, cream-tinted with age, which was on a level with his face.

She knew, however, that he was not examining the carving from the standpoint of a critic; and she waited silently for whatever was coming.

It came when he ceased his scrutiny of the classical figures in high relief, that appeared upon the marble slab.

"Beatrice, my beloved," said he, and her face brightened. Nothing that commenced with the assumption that she was his beloved could be very bad. "I have been in great trouble—I am in great trouble still."

She was by his side in a moment, and had taken one of his hands in hers. She held it, looking up to his face with her eyes full of sympathy and concern.

"My dearest," he said, "you are all that is good and gracious. We must part, and for ever."

She laughed, still looking at his face. There really was something laughable in the sequence of his words. But her laugh did not make his task any easier.

"When I told you that I loved you, Beatrice, I told you the truth," said he. "If I were to tell you anything else now it would be a falsehood. But I had no right ever to speak to you of love. I am absolutely penniless."

"That is no confession," said she. "I knew all along that you were dependent upon your father for everything. I felt for you—so did Mr. Airey."

"Mr. Airey?" said he. "Mr. Airey mentioned to you that I was a beggar?"

"Oh, he didn't say that. He only said—what did he say?—something about the affairs of the world being very badly arranged, otherwise you should have thousands—oh, he said he felt for you with all his heart."

"'With all his appreciation of the value of an opportunity,' he should have said. Never mind Edmund Airey. You, yourself, can see, Beatrice, how impossible it would be for any man with the least sense of honour, situated as I am, to ask you to wait—to wait for something indefinite."

"You did not ask me to wait for anything. You did not ask me to wait for your love—you gave it to me at once. There is nothing indefinite in love."

"My Beatrice, you cannot think that I would ask you for your love without hoping to marry you?"

"Then let us be married to-morrow."

She did not laugh, speaking the words. He could see that she would not hesitate to marry him at any moment.

"Would to heaven that we could be, my dearest! But could there be anything more cruel than for a penniless man, such as I am, to ask a girl, such as you are, to marry him?"

"I cannot see where the cruelty would be. People have been very happy together before now, though they have had very little money between them."

"My dear Beatrice, you were not meant to pass your life in squalid lodgings, with none of the refinements of life around you; and I—well, I have known what roughing it means; I would face the worst alone; but I am not selfish enough to seek to drag you down to my level—to ask you to face hardship for my sake."

"But I——"

"Do not say anything, darling: anything that you may say will only make it the harder to part. I can do it, Beatrice; I am strong enough to say good-bye."

"Then say it, Harold."

She stood facing him, with her wonderful eyes looking steadily into his. The message that they conveyed to him was such as he could not fail to read aright. He knew that if he had said goodbye, he would never have a chance of looking into those eyes again.

And yet he made the attempt to speak—to say the word that she had challenged him to utter. His lips were parted for more than a moment. He suddenly dropped her hand—he had been holding it all the time—and turned away from her with a passionate gesture.

"I cannot say it—God help me! I cannot say good-bye," he cried.

He had flung himself into a sofa and had buried his face in his hands.

For a short time he had actually felt that he was desirous to part from her. For some minutes he had been quite sincere. The force of the words he had made use of to show Beatrice how absolutely necessary it was that they should part, had not been felt by her; those words had, however, affected him. He had felt—for the first time, in spite of his previous self-communing—that he must say good-bye to her, but he found that he was too weak to say it.

He felt a hand upon his shoulder. He could feel her gracious presence near to him, before her voice came.

"Harold," she said, "if you had said it, I should never have had an hour's happiness in my life. I would never have seen you again. I felt that all the happiness of my life was dependent upon your refraining from speaking those words. Cannot you see, my love, that the matter has passed out of our hands—that it is out of our power to part now? Harold, cannot you see that, let it be for good or evil—for heaven or doom—we must be together? Whatever is before us, we are not two but one—our lives are joined beyond the power of separation. I am yours; you are mine."

He sprang to his feet. He saw that tears were in her eyes. "Let it be so," he cried. "In God's name let it be so. Whatever may happen, no suggestion of parting shall come from me. We stand together, and for ever, Beatrice."

"For ever and ever," she said.

That was how their interview came to a close.

Did he know when he had set out for her home that this would be the close of their interview—this clasping of the hands—this meeting of the lips?

Perhaps he did not. But one thing is certain: if it had not had this ending, he would have been greatly mortified.

His vanity would have received a great blow.

CHAPTER XXXIV
ON THE MESSAGE OF THE LILY

WALKING Westward to his rooms, he enjoyed once again the same feeling of exultation, which had been his on the evening of the return from the seal-hunt. He felt that she was wholly his.

He had done all that was in his power to show her how very much better it would be for her to part from him and never to see him again—how much better it would be for her to marry the wealthy and distinguished man who had, out of the goodness of his heart, expressed to her a deep sympathy for his, Harold's, unfortunate condition of dependence upon a wicked father. But he had not been able to convince her that it would be to her advantage to adopt this course.

Yet, instead of feeling deeply humiliated by reason of the failure of his arguments, he felt exultant.

"She is mine—she is mine!" he cried, when he found himself alone in his room in St. James's. "There is none like her, and she is mine!"

He reflected for a long time upon her beauty. He thought of Mrs. Mowbray, and he smiled, knowing that Beatrice was far lovelier, though her loveliness was not of the same impressive type. One did not seem to breathe near Beatrice that atmosphere heavy with the scent of roses, which Mrs. Mowbray carried with her for the intoxication of the nations. Still, the beauty of Beatrice was not a tame thing. It had stirred him, and it had stirred other men.

Yes, it had stirred Edmund Airey—he felt certain of it, although he did not doubt the truth of Mrs. Mowbray's communication on this subject.

Even though Edmund Airey had been in a plot with Helen, still Harold felt that he had been stirred by the beauty of Beatrice.

He thought over this point for some time, and the conclusion that he came to was, that he could easily find out if Edmund meant to play no more important a rôle than that of partner in Helen Craven's plot. It was perfectly clear, that if Edmund had merely acted as he had done at the suggestion of

Helen, he would cease to take any further interest in Beatrice, unless it was his intention to devote his life to carrying out the plot.

In the course of some weeks, he would learn all that could be known on this point; but meantime his condition was a peculiar one.

He would have felt mortified had he been certain that Edmund Airey had not really been stirred by the charm of Beatrice; but he would have been somewhat uneasy had he felt certain that Edmund was deeply in love with her. He trusted her implicitly—he felt certain of himself in this respect. Had he not a right to trust her, after the way in which she had spoken to him—the way in which she had given herself up to him? But then he felt that he had made use of such definite arguments to her, in pointing out the advisability of their parting, as caused it to be quite possible that she might begin to perceive—after a year or two of waiting—that there was some value in those arguments of his, after all.

By the time that he had dined with some people, who had sent him a card on his return to London, and had subjected himself to the mortifying influence of some unfamiliar *entrées*, and a conversation with a woman who was the survivor of the wreck of spiritualism in London, he was no longer in the exultant mood of the afternoon.

"A Fool's Paradise—a Fool's Paradise!" he murmured, as he sat in an easy-chair, and gazed into his flickering fire. It had been very glorious to think that he was beloved by that exquisite girl—to think of the kisses of her mouth; but whither was the love leading him?

His father's words could not be forgotten—those words which he had spoken from beneath the eiderdown of his bed at Castle Innisfail; and Harold knew that, should he marry Beatrice, his father would certainly carry out his threat of cutting off his allowance.

Thus it was that he sat in his chair feeling that, even though Beatrice had refused to be separated from him, still they were as completely parted by circumstances as if she had immediately acknowledged the force of his arguments, and had accepted, his invitation to say good-bye for ever.

Thus it was that he cried, "A Fool's Paradise—a Fool's Paradise!" as he thought over the whole matter.

What were the exact elements of the Paradise in which his exclamation suggested that he was living, he might have had some difficulty in defining.

But then the site of the original Paradise is still a matter of speculation.

The next day he went to take lunch with her and her father—he had promised to do so before he had left her, when they had had their interview.

It so happened, however, that he only partook of lunch with Beatrice; for Mr. Avon had, he learned, been compelled to go to Dublin for some days, to satisfy himself regarding a document which was in a library in that city.

Harold did not grumble at the prospect of a long afternoon by her side; only he could not help feeling that the *ménage* of the Avon family was one of the most remarkable that he had ever known. The historical investigations of Mr. Avon did not seem to induce him to take a conventional view of his obligations, as the father of an extremely handsome girl—assuming that he was aware of the fact of her beauty—or a pessimistic view of modern society. He seemed to allow Beatrice to be in every way her own mistress— to receive whatever visitors she pleased; and to lay no narrow-minded prohibition upon such an incident as lunching *tête-à-tête* with a young man, or perhaps—but Harold had no knowledge of such a case—an old man.

He wondered if the historian had ever been remonstrated with on this subject, by such persons as had not had the advantage of scrutinizing humanity through the medium of state papers.

Harold thought that, on the whole, he had no reason to take exception to the liberality of Mr. Avon's system. He reflected that it was to this system he was indebted for what promised to be an extremely agreeable afternoon.

What he did not reflect upon, however, was, that he was indebted to Mr. Avon's peculiarities—some people would undoubtedly call the system a peculiar one—for a charmingly irresponsible relationship toward the historian's daughter. He did not reflect upon the fact, that if the girl had had the Average Father, or the Vigilant Mother, to say nothing of the Athletic Brother, he would not have been able, without some explanation, to visit her, and, on the strength of promising to love her, to kiss her, as he had now repeatedly done, on the mouth—or even on the forehead, which is somewhat less satisfying. Everyone knows that the Vigilant Mother would, by the application of a maternal thumb-screw which she always carries attached to her bunch of keys, have extorted from Beatrice a full confession as to the incidents of the seal-hunt—all except the hunting of the seals—and that this confession would have led to a visit to the study of the Average Father, in one corner of which reposes the rack, in working order, for the reception of the suitor. Everyone knows so much, and also that the alternative of the paternal rack, is the fist of the Athletic Brother.

But Mr. Harold Wynne did not seem to reflect upon these points, when he heard the lightly uttered excuses of Beatrice for her father's absence, as they seated themselves at the table in the large dining-room.

His practised eye made him aware of the fact that Beatrice understood what he considered to be the essentials of a *recherché* lunch: a lunch appeals to the eye; but wine appeals to other senses than the sense of seeing; and the result of his judgment was to convince him that, if Mr. Avon was as careless in the affairs of the cellar as he was in the affairs of the drawing-room, he was to be congratulated upon having about him someone who understood still hock at any rate.

In the drawing-room, she busied herself in arranging, in Wedgwood bowls, some flowers that he had brought her—trifles of sprawling orchids, Eucharis lilies, and a fairy tropical fern or two, all of which are quite easy to be procured in London in October for the expenditure of a few sovereigns. The picture that she made bending over her bowls was inexpressibly lovely. He sat silent, watching her, while she prattled away with the artless high spirits of a child. She was surely the loveliest thing yet made by God. He thought of what the pious old writer had said about a particular fruit, and he paraphrased it in his own mind, saying, that doubtless God could make a lovelier thing, but certainly He had never made it.

"I am delighted to have such sweet flowers now," she cried, as she observed, with critical eyes, the effect of a bit of flaming crimson—an orchid suggesting a flamingo in flight—over the turquoise edge of the bowl. "I am delighted, because I have a prospect of other visitors beside yourself, my lord."

"Other visitors?" said he. He wondered if he might venture to suggest to her the inadvisability of entertaining other visitors during her father's absence.

"Other visitors indeed," she replied. "I did not tell you yesterday all that I had to tell. I forget now what we talked about yesterday. How did we put in our time?"

She looked up with laughing eyes across the bowl of flowers, that she held up to her face.

"I don't forget—I shall never forget," said he, in a low voice.

"You must never forget," said she. "But to my visitors—who are they, do you fancy? Don't try to guess, for if you should succeed I should be too mortified to be able to tell you that you were right. I will tell you now. Three days ago—while we were still on the Continent—Miss Craven called. She promised faithfully to do so at Castle Innisfail—indeed, she suggested doing so herself; and I found her card waiting for me on my return with a few words scrawled on it, to tell me that she would return in some days. I don't think that anything should be in the same bowl with a Eucharis lily—even the Venus-hair fern looks out of place beside it."

She had strayed from her firebrand orchids to the white lilies.

"You are quite right, indeed," said he. "A lily and you stand alone—you make everything else in the world seem tawdry."

"That is not the message of the lily," said she. "But supposing that Miss Craven should call upon me to-day—would you be glad of such a third person to our party?"

"I should kill her, if she were a thousand times Helen Craven," said he, with a laugh. "But she is only one visitor; who are the others?"

"Oh, there is only one other, and he is interesting to me only," she cried. "Yes, I found Mr. Airey's card also waiting for me, and on it were scrawled almost the very words that were on Miss Craven's card, so that he may be here at any moment." Harold did not say a word. He sat watching her as her hands mingled with their sister-lilies on the table. Something cold seemed to have clasped his heart—a cold doubt that made him dumb.

"Yes," she continued; "Mr. Airey asked me one night at Castle Innisfail to let him know where we should go after leaving Ireland."

"Yes," said he, in a slow way; "I heard him make that request of you."

"You heard him? But you were taking part in the *tableaux* in the hall."

"I had left the platform and had strayed round to one of the doors. You told him where you were going?"

"I told him that we should be in this house in October, and he said that he would make it a point to be in town early in October, though Parliament was not to sit until the middle of January. He has kept his word."

"Yes, he has kept his word."

Harold felt that cold hand tightening upon his heart. "I think that he was interested in me," continued the girl. "I know that I was interested in him. He knows so much about everything. He is a close friend of yours, is he not?"

"Yes," said Harold, without much enthusiasm. "Yes, he was a close friend of mine. You see, I had my heart set upon going into Parliament—upon so humble an object may one's aspirations be centred—and Edmund Airey was my adviser."

"And what did he advise you to do?" she asked.

"He advised me to—well, to go into Parliament." He could not bring himself to tell her what form exactly Edmund Airey's advice had assumed.

"I am sure that his advice was good," said she. "I think that I would go to him if I stood in need of advice."

"Would you, indeed, Beatrice?" said he. He was at the point of telling her all that he had learned from Mrs. Mowbray; he only restrained himself by an effort.

"I believe that he is both clever and wise."

"The two do not always go together, certainly."

"They do not. But Mr. Airey is, I think, both."

"He has been better than either. To be successful is better than to be either wise or clever. Mr. Airey has been successful. He will get an Under-Secretaryship if the Government survives the want of confidence of the Opposition."

"And you will go into Parliament, Harold?"

He shook his head.

"That aspiration is past," said he; "I have chosen the more excellent career. Now, tell me something of your aspirations, my beloved."

"To see you daily—to be near you—to—"

But the enumeration of the terms of her aspirations is unnecessary.

How was it that some hours after this, Harold Wynne left the house with that cold feeling still at his heart?

Was it a pang of doubt in regard to Beatrice, or a pang of jealousy in regard to Edmund Airey?

CHAPTER XXXV
ON THE HOME

HAROLD WYNNE remembered how he had made up his mind to judge whether or not Edmund Airey had been simply playing, in respect of Beatrice, the part which, according to Mrs. Mowbray's story, had been assigned to him by Helen Craven. He had made up his mind that unless Edmund Airey meant to go much further than—according to Mrs. Mowbray's communication—Helen Craven could reasonably ask him to go, he would not take the trouble to see Beatrice again.

Helen could scarcely expect him to give up his life to the furtherance of her interests with another man.

Well, he had found that Edmund, so far from showing any intention of abandoning the position—it has already been defined—which he had assumed toward Beatrice, had shown, in the plainest possible way, that he did not mean to lose sight of her.

And for such a man as he was, to mean so much, meant a great deal, Harold was forced to acknowledge.

He spent the remainder of the day which had begun so auspiciously, wondering if his friend, Edmund Airey, meant to tell Beatrice some day that he loved her, and, what was very much more important, that he was anxious to marry her.

And then that unworthy doubt of which he had become conscious, returned to him.

If Edmund Airey, who, at first, had merely been attracted to Beatrice with a view of furthering what Helen Craven believed to be her interests, had come to regard her differently—as he, Harold, assumed that he had— might it not be possible, he asked himself, that Beatrice, who had just admitted that she had always had some sort of admiration for Edmund Airey, would — — —-

"Never, never, never!" he cried. "She is all that is good and true and faithful. She is mine—altogether mine!"

But his mind was in such a condition that the thought which he had tried to crush down, remained with him to torture him.

It should not have been a torturing thought, considering that, a few days before, he had made up his mind that it was his duty to relinquish Beatrice—to go to her and bid her good-bye for ever. To be sure, he had failed to realize this honourable intention of his; but what was honourable at one time was honourable at another, so that the thought of something occurring to bring about the separation for which he had professed to be so anxious, should not have been a great trouble to him—it should have been just the contrary.

The next day found him in the same condition. The thought occurred to him, "What if, at this very moment, Edmund Airey is with her, endeavouring to increase that admiration which he must know Beatrice entertains for him?" The thought was not a consoling one. Its effect was to make him think very severely of the laxity of Mr. Avon's *ménage*, which would make possible such an interview as he had just imagined. It was a terrible thing, he thought, for a father to show so utter a disregard for his responsibilities as to— —-

But here he reflected upon something that had occurred to him in connection with *tête-à-tête* interviews, and he thought it better not to pursue his course of indignant denunciation of the eminent historian.

He put on an overcoat and went to pay a visit to his sister, who, he had heard the previous day, was in town for a short time. In another week she would be entertaining a large party for the pheasant-shooting at her country-house in Brackenshire, and Harold was to be her guest as well as Edmund Airey and Helen Craven. It was to this visit that Lord Fotheringay had alluded in the course of his chamber interview with his son at Castle Innisfail.

Harold had now made up his mind that he would not be able to join his sister's party, and he thought it better to tell her so than to write to her to this effect.

Mrs. Lampson was not at home, the servant said, when he had knocked at the door of the house in Eaton Square. A party was expected for lunch, however, so that she would probably return within half an hour.

Harold said he would wait for his sister, and went upstairs.

There was one person already in the drawingroom and that person was Lord Fotheringay.

Harold greeted him, and found that he was in an extremely good humour. He had never been in better health, he declared. He felt, he said, as young as the best of them—he prudently refrained from defining them—and he was still of the opinion that the Home—the dear old English Home—was where true and lasting happiness alone was to be found; and he meant to try the Principality of Monaco later on; for November was too awful in any part of Britain. Yes, he had seen the influence of the Home upon exiles in various parts of the world. Had he not seen strong men weep like children—like innocent children—at the sight of an English post-mark—the post-mark of a simple English village? Why had they wept, he asked his son, with the well-gloved forefinger of the professional moralist outstretched?

His son declined to hazard an answer.

They had wept those tears—those bitter tears—Lord Fotheringay said, with solemn emphasis, because their thoughts went back to that village home of theirs—the father, the mother, perhaps a sister—who could tell?

"Ah, my boy," he continued, "'Mid pleasures and palaces'—"mid pleasures and'—by the way, I looked in at the Rivoli Palace last night. I heard that there was a woman at that place who did a new dance. I saw it. A new dance! My dear boy, it wasn't new when I saw it first, and that's—ah, never mind—it's some years ago. I was greatly disappointed with it. There's nothing indecent in it—I will say that for it—but there's nothing enlivening. Ah, the old home of burlesque—the old home—that's what I was talking about—the Home—the sentiment of the Home—"

"Of burlesque?" suggested Harold.

"Of the devil, sir," said his father. "Don't try to be clever; it's nearly as bad as being insolent. What about that girl—Helen Craven, I mean? Have you seen her since you came to town? She's here. She'll be at Ella's next week. Perhaps it will be your last chance. Heavens above! To think that a pauper like you should need to be urged to marry such a girl! A girl with two hundred thousand pounds in cash—a girl belonging to one of the best families in all—in all Birmingham. Harold, don't be a fool! Such a chance doesn't come every day."

Just then Mrs Lampson entered the room and with her, her latest discovery, the Coming Dramatist.

Mrs Lampson was invariably making discoveries. But they were mostly discoveries of quartz; they contained a certain proportion of gold, to be sure; but when it came to the crushing, they did not yield enough of the precious metal to pay the incidental expenses of the plant for the working.

She had discovered poets and poetesses—the latter by the score. She had discovered at least one Genius in black and white—his genius being testified by his refusal to work; and she had discovered a pianoforte Genius—his genius being proved by the dishevelment of his hair. The man who had the reputation for being the Greatest Living Atheist was a welcome guest at her house, and the most ridiculous of living socialists boasted of having dined at her table.

She was foremost in every philanthropic movement, and wrote articles to the magazines, lamenting the low tone of modern society in London.

She also sneered (in private) at Lady Innisfail. Her latest discovery, the Coming Dramatist, had had, he proudly declared, his plays returned to him by the best managers in London, and by the one conscientious manager in the United States—the last mentioned had not prepaid the postage, he lamented.

He was a fearful joy to cherish; but Mrs. Lampson listened to his egotism at lunch, and tried to prevent her other guests from listening to him.

They would not understand him, she thought, and she did not make a mistake in this matter.

She got rid of him as soon as possible, and once more breathed freely. He had not disgraced her—that was so much in his favour. The same could not always be said of her discoveries.

The Christian Dynamitard was, people said, the only gentleman who had ever been introduced ta society by Mrs. Lampson.

When Harold found his sister alone, he explained to her that it would be impossible for him to join her party at Abbeylands—Mr. Lampson's Bracken-shire place—and his sister laughed and said she supposed that he had something better on his hands. He assured her that he had nothing better, only—

"There, there," said she, "I don't want you to invent an excuse. You would only have met people whom you know."

"Of course," said Harold, "you're not foolish enough to ask your discoveries down to shoot pheasants. I should like to see some of them in a *battue* with my best enemies. Yes, I'd hire a window, with pleasure."

"Didn't he behave well—the Coming Dramatist?" said she, earnestly. "You cannot say he didn't behave well—at least for a Coming Person."

"He behaved—wonderfully," said Harold. "Good-bye."

She followed him to the door of the room—nay, outside.

"By the bye," said she, in a whisper; "do you know anything of a Miss Avon?"

"Miss Avon?" said Harold. "Miss Avon. Why, if she is the daughter of Julius Anthony Avon, the historian, we met her at Castle Innisfail. Why do you ask me, Ella?"

"It is so funny," said she. "Yesterday Mr. Airey called upon me, and before he left he begged of me to call upon her, and even hinted—he has got infinite tact—that she would make a charming addition to our party at Abbeylands."

"Ah," said Harold.

"And just now papa has been whispering to me about this same Miss Avon. He commanded me—papa has no tact—to invite her to join us for a week. I wonder what that means."

"What what means?"

"That—Mr. Airey and papa."

"Great Heaven! Ella, what should it mean, except that two men, for whom we have had a nominal respect, have gone over to the majority of fools?"

"Oh, is that all? I was afraid that—ah, good-bye."

"Good-bye."

CHAPTER XXXVI
ON THE INFLUENCE OF A MAN OF THE WORLD

It was true then—what he had surmised was true! Edmund Airey had shown himself to be actuated by a stronger impulse than a desire to assist Helen Craven to realize her hopes—so much appeared perfectly plain to Harold Wynne, as he strolled back to his rooms.

He was now convinced that Edmund Airey was serious in his attitude in respect of Beatrice. At Castle Innisfail he had been ready enough to play the game with counters, on his side at least, as stakes, but now he meant to play a serious game.

Harold recalled what proofs he had already received, to justify his arriving at this conclusion, and he felt that they were ample—he felt that this conclusion was the only one possible to be arrived at by anyone acquainted with all that had come under his notice.

He was quite astounded to hear from his sister that Edmund Airey had taken so extreme a step as to beg of her to call upon Beatrice, and invite her to join the Abbeylands party. Whether or not he had approached Mrs. Lampson in confidence on this matter, the fact of his having approached her was, in some degree, compromising to himself, and no one was better aware of this fact than Edmund Airey. He was not an eager boy to give way to a passion without counting the cost. There was no more subtle calculator of costs than Edmund Airey, and Harold knew it.

What, then, was left for Harold to infer?

Nothing, except what he had already inferred.

What then was left for him to do to checkmate the man who was menacing him?

He had lived so long in that world, the centre of which is situated somewhere about Park Lane, and he had come to believe so thoroughly that the leading characteristic of this world is worldliness, that he had lost the capacity to trust anyone implicitly. He was unable to bring himself to risk everything upon the chance of Beatrice's loving him, in the face of the worst that might occur.

Thus it was that the little feeling of distrust which he experienced the previous day remained with him. It did not increase, but it was there. Now and again he could feel its cold finger upon his heart, and he knew that it was there.

He could not love with that blind, unreasoning, uncalculating love— that love which knows only heaven and hell, not earth. That perfect love, which casteth out distrust, was not the love of his world.

And thus it was that he walked to his rooms, thinking by what means he could bind that girl to him, so that she should be bound beyond the possibility of chance, or craft, or worldliness coming between them.

He had not arrived at any satisfactory conclusion on this subject when he reached his rooms.

He was surprised to find waiting for him Mr. Playdell, but he greeted the man cordially—he had acquired a liking for him, for he perceived that, with all his eccentricities—all his crude theories that he tried to vivify by calling them principles, he was still acting faithfully toward Archie Brown, and was preventing him from squandering hundreds of pounds where Archie might have squandered thousands.

"You are naturally surprised to see me, Mr. Wynne," said Playdell. "I dare say that most men would think that I had taken a liberty in making an uninvited call like this."

"I, at any rate, think nothing of the sort, Mr. Playdell," said Harold.

"I am certain that you do not," said Mr. Play-dell. "I am certain that you are capable of doing me justice—yes, on some points."

"I hope that I am, Mr. Playdell."

"I know that you are, Mr. Wynne. You are not one of those silly persons, wise in their own conceit, who wink at one another when my name is mentioned, and suggest that the unfrocked priest is making a very fair thing out of his young patron."

"I believe that your influence over him is wholly for good, Mr. Playdell. If he were to allow you the income of a Bishop instead of that of a Dean I believe that he would still save money—a great deal of money—by having you near him."

"And you are in no way astray, Mr. Wynne. I was prepared for what people would say when I accepted the situation that Archie offered me, but the only stipulation that I made was that my accounts were to be audited by a professional man, and monthly. Thus it is that I protect myself. Every penny that I receive is accounted for."

"That is a very wise plan, Mr. Playdell, but—"

"But it has nothing to do with my coming here to-day? That is what you are too polite to say. You are right, Mr. Wynne. I have not come here to talk about myself and my systems, but about our friend Archie. You have great influence over him."

"I'm afraid I haven't much. If I had, I wouldn't hesitate to tell him that he is making an ass of himself."

"You have come to the point at once, Mr. Wynne."

Mr. Playdell had risen from his chair and was walking up and down the room with his head bent. Now he stood opposite to Harold.

"The point?" said Harold.

"The point is that he is being robbed right and left through the medium of the Legitimate Theatre, and a stop must be put to it," said Playdell.

"And you think that I should make the attempt to put a stop to this foolishness of his? My dear Mr. Playdell, if I were to suggest to Archie that he is making an ass of himself over this particular matter, I should never have another chance of exercising my influence over him for good or bad. I have always known that Mrs. Mowbray is one of the most expensive tastes in England. But when the beauty of Mrs. Mowbray is to be exploited with the beauty of the poetry of Shakespeare, and when these gems are enclosed in so elaborate a setting as the Legitimate Theatre—well, I suppose Archie's millions will hold out. There's a deal of spending in three millions, Mr. Playdell."

"His millions will hold out," said Mr. Playdell. "And so will he," laughed Harold. "I have known Mrs. Mowbray for several years, and she has never ruined any man except her husband, and he is not worth talking about. She has always liked young men with wealth so enormous that even her powers of spending money can make no impression on it."

"Mr. Wynne, you can have no notion what that theatre has cost Archie—what it is daily costing him. Eight hundred pounds a week wouldn't cover the net loss of that ridiculous business—that trailing of Shakespeare in the mire, to gratify the vanity of a woman. I know what men are when they are very young. If I were to talk to Archie seriously on this subject, he would laugh at me; if he did not, he would throw something at me. The result would be *nil*."

"Unless he was a good shot with a casual missile."

"Mr. Wynne, he would not listen to me; but he would listen to you—I know that he would. You could talk to him with all the authority of a man of the world—a man in Society."

"Mr. Playdell," said Harold, shaking his head, "if there's no fool like the old fool, there's no ass like the young ass. Now, I can assure you, on the authority of a man of the world—you know what such an authority is worth—that to try and detach Archie from his theatre nonsense just now by means of a lecture, would be as impossible as to detach a limpet from a rock by a sermon on—let us say—the flexibility of the marriage bond."

"Alas! alas!" said Mr. Playdell.

"The only way that Archie can be induced to throw over Mrs. Mowbray and Shakespeare and suchlike follies, is by inducing him to form a stronger attachment elsewhere."

"The last state of that man might be worse than the first, Mr. Wynne."

"Might—yes, it might be, but that is no reason why it should be. The young ass takes to thistles, because it has never known the enjoyment of a legitimate pasture."

"The legitimate pasture is some distance away from the Legitimate Theatre, Mr. Wynne."

"I agree with you. Now, the thought has just occurred to me that I might get Archie brought among decent people, for the first time in his life. My sister, Mrs. Lampson, is having a party down at her husband's place in Brackenshire, for the pheasant-shooting. Why shouldn't Archie be one of the party? There are a number of decent men going, and decent women also. None of the men will try to get the better of him."

"And the women will not try to make a fool of him?"

"I won't promise that—the world can't cease to revolve on its axis because Archie Brown has a tendency to giddiness."

Mr. Playdell was grave. Then he said, thoughtfully, "Whatever the women may be, they can't be of the stamp of Mrs. Mowbray."

"You may trust my sister for that. You may also trust her to see that they are less beautiful than Mrs. Mowbray," remarked Harold.

Mr. Playdell pondered.

"Pheasant-shooting is expensive in its way," said he. "The preservation of grouse runs away with a good deal of money also, I am told. Race horses, it is generally understood, entail considerable outlay. Put them all together, and you only come within measurable distance of Mrs. Mowbray and

Shakespeare as a pastime—with nothing to show for the money—absolutely nothing to show for the money."

"Except Mrs. Mowbray and Shakespeare."

"Mr. Wynne, I believe that your kind suggestion may be the saving of that lad," said Playdell.

"Oh, it's the merest chance," said Harold. "He may grow sick of the whole business after the first *battue*."

"He won't. I've known men saved from destruction by scoring a century in a first-class cricket match: they gave themselves up to cricket, to the exclusion of other games less healthy. If Archie takes kindly to the pheasants, he may make up his mind to buy a place and preserve them. That will be a healthy occupation for him. You will give him to understand that it's the proper thing to do, Mr. Wynne."

"You may depend upon me. I'll write to my sister to invite him. It's only an experiment."

"It will succeed, Mr. Wynne—it will succeed, I feel that it will. If you only knew, as I do, how he is being fooled, you would understand my earnestness—you have long ago forgiven my intrusion. Give me a chance of serving you in return, Mr. Wynne. That's all I ask."

CHAPTER XXXVII
ON THE DEFECTIVE LINK

HAROLD had a note written to Mrs. Lampson, begging her to invite his friend, Mr. Archie Brown, to join her party at Abbeylands, almost before Mr. Playdell had left the street. He knew that his sister would be very glad to have Archie. All the world had a general notion of Archie's millions; and Abbeylands was one of those immense houses that can accommodate a practically unlimited number of guests. The property had been bought from a nobleman, who had been brought to the verge of bankruptcy by trying to maintain it. Mr. Lampson, a patriotic American, had come to his relief, and had taken the place off his hands.

That is what all truly patriotic Americans do when they have an opportunity.

The new-world democracy comes to the rescue of the old-world aristocracy, and thus a venerable institution is preserved from annihilation.

Harold posted his letter as he went out to dine with a man who was a member of the Carlton Club, and zealous in heating up recruits for the Conservative party. He thought that Harold might possibly be open to conviction, not, of course, on the question of the righteousness of certain principles, but on the question of the direction in which the cat was about to jump. The jumping cat is the dominant power in modern politics.

Harold ate his dinner, and listened patiently to the man whose acquaintance with the tendencies of every genus of the political *felis* was supposed to be extraordinary. He said little. Before he had gone to Castle Innisfail the subject would have interested him greatly, but now he thought that Archie Brown's inanities were preferable to those of the politician.

He was just enough to acknowledge, however, that the cigar with which he left the Carlton was as good a one as he had ever smoked. So that there was some advantage in being a Conservative after all.

He walked round St. James's Square, for the night was warm and fine. His mind was not conscious of having received anything during the previous two hours upon which it would be profitable to ponder. He thought over the question which he had put to himself previously—the question of how he could bind Beatrice to him—how he could make her certainly his own, and thus banish that cold distrust of which he now and again became aware— no, it was not exactly distrust, it was only a slightly defective link in the chain of complete trust.

She loved him and she promised to love him. He reflected upon this, and he asked himself what more could he want. What bond stronger than her word could he desire to have?

"Oh, I will trust her for ever—for ever," he murmured. "If she is not true, then there never was truth on earth."

He fancied that he had dismissed the matter from his mind with this exorcism.

And so he had.

But it so happens that some persons are so constituted that there is but the slenderest connection between their mind and their heart. Something that appeals very forcibly to their mind will not touch their heart in the least. They are Nature's "sports."

Harold Wynne was one of these people. He had made up his mind that, on the question of implicitly trusting Beatrice, nothing more remained to be said. There was still, however, that cold finger upon his heart.

But having made up his mind that nothing more remained to be said on the question, he was logical enough—for logic is also a mental attribute, though by no means universally distributed—to think of other matters.

He began to think about Mr. Playdell, and his zeal for the reform of Archie. Harold's respect for Mr. Playdell had materially increased since the morning. At first he had been inclined to look with suspicion upon the man who had, by the machinery of the Church, been prohibited from discharging the functions of a priest of that Church, though, of course, he was free to exercise that unimportant function known as preaching. He could not preach within a church, however. If he wished to try and save souls by preaching, that was his own business. He would not do so with the sanction of the Church. He was anxious to save the soul of Archie Brown, at any rate. He assumed that Archie had a soul in embryo, ready to be hatched, and it was clear to Harold that Mr. Playdell was anxious to save it from being addled before it had pecked its way out of its shell. Therefore Harold had a considerable respect for Mr. Playdell, though he had been one of the unprofitable servants of the Church.

He thought of the earnest words of the man—of the earnest way in which he had begged to be given the chance of returning the service, which he believed was about to be done to him by Harold.

He had been greatly in earnest; but that fact only made his words the more ridiculous.

"What service could he possibly do me?" Harold thought, when he had had his laugh, recalling the outstretched hand of Mr. Playdell, and his eager eyes. *"What service could he possibly do me? What service?"*

He was rooted to the pavement. The driver of a passing hansom pulled up opposite him, taking the fact of his stopping so suddenly as an indication that he wanted a hansom.

He took no notice of the hansom, and it passed up the square. He remained so long lost in thought, that his cigar, so strongly impregnated with sound Conservative principles, went out like any Radical weed, or the penny Pickwick of the Labour Processionist.

He dropped the unsmoked end, and felt for his pocket-handkerchief. He raised his hat and wiped his forehead.

Then he took a stroll into Piccadilly and on to Knightsbridge. He went down Sloane Street, and into Chelsea, returning by the Embankment to Westminster—the clock was chiming the hour of 2 a.m. as he passed.

But the same clock had struck three before he got into bed, and five before he fell asleep.

VOLUME 3

CHAPTER XXXVIII
ON A KNOWLEDGE OF THE WORLD

SHORTLY after noon he was with her. He had left his rooms without touching a morsel of breakfast, and it was plain that such sleep as he had had could not have been of a soothing nature. He was pale and haggard; and she seemed surprised—not frightened, however, for her love was that which casteth out fear—at the way he came to her—with outstretched hands which caught her own, as he said, "My beloved—my beloved, I have a strange word for you—a strange proposal to make. Dearest, can you trust me? Will you marry me—to-morrow—to-day?"

She scarcely gave a start. He was only conscious of her hands tightening upon his own. She kept her eyes fixed upon his. The silence was long. It was made the more impressive by the distinctness with which the jocularity of the fishmonger's hoy with the cook at the area railings, was heard in the room.

"Harold," she said, in a voice that had no trace of distrust, "Harold, you are part of my life—all my life! When I said that I loved you, I had given myself to you. I will marry you any time you please—to-morrow—to-day—this moment!"

She was in his arms, sobbing.

His "God bless you, my darling!" sounded like a sob also.

In a few moments she was laughing through her tears.

He was not laughing.

"Now, tell me what you mean, my beloved," said she, with a hand on each of his shoulders.

"Tell me what you mean by coming to frighten me like this. What has happened?"

"Nothing has happened, only I want to feel that you are my own—my own beyond the possibility of being separated from me by any power on earth. I do not want to take you away from your father's house—I cannot offer you any home. It may be years before we can live together as those who love one another as we love, may live with the good will of heaven. I only want you to become my wife in name, dearest. Our marriage must be kept a secret."

"But my own love," said she, "why should you wish to go through this ceremony? Are we not united by the true bond of love? Can we be more closely united than we are now? The strength of the marriage bond is only strong in proportion as the love which is the foundation of marriage is strong. Now, why should you wish for the marriage rite before we are prepared to live for ever under the same roof?"

"Why, why?" he cried passionately, as he looked into the depths of her eyes.

He left her and went across the room to one of the windows and looked out. (It was the greengrocer's boy who was now jocular with the cook at the area railings.)

"My Beatrice—" Harold had returned to her from his scrutiny of the pavement. "My Beatrice, you have not seen all that I have seen in the world. You do not know—you do not know me as I know myself. Why should there come to me sometimes an unworthy thought—no, not a doubt—oh, I have seen so much of the world, Beatrice, I feel that if anything should come between us it would kill me. I must—I must feel that we are made one—that there is a bond binding us together that nothing can sever."

"But, my Harold—no, I will not interpose any buts. You would not ask me to do this if you had not some good reason. You say that you know the world. I admit that I do not know it. I only know you, and knowing you and loving you with all my heart—with all my soul—I trust you implicitly—without a question—without the shadow of a doubt."

"God bless you, my love, my love! You will never have reason to regret loving me—trusting me."

"It is my life—it is my life, Harold."

Once again he was standing at the window. This time he remained longer with his eyes fixed upon the railings of the square enclosure.

"It must be to-morrow," he said, returning to her. "I shall come here at noon. A few words spoken in this room and nothing can part us. You will still call yourself by your own name, dearest, God hasten the day when you can come to me as my wife in the sight of all the world and call yourself by my name."

"I shall be here at noon to-morrow," said she.

"Unless," said he, returning to her after he had kissed her forehead and had gone to the door. "Unless"—he framed her face with his hands, and looked down into the depths of her eyes.—"Unless, when you have thought over the whole matter, you feel that you cannot trust me."

She laughed.

"Ah, my love, my love, you do not know the world," said he.

He knew the world.

Another man who knew the world was Pontius Pilate.

This was why he asked "What is Truth?"

Harold Wynne was in Archie Brown's room in Piccadilly within half an hour.

Archie was at the Legitimate Theatre, Mr. Playdell said—Mr. Playdell was seated at the dining-room table surrounded by papers. A trifling difference of opinion had arisen between Mrs. Mowbray and her manager, he added, and (with a smile) Archie had hurried to the theatre to set matters right.

"It is kind of you to call, Mr. Wynne," continued Mr. Playdell. "But I hope it is not to tell me that you regret the suggestion that you made yesterday—that you do not see your way to write to your sister to invite Archie to her place."

"I wrote to her the moment you left me," said Harold. "Archie will get his invitation this evening. It is not about him that I came here to-day, Mr. Playdell. I came to see you. You asked me yesterday to give you an opportunity of doing something for me. I can give you that opportunity."

"And I promise you that I shall embrace it with gladness, Mr. Wynne," said Playdell, rising from the table. "Tell me how I can serve you and you will find how ready I am."

"You still hold to your original principles regarding marriage, Mr. Playdell?"

"How could I do otherwise than hold to them, Mr. Wynne? They are the result of thought; they are not merely a fad to gain notoriety. Let me prove the position that I take up on this matter."

"You need not, Mr. Playdeil. I heard all your case when it was published. I confess that I now think differently respecting you from what I thought at that time. Will you perform the ceremony of marriage between a lady who has promised to marry me and myself?"

"There is only one condition that I make, Mr. Wynne. You must take an oath that you consider the rite, as I perform it, to be binding upon you, and that you will never recognize a divorce."

"I will take that oath willingly, Mr. Playdeil. I have promised my *fiancée* that we shall be with her at noon to-morrow. She will be prepared for us. By the way, do you require a ring for the ceremony as performed by you?"

Mr. Playdeil looked grave—almost scandalized.

"Mr. Wynne," said he, "that question suggests to me a certain disbelief on your part in the validity in the sight of heaven of the rite of marriage as performed by a man with a full sense of his high office, even though unfrocked by a Church that has always shown too great a readiness to submit to secular guidance—secular restrictions in matters that were originally, like marriage, purely spiritual. The Church has not only submitted to civil restrictions in the matter of the celebration of the holy rite of matrimony, but, while declaring at the altar that God has joined them whom the Church has joined, and while denying the authority of man to put them asunder, she recognizes the validity of divorce. She will marry a man who has been divorced from his wife, when he has duly paid the Archbishop a sum of money for sanctioning what in the sight of God is adultery."

"My dear Mr. Playdell," said Harold, "I recollect very clearly the able manner in which you defended your—your—principles, when they were called in question. I do not desire to call them in question now. I believe in your sincerity in this matter and in other matters. I shall drive here for you at half past eleven o'clock to-morrow. I need scarcely say that I mean my marriage to be kept a secret."

"You may depend upon my good faith in that respect," said Mr. Playdell. "Mr. Wynne," he added, impressively, "this land of ours will never be a moral one so long as the Church is content to accept a Parliamentary definition of morality. The Church ought certainly to know her own business."

"There I quite agree with you," said Harold.

He refrained from asking Mr. Playdell if the Church, in dispensing with his services as one of her priests, had not made an honest attempt to vindicate her claims to know her own business. He merely said, "Half past eleven to-morrow," after shaking hands with Mr. Playdell, who opened the door for him.

CHAPTER XXXIX
ON CONSCIENCE AND THE RING

HAROLD WYNNE shut himself up in his rooms without even lunching. He drew a chair in front of the fire and seated himself with the sigh of relief that is given by a man who has taken a definite step in some matter upon which he has been thinking deeply for some time. He sat there all the day, gazing into the fire.

Yes, he had taken the step that had suggested itself to him the previous night. He had made up his mind to take advantage of the opportunity that was afforded him of binding Beatrice to him by a bond which she at least would believe incapable of rupture. The accident of his meeting with the man whose views on the question of marriage had caused him to be thrust out of the Church, and whose practices left him open to a criminal prosecution, had suggested to him the means for binding to him the girl whose truth he had no reason to doubt.

He meant to perpetrate a fraud upon her. He had known of men entrapping innocent girls by means of a mock marriage, and he had always regarded such men as the most unscrupulous of scoundrels. He almost succeeded, after a time, in quieting the whisperings by his conscience of the word "fraud"—its irritating repetitions of this ugly word—by giving prominence to the excellence of his intentions in the transaction which he was contemplating. It was not a mock marriage—no, it was not, as ordinary mock marriages, to be gone through in order to give a man possession of the body of a woman, and to admit of his getting rid of her when it would suit his convenience to do so. It was, he assured his conscience, no mock marriage, since he was seeking it for no gross purpose, but simply to banish the feeling of cold distrust which he had now and again experienced. Had he not offered to free the girl from the promise which she had given to him? Was that like the course which would be adopted by a man endeavouring to take advantage of a girl by means of a mock marriage? Was there anything on earth that he desired more strongly than a real marriage with that same girl? There was nothing. But it was, unfortunately, the case that a real marriage would mean ruin to him; for he knew that his father would keep his word—when it suited his own purpose—and refuse him his allowance upon the day that he refused to sign a declaration to the effect that he was unmarried.

The rite which Mr. Playdell had promised to perform between him and Beatrice would enable him to sign the declaration with—well, with a clear conscience.

But in the meantime this same conscience continued gibing him upon his defence of his conduct; asking him with an irritating sneer, if he would mind explaining his position to the girl's father?—if he was not simply taking advantage of the peculiar circumstances of the girl's life—of the remarkable independence which she enjoyed, apparently with the sanction of her father, to perpetrate a fraud upon her?

For bad taste, for indelicacy, for vulgarity, for disregard of sound argument—that is, argument that sounds well—and for general obstinacy, there is nothing to compare with a conscience that remains in moderately good working order.

After all his straightforward reasoning during the space of two hours, he sprang from his seat crying, "I'll not do it—I'll not do it!"

He walked about his room for an hour, repeating every now and again the words, "I'll not do it—I'll not do it!"

In the course of another hour, he turned on his electric lamp, and wrote a note of half a dozen lines to Mr Playdell, telling him that, on second thoughts, he would not trouble him the next day. Then he wrote an equally short note to Beatrice, telling her that he thought it would be advisable to have a further talk with her before carrying out the plan which he had suggested to her for the next day. He put each note into its cover; but when about to affix stamps to them, he found that his stamp-drawer was empty. This was not a serious matter; he was going to his club to dine, and he knew that he could get stamps from the hall-porter.

He felt very much lighter at heart leaving his rooms than he had felt on entering some hours before. He felt that he had been engaged in a severe conflict, and that he had got the better of his adversary.

At the door of the club he found Mr. Durdan standing somewhat vacantly. He brightened up at the appearance of Harold.

"I've just been trying to catch some companionable fellow to dine with me," he cried.

"I'm sorry that I can't congratulate you upon finding one," said Harold.

"Then I congratulate myself," said Mr. Durdan, brightly. "You're the most companionable man that I know in town at present."

"Ah, then you're not aware of the fact that Edmund Airey is here just now," said Harold with a shrewd laugh.

"Edmund Airey? Edmund Airey?" said Mr. Durdan. "Let me tell you that your friend Edmund Airey is——"

"Don't say it in the open air," said Harold.

"Come inside and make the revelation to me."

"Then you will dine with me? Good! My dear fellow, my medical man has warned me times without number of the evil of dining alone, or with a newspaper—even the *Telegraph*. It's the beginning of dyspepsia, he says; so I wait at the door any time I am dining here until I get hold of the right man."

"If I can play the part of a priest and exorcise the demon that you're afraid of, you may reckon upon my services," said Harold. "But to tell you the truth, I'm a bit down myself to-night."

"What's the matter with you—nothing serious?" said Mr. Durdan.

"I've been working out some matters," said Harold.

"I know what's the matter with you," said the other. "That friend of yours has been trying to secure you for the Government, and you were too straightforward to be entrapped? Airey is a clever man—I don't deny his cleverness for a moment. Oh, yes; Mr. Airey is a very clever man." It seemed that he was now levelling an accusation against Mr. Airey that his best friends would find difficulty in repudiating. "Yes, but you and I, Wynne, are not to be caught by a phrase. The moment he fancied that I was attracted to her—I say, fancied, mind—and that he fancied—it may have been the merest fancy—that she was not altogether indifferent to me, he forced himself forward, and I have good reason to believe that he is now in town solely on her account. I give you my word, Wynne, I never spoke a sentence to Miss Avon that all the world mightn't hear. Oh, there's nothing so contemptible as a man like Airey—a fellow who is attracted to a girl only when he sees that she is attracting other men. Yes, I met a man yesterday who told me that Airey was in town. 'Why should he be in town now?' I inquired. 'There's nothing going on in town.' He winked and said, '*cherchez la femme*'—he did upon my word. Oh, the days of the Government are numbered. Will you try Chablis or Sauterne?"

Harold said that he rather thought that he would try Chablis.

For another hour-and-a-half he was forced to listen to Mr. Durdan's prosing about the blunders of the Administration, and the designs of Edmund Airey. He left the club without asking the hall-porter for any stamps.

He had made up his mind that he would not need any stamps that night.

Before he reached his rooms he took out of the pocket of his overcoat the two letters which he had written, and he tore them both into small pieces.

With the chatter of Mr. Durdan there had come back to him that feeling of distrust.

Yes, he would make sure of her.

He unlocked one of the drawers in his writing-table and brought out a small *boule* case. When he had found—not without a good deal of searching—the right key for the box, he opened it. It contained an ivory miniature of his mother, in a Venetian mounting, a few jewels, and two small rings. One of them was set with a fine chrysoprase cameo of Eros, and surrounded by rubies. The other was an old *in memoriam* ring.

He picked up the cameo and scrutinized it attentively for some time, slipping it down to the first joint of his little finger. He kept turning it over for half an hour before he laid it on the desk and relocked the box and the drawer.

"It will be hers," he said. "Would I use my mother's ring for this ceremony if I meant it to be a fraud—if I meant to take advantage of it to do an injury to my beloved one? As I deal with her, so may God deal with me when my hour comes." It was a ring that had been left to him with a few other trinkets by his mother, and he had now chosen it for the ceremony which was to be performed the next day.

Curiously enough, the fact of his choosing this ring did more to silence the whispering jeers of his conscience than all his phrases of argument had done.

The next day he called for Mr. Playdell in a hansom, and shortly after noon, the words of the marriage service of the Church of England had been repeated in the Bloomsbury drawing-room by the man who had once been a priest and who still wore the garb of a priest. He, at any rate, did not consider the rite a mockery.

Harold could not shake off the feeling that he was acting a part in a dream. When it was all over he dropped into a chair, and his head fell forward until his face was buried in his hands.

It was left for Beatrice to comfort this sufferer in his hour of trial.

Her hand—his mother's ring was upon the third finger—was upon his head, and he heard her low sympathetic voice saying, "My husband— my husband—I shall be a true wife to you for ever and ever. We shall live trusting one another for ever, my beloved!"

They were alone in the room. He did not raise his face from his hands for a long time. She knelt beside where he was sitting and put her head against his.

In an instant he had clasped her passionately. He held her close to him, looking into her eyes.

"Oh, my love, my love," he cried. "What am I that you should have given to me that divine gift of your love? What am I that I should have asked you to do this for my sake? Was there ever such love as yours, Beatrice? Was there ever such baseness as mine? Will you forgive me, Beatrice?"

"Only once," said she, "I felt that—I scarcely know what I felt, dear—I think it was that your hurrying on our marriage showed—was it a want of trust?"

"I was a fool—a fool!" he said bitterly. "The temptation to bind you to me was too great to be resisted. But now—oh, Beatrice, I will give up my life to make you happy!"

CHAPTER XL
ON SOCIETY AND THE SEAL

THE next afternoon when Harold called upon Beatrice, he found her with two letters in her hand. The first was a very brief one from her father, letting her know that he would have to remain in Dublin for at least a fortnight longer; the second was from Mrs. Lampson—she had paid Beatrice a ten minutes' visit the previous day—inviting her to stay for a week at Abbeylands, from the following Tuesday.

"What am I to do in the matter, my husband—you see how quickly I have come to recognize your authority?" she cried, while he glanced at his sister's invitation.

"My dearest, you had better recognize the duty of a wife in this and other matters, by pleasing yourself," said he.

"No," said she. "I will only do what you advise me. That, you should see as a husband—I see it clearly as a wife—will give me a capital chance of throwing the blame on you in case of any disappointment. Oh, yes, you may be certain that if I go anywhere on your recommendation and fail to enjoy myself, all the blame will be laid at your door. That's the way with wives, is it not?"

"I can't say," said he. "I've never had one from whom to get any hints that would enable me to form an opinion."

"Then what did you mean by suggesting to me that it was wife-like to please myself?" said she, with an affectation of shrewdness that was extremely charming.

"I've seen other men's wives now and again," said he. "It was a great privilege."

"And they pleased themselves?"

"They did not please me, at any rate. I don't see why you shouldn't go down to my sister's place next week. You should enjoy yourself."

"You will be there?"

He shook his head.

"I was to have been there," said he; "but when I promised to go I had not met you. When I found that you were to be in town, I told Ella, my sister, that it was impossible for me to join her party."

"Of course that decides the matter," said she. "I must remain here, unless you change your mind and go to Abbeylands."

He remained thoughtful for a few moments, and then he turned to where she was opening the old mahogany escritoire.

"I particularly want you to go to my sister's," he said. "A reason has just occurred to me—a very strong reason, why you should accept the invitation, especially as I shall not be there."

"Oh, no," said she, "I could not go without you."

"My dear Beatrice, where is that wifely obedience of which you mean to be so graceful an exponent?" said he, standing behind her with a hand on each of her shoulders. "The fact is, dearest, that far more than you can imagine depends on your taking this step. It is necessary to throw people— my relations in particular—off the notion that something came of our meeting at Castle Innisfail. Now, if you were to go to Abbeylands while it was known that I had excused myself, you can understand what the effect would be."

"The effect, so far as I'm concerned, would be that I should be miserable, all the time I was away from you."

"The effect would be, that those people who may have been joining our names together, would feel that they have been a little too precipitate in their conclusions."

"That seems a very small result for so much self-sacrifice on our part, Harold."

"It's not so small as it may seem to you. I see now how important it would be to me—to both of us—if you were to go for a week to Abbeylands while I remain in town."

"Then of course I'll go. Yes, dear; I told you that I would trust you for ever. I placed all my trust in you yesterday. How many people would condemn me for marrying you in such indecent haste—that is what they would call it—and without a word of consultation with my father either? When I showed my trust in you at that time—the most important in my life—you may, I think, have confidence that I will trust you in everything. Yes, I'll go."

He had turned away from her. How could he face her when she was talking in this way about her trust in him?

"There has never been trust like yours, my beloved," said he, after a pause. "You will never regret it for a moment, my love—never, never!"

"I know it—I know it," said she.

"The fact is, Beatrice," said he, after another pause, "my relatives think that if I were to marry Helen Craven I should be doing a remarkably good stroke of business. They were right: it would be a good stroke—of business."

"How odd," cried Beatrice. She had become thoroughly interested. "I never thought of such a possibility at Castle Innisfail. She is nice, I think; only she does not know how to dress."

In an instant there came to his memory Mrs. Mowbray's cynical words regarding the extent of a woman's forgiveness.

"The question of being nice or of dressing well does not make any difference so far as my friends are concerned," said he. "All that is certain is that Helen Craven has several thousands of pounds a year, and they think that I should be satisfied with that."

"And so you should," she cried, with the light of triumph in her eyes. "I wonder if Mr. Airey knew what the wishes of your relatives were in this matter. I should like to know that, because I now recollect that he suggested something in that way when we talked together about you one evening at the Castle."

"Edmund Airey gave me the strongest possible advice on the subject," said Harold. "Yes, he advised me to ask Helen Craven to be my wife. More than that—I only learnt it a few days ago—so soon as you appeared at the Castle, and he saw—he sees things very quickly—that I was in love with you, he thought that if he were to interest you greatly, and that if you found out that he was wealthy and distinguished, you might possibly decline to fall in love with me, and so——"

"And so fall in love with him?" she cried, starting up from her chair at the desk. "I see now all that he meant. He meant that I should be interested in him—I was, too, greatly interested in him—and that I should be attracted to him, and away from you. But all the time he had no intention of allowing himself to be attracted by me to the point of ever asking me to marry him. In short, he was amusing himself at my expense. Oh, I see it all now. I must confess that, now and again, I wondered what Mr. Airey meant by placing himself so frequently by my side. I felt flattered—I admit that I felt flattered.

Can you imagine anything so cruel as the purpose that he set himself to accomplish?"

Her face had become pale. This only gave emphasis to the flashing of her eyes. She was in a passion of indignation.

"Edmund Airey and his tricks were defeated," said Harold in a low voice. "Yes, we have got the better of him, Beatrice, so much is certain."

"But the cruelty of it—the cruelty—oh, what does it matter now?" she cried. Then her paleness vanished into a delicate roseate flush, as she gave a laugh, and said, "After all, I believe that my indignation is due only to my wounded vanity. Yes, all girls are alike, Harold. Our vanity is our dominant quality."

"It is not so with you, Beatrice," he said. "I know you truly, my dear. I know that you would be as indignant if you heard of the same trickery being carried on in respect of another girl."

"I would—I know I would," she cried. "But what does it matter? As you say, I—we—have defeated this Mr. Airey, so that my vanity at least can find sweet consolation in reflecting that we have been cleverer than he was. I don't suppose that he could imagine anyone existing cleverer than himself."

"Yes, I think that we have got the better of him," said Harold. He was a little surprised to find that she felt so strongly on the subject of Edmund's attitude in regard to herself. He did not think it wise to tell her that that attitude was due to the timely suggestion of Helen. He could not bring himself to do so. He felt that his doing so would be to place himself on a level with the man who gives his wife during the first year of their married life, a circumstantial account of the many wealthy and beautiful young women who were anxious—to a point of distraction—to marry him.

He felt that there was no need for him to say anything about Helen—he almost wished that he had said nothing about Edmund.

"We got the better of him," he said a second time. "Never mind Edmund Airey. You must go to Abbeylands and amuse yourself. You will most likely meet with Archie Brown there. Archie is the plainest looking and probably the richest man of his age in England. He is to be made the subject of an experiment at Abbeylands."

"Is he to be vivisected?" said she. She was now neither pale nor roseate. She was herself once more.

"There's no need to vivisect poor Archie," said he. "Everyone knows that there's nothing particular about Archie. No; we are merely trying a new cure for him. He has not been in a very healthy state lately."

"If he is delicate, I suppose he will be thrown a good deal with us—the females, the incapables—while the pheasant-shooting is going on."

"You will see how matters are managed at Abbeylands," said Harold. "If you find that Archie is attracted toward any girl who is distinctly nice, you might—how does a girl assist her weaker sister to make up her mind to look with friendly eyes upon such a one as Archie?"

"Let me see," said she. "Wouldn't the best way be for girl number one to look with friendly eyes on him herself?"

Harold lay back on his chair and laughed at first; then he gazed at her in wonder.

"You are cleverer than Edmund Airey and Helen Craven when they combine their wisdom," said he. "Your woman's instinct is worth more than their experience."

"I never knew what the instincts of a woman were before this morning," said she. "I never felt that I had any need to exercise the instinct of defence. I suppose the young seal, though it has never been in the water, jumps in by instinct should it be attacked. Oh, yes, I dare say I could swim as well as most girls of my age."

It was only when he had returned to his rooms that he fully comprehended the force of her parable of the young seal.

CHAPTER XLI
ON DRY CHAMPAGNE AND A CRISIS

THE next morning Archie drove one of his many machines round to Harold's rooms and broke in upon him before he had finished his breakfast.

"Hallo, my tarty chip," cried Archie; "what's the meaning of this?"

He threw on the table an envelope addressed to him in the handwriting of Mrs. Lampson.

"What's the meaning of what?" said Harold. "Have you got beyond the restraint of Mr. Playdell alcoholically, that you ask me what's the meaning of that envelope?"

"I mean what does the inside mean?" said Archie.

"I'm sure you know better than I do, if you've read what's inside it."

"Oh, you're like one of the tarty chips in the courts that cross-examine other tarty chips until their faces are blue," said Archie. "There's no show for that sort of thing here. So just open the envelope and see what's inside."

"How can I do that and eat my kidneys?" said Harold. "I wish to heavens you wouldn't come here bothering me when I'm trying to get through a tough kidney and a tougher leading article. What's the matter with the letter, Archie, my lad?"

"It's all right," said Archie. "It's an invite from your sister for a big shoot at Abbeylands. What does it mean—that's what I'd like to know? Does it mean that decent people are going to make me the apple of their eye, after all?"

"I don't think it goes quite so far as that," said Harold. "I expect it means that my sister has come to the end of her discoveries and she's forced to fall back on you."

"Oh, is that all?" Archie looked disappointed. "All? Isn't it enough?" said Harold. "Why, you're in luck if you let her discover you. I knew that her atheists couldn't hold out. She used them up too quickly. One should he economical of one's genuine atheists nowadays."

"Great Godfrey! does she take me for an atheist?" shouted Archie.

"Did you ever hear of an atheist shooting pheasants?" said Harold. "Not likely. An atheist is a man that does nothing except talk, and talks about nothing except himself. Now, you're asked to the shoot, aren't you?"

"That's in the invite anyway."

"Of course. And that shows that you're not taken for an atheist."

"I'm glad of that. I draw the line at atheism," Archie replied with a smile.

"I hope you'll have a good time among the pheasants."

"Do you suppose that I'll go?"

"I'm sure you will. I may have thought you a bit of a fool before I came to know you, Archie—"

"And since you heard that I had taken the Legitimate."

"Well, yes, even after that masterpiece of astuteness. But I would never think that you'd be fool enough to throw away this chance."

"Chance—chance of what?"

"Of getting among decent people. I told you that my sister has nothing but decent people when there's a shoot—there's no Coming Man in anything among the house-party. Yes, it's sure to be comfortable. It's the very thing for you."

"Is it? I'm not so certain about it. The people there are pretty sure to allude in a friendly spirit to my red hair."

"Well, yes, I think you may depend upon that. That means that you'll get on so well among them that they will take an interest in your personality. If you get on particularly well with them they may even allude to the simplicity of your mug. If they do that, you may be certain that you are a great social success."

Archie mused.

It was in this musing spirit that he took in a contemplative way a lump of sugar out of the sugar bowl, turned it over between his fingers as though it was something altogether new to him. Then he threw the lump up to the ceiling, his face became one mouth, and the sugar disappeared.

"I think I'll go," he said, as he crunched the lump. "Yes, I'll be hanged if I don't go."

"That's more than probable," said Harold.

"Yes, I'd like to clear off for a bit from this kennel."

"What kennel?"

"This kennel—London. Do you go the length of denying that London's a kennel?"

"I don't do anything of the sort."

"You'd best not. I was thinking if a run to Australia, or California, or Timbuctoo would not be healthy just now."

"Oh."

"Yes, I made up my mind yesterday, that if I don't have better hands soon, I'll chuck up the whole game. That's the sort of new potatoes that I am."

"The Legitimate?"

"The Legitimate be frizzled! Am I to continue paying for the suppers that other tarty chips eat? That's what I want you to tell me. You know what a square deal is, Wynne, as well as most people."

"I believe I do."

"Well, then, you can tell me if I'm to pay for dry champagne for her guests."

"Whose guests?"

"Great Godfrey! haven't I been telling you? Mrs. Mowbray's guests. Who else's would they be? Do you mean to tell me that, in addition to giving people free boxes at the Legitimate every night to see W. S. late of Stratford upon Avon, it's my business to supply dry champagne all round after the performance?"

"Well," said Harold, "to speak candidly to you, I've always been of the opinion that the ideal proprietor of a theatre is one who supplies really comfortable stalls free, and has really sound champagne handed round at intervals during the performance. I also frankly admit that I haven't yet met with any manager who quite realized my ideas in this matter. Archie, my lad, the sooner you get down to Abbeylands the better it will be for yourself."

"I'll go. Mind you, I don't cry off when I know the chaps that she asks to supper—I'll flutter the dimes for anyone I know; but I'm hanged if I do it for the chaps that chip in on her invite. They'll not draw cards from my pack, Wynne. No, I'll see them in the port of Hull first. That's the sort of new potatoes that I am."

"Give me your hand, Archie," cried Harold. "I always thought you nothing better than a millionaire, but I find that you're a man after all."

"I'll make things hum at the Legitimate yet," said Archie—his voice was fast approaching the shouting stage. "I'll send them waltzing round. I thought once upon a time that, when she laid her hand upon my head and said, 'Poor old Archie,' I could go on for ever—that to see the decimals fluttering about her would be the loveliest sight on earth for the rest of my life. But I'm tired of that show now, Wynne. Great Godfrey! I can get my hair smoothed down at a barber's for sixpence, and yet I believe that she charged me a thousand pounds for every time she patted my head. A decimal for a pat—a pat!"

"You could buy the whole Irish nation for less money, according to some people's ideas—but they're wrong," said Harold.

"Wynne," said Archie, solemnly. "I've been going it blind for some time. Shakespeare's a fraud. I'll shoot those pheasants."

He had picked up his hat, and in another minute Harold saw him sending his pair of chestnuts down the street at a pace that showed a creditable amount of self-restraint on the part of Archie.

Three days afterwards Harold got a letter from Mrs. Lampson, giving him a number of commissions to execute for her—delicate matters that could not be intrusted to any one except a confidential agent. The postscript mentioned that Archie Brown had arrived a few days before and had charmed every one with his shyness. On this account she could scarcely believe, she said, that he was a millionaire. She added that Lady Innisfail and her daughter had just arrived at Abbeylands, that the Miss Avon about whom she had inquired, had accepted her invitation and was coming to Abbeylands on the next day; and finally, Mrs. Lampson said that her father was dull enough to make people believe that he was really reformed. He was inquiring when Miss Avon was coming, and he shared the fate of all men (and women) who were unfortunate enough to be reformed: he had become deadly dull. Lady Innisfail had assured her, however, that it was very rarely that a Hardened Reprobate permanently reformed—even with the incentive of acute rheumatism—before he was sixty-five, so that it would be unwise to be despondent about Lord Fotheringay. If this was so—and Lady Innisfail was surely an authority—Mrs. Lampson said that she looked forward to such a lapse on the part of her father as would restore him to the position of interest which he had always occupied in the eyes of the world.

Harold lay back in his chair and laughed heartily at the reference made by his sister to the shyness of Archie, and also to the fact of Norah Innisfail's sitting at the table with the Young Reprobate as well as the Old.

He wondered if the conversation had yet turned upon the management of the Legitimate Theatre.

It was after he had lunched on the next Tuesday that Harold received this letter—written by his sister the previous day. He had passed an hour with Beatrice, who was to start by the four-twenty train for Abbeylands station. He had said goodbye to her for a week, and already he was feeling so lonely that he was soon pacing his room calling himself a fool for having elected to remain in town while she was to go.

He thought how they might have had countless strolls through the fine park at Abbeylands—through the picturesque ruins of the old Abbey—on the banks of the little trout stream. Instead of being by her side among those interesting scenes, he would have to remain—he had been foolish enough to make the choice—in the neighbourhood of nothing more joyous than St. James's Palace.

This was bad enough; but not merely would he be away from the landscapes at Abbeylands, the elements of life in those landscapes would be represented by Beatrice and Another.

Yes; she would certainly appear with someone at her side—in the place he might have occupied if he had not been such a fool.

An hour had passed before he had got the better of his impulse to call a hansom and drive to the railway terminus and take a seat beside her in the train. When the clock had struck four, and it was therefore too late for him to entertain the idea of going with her, he became more inclined to take a reasonable view of the situation.

"I was right." he said, as he seated himself in front of the fire, and stared into the smouldering coals. "Yes, I was right. No one must suspect that we are—bound to one another"—the words were susceptible of a sufficiently liberal interpretation. "The penetration of Edmund Airey will be at fault for the first time, and the others who had so many suspicions at Castle Innisfail, will find themselves completely at fault."

He began to think how, though he had been cruelly dealt with by Fate in some respects—in respect of his own father, for instance, and also in respect of his own poverty—he had still much to be thankful for.

He was beloved by the loveliest woman whom he had ever seen— the only woman for whom he had ever felt a passion. And the peculiar position which she occupied, had enabled him to see her every day and to kiss her exquisite face—there was none to make him afraid. Such obstacles in the way of a lover's freedom as the Average Father, the Vigilant Mother and the Athletic Brother he had never encountered. And then a curious circumstance—the thought of Beatrice as a part of the landscapes around Abbeylands caused him to lay special emphasis upon this—had enabled him to bind the girl to him with a bond which in her eyes at least—yes, in his eyes too, by heaven, he felt—was not susceptible of being loosened.

Yes, the ways of Providence were wonderful, he felt. If he had not met Mr. Playdell.... and so forth.

But now Beatrice was his own. She might stray through the autumn woods by the side of Edmund Airey or any man whom she might meet at Abbeylands; she would feel upon her finger the ring that he had placed there—the ring that— —

He sprang to his feet with a sudden cry.

"Good God! the Ring! the Ring!"

He looked at the clock on the mantelpiece. It pointed to four-seventeen.

He pulled out his watch. It pointed to four-twenty-two.

He rushed to the sofa where an overcoat was lying. He had it on him in a moment. He snatched up a railway guide and stuffed it into his pocket.

In another minute he was in a hansom, driving as fast as the hansomeer thought consistent with public safety—a trifle over that which the police authorities thought consistent with public safety—in the direction of the Northern Railway terminus.

CHAPTER XLII
ON THE RING AND THE LOOK

HE tried, while in the hansom, to unravel the mysteries of the system by which passengers were supposed to reach Brackenshire. He found the four-twenty train from London indicated in its proper order. This was the train by which he had invariably travelled to Abbeylands—it was the last train in the day that carried passengers to Abbeylands Station, for the station was on a short branch line, the junction being Mowern.

On reaching the terminus he lost no time in finding a responsible official—one whose chastely-braided uniform looked repressful of tips.

"I want to get to Mowern Junction before the four-twenty train from here goes on to Abbeylands. Can I do it?" said Harold.

"Next train to the Junction five-thirty-two, sir," said the official.

"That's too late for me," said Harold. "The train leaves the Junction for Abbeylands a quarter of an hour after arriving at Mowern. Is there no local train that I might manage to catch that would bring me to the Junction?"

"None that would serve your purpose, sir."

Harold clearly saw how it was that this company could never get their dividend over four per cent.

"Why is there so long a wait at Mowern?" he asked.

"Waits for Ditchford Mail, sir."

"And at what time does a train start for Ditch-ford?"

"Can't tell, sir. Ditchford is on the Nethershire system—they have running powers over our line to Mowern."

Harold whipped out his guide, and found Ditch-ford in the index. By an inspiration he turned at once to the page devoted to the Nethershire service of trains. He found that, by an exquisite system of timing the trains, it was possible to reach a station a mile from Ditchford on the one line, just six minutes after the departure of the last local train to Ditchford on the other line. It took a little ingenuity, no doubt, on the part of the Directors of both lines to accomplish this, but still they managed to do it.

"I beg pardon, sir," said an official wearing a uniform that suggested tolerance of views in the matter of tips—the more important official had moved away. "I beg pardon, sir. Why not take the four-fifty-five to Mindon, and change into the Ditchford local train—that'll reach the junction four minutes before the express? I know it, sir. I was stationed at change into the Ditchford local train—that'll reach the junction four minutes before the express? I know it, sir. I was stationed at that part of the system."

To glance at the clock, and to perceive that he had time enough to drive to the Nethershire terminus, and to transfer a coin to the unconscious but not reluctant hand of the official of the liberal views, occupied Harold but a moment. At four-fifty-five he was in the Nethershire train on his way to Mindon.

He had not waited to verify the man's statement as to the trains, but in the railway carriage he did so, and he found that the beautiful complications of the two systems were at least susceptible of the interpretation put on them.

For the next two hours Harold felt that he could devote himself, if he had the mind, to the problem of the ring that had been so suddenly suggested to him.

It did not require him to spend more than the merest fraction of this time in order to convince him that the impulse upon which he had acted, was one that he would have been a fool to repress.

The ring which he had put on her finger, and which she had worn since, and would most certainly wear—he had imagined her doing so—at Abbeylands, could not fail to be recognized both by his father and his sister. It had belonged to his mother, and it was unique. It had flashed upon him suddenly that, unless he was content that his father and sister should learn that he had given her that ring, it would be necessary for him to prevent Beatrice from wearing it even for an hour at Abbeylands.

Apart altogether from the question of the circumstances under which he had put the ring upon her finger—circumstances which he had good reason for desiring to conceal—the fact that he had given to her the object which he valued most highly in the world, and which his father and sister knew that he so valued, would suggest to both these persons as much as would ruin him.

His father would, he knew, be extremely glad to discover some pretext to cut off the last penny of his allowance; and assuredly he would regard this gift of the ring as an ample pretext for adopting such a course of action.

Indeed, Lord Fotheringay had never been at a loss for a pretext for reducing his son's allowance; and now that he was posing—with but indifferent success, as Harold had learned from Mrs. Lampson's postscript—as a Reformed Sinner, he would, his son knew, think that, in cutting off his son's allowance, he was only acting consistently with the traditions of Reformed Sinners.

The Reformed Sinner is usually a sinner whose capacity to enjoy the pleasures of sin has become dulled, and thus he is intolerant of the sins of others, and particularly intolerant of the capacity of others to enjoy sin. This is why he reduces the allowances of his children. Like the man who advances to the position of teetotal lecturer, after having served for some time as the teetotal lecturer's Example, he knows all about the evil which he means to combat—to be more exact, which he means his children to combat.

All this Harold knew perfectly well. He knew that the only difference that the reform of his father would make to him, was that, while his father had formerly cut down his allowance with a courteously worded apology, he would now stop it altogether without an apology.

How could he have failed to remember, when he put that ring upon her finger, how great were the chances that it would be seen there by his father or his sister?

The truth was, that he had at that time not considered the possibility of her going to Abbey-lands. He knew that Mrs. Lampson intended inviting her; but he felt certain that, when she heard that he was not going, she would not accept the invitation. She would not have accepted it, if it had not suddenly occurred to him that the fact of her going while he remained in town would be to his advantage.

Would he be in time to prevent the disaster which he foresaw would occur if she appeared in the drawing-room at Abbeylands wearing the ring?

He looked at his watch. The train was three minutes late in reaching several of the stations on its route, and it was delayed for another three minutes when there was only a single line of rails. How would it be possible for the train to make up so great a loss during the remainder of the journey?

He reminded the guard at one of many intolerable stoppages, that the train was long behind its time. The guard could not agree with him, it was only about seven minutes late, he assured Harold.

On it went, and it seemed as if the engine-driver had a clearer sense of his responsibilities than the guard, for during the next thirty miles, he managed to save over two minutes. All this Harold noticed with more interest than he had ever taken in the details of any railway journey.

When at last Mindon was reached, and he left the train to change into the one which was to carry him on to the Junction, he found that this train had not yet come up. Here was another point to be considered. Would the train come up in time?

He was not left for long in suspense. The long row of lighted carriages ran up to the platform before he had been waiting for two minutes, and in another two minutes the train was steaming away with him.

He looked at his watch once more, and then he was able to give himself a rest, for he saw that unless some accident were to happen, he would be at Mowern Junction before the train should leave for Abbeylands Station on the branch line.

In running into the Junction, the train went past the platform of the branch line. A number of carriages were there, and at the side glass of one compartment he saw the profile of Beatrice.

The little cry that she gave, when he opened the door of the compartment and spoke her name, had something of terror as well as delight in it.

"Harold! How on earth—" she began.

"I have a rather important message for you," he said. "Will you take a turn with me on the platform? There is plenty of time. The train does not start for six minutes."

She was out of the carriage in a moment. "Mr. Wynne has a message for me—it is probably from Mrs. Lampson," she said to her maid, who was in the same compartment.

CHAPTER XLIII
ON THE SON OF APHRODITE

WHAT can be the matter? How did you manage to come here? You must have travelled by the same train as we came by. Oh, Harold, my husband, I am so glad to see you. You have changed your mind—you are coming on with me? Oh, I see it all now. You meant all along to give me this delightful surprise."

The words came from her in a torrent as she put her hand on his arm—he could feel the ring on her finger.

"No, no," said he; "everything remains as it was this morning. I only wish that I were going on with you. Providentially something occurred to me when I was sitting alone after lunch. That is why I came. I managed to catch a train that brought me here just now—the train I was in ran past this platform and I saw your face."

"What can have occurred to you that you could not tell me in a letter?" she asked, her face still bearing the look of glad surprise that had come to it when she had heard the sound of his voice.

"We shall have to go into a waiting-room, or—better still—an empty carriage," said he. "I see several men whom I know, and—worse luck! women—they are on their way to Abbeylands, and if they saw us together in this confidential way, they would never cease chattering when they arrived. We shall get into a compartment—there is one that still remains unlighted, it will be the best for our purpose; there will be no chance of a prying face appearing at the window."

"Shall we have time?" she asked.

"Plenty of time. By getting into the carriage you will run no chance of being left behind—the worst that can happen is that I may be carried on with you."

"The worst? Oh, that is the best—the best." They had strolled to the end of the platform where it was dimly lighted, and in an instant, apparently unobserved by anyone, they had got into an unlighted compartment at the rear of the train, and Harold shut the door quietly, so as not to attract the attention of the three or four men in knickerbockers who were stretching their legs on the platform until the train was ready to start.

"We are fortunate," said he. "Those men outside will be your fellow-guests for the week. None of them will think of glancing into a dark carriage; but if one of them does so, he will be nothing the wiser."

"And now—and now," she cried.

"And now, my dearest, you remember the ring that I put upon your finger?"

"This ring? Do you think it likely that I have forgotten it already?" she whispered.

"No, no, dearest; it was I who forgot it," he said. "It was I who forgot that my father and my sister are perfectly certain to recognize that ring if you wear it at Abbeylands: they will be certain to see it on your linger, and they will question you as to how it came into your possession."

"Of course they will," she said, after a pause. "You told me that it was a ring that belonged to your mother. There can only be one such ring in the world. Oh, they could not fail to recognize it. The little chubby wicked Eros surrounded by the rubies—I have looked at the design every day—every night—sometimes the firelight gleaming upon the circle of rubies has made them seem to me a band of blood. Was that the idea of the artist who made the design, I wonder—a circle of blood with the god Eros in the centre."

She had taken off her glove, and had laid the hand with the ring in one of his hands.

He had never felt her hand so soft and warm before. His hand became hot through holding hers. His heart was beating as it had never beaten before.

The force of his grasp pressed the sharply cut cameo into his flesh. The image of that wicked little god, the son of Aphrodite, was stamped upon him. It seemed as if some of his blood would mingle with the blood that sparkled and beat within the heart of the rubies.

He had forgotten the object of his mission to her. Still holding her hand with the ring, he put his arm under the sealskin coat that reached to her feet, and held her close to him while he kissed her as he had never before kissed her.

Suddenly he seemed to recollect why he was with her. He had not hastened down from London for the sake of the kiss.

"My beloved, my beloved!" he murmured—each word sounded like a sob—"I should like to remain with you for ever."

She did not say a word. She did not need to say a word. He could feel the tumult of her heart, and she knew it.

"For God's sake, Beatrice, let me speak to you," he said.

It was a strange entreaty. His arm was about her, his hand was holding one of hers, she was simply passive by his side; and yet he implored of her to let him speak to her.

It was some moments before she could laugh, however; which was also strange, for the humour of the matter which called for that laugh, was surely capable of being appreciated by her immediately.

She gave a laugh and then a sigh.

The carriage was dark, but a stray gleam of light from a side platform now and again came upon her face, and her features were brought into relief with the clearness and the whiteness of a lily in a jungle.

As she gave that laugh—or was it a sigh?—he started, perceiving that the expression of her features was precisely that which the artist in the antique had imparted to the features of the little chrysoprase Eros in the centre of that blood-red circle of the ring.

"Why do you laugh, Beatrice?8 said he.

"Did I laugh, Harold?" said she. "No—no—I think—yes, I think it was a sigh—or was it you who sighed, my love?"

"God knows," said he. "Oh, the ring—the ring!"

"It feels like a band of burning metal," she said.

"It is almost a pain for me to wear it. Have you not heard of the curious charms possessed by rings, Harold—the strange spells which they carry with them? The ring is a mystery—a mystic symbol. It means what has neither beginning nor ending—it means perfection—completeness—it means love—love's completeness."

"That is what your ring must mean to us, my beloved," said he. "Whether you take it from your finger or let it remain there, it will still mean the completeness of such love as is ours."

"And I am to take it off, Harold?"

"Only so long as you stay at Abbeylands, Beatrice. What does it matter for one week? You will see, dearest, how my plans—my hopes—must certainly he destroyed if that ring is seen on your finger by my father or my sister. It is not for the sake of my plans only that I wish you to refrain from wearing it for a week; it is for your sake as well."

"Would they fancy that I had stolen it, dear?" she asked, looking up to his face with a smile.

"They might fancy worse things than that, Beatrice," said he. "Do not ask me. You may be sure that I am advising you aright—that the consequences of that ring being recognized on your finger would be more serious than you could understand."

"Did I not say something to you a few days ago about the completeness of my trust in you, Harold?" she whispered. "Well, the ring is the symbol of this completeness also. I trust you implicitly in everything. I have given myself up to you. I will do whatever you may tell me. I will not take the ring off until I reach Abbeylands, but I shall take it off then, and only replace it on my finger every night."

"My darling, my darling! Such love as you have given to me is God's best gift to the world."

He had committed himself to an opinion practically to the same effect upon more than one previous occasion.

And now, as then, the expression of that opinion was followed by a long silence, as their faces came together.

"Beatrice," he said, in a tremulous voice.

"Harold."

"I shall go on with you to Abbeylands. Come what may, we shall not now be separated."

But they were separated that very instant. The carriage was flooded with light—the chastened flood that comes from an oil lamp inserted in a hollow in the roof—and they were no longer in each others arms. They heard the sound of the porter's feet on the roof of the next carriage.

"It is so good of you to come," said she.

There was now perhaps three inches of a space separating them.

"Good?" said he. "I'm afraid that's not the word. We shall be under one roof."

"Yes," she said slowly, "under one roof."

"Tickets for Ashmead," intoned a voice at the carriage window.

"We are for Abbeylands Station," said Harold.

"Abb'l'ns," said the guard. "Why, sir, you know the Abb'l'ns train started six minutes ago."

CHAPTER XLIV
ON THE SHORTCOMINGS OF A SYSTEM

HAROLD was out of the compartment in a moment. Did the guard mean that the train had actually left for Abbeylands? It had left six minutes before, the guard explained, and the station-master added his guarantee to the statement.

Harold looked around—from platform to platform—as if he fancied that there was a conspiracy between the officials to conceal the train.

How could the train leave without taking all its carriages with it?

It did nothing of the kind, the station-master said, firmly but respectfully.

The guard went on with his business of cutting neat triangles out of the tickets of the passengers in the carriages that were alongside the platform—passengers bound for Ashmead.

"But I—we—my—my wife and I got into one of the carriages of the Abbeylands train," said Harold, becoming indignant, after the fashion of his countrymen, when they have made a mistake either on a home or foreign railway. "What sort of management is it that allows one portion of a train to go in one direction and another part in another direction?"

"It's our system, sir," said the official. "You see, sir, there're never many passengers for either the Abbeyl'n's"—being a station-master he did not do an unreasonable amount of clipping in regard to the names—"or the Ashm'd branch, so the Staplehurst train is divided—only we don't light the lamps in the Ashm'd portion until we're ready to start it. Did you get into a carriage that had a lamp, sir?"

"I've seen some bungling at railway stations before now," said Harold, "but bang me if I ever met the equal of this."

"This isn't properly speaking a station, sir, it's a junction," said the official, mildly, but with the force of a man who has said the last word.

"That simply means that greater bungling may be found at a junction than at a station," said Harold. "Is it not customary to give some notice of the departure of a train at a junction as well as a station, my good man?"

The official became reasonably irritated at being called a good man.

"The train left for Abbeyl'n's according to reg'lation, sir," said he. "If you got into a compartment that had no lamp— —"

"Oh, I've no time for trifling," said Harold. "When does the next train leave for Abbey-lands?"

"At eight-sixteen in the morning," said the official.

"Great heavens! You mean to say that there's no train to-night?"

"You see, if a carriage isn't lighted, sir, we— —"

The man perceived the weakness of Harold's case—from the standpoint of a railway official—and seemed determined not to lose sight of it. "Contributory negligence" he knew to be the most valuable phrase that a railway official could have at hand upon any occasion.

"And how do you expect us to go on to Abbeylands to-night?" asked Harold.

"There's a very respectable hotel a mile from the junction, sir," said the man. "Ruins of the Priory, sir—dates back to King John, page 84 *Tourist's Guide to Brackenshire.*"

"Oh," said Harold, "this is quite preposterous." He went to where Beatrice was seated watching, with only a moderate amount of interest, the departure of five passengers for Ashmead.

"Well, dear?" said she, as Harold came up.

"For straightforward, pig-headed stupidity I'll back a railway company against any institution in the world," said he. "The last train has left for Abbeylands. Did you ever know of such stupidity? And yet the shareholders look for six per cent, out of such a system."

"Perhaps," said she timidly—"perhaps we were in some degree to blame."

He laughed. It was so like a woman to suggest the possibility of some blame attaching to the passengers when a railway company could be indicted. To the average man such an idea is as absurd as beginning to argue with a person at whom one is at liberty to swear.

"It seems that there is a sort of hotel a mile away," said he. "We cannot be starved, at any rate."

"And I—you—we shall have to stay there?" said she.

He gave a sort of shrug—an Englishman's shrug—about as like the real thing as an Englishman's bow, or a Chinaman's cheer.

"What can we do?" said he. "When a railway company such as this— oh, come along, Beatrice. I am hungry—hungry—hungry!"

He caught her by the arm.

"Yes, Harold—husband," said she.

He started.

"Husband! Husband!" he said. "I never thought of that. Oh, my beloved—my beloved!"

He stood irresolute for a moment.

Then he gave a curious laugh, and she felt his hand tighten upon her arm for a moment.

"Yes," he whispered. "You heard the words that—that man said while our hands were together? 'Whom God hath joined'—God—that is Love. Love is the bond that binds us together. Every union founded on Love is sacred—and none other is sacred—in the sight of heaven."

"And you do not doubt my love," she said.

"Doubt it? oh, my Beatrice, I never knew what it was before now." They left the station together, after he had written and despatched in her name a telegram to her maid, directing her to explain to Mrs. Lampson that her mistress had unfortunately missed the train, but meant to go by the first one in the morning.

By chance a conveyance was found outside, and in it they drove to the Priory Hotel which, they were amazed to find, promised comfort as well as picturesqueness.

It was a long ivy-covered house, and bore every token of being a portion of the ancient Priory among the ruins of which it was standing. Great elms were in front of the house, and on one side there were apple trees, and at the other there was a garden reaching almost to where a ruined arch was held together by its own ivy.

As they were in the act of entering the porch, a ray of moonlight gleamed upon the ruins, and showed the trimmed grass plots and neat gravel walks among the cloisters.

Harold pointed out the picturesque effect to Beatrice, and they stood for some moments before entering the house.

The old waiter, whose moderately white shirt front constituted a very distinctive element of the hall with its polished panels of old oak, did not bustle forward when he saw them admiring the ruins.

"Upon my word," said Harold, entering, "this is a place worth seeing. That touch of moonlight was very effective."

"Yes, sir," said the waiter; "I'm glad you're pleased with it. We try to do our best in this way for our patrons. Mrs. Mark will be glad to know that you thought highly of our moonlight, sir."

The man was only a waiter, but he was as solemn as a butler, as he opened the door of a room that seemed ready to do duty as a coffee-room. It had a low groined ceiling, and long narrow windows.

An elderly maid was lighting candles in sconces round the walls.

"Really," said Harold, "we may be glad that the bungling at the junction brought us here."

"Yes, sir," said the man with waiter-like acquiescence; "they do bungle things sometimes at that junction."

"We were on our way to Abbeylands," said Harold, "but those idiots on the platform allowed us to get into the wrong carriages—the carriages that were going to Ashmead. We shall stay here for the night. The station-master recommended us to go here, and I'm much obliged to him. It's the only sensible—"

"Yes, sir: he's a brother to Mrs. Mark—Mrs. Mark is our proprietor," said the waiter.

"*Mrs.* Mark," said Harold.

"Yes, sir: she's our proprietor."

Harold thought that, perhaps, when the owner of an hotel was a woman, she might reasonably be called the proprietor.

"Oh, well, perhaps a maid might show my—my wife to a room, while I see what we can get for dinner—supper, I suppose we should call it."

The middle-aged woman who was lighting the candles came forward smiling, as she adroitly extinguished the wax taper by the application of her finger and thumb. With her Beatrice disappeared.

Harold quite expected that he was about to come upon the weak element in the management of this picturesque inn. But when he found that a cold pheasant as well as some hot fish was available for supper, he admitted that the place was perfect. There was no wine card, but the old waiter promised a Champagne for which, he said, Mr. Lampson, of Abbeylands, had once made an offer.

"That will do for us very well," said Harold. "Mr. Lampson would not make an offer for anything—wine least of all—of which he was uncertain."

The waiter went off in the leisurely style that was only consistent with the management of an establishment that dated back to King John; and in a few minutes Beatrice appeared, having laid aside her sealskin coat, and her hat.

How exquisite she seemed as she stood for an instant in the subdued light at the door!

And she was his.

CHAPTER XLV
ON MOONLIGHT AND MORALS

SHE was his.

He felt the joy of it as she stood at the door in her beautifully fitting travelling dress.

The thought sent an exultant glow through his veins, as he looked at her from where he was standing at the hearth. (There was no "cosy corner" abomination.)

She was his.

He went forward to meet her, and put out both his hands to her.

She placed a hand in each of his.

"How delightfully warm you are," she said. "You were standing at the fire."

"Yes," he said. "I was at the fire; in addition, I was also thinking that you are mine."

"Altogether yours now," she said looking at him with that trustful smile which should have sent him down on his knees before her, but which did not do more than cause his eyes to look at her throat instead of gazing straight into her eyes.

They seated themselves on one of the old window-seats, and talked face to face, listlessly watching the old waiter lay a white cloth on a portion of the black oak table.

When they had eaten their fish and pheasant—Harold wondered if the latter had come from the Abbeylands' preserves, and if Archie Brown had shot it—they returned to the window-seat, and there they remained for an hour.

He had thrown all reserve to the winds. He had thrown all forethought to the winds. He had thrown all fear of God and man to the winds.

She was his.

The old waiter re-entered the room and laid on the table a flat bedroom candlestick with a box of matches.

"Can I get you anything before I go to bed, sir?" he inquired.

"I require nothing, thank you," said Harold.

"Very good, sir," said the waiter. "The candles in the sconces will burn for another hour. If that will not be long enough—"

"It will be quite long enough. You have made us extremely comfortable, and I wish you goodnight," said Harold.

"Good-night, sir. Good-night, madam."

This model servitor disappeared. They heard the sound of his shoes upon the stairs.

"At last—at last!" whispered Harold, as he put an arm on the deep embrasure of the window behind her.

She let her shapely head fall back until it rested on his shoulder. Then she looked up to his face.

"Who could have thought it?" she cried. "Who could have predicted that evening when I stood on the cliffs and sent my voice out in that wild way across the lough, that we should be sitting here to-night?"

"I knew it when I got down to the boat and drew your hands into mine by that fishing-line," said he. "When the moon showed me your face, I knew that I had seen the face for which I had been searching all my life. I had caught glimpses of that face many times in my life. I remember seeing it for a moment when a great musician was performing an incomparable work—a work the pure beauty of which made all who listened to it weep. I can hear that music now when I look upon your face. It conveys to me all that was conveyed to me by the music. I saw it again when, one exquisite dawn, I went into a garden while the dew was glistening over everything. There came to me the faint scent of violets. I thought that nothing could be lovelier; but in another moment, the glorious perfume of roses came upon me like a torrent. The odour of the roses and the scent of the violets mingled, and before my eyes floated your face. When the moonlight showed me your face on that night beside the Irish lough I felt myself wondering if it would vanish."

"It has come to stay," she whispered, in a way that gave the sweetest significance to the phrase that has become vulgarized.

"It came to stay with me for ever," he said. "I knew it, and I felt myself saying, 'Here by God's grace is the one maid for me.'"

He did not falter as he looked down upon her face—he said the words "God's grace" without the least hesitancy.

The moonlight that had been glistening on the ivy of the broken arches of the ancient Priory, was now shining through the diamond panes of the window at which they were sitting. As her head lay back it was illuminated by the moon. Her hair seemed delicate threads of spun glass through which the light was shining.

One of the candles flared up for a moment in its socket, then dwindled away to a single spark and then expired.

"You remember?" she whispered.

"The seal-cave," he said. "I have often wondered how I dared to tell you that I loved you."

"But you told me the truth."

"The truth. No, no; I did not love you then as I regard loving now. Oh, my Beatrice, you have taught me what 'tis to love. There is nothing in the world but love, it is life—it is life!"

"And there are none in the world who love as you and I do."

His face shut out the moonlight from hers. There was a long silence before she said, "It was only when you had parted from me every day that I knew what you were to me, Harold. Ah, those bitter moments! Those sad Good-byes—sad Good-nights out of the moonlight from hers. There was a long silence before she said, "It was only when you had parted from me every day that I knew what you were to me, Harold. Ah, those bitter moments! Those sad Good-byes—sad Good-nights!"

"They are over, they are over!" he cried. The lover's triumph rang through his words. "They are over. We have come to the night when no more Good-nights shall be spoken. What do I say? No more Good-nights? You know what a poet's heart sang—a poet over whose head the waters of passion had closed? I know the song that came from his heart—beloved, the pulses of his heart beat in every line:"=

"'Good-night! ah, no, the hour is ill
That severs those it should unite:
Let us remain together still,
Then it will be good night.=
"' How can I call the lone night good,
Though thy sweet wishes wing its flight?
Be it not said—thought—understood;

A Gray Eye Or So — Complete | 233

Then it will be good night.=

"'To hearts that near each other move

From evening close to morning light,

The night is good because, oh, Love,

They never say Good-night.'"=

His whispering of the last lines was very tremulous. Her eyes were closed and her lips were parted with the passing of a sigh—a sigh that had something of a sob about it. Then both her arms were flung round his neck, and he felt her face against his. Then.... he was alone.

How had she gone?

Whither had she gone?

How long had he been alone?

He got upon his feet, and looked in a dazed way around the room.

Had it all been a dream? Was it only in fancy that she had been in his arms? Had he been repeating Shelley's poem in the hearing of no one?

He opened a glass door by which access was had to the grounds of the old Priory, and stood, surpliced by the moonlight, beside the ruined arch where an oriel window had once been. He turned and looked at the house. It was black against the clear sky that overflowed with light, but one window above the room where he had been sitting was illuminated.

It had no drapery—he could see through it half way into the room beyond.

Just above where a silver sconce with three lighted candles hung from the wall, he could see that the black panel bore in high relief a carved Head of the Virgin, surrounded with lilies.

He kept his eyes fixed upon that carving until—until....

There came before his eyes in that room the Temptation of Saint Anthony.

His eyes became dim looking at her loveliness, shining with dazzling whiteness beneath the light of the candles.

He put his hands before his eyes and staggered to the door through which he had passed. There he stood, his breath coming in sobs, with his hand on the handle of the door.

There was not a sound in the night. Heaven and earth were breathlessly watching the struggle.

It was the struggle between Heaven and Hell for a human soul.

The man's fingers fell from the handle of the door. He clasped his hands across the ivy of the wall and bowed his head upon them.

Only for a few moments, however. Then, with a cry of agony, he started up, and with his clasped hands over his eyes, fled—madly—blindly—away from the house.

Before he had gone far, he tripped and fell over a stone—he only fell upon his knees, but his hands were clutching at the ground.

When he recovered himself, he found that he was on his knees at the foot of an ancient prostrate Cross.

He stared at it, and some time had passed before there came from his parched lips the cry, "Christ have mercy upon me!"

He bowed his head to the Cross, and his lips touched the cold, damp stone.

This was not the kiss to which he had been looking forward.

He sprang to his feet and fled into the distance.

She was saved!

And he—he had saved his soul alive!

CHAPTER XLVI
ON A BED OF LOGS

ONWARD he fled, he knew not whither; he only knew that he was flying for the safety of his soul.

He passed far beyond the limits of the Priory grounds, but he did not reach the high road. He crossed a meadow and came upon a trout stream. He walked beside it for an hour. At the end of that time there was no moonlight to glitter upon its surface. Clouds had come over the sky and drops of rain were beginning to fall.

He crossed the stream by a little bridge, and reached the border of a wood. It was now long past midnight. He had been walking for two hours, but he had no consciousness of weariness. It was not until the rain was streaming off his hair that he recollected that he had no hat. But on still he went through the darkness and the rain, as though he were being pursued, and that every step he took was a step toward safety.

He came upon a track that seemed to lead through the wood, and upon this track he went for several miles. The ground was soft, and at some places the rain had turned it into a morass. The autumn leaves lay in drifts, sodden and rotting. Into more than one of these he stumbled, and when he got upon his feet again, the damp leaves and the mire were clinging to him.

For three more hours he went on by the winding track through the wood. In the darkness he strayed from it frequently, but invariably found it again and struggled on, until he had passed right through the wood and reached a high road that ran beside it.

As though he had been all the night wandering in search for this road, so soon as he saw it he cried, "Thank God, thank God!"

But something else may have been in his mind beyond the satisfaction of coming upon the road.

At the border of the wood where the track broadened out, there was a woodcutter's rough shed. It was piled up with logs of various sizes, and with trimmed boughs awaiting the carts to come along the road to carry them away. He entered the shed, and, overpowered with weariness, sank down upon a heap of boughs; his head found a resting place in a forked branch and in a moment he was sound asleep.

His head was resting upon the damp bark of the trimmed branch, when it might have been close to that whiteness which he had seen through the window.

True; but his soul was saved.

He awoke, hearing the sound of voices around him.

The cold light of a gray, damp day was struggling with the light that came from a fire of faggots just outside, and the shed was filled with the smoke of the burning wood. The sound of the crackling of the small branches came to his ears with the sound of the voices.

He raised his head, and looked around him in a dazed way. He did not realize for some time the strange position in which he found himself. Suddenly he seemed to recall all that had occurred, and once more he said, "Thank God, thank God!"

Three men were standing in the shed before him. Two of them held bill-hooks in a responsible way; the third had the truncheon of a constable. He also wore the helmet of a constable.

The men with the bill-hooks seemed preparing to repel a charge. They stood shoulder to shoulder with their implements breast high.

The man with the truncheon seemed willing to trust a great deal to them, whether in regard to attack or defence.

"Well, you're awake, my gentleman," said the man with the truncheon.

The speech seemed a poor enough accompaniment to such a show of strength, aggressive or defensive, as was the result of the muster in the shed.

"Yes, I believe I'm awake," said Harold. "Is the morning far advanced?"

"That's as may be," said the truncheon-holder, shrewdly, and after a pause of considerable duration.

"You're not the man to compromise yourself by a hasty statement," said Harold.

"No," said the man, after another pause.

"May I ask what is the meaning of this rather imposing demonstration?" said Harold.

"Ay, you may, maybe," replied the man. "But it's my business to tell you that—" here he paused and inflated his lungs and person generally— "that all you say now will be used as evidence against you."

"That's very official," said Harold. "Does it mean that you're a constable?"

"That it do; and that you're in my charge now. Close up, bill-hooks, and stand firm," the man added to his companions.

"Don't trumle for we," said one of the billhook-holders.

"You see there's no use broadening vi'lent-like," said the truncheon-holder.

"That's clear enough," said Harold. "Would it be imprudent for me to inquire what's the charge against me?"

"You know," said the policeman.

"Come, my man," said Harold; "I'm not disposed to stand this farce any longer. Can't you see that I'm no vagrant—that I haven't any of your logs concealed about me. What part of the country is this? Where's the nearest telegraph office?"

"No matter what's the part," said the constable; "I've arrested you before witnesses of full age, and I've cautioned you according to the Ack o' Parliament."

"And the charge?"

"The charge is the murder."

"Murder—what murder?"

"You know—the murder of the Right Honourable Lord Fotheringay."

"What!" shouted Harold. "Lord—oh, you're mad! Lord Fotheringay is my father, and he's staying at Abbeylands. What do you mean, you idiot, by coming to me with such a story?" The policeman winked in by no means a subtle way at the two men with the bill-hooks; he then looked at Harold from head to foot, and gave a guffaw.

"The son of his lordship—the murdered man—you heard that, friends, after I gave the caution according to the Ack o' Parliament?" he said.

"Ay, ay, we heard—leastways to that effeck," replied one of the men.

"Then down it goes again him," said the constable. "He's a gentleman-Jack tramp—and that's the worst sort—without hat or head gear, and down it goes that he said he was his lordship's son."

"For God's sake tell me what you mean by talking of the murder of Lord Fotheringay," said Harold. "There can be no truth in what you said. Oh, why do I wait here talking to this idiot?" He took a few steps toward one end of the shed. The men raised their bill-hooks, and the constable made an aggressive demonstration with his truncheon.

Against Stupidity the gods fight in vain, but now and again a man with good muscles can prevail against it. Harold simply dealt a kick upon the heavy handle of the bill-hook nearest to him, and it swung round and caught in the stomach the second man, who immediately dropped his implement. He needed both hands to press against his injured person.

The constable ran to the other end of the shed and blew his whistle.

Harold went out in the opposite direction and got upon the high road; but before he had quite made up his mind which way to go, he heard the clatter of a horse galloping. He saw that a mounted constable was coming up, and he also noticed with a certain amount of interest, that he was drawing a revolver.

Harold stood in the centre of the road and held up his hand.

One of the few occasions when a man of well developed muscles, if he is wise, thinks himself no better than the gods, is when Stupidity is in the act of drawing a revolver.

"Are you the sergeant of constabulary?" Harold inquired, when the man had reined in. He still kept his revolver handy.

"Yes, I'm the sergeant of constabulary. Who are you, and what are you doing here?" said the man.

"He's the gentleman-Jack tramp that the lads found asleep in the shed, sergeant," said the constable, who had hurried forward with the naked truncheon. "The lads came on him hiding here, when they were setting about their day's work. They ran for me, and that's why I sent for you. I've arrested him and cautioned him. He was nigh clearing off just now, but I never took an eye off him. Is there a reward yet, sergeant?"

"Officer," said Harold. "I am Lord Fotheringay's son. For God's sake tell me if what this man says is true—is Lord Fotheringay dead—murdered?"

"He's dead. You seem to know a lot about it, my gentleman," said the sergeant. "You're charged with his murder. If you make any attempt at resistance, I'll shoot you down like a dog."

The man had now his revolver is his right hand. Harold looked first at him, and then at the foolish man with the truncheon. He was amazed. What could the men mean? How was it that they did not touch their helmets to him? He had never yet been addressed by a policeman or a railway porter without such a token of respect. What was the meaning of the change?

This was really his first thought.

His mind was not in a condition to do more than speculate upon this point. It was not capable of grasping the horrible thing suggested by the men.

He stood there in the middle of the road, dazed and speechless. It was not until he had casually looked down and had seen the condition of his feet and legs and clothes that, passing from the amazed thought of the insolence of the constables, into the amazement produced by his raggedness—he was apparently covered with mire from head to foot—the reason of his treatment flashed upon him; and in another instant every thought had left him except the thought that his father was dead. His head fell forward on his chest. He felt his limbs give way under him. He staggered to the low hank at the side of the road and managed to seat himself. He supported his head on his hands, his elbows resting on his knees.

There he remained, the four men watching him; for the interest which attaches to a distinguished criminal in the eyes of ignorant rustics, is almost as great as that which he excites among the leaders of society, who scrutinize him in the dock through opera glasses, and eat *pâté de foie gras* sandwiches beside the judge.

CHAPTER XLVII
ON THE PLEASURES OF MEMORY

SOME minutes had passed before Harold had sufficiently recovered to be able to get upon his feet. He could now account for everything that had happened. His father must have been found dead under suspicious circumstances the previous day, and information had been conveyed to the county constabulary. The instinct of the constabulary being to connect all crime with tramps, and his own appearance, after his night of wandering, as well as the conditions under which he had been found, suggesting the tramp, he had naturally been arrested.

He knew that he could only suffer some inconvenience for an hour or so. But what would be the sufferings of Beatrice?

"The circumstances under which I am found are suspicious enough to justify my arrest," he said to the mounted man. "I am Lord Fotheringay's son."

"Gammon! but it'll be took down," said the constable with the truncheon.

"Hold your tongue, you fool!" cried the sergeant to his subordinate.

"I can, of course, account for every movement of mine, yesterday and the day before," said Harold. "What hour is the crime supposed to have taken place? It must have been after four o'clock, or I should have received a telegram from my sister, Mrs. Lampson. I left London shortly before five last evening."

"If you can prove that, you're all right," said the sergeant. "But you'll have to give us your right name."

"You'll find it on the inside of my watch," said Harold.

He slipped the watch from the swivel clasp and handed it to the sergeant.

"You're a fool!" said the sergeant, looking at the hack of the watch. "This is a watch that belonged to the murdered man. It has a crown over a crest, and arms with supporters."

"Of course," said Harold. "I forgot that it was my father's watch before he gave it to me." The sergeant smiled. The constable and the two bill-hook men guffawed.

"Give me the watch," said Harold.

The sergeant slipped it into his own pocket.

"You've put a rope round your neck this minute," said he. "Handcuffs, Jonas."

The constable opened the small leathern pouch on his belt. Harold's hands instinctively clenched. The sergeant once more whipped his revolver out of its case.

"It has never occurred before this minute," said the constable.

"What do you mean? Where's the handcuffs?" cried the sergeant.

"Never before," said the constable, "I took them out to clean them with sandpaper, sergeant—emery and oil's recommended, but give me sandpaper—not too fine but just fine enough. Is there any man in the county that can show as bright a pair of handcuffs as myself, sergeant? You know."

"Show them now," said the sergeant.

"You'll have to come to the house with me, for there they be to be," replied the constable. "Ay, but I've my truncheon."

"Which way am I to go with you?" said Harold. "You don't think that I'm such a fool as to make the attempt to resist you? I can't remain here all day. Every moment is precious."

"You'll be off soon enough, my good man," said the sergeant. "Keep alongside my horse, and if you try any game on with me, I'll be equal to you." He wheeled his horse and walked it in the direction whence he had come. Harold kept up with it, thinking his thoughts. The man with the truncheon and the two men who had wielded the billhooks marched in file beside him. Marching in file had something official about it.

It was a strange procession that appeared on the shining wet road, with the dripping autumn trees on each side, and the gray sodden clouds crawling up in the distance.

How was he to communicate with her? How was he to let Beatrice know that she was to return to London immediately?

That was the question which occupied all his thoughts as he walked with bowed head along the road. The thought of the position which he occupied—the thought of the tragic incident which had aroused the vigilance of the constable—the desire to learn the details of the terrible thing that had occurred—every thought was lost in that question:

"How am I to prevent her from going on to Abbeylands?"

Was it possible that she might learn at the hotel early in the morning, that Lord Fotheringay had been murdered? When the news of the murder had spread round the country—and it seemed to have done so from the course that the woodcutters had adopted on coming upon him asleep—it would certainly be known at the hotel. If so, what would Beatrice do?

Surely she would take the earliest train back to London.

But if she did not hear anything of the matter, would she then remain at the hotel awaiting his return?

What would she think of him? What would she think of his desertion of her at that supreme moment?

Can a woman ever forgive such an act of desertion? Could Beatrice ever forgive his turning away from her love?

Was he beginning to regret that he had fled away from the loveliest vision that had ever come before his eyes?

Did Saint Anthony ever wish that he had had another chance?

If for a single moment Harold Wynne had an unworthy thought, assuredly it did not last longer than a single moment.

"Whatever may happen now—whether she forgives me or forsakes me—thank God—thank God!"

This was what his heart was crying out all the time that he walked along the road with bowed head. He felt that he had been strong enough to save her—to save himself.

The procession had scarcely passed over more than a quarter of a mile of the road, when a vehicle appeared some distance ahead.

"Steady," said the sergeant. "It's the Major in his trap. I sent a mounted man for him. You'll be in trouble about the handcuffs, Jonas, my man."

"Maybe the murderer would keep his hands together to oblige us," suggested the constable.

"I'll not be a party to deception," said his superior. "Halt!"

Harold looked up and saw a dog-cart just at hand. It was driven by a middle-aged gentleman, and a groom was seated behind. Harold had an impression that he had seen the driver previously, though he could not remember when or where he had done so. He rather thought he was an officer whom he had met at some place abroad.

The dog-cart was pulled up, and the officials saluted in their own way, as the gentleman gave the reins to his groom and dismounted.

"An arrest, sir," said the sergeant. "The two woodcutters came upon him hiding in their shed at dawn, and sent for the constable. Jonas, very properly, sent for me, and I despatched a man for you, sir. When arrested, he made up a cock-and-bull story, and a watch, supposed to be his murdered lordship's, was found concealed about his person. It's now in my possession."

"Good," said the stranger. Then he subjected Harold to a close scrutiny.

"I know now where I met you," said Harold. "You are Major Wilson, the Chief Constable of the County, and you lunched with us at Abbeylands two years ago."

"What! Mr. Wynne!" cried the man. "What on earth can be the meaning of this? Your poor father—"

"That is what I want to learn," said Harold eagerly. "Is it more than a report—that terrible thing?"

"A report? He was found at six o'clock last evening by a keeper on the outskirts of one of the preserves."

"A bullet—an accident? he may have been out shooting," said Harold.

"A knife—a dagger."

Harold turned away.

"Remain where you are, sergeant," said Major Wilson. "Let me have a word with you, Mr. Wynne," he added to Harold.

"Certainly," said Harold. His voice was shaky. "I wonder if you chance to have a flask of brandy in your cart. You can understand that I'm not quite—"

"I'm sorry that I have no brandy," said Major Wilson. "Perhaps you wouldn't mind sitting on the bank with me while you explain—if you wish—I do not suggest that you should—I suppose the constables cautioned you."

"Amply," said Harold. "I find that I can stand. I don't suppose that any blame attaches to them for arresting me. I am, I fear, very disreputable looking. The fact is that I was stupid enough to miss the train from Mowern junction last night, and I went to the Priory Hotel. I came out when the night was fine, without my hat, and I— — had reasons of my own for not wishing to return to the hotel. I got into the wood and wandered for several hours along a track I found. I got drenched, and taking shelter in the woodcutters' shed, I fell asleep. That is all I have to say. I have not the least idea what part of the country this is: I must have walked at least twenty miles through the night."

"You are not a mile from the Priory Hotel," said Major Wilson.

"That is impossible," cried Harold. "I walked pretty hard for five hours."

"Through the wood?"

"I practically never left the track."

"You walked close upon twenty miles, but you walked round the wood instead of through it. That track goes pretty nearly round Garstone Woods. Mr. Wynne, this is the most unfortunate occurrence I ever heard of or saw in my life."

"Pray do not fancy for a moment that, so far as I am concerned, I shall be inconvenienced for long," said Harold. "It is a shocking thing for a son to be suspected even for a moment of the murder of his own father; but sometimes a curious combination of circumstances— —"

"Of course—of course, that is just it. Do not blame me, I beg of you. Did you leave London yesterday?"

"Yes, by the four-fifty-five train."

"Have you a portion of your ticket to Abbeylands?"

"I took a return ticket to Mowern. I gave one portion of it to the collector, the return portion is in my pocket."

He produced the half of his ticket. Major Wilson examined the date, and took a memorandum of the number stamped upon it.

"Did you speak to anyone at the junction on your arrival?" he then inquired.

"I'm afraid that I abused the station-master for allowing the train to go to Abbeylands without me," said Harold. "That was at ten minutes past seven o'clock. Oh, you need not fear for me. I made elaborate inquiries from the railway officials in London between half past four and the hour of the train's starting. I also spoke to the station-master at Mindon, asking him if he was certain that the train would arrive at the junction in time." Major Wilson's face brightened. Before it had been somewhat overcast.

"A telegram, as a matter of form, will be sufficient to clear up everything," said Major Wilson. "Yes, everything except—wasn't that midnight walk of yours a very odd thing, Mr. Wynne?"

"Yes," said Harold, after a pause. "It was extremely odd. So odd that I know that you will pardon my attempting to explain it—at least just now. You will, I think, be satisfied if you have evidence that I was in London yesterday afternoon. I am anxious to go to my sister without delay. Surely some clue must be forthcoming as to the ruffian who did the deed."

"The only clue—if it could be termed a clue—is the sheath of the dagger," replied Major Wilson. "It is the sheath of an ordinary belt dagger, such as is commonly worn by the peasantry in Southern Italy and Sicily. Lord Fotheringay lived a good deal abroad. Do you happen to know if he became involved in any quarrel in Italy—if there was any reason to think that his life had been threatened?"

Harold shook his head.

"My poor father returned from abroad a couple of months ago, and joined Lady Innisfail's party in Ireland. I have only seen him once in London since then. He must have been followed by some one who fancied that—that—"

"That he had been injured by your father?"

"That is what I fear. But my father never confided his suspicions—if he had any on this matter—to me."

They had walked some little way up the road. They now returned slowly and silently.

A one-horse-fly appeared in the distance. When it came near, Harold recognized it as the one in which he had driven with Beatrice from the station to the hotel.

"If you will allow me," said Harold to Major Wilson, "I will send to the hotel for my overcoat and hat."

"Do so by all means," said Major Wilson. "There is a decent little inn some distance on the road, where you will be able to get a brush down—you certainly need one. I'll give my sergeant instructions to send some telegrams at the junction."

"Perhaps you will kindly ask him to return to me my watch," said Harold. "I don't suppose that he will need it now."

Harold stopped the fly, and wrote upon a card of his own the following words, "*A shocking thing has happened that keeps me from you. My poor father is dead. Return to town by first train.*"

He instructed the driver to go to the Priory Hotel and deliver the card into the hand of the lady whom he had driven there the previous evening, and then to pay Harold's bill, drive the lady to the junction, and return with the overcoat and hat to the inn on the road.

Harold gave the man a couple of sovereigns, and the driver said that he would be able easily to convey the lady to the junction in time for the first train.

While the sergeant went away to send the Chief Constable's telegrams, Major Wilson and Harold drove off together in the dog-cart—the man with the truncheon and the men who had carried the bill-hooks respectfully saluted as the vehicle passed.

In the course of another half hour, Harold was in the centre of a cloud of dust, produced by the vigorous action of an athlete at the little inn, who had been engaged to brush him down. When he caught sight of himself in a looking-glass on entering the inn, Harold was as much amazed as he had been when he heard from the Chief Constable that he had been wandering round the wood all night. He felt that he could not blame the woodcutters for taking him for a tramp.

He managed to eat some breakfast, and then he fly came up with his overcoat and hat. He spoke only one sentence to the driver.

"You brought her to the train?"

"Yes, sir. She only waited to write a line. Here it is, sir."

He handed Harold an envelope.

Inside was a sheet of paper.

"*Dearest—dearest—You have all my sympathy—all my love. Come to me soon.*"

These were the words that he read in the handwriting of Beatrice.

He was in a bedroom when he read them. He sat down on the side of the bed and burst into tears.

It was ten years since he had wept.

Then he buried his face in his hands and said a prayer.

It was ten years since he had prayed.

CHAPTER XLVIII
ON MURDER AS A SOCIAL INCIDENT

THIS is not the story of a murder. However profitable as well as entertaining it would be to trace through various mysteries, false alarms, and intricacies the following up of a clue by the subtle intelligence of a detective, until the rope is around the neck of the criminal, such profit and entertainment must be absent from this story of a man's conquest of the Devil within himself. Regarding the incident of the murder of Lord Fotheringay much need not be said.

The sergeant appeared at the inn with replies to the telegrams that he had been instructed to send to the railway officials, and they were found to corroborate all the statements made by Harold. A ticket of the number of that upon the one which Harold still retained, had been issued previous to the departure of the four-fifty-five train from London.

"Of course, I knew what the replies would be," said Major Wilson. "But you can understand my position."

"Certainly I can," said Harold. "It needs no apology."

They drove to the junction together to catch the train to Abbeylands station. An astute officer from Scotland Yard had been telegraphed for, to augment the intelligence of the County Constabulary Force in the endeavour to follow up the only clue that was available, and Major Wilson was to travel with the London officer to the scene of the crime.

In a few minutes the London train came up, and the passengers for the Abbeylands line crossed to the side platform. Among them Harold perceived his own servant. The man was dressed in black, and carried a portmanteau and hat-box. He did not see his master until he had reached the platform. Then he walked up to Harold, laid down the portmanteau and endeavoured—by no means unsuccessfully—to impart some emotion—respectful emotion, and very respectful sympathy, into the act of touching his hat.

"I heard the sad news, my lord," said the man, "and I took the liberty of packing your lordship's portmanteau and taking the first train to Abbeylands. I took it for granted that you would be there, my lord."

"You acted wisely, Martin," said Harold. "I will ask you not to make any change in addressing me for some days, at least."

"Very good, my lord—I mean, sir," said the man.

He had not acquired for more than a minute the new mode of address, and yet he had difficulty in relinquishing it.

Abbeylands was empty of the guests who, up to the previous evening, had been within its walls. From the mouth of the gamekeeper, who had found the body of Lord Fotheringay, Harold learned a few more particulars regarding his ghastly discovery, but they were of no importance, though the astute Scotland Yard officer considered them—or pretended to consider them—to be extremely valuable.

For a week the detectives were very active, and the newspapers announced daily that they had discovered a clue, and that an arrest might be looked for almost immediately.

No arrest took place, however; the detectives returned to their head-quarters, and the mild sensation produced by the heading of a newspaper column, "The Murder of Lord Fotheringay" was completely obliterated by the toothsome scandal produced by the appearance of a music-hall artist as the co-respondent in a Duchess's divorce case. It was eminently a case for sandwiches and plovers' eggs; and the costumes which the eaters of these portable comestibles wore, were described in detail by those newspapers which everyone abuses and—reads. The middle-aged rheumatic butterfly was dead and buried; and though many theories were started—not by Scotland Yard, however—to account for his death, no arrests were made. Whoever the murderer was, he remained undetected. (A couple of years had passed before Harold heard a highly circumstantial story about the appearance of a foreign gentleman with extremely dark eyes and hair, in the neighbourhood of Castle Innisfail, inquiring for Lord Fotheringay a few days after Lord Fotheringay had left the Castle).

Mrs. Lampson, the only daughter of the deceased peer, had received so severe a shock through the tragic circumstances of her father's death, that she found it necessary to take a long voyage. She started for Samoa with her husband in his steam yacht. It may be mentioned incidentally, however, that, as the surface of the Bay of Biscay was somewhat ruffled when the yacht was going southward, it was thought advisable to change the cruise to one in the Mediterranean. Mrs. Lampson turned up on the Riviera in the spring, and, after entertaining freely there for some time, an article appeared above her signature in a leading magazine deploring the low tone of society at Monte Carlo and on the Riviera generally.

It was in the railway carriage on their way to London from Abbeylands—the exact time was when Harold was in the act of repeating the stanzas from Shelley—that Helen Craven and Edmund Airey conversed together, sitting side by side for the purpose.

"He is Lord Fotheringay now," remarked Miss Craven, thoughtfully.

Edmund looked at her with something of admiration in his eyes. The young woman who, an hour or two after being shocked at the news of a tragedy enacted at the very door of the house where she had been a guest, could begin to discuss its social bearing, was certainly a young woman to be wondered at—that is, to be admired.

"Yes," said Edmund, "he is now Lord Fotheringay, whatever that means."

"It means a title and an income, does it not?" said she.

"Yes, a sort of title and, yes, a sort of income," said he.

"Either would be quite enough to marry and live on," said Helen.

"He contrived to live without either up to the present."

"Yes, poorly."

"Not palatially, certainly, but still pleasantly."

"Will he ask her to marry him now, do you think?"

"Her?"

"Yes, you know—Beatrice Avon."

"Oh—I think that—that I should like to know what you think about it."

"I think he will ask her."

"And that she will accept him?"

She did not know how much thought he had been giving to this question during some hours—how eagerly he was waiting her reply.

"No." she said; "I believe that she will not accept him, because she means to accept you—if you give her a chance."

The start that he gave was very well simulated. Scarcely so admirable from a standpoint of art was the opening of his eyes accompanied by a little exclamation of astonishment.

"Why are you surprised?" she said, as if she was surprised at his surprise—so subtly can a clever young woman flatter the cleverest of men.

He shook his head.

"I am surprised because I have just heard the most surprising sentence that ever came upon my ears. That is saying a good deal—yes, considering how much we have talked together."

"Why should it be surprising?" she said. "Did you not call upon her in town?"

"Yes, I called upon her," he replied, wondering how she had come to know it. (She had merely guessed it.)

"That would give her hope."

"Hope?"

"Hope. And it was this hope that induced her to accept Mrs. Lampson's invitation, although she must have known that Mrs. Lampson's brother was not to be of the party. I have often wondered if it was you or Lord Fotheringay who asked Mrs. Lampson to invite her?"

"It was I," said Edmund.

Her eyes brightened—so far as it was possible for them to brighten.

"I wonder if she came to know that," said Helen musingly. "It would be something of a pity if she did not know it."

"For that matter, nearly everything that happens is a pity," said he.

"Not everything," said she. "But it is certainly a pity that the person who had the bad taste to stab poor Lord Fotheringay did not postpone his crime for at least one day. You would in that case have had a chance of returning by the side of Beatrice Avon instead of by the side of some one else."

"Who is infinitely cleverer," said Edmund.

At this point their conversation ended—at least so far as Harold and Beatrice were concerned.

Helen felt, however, that even that brief exchange of opinions had been profitable. Her first thought on hearing of the ghastly discovery of the gamekeeper, was that all her striving to win Harold had been in vain—that all her contriving, by the help of Edmund Airey, had been to no purpose. Harold would now be free to marry Beatrice Avon—or to ask her to marry him; which she believed was much the same thing.

But in the course of a short time she did not feel so hopeless. She believed that Edmund Airey only needed a little further flattery to induce him to resume his old attitude in regard to Beatrice; and the result of her little chat with him in the train showed her not merely that, in regard to flattery, he was pretty much as other men, only, of course, he required it to be subtly administered—but also that he had no intention of allowing his compact in regard to Beatrice to expire with their departure from Castle Innisfail. He admitted having called upon her in London, and this showed Helen very plainly that his attitude in respect of Beatrice was the result of a rather stronger impulse than the desire to be of service to her, Helen, in accordance with the suggestions which she had ventured to make during her first frank interview with him.

She made up her mind that he would not require in future to be frequently reminded of that frank interview. She knew that there exists a more powerful motive for some men's actions than a desire to forward the happiness of their fellow-men.

This was her reflection at the precise moment that Harold's face was bent down to the face of Beatrice, while he whispered the words that thrilled her.

As for Edmund Airey, he, too, had his thoughts, and, like Helen, he considered himself quite capable of estimating the amount of importance to be attached to such an incident as the murder of Lord Fotheringay, as a factor in the solution of any problem that might suggest itself. A murder is, of course, susceptible of being regarded from a social standpoint. The murder of Lord Fotheringay, for instance, had broken up what promised to be an exceedingly interesting party at Abbeylands. A murder is very provoking sometimes; and when Edmund Airey heard Lady Innisfail complain to Archie Brown—Archie had become a great friend of hers—of the irritating features of that incident—when he heard an uncharitable man declare that it was most thoughtless of Lord Fotheringay to get a knife stuck into his ribs just when the pheasants were at their best, he could not but feel that his own reflections were very plainly expressed.

He had not been certain of himself during the previous two months. For the first time in his life he did not see his way clearly. It was in order to improve his vision that he had begged Mrs. Lampson—with infinite tact, she admitted to her brother—to invite Beatrice to Abbeylands. He rather thought that, before the visit of Beatrice should terminate, he would be able to see his way clearly in certain directions.

But now, owing to the annoying incident that had occurred, the opportunity was denied him of improving his vision in accordance with the prescription which he had prepared to effect this purpose; therefore— —

He had reached this point in his reflections when the special train, which Mr. Lampson had chartered to take his guests back to town, ran alongside the platform at the London terminus.

This was just the moment when Harold looked up to the window from the Priory grounds and saw that vision of white glowing beauty.

CHAPTER XLIX
ON THE ADVANTAGES OF CONFESSION

HE stood silent, without taking a step into the room, when the door had been closed behind him.

With a cry she sprang from her seat in front of the fire and put out her hands to him.

Still he did not move a step toward her. He remained at the door.

Something of fear was upon her face as she stood looking at him. He was pale and haggard and ghostlike. She could not but perceive how strongly the likeness to his father, who had been buried the previous day, appeared upon his face now that it was so worn and haggard—much more so than she had ever seen his father's face.

"Harold—Harold—my beloved!" she cried, and there was something of fear in her voice. "Harold—husband—"

"For God's sake, do not say that, Beatrice!"

His voice was hoarse and quite unlike the voice that had whispered the lines of Shelley, with his face within the halo of moonlight that had clung about her hair.

She was more frightened still. Her hands were clasped over her heart—the lamplight gleamed upon the blood-red circle of rubies on the one ring that she wore—it had never left her finger.

He came into the room. She only retreated one step.

"For God's sake, Beatrice, do not call me husband! I am not your husband!"

She came toward him; and now the look of fear that she had worn, became one of sympathy. Her eyes were full of tears as she said, "My poor Harold, you have all the sympathy—the compassion—the love of my heart. You know it."

"Yes," he said, "I know it. I know what is in your heart. I know its purity—its truth—its sweetness—that is why I should never have come here, knowing also that I am unworthy to stand in your presence."

"You are worthy of all—all—that I can give you."

"Worthy of contempt—contempt—worthy of that for which there is no forgiveness. Beatrice, we have not been married. The form through which we went in this room was a mockery. The man whom I brought here was not a priest. He was guilty of a crime in coming here. I was guilty of a crime in bringing him."

She looked at him for a few moments, and then turned away from him.

She went without faltering in the least toward the chair that still remained in front of the fire. But before she had taken more than a few steps toward it, she looked back at him—only for a second or two, however; then she reached the chair and seated herself in it with her back to him. She looked into the fire.

There was a long silence before he spoke again.

"I think I must have been mad," he said. "Mad to distrust you. It was only when I was away from you that madness came upon me. The utter hopelessness of ever being able to call you mine took possession of me, body and soul, and I felt that I must bind you to me by some means. An accident suggested the means to me. God knows, Beatrice, that I meant never to take advantage of your belief that we were married. But when I felt myself by your side in the train—when I felt your heart beating against mine that night—I found myself powerless to resist. I was overcome. I had cast honour, and truth, yes, and love—the love that exists for ever without hope of reward—to the winds. Thank God—thank God that I awoke from my madness. The sight which should have made me even more powerless to resist, awoke me to a true sense of the life which I had been living for some hours, and by God's grace I was strong enough to fly."

Again there was a long silence. He could see her finely-cut profile as she sat upright, looking into the fire. He saw that her features had undergone no change whatever while he was speaking. It seemed as if his recital had in no respect interested her.

The silence was appalling.

She put out her hand and took from a small table beside her, the hook which apparently she had been reading when he had entered. She turned over the leaves as if searching for the place at which she had been interrupted.

He came beside her.

"Have you no word for me—no word of pity—of forgiveness—of farewell?" he said.

She had apparently found her place. She seemed to be reading.

"Beatrice, Beatrice, I implore of you—one word—one word—any word!"

He had clutched her arm as he fell on his knees passionately beside her. The book dropped to the floor. She was on her feet at the same instant.

"Oh God—oh God, what have I done that I should be the victim of these men?" she cried, not in a strident voice, but in a low tone, tremulous with passion. "One man thinks it a good thing to amuse himself by pretending that I interest him, and another whom I trusted as I would have trusted my God, endeavours to ruin my life—and he has done it—he has done it! My life is ruined!"

She had never looked at him while he was speaking to her. She had not been able for some time to comprehend the full force of the revelation he had made to her; but so soon as she had felt his hand upon her arm, she seemed in a moment to understand all.

Now she looked at him as he knelt at her feet with his head bowed down to the arm of the chair in which she had been sitting—she looked down upon him; and then with a cry as of physical pain, she flung herself wildly upon a sofa, sobbing hysterically.

He was beside her in a moment.

"Oh, Beatrice, my love, my love, tell me what reparation I can make," he cried. "Beatrice, have pity upon me! Do not say that I have ruined your life. It was only because I could not bear the thought that there was a chance of losing you, that I did what I did. I could not face that, Beatrice!"

She still lay there, shaken with sobs. He dared not put his hand upon her. He dared not touch one of her hands with his. He could only stand there by her side. Every sob that she gave was like a dagger's thrust to him. He suffered more during those moments than his father had done while the hand of the assassin was upon him.

The long silence was broken only by her sobs.

"Beatrice—Beatrice, you will say one word to me—one word, Beatrice, for God's sake!"

Some moments had passed while she struggled hard to control herself.

It was long before she was successful.

"Go—go—go!" she cried, without raising her head from the satin cushion of the sofa. "Oh, Harold, Harold, go!"

"I will go," he said, after another long pause. "I will go. But I leave here all that I love in the world—all that I shall ever love. I was false to myself once—only once; I shall never be so again. I shall never cease loving you while I live, Beatrice. I never loved you as I do now."

She made no sign.

Even when she heard the door of the room open and close, she did not rise.

And the fire burnt itself out, and the lamp burnt itself out, but still she lay there in her tears.

CHAPTER L
ON CONSOLATION AS A FINE ART

HIS worst forebodings had come to pass. That was the one feeling which Harold had on leaving her.

He had scarcely ventured to entertain a hope that the result of his interview with her and of his confession to her would be different.

He knew her.

That was why he had gone to her without hope. He knew that her nature was such as made it impossible for her to understand how he could have practised a fraud upon her; and he knew that understanding is the first step toward forgiving.

Still, there ever pervades the masculine mind an idea that there is no limit to a woman's forgiveness.

The masculine mind has the best of reasons for holding fast to this idea. It is the result of many centuries of experience of woman—of many centuries of testing the limits of woman's forgiveness. The belief that there is nothing that a woman will not forgive in a man whom she loves, is the heritage of man—just as the heritage of woman is to believe that nothing that is done by a man whom she loves, stands in need of forgiveness.

Thus it is that men and women make (occasionally) excellent companions for one another, and live together (frequently) in harmony.

Thus it was that, in spite of the fact that his reason and his knowledge of the nature of Beatrice assured him that his confession of the fraud in which he had participated against her would not be forgiven by her, there still remained in the mind of Harold Wynne a shadowy hope that she might yet be as other women, who, understanding much, forgive much.

He left her presence, feeling that she was no as other women are.

That was the only grain of comfort that remained with him. He loved her more than he had ever done before, because she was not as other women are.

She could not understand how that cold distrust had taken possession of him.

She knew nothing of that world in which he had lived all his life—a world quite full of worldliness—and therefore she could not understand how it was that he had sought to bind her to him beyond the possibility (as he meant her to think) of ever being separated from him. She had laid all her trust in him. She had not even claimed from him the privilege of consulting with someone—her father or someone with whom she might be on more confidential terms—regarding the proposition which he had made to her. No, she had trusted him implicitly, and yet he had persevered in regarding her as belonging to the worldly ones among whom he had lived all his life.

He had lost her.

He had lost her, and he deserved to lose her. This was his thought as he walked westward. He had not the satisfaction of feeling that he was badly treated.

The feeling on the part of a man that he has been badly treated by a woman, usually gives him much greater satisfaction than would result from his being extremely well treated by the same, or, indeed, by any other woman.

But this blessed consciousness of being badly treated was denied to Harold Wynne. He had been the ill-treater, not the ill-treated. He reflected how he had taken advantage of the peculiar circumstances of the girl's life—upon the absence of her father—upon her own trustful innocence—to carry out the fraud which he had perpetrated upon her. Under ordinary circumstances and with a girl of an ordinary stamp, such a fraud would have been impossible. He was well aware that a girl living under the conditions to which most girls are subjected, would have laughed in his face had he suggested the advisability of marrying him privately.

Yes, he had taken a cruel advantage of her and of the freedom which she enjoyed, to betray her; and the feeling that he had lost her did not cause him more bitterness than deserved to fall to his lot.

One bitterness of reflection was, however, spared to him, and this was why he cried again, as he threw himself into a chair, "Thank God—thank God!"

He had not been seated for long, before his servant entered with a card.

"I told the lady that you were not seeing any one, my lord," said Martin.

"The lady?"

Not for a single instant did it occur to his mind that Beatrice had come to him.

"Yes, my lord; Miss Craven," said Martin, handing him the card. "But she said that perhaps you would see her."

"*Only for a minute*," were the words written in pencil on Miss Craven's card.

"Yes, I will certainly see Miss Craven," said Harold.

"Very good, my lord."

She stood at the door. The light outside was very low; so was the light in the room.

Between two dim lights was where Helen looked her best. A fact of which she was well aware.

She seemed almost pretty as she stood there.

She had made up pale, which she considered appropriately sympathetic on her part. And, indeed, there can scarcely be a difference of opinion on this point.

In delicate matters of taste like this she rarely-made a mistake.

"It was so good of you to come," said he, taking her hand.

"I could not help it, Harold," said she.

"Mamma is in the brougham; she desired me to convey to you her deepest sympathy."

"I am indeed touched by her thoughtfulness," said Harold. "You will tell her so."

"Mamma is not very strong," said Helen. "She would not come in with me. She, too, has suffered deeply. But I felt that I must tell you face to face how terribly shocked we were—how I feel for you with all my heart. We have always been good friends—the best of friends, Harold—at least, I do not know where I should look in the world for another such friend as you."

"Yes, we were always good friends, Helen," said he; "and I hope that we shall always remain so."

"We shall—I feel that we shall, Harold," said she.

Her eyes were overflowing with tears, as she put out a hand to him—a hand which he took and held between both his own, but without speaking a word. "I felt that I must go to you if only for a moment—if only to say to you as I do now, 'I feel for you with all my heart. You have all my sympathy.'

That is all I have to say. I knew you would allow me to see you, and to give you my message. Good-bye."

"You are so good—so kind—so thoughtful," said he. "I shall always feel that you are my friend—my best friend, Helen."

"And you may always trust in my friendship—my—my—friendship," said she. "You will come and see us soon—mamma and me. We should be so glad. Lady Innisfail wanted me to go with her to Netherford Hall—several of your sister's party are going with Lady Innisfail; but of course I could not think of going. I shall go nowhere for some time—a long time, I think. We shall be at home whenever you call, Harold."

"And you may be certain that I shall call soon," said he. "Pray tell Mrs. Craven how deeply touched—how deeply grateful I am for her kindness. And you—you know that I shall never forget your thoughtfulness, Helen."

Her eyes were still glistening as he took her hand and pressed it. She looked at him through her tears; her lips moved, but no words came. She turned and went down the stairs. He followed her for a few steps, and then Martin met her, opened the hall-door, and saw her put into the brougham by her footman.

"Well," said her mother, when the brougham got upon the wood pavement. "Well, did you find the poor orphan in tears and comfort him?" Mrs. Craven was not devoid of an appreciation of humour of a certain form. She had lived in Birmingham for several years of her life.

"Dear mamma," said Helen, "I think you may always trust to me to know what is right to do upon all occasions. My visit was a success. I knew that it would be a success. I know Harold Wynne."

"I know one thing," said Mrs. Craven, "and that is, that he will never marry you. Whatever Harold Wynne might have done, Lord Fotheringay will never marry you, my dear. Make up your mind to that."

Her daughter laughed in the way that a daughter laughs at a prophetic mother clad in sables, with a suspicion of black velvet and beads underneath.

CHAPTER LI
ON THE WAYS OF PROVIDENCE AND OTHERS

DURING the next few days Harold had numerous visitors. A man cannot have his father murdered without attracting a considerable amount of attention to himself. Cards *"With deepest sympathy"* were left upon him by the hundred, and the majority of those sympathizers drove away to say to their friends at their clubs what a benefactor to society was the person who had run that knife into the ribs of Lord Fotheringay. Some suggested that a presentation should be got up for that man; and when someone asked what the police meant by taking so much trouble to find the man, another ventured to formulate the very plausible theory that they were doing so in order to force him to give sittings to an eminent sculptor for a statue of himself with the knife in his hand, to be erected by public subscription outside the House of Lords.

"Yes; *pour encourager les autres!*" said one of the sympathizers.

Another of the sympathizers inquired where were the Atheists now?

It was generally admitted that, as an incentive to orthodoxy, the tragic end of Lord Fotheringay could scarcely be over-estimated.

It threw a flood of light upon the Ways of Providence.

The Scotland Yard people at first regarded the incident from such a standpoint.

They assumed that Providence had decreed a violent death to Lord Fotheringay, in order to give the detective force an opportunity of displaying their ingenuity.

They had many interviews with Harold, and they asked him a number of questions regarding the life of his father, his associates, and his tastes.

They wondered if he had an enemy.

They feared that the deed was the work of an enemy; and they started the daring theory that if they only had a clue to this supposititious enemy they would be on the track of the assassin.

After about a week of suchlike theorizing, they were not quite so sure of Providence.

Some newspapers interested in the Ways of Providence, declared through the medium of leading articles, that Lord Fotheringay had been murdered in order that the world might be made aware of the utter incapacity of Scotland Yard, and the necessity for the reorganization of the detective force.

Other newspapers—they were mostly the organs of the Opposition—sneered at the Home Secretary.

Mr. Durdan was heard to affirm in the solitude of the smoking-room of his club, that the days of the Government were numbered.

Then Harold had also to receive daily visits from the family lawyers; and as family lawyers take more interest in the affairs of the family than any of its members, he found these visits very tiresome; only he was determined to find out what was his exact position financially, and to do so involved the examination of the contents of several tin boxes, as well as the columns of some bank books. On the whole, however, the result of his researches under the guidance of the lawyers was worth the trouble that they entailed.

He found that he would be compelled to live on an income of twelve thousand pounds a year, if he really wished—as he said he did—to make provision for the paying off of certain incumbrances, and of keeping in repair a certain mansion on the borders of a Welsh county.

Having lived for several years upon an allowance of something under twelve hundred pounds a year, he felt that he could manage to subsist on twelve thousand. This was the thought that came to him automatically, so soon as he had discovered his financial position. His next thought was that, by his own folly, he had rendered himself incapable of enjoying this sudden increase in revenue.

If he had only been patient—if he had only been trustful for one week longer!

He felt very bitterly on the subject of his folly—his cruelty—his fraud; the fact being that he entertained some preposterous theory of individual responsibility.

He had never had inculcated on him the principles of heredity, otherwise he would have understood fully that he could no more have avoided carrying out a plan of deception upon a woman, than the pointer puppy—where would the Evolutionists be without their pointer puppy?—can avoid pointing.

Whether the adoption of the scientific explanation of what he had done would have alleviated his bitterness or not, is quite another question. The philosophy that accounts for suffering does not go the length of relieving suffering. The science that gives the gout a name that few persons can pronounce, does not prevent an ordinary gouty subject from swearing; which seems rather a pity.

Among the visitors whom Harold saw in these days was Edmund Airey. Mr. Airey did not think it necessary to go through the form of expressing his sympathy for his friend's bereavement. His only allusion to the bereavement was to be found in a sneer at Scotland Yard.

Could he do anything for Harold, he wondered. If he could do anything, Harold might depend on his doing it.

Harold said, "Thank you, old chap, I don't think I can reasonably ask you to work out for me, in tabulated form, the net value of leases that have yet to run from ten to sixty years."

"Therein the patient must minister to himself," said Edmund. "I suppose it is, after all, only a question of administration. If you want any advice— well, you have asked my advice before now. You have even gone the length of taking my advice—yes, sometimes. That's more than the majority of people do—unless my advice bears out their own views. Advice, my dear Harold, is the opinion asked by one man of another when he has made up his mind what course to adopt."

"I have always found your counsel good," said Harold. "You know men and their motives. I have often wondered if you knew anything about women."

Mr. Airey smiled. It was rather ridiculous that anyone so well acquainted with him as Harold was, should make use of a phrase that suggested a doubt of his capacity.

"Women—and their motives?" said he.

"Quite so," said Harold. "Their motives. You once assured me that there was no such thing as woman in the abstract. Perhaps, assuming that that is your standpoint, you may say that it is ridiculous to talk of the motives of woman; though it would be reasonable—at least as reasonable as most talk of women—to speak of the motives of a woman."

"What woman do you speak of?" said Edmund, quickly.

"I speak as a fool—broadly," said Harold. "I feel myself to be a fool, when I reflect upon the wisdom of those stories told to us by Brian the boatman. The first was about a man who defrauded the revenue of the country, the other was about a cow that got jammed in the doorway of an Irish cabin. There was some practical philosophy in both those stories, and they put all questions of women and their motives out of our heads while Brian was telling them."

"There's no doubt about that," said Edmund.

"By the way, didn't you ask me for my advice on some point during one of those days on the Irish lough?"

"If I did, I'm certain that I received good counsel from you," said Harold.

"You did. But you didn't take it," said Edmund, with a laugh.

"I told you once that you hadn't given me time. I tell you so again," said Harold.

"Has she been to see you within the past few days? asked Edmund.

"You understand women—and their motives," said Harold. "Yes, Miss Craven was here. By the way, talking of motives, I have often wondered why you suggested to my sister that Miss Avon would make an agreeable addition to the party at Abbeylands."

Not for a second did Edmund Airey change colour—not for a second did his eyes fall before the searching glance of his friend.

"The fact was," said he—and he smiled as he spoke—"I was under the impression that your father—ah, well, if he hadn't that mechanical rectitude of movement which appertains chiefly to the walking doll and other automata, he had still many good points. He told me upon one occasion that it was his intention to marry Miss Avon. I was amused."

"And you wanted to be amused again? I see. I think that I, too, am beginning to understand something of men—and their motives," remarked Harold.

"If you make any progress in that direction, you might try and fathom the object of the Opposition in getting up this agitation about Siberia. They are going to arouse the country by descriptions of the horrors of exile in Siberia. They want to make the Government responsible for what goes on there. And the worst of it is that they'll do it, too. Do you remember Bulgaria?"

"Perfectly. The country is a fool. The Government will need a strong programme to counteract the effects of the Siberian platform."

"I'm trying to think out something at the present moment. Well, good-bye. Don't fail to let me know if I can do anything for you."

He had been gone some time before Harold smiled—not the smile of a man who has been amused at something that has come under his notice, but the sad smile of a man who has found that his sagacity has not been at fault when he has thought the worst about one of his friends.

There are times when a certain imperturbability of demeanour on the part of a man who has been asked a sudden searching question, conveys as much to the questioner as his complete collapse would do. The perfect composure with which Edmund had replied to his sudden question regarding his motive in suggesting to Mrs. Lampson—with infinite tact— that Beatrice Avon might be invited to Abbeylands, told Harold all that he had an interest to know.

Edmund Airey's acquaintance with men—and women—had led him to feel sure that Mrs. Lamp-son would tell her brother of the suggestion made by him, Edmund; and also that her brother would ask him if he had any particular reason for making that suggestion. This was perfectly plain to Harold; and he knew that his friend had been walking about for some time with that answer ready for the question which had just been put to him.

"He is on his way to Beatrice at the present moment," said Harold, while that bitter smile was still upon his features.

And he was right.

CHAPTER LII
ON THE FLUSH, THE FOOL, AND FATE

MR. AIREY had called on Beatrice since his return from that melancholy entertainment at Abbeylands, but he had not been fortunate enough to find her at home. Now, however, he was more lucky. She had already two visitors with her in the big drawing-room, when Mr. Airey was announced.

He could not fail to notice the little flush upon her face as he entered. He noticed it, and it was extremely gratifying to him to do so; only he hoped that her visitors were not such close observers as he knew himself to be. He would not have liked them—whoever they were—-to leave the house with the impression that he was a lover. If they were close observers and inclined to gossip, they might, he felt, consider themselves justified in putting so liberal an interpretation upon her quick flush as he entered.

He did not blush: he had been a Member of Parliament for several years.

Yes, she was clearly pleased to see him, and her manifestation of pleasure made him assured that he had never seen a lovelier girl. It was so good of him not to forget her, she declared. He feared that her flush would increase, and suggest the peony rather than the peach. But he quickly perceived that she had recovered from the excitement of his sudden appearance, and that, as a matter of fact, she was becoming pale rather than roseate.

He noticed this when her visitors—they were feeble folk, the head of a department in the Museum and his sister—had left the house.

"It is delightful to be face to face with you once more," he said. "I seem to hear the organ-music of the Atlantic now that I am beside you again."

She gave a little laugh—did he detect something of scorn in its ring?—as she said, "Oh, no; it is the sound of the greater ocean that we have about us here. It is the tide of the affairs of men that flows around us."

No, her laugh could have had nothing of scorn about it.

"I cannot think of you as borne about on this full tide," said he. "I see you with your feet among the purple heather—I wonder if there was a sprig of white about it—along the shores of the Irish lough. I see you in the midst of a flood of sunset-light flowing from the west, making the green one red."

She saw that sunset. He was describing the sunset that had been witnessed from the deck of the yacht returning from the seal-hunt beyond the headlands. Did he know why she got up suddenly from her seat and pretended to snuff one of the candles on the mantelshelf? Did he know how close the tears were to her eyes as she gave another little laugh?

"So long as you do not associate me with Mr. Durdan's views on the Irish question, I shall be quite satisfied," said she. "Poor Mr. Durdan! How he saw a bearing upon the Irish question in all the phenomena of Nature! The sunset—the sea—the clouds—all had more or less to do with the Irish question."

"And he was not altogether wrong," said Edmund. "Mr. Durdan is a man of scrupulous inaccuracy, as a rule, but he sometimes stumbles across a truth. The sea and sky are eternal, and the Irish question——"

"Is the rock upon which the Government is to be wrecked, I believe," said she. "Oh, yes; Mr. Durdan confided in me that the days of the Government are numbered."

"He became confidential on that topic to a considerable number of persons," said Edmund.

"And we are confidential on Mr. Durdan as a topic," said she.

"We have talked confidentially on more profitable topics, have we not?" said he.

"We have talked confidently at least."

"And confidingly, I hope. I told you all my aspirations, Miss Avon."

"All?"

"Well, perhaps, I made some reservations."

"Oh."

"Perhaps I shall tell you confidentially of some other aspirations of mine—some day."

He spoke slowly and with an emphasis and suggestiveness that could not be overlooked.

"And you will speak confidently on that subject, I am sure."

She was lying back in her chair, with the firelight fluttering over her. The firelight was flinging rose leaves about her face.

That was what the effect suggested to him.

He noticed also how beautiful was the effect of the light shining through her hair. That was an effect which had been noticed before.

She turned her eyes suddenly upon him, when he did not reply to her word, "confidently."

He repeated the word.

"Confidently—confidently;" then he shook his head. "Alas! no. A man who speaks confidently on the subject of his aspirations—on the subject of a supreme aspiration—is a fool."

"And yet I remember that you assured me upon one occasion that man was master of his fate," said she.

"Did I?" said he. "That must have been when you first appeared among us at Castle Innisfail. I have learned a great deal since then."

"For example?" said she.

"Modesty in making broad statements where Fate is concerned," he replied, with scarcely a pause.

She withdrew her eyes from his face, and gave a third laugh, closely resembling in its tone her first—that one which caused him to wonder if there was a touch of scorn in its ripple.

He looked at her very narrowly. She was certainly the loveliest thing that he had ever seen. Could it be possible that she was leading him on?

She had certainly never left herself open to the suspicion of leading him on when at Castle Innis-fail—among the purple heather or the crimson sunsets about which he had been talking—and yet he had been led on. He had a suspicion now that he was in peril. He had so fine an understanding of woman and her motives, that he became apprehensive of the slightest change. He was, in respect of woman, what a thermometer is when aboard a ship that is approaching an iceberg. He was appreciative of every change—of every motive.

"I was looking forward to another pleasant week near you," said he, and his remark somehow seemed to have a connection with what he had been saying—had he not been announcing an acquirement of modesty?—"Yes, if you had been with us at Abbeylands you might have become associated in my mind with the glory of the colour of an autumn woodland. But it was, of course, fortunate for you that you got the terrible news in time to prevent your leaving town."

He felt that she had become suddenly excited. There was no ignoring the rising and falling of the lace points that lay upon the bosom of her gown. The question was: did her excitement proceed from what he had said, or from what she fancied he was about to say?

It was a nice question.

But he bore out his statement regarding his gain in modesty, by assuming that she had been deeply affected by the story of the tragic end of Lord Fotheringay, so that she could not now hear a reference to it without emotion.

"I wonder if you care for German Opera," said he. There could scarcely be even the most subtle connection between this and his last remark. She looked at him with something like surprise in her eyes when he had spoken. Only to some minds does a connection between criminality and German Opera become apparent.

"German Opera, Mr. Airey?"

"Yes. The fact is that I have a box for the winter season at the Opera House, and my cousin, Mrs. Carroll, means to go to every performance, I believe; she is an enthusiast on the subject of German Opera—she has even sat out a performance of 'Parsifal'—and I know that she is eager to make converts. She would be delighted to call upon you when she returns from Brighton."

"It is so kind of you to think of me. I should love to go. You will be there—I mean, you will be able to come also, occasionally?"

He looked at her. He had risen from his seat, being about to take leave of her. She had also risen, but her eyes drooped as she exclaimed, "You will be there?"

She did not fail to perceive the compromising sequence of her phrases, "I should love to go. You will be there?" She was looking critically at the toe of her shoe, turning it about so that she could make a thorough examination of it from every standpoint. Her hands, too, were busy tying knots on the girdle of her gown.

He felt that it would be cruel to let her see too plainly that he was conscious of that undue frankness of hers; so he broke the awkward silence by saying—not quite casually, of course, but still in not too pointed a way, "Yes, I shall be there, occasionally. Not that my devotion will be for German Opera, however." The words were well chosen, he felt. They were spoken as the legitimate sequence to those words that she had uttered in that girlish enthusiasm, which was so charming. Only, of course, being a man, he could choose his words. They were artificial—the result of a choice; whereas it was plain that she could not choose but utter the phrases that had come from her. She was a girl, and so spoke impulsively and from her heart.

"Meantime," said she—she had now herself almost under control again, and was looking at him with a smile upon her face as she put out her hand to meet his. "Meantime, you will come again to see me? My father is greatly occupied with his history, otherwise he also would, I know, be very pleased to see you."

"I hope that you will be pleased," said he. "If so, I will call— occasionally—frequently."

"Frequently," said she, and once again—but only for a moment this time—she scrutinized her foot.

"Frequently," said he, in a low tone. Being a man he could choose his tones as well as his words.

He went away with a deep satisfaction dwelling within him—the satisfaction of the clever man who feels that he has not only spoken cleverly, but acted cleverly—which is quite a different thing.

Later on he felt that he need not have been in such a hurry calling upon her. He had gone to her directly after visiting Harold. He had been under the impression that he would do well to see her and make his proposal to her regarding the German Opera season without delay. The moment that he had heard of Lord Fotheringay's death, it had occurred to him that he would do well to lose no time in paying her a visit. After due consideration, he had thought it advisable to call upon Harold in the first instance. He had done so, and the result of his call was to make him feel that he should not any longer delay his visit to Beatrice.

Now, as has been said, he felt that he need not have been in such a hurry.

"*I should love to go—you will be there.*"

Yes, those were the words that had sprung from her heart. The sequence of the phrases had not been the result of art or thought.

He had clearly under-estimated the effect of his own personality upon an impressionable girl who had a great historian for a father. The days that he had passed by her side—carrying out the compact which he had made with Helen Craven—had produced an impression upon her far more powerful than he had believed it possible to produce within so short a space of time.

In short, she was his.

That is what he felt within an hour of parting from her; and all his resources of modesty and humility were unequal to the task of changing his views on this point.

Was he in love with her?

He believed her to be the most beautiful woman whom he had ever seen.

CHAPTER LIII
ON A SUPREME ASPIRATION

IT was commonly reported that Mr. Durdan had stated with some degree of publicity that the days of the Government were numbered.

There were a good many persons who were ready to agree with him before the month of December had passed; for the agitation on the subject of Siberia was spreading through the length and breadth of the land. The active and observant Leader of the Opposition knew the people of England, Scotland, and perhaps—so far as they allowed themselves to be understood—of Wales, thoroughly. Of course Ireland was out of the question altogether.

Knowing the people so well, he only waited for a sharp frost to open his campaign. He was well aware that it would be ridiculous to commence an agitation on the subject of Siberia unless in a sharp frost. To try to move the constituencies while the water-pipes in their dwellings remained intact, would be a waste of time. It is when his pipes are burst that the British householder will join in any agitation that may be started. The British farmer invariably turns out the Government after a bad harvest; and there can be but little doubt that a succession of wet summers would make England republican.

It was because all the water-pipes in England were burst, that the atrocities in Bulgaria stirred the great sympathetic heart of this England of ours, and the strongest Government that had existed for years became the most unpopular. A strong Government may survive a year of great commercial depression; but the strongest totters after a wet summer, and none has ever been known to survive a frost that bursts the household water-pipes.

The campaign commenced when the thermometer fell to thirty-two degrees Fahrenheit. That was the time to be up and doing. In every quarter the agitation made itself felt.

"The sympathetic pulse of the nation was not yet stilled," we were told. "Six years of inefficient Government had failed to crush down the manhood of England," we were assured. "The Heart was still there—it was beating still; and wherever the Heart of an Englishman beats there was found a foe—a determined, resolute foe—nay, an irresistible foe, to tyranny, and what tyranny had the world ever known that was equal to that which sent thousands and tens of thousands of noble men and women—women—women—to a living death among the snows of Siberia? Could any one present form an idea of the horrors of a Siberian winter?" (Cries of "Yes, yes," from householders whose water-pipes had burst.) "Well, in the name of our common humanity—in the name of our common sympathies—in the name of England (cheers)—England, mind you, with her fleet, that in spite of six years of gross mismanagement on the part of the Government, was still the mistress of the main—(loud cheers) England, mind you, whose armies had survived the shocking incapacity of a Government that had refused a seven-hours day to the artisans at Woolwich and Aldershot—(tremendous cheers) in the name of this grand old England of ours let those who were responsible for Siberia—that blot upon the map of Europe"—(the agitator is superior to geography)—"let them be told that their day is over. Let the Government that can look with callous eyes upon such horrors as are enacted among the frosts and snows of Siberia be told that its day is over (cheers). Did anyone wish to know something of these horrors?" ('Yes, yes!') "Well, here was a book written by a correspondent to a New York journal, and which, consequently, was entitled to every respect".... and so forth.

That was the way the opponents of the Government talked at every meeting. And in the course of a short time they had successfully mixed up the labour question, the army and navy retrenchment question, the agricultural question, and several other questions, with the stories of Siberian horrors, and the aggregate of evil was laid to the charge of the Government.

The friends of the Government were at their wits' end to know how to reply to this agitation. Some foolish ones endeavoured to make out that England was not responsible for what was done in Siberia. But this sophistry was too shallow for the people whose water-pipes were burst, and those who were responsible for it were hooted on every platform.

It was at this critical time that the Prime Minister announced at a Dinner at which he was entertained, that, while the Government was fully sensible of the claims of Siberia, he felt certain that he was only carrying out the desire of the people of England, in postponing consideration of this vast question until a still greater question had been settled. After long and careful deliberation, Her Majesty's Ministers had resolved to submit to the country a programme the first item of which was the Conversion of the Jews.

The building where this announcement was made rang with cheers. The friends of the Government no longer looked gloomy. In a few days they knew that the Nonconformist Conscience would be awake, and as a political factor, the Nonconformist Conscience cannot be ignored. A Government that had for its policy the Conversion of the Jews would be supported by England—this great Christian England of ours.

"My Lords and Gentlemen," said the Prime Minister, "the contest on which we are about to enter is very limited in its range. It is a contest of England and Religion against the Continent and Atheism. My Lords and Gentlemen, come what may, Her Majesty's Ministers will be on the side of Religion."

It was felt that this timely utterance had saved the Government.

It was not to be expected that, when these tremendous issues were broadening out, Mr. Edmund Airey should have much time at his disposal for making afternoon calls; still he managed to visit Beatrice Avon pretty frequently—much more frequently than he had ever visited anyone in all his life. The season of German Opera was a brilliant one, and upon several occasions Beatrice appeared in Mr. Airey's box by the side of the enthusiastic lady, who was pointed out in society as having remained in her stall from the beginning to the end of "Parsifal." Mr. Airey never missed a performance at which Beatrice was present. He missed all the others.

Only once did he venture to introduce Harold's name in her drawing-room. He mentioned having seen him casually in the street, and then he watched her narrowly as he said, "By the way, I have never come upon him here. Does he not call upon you?"

There was only a little brightening of her eyes—was it scorn?—as she replied: "Is it not natural that Lord Fotheringay should be a very different person from Mr. Harold Wynne? Oh, no, he never calls now."

"I have heard several people say that they had found him greatly changed, poor fellow!" said Edmund.

"Greatly changed—not ill?" she said.

He wondered if the tone in which she spoke suggested anxiety—or was it merely womanly curiosity?

"Oh, no; he seems all right; but it is clear that his father's death and the circumstances attending it affected him deeply."

"It gave him a title at any rate."

The suspicion of scorn was once more about her voice. Its tone no longer suggested anxiety for the health of Lord Fotheringay.

"You are too hard on him, Beatrice," said Edmund. She had come to be Beatrice to him for more than a week—a week in which he had been twice in her drawing-room, and in which she had been twice in his opera box.

"Too hard on him?" said she. "How is it possible for you to judge what is hard or the opposite on such a point?"

"I have always liked Harold," said he; "that is why I must stand up for him."

"Ah, that is your own kindness of heart," said she. "I remember how you used to stand up for him at Castle Innisfail. I remember that when you told me how wretchedly poor he was, you were very bitter against the destiny that made so good a fellow poor, while so many others, not nearly so good, were wealthy."

"I believe I did say something like that. At any rate I felt that. Oh, yes, I always felt that I must stand up for him; so even now I insist on your not being too hard on him."

He laughed, and so did she—yes, after a little pause.

"Come again—soon," she said, as she gave him her hand, which he retained for some moments while he looked into her eyes—they were more than usually lustrous—and said,

"Oh, yes, I will come again soon. Don't you remember what I said to you in this room—it seems long ago, we have come to be such close friends since—what I said about my aspirations—my supreme aspiration?"

"I remember it," said she—her voice was very low.

"I have still to reveal it to you, Beatrice," said he.

Then he dropped her hand and was gone.

He made another call the same afternoon. He drove westward to the residence of Helen Craven and her mother, and in the drawing-room he found about a dozen people drinking tea, for Mrs. Craven had a large circle.

It took him some time to get beside Helen; but a very small amount of manoeuvring on her part was sufficient to secure comparative privacy for him and herself in a dimly-lighted part of the great room—an alcove that made a moderately valid excuse for a Moorish arch and hangings.

"The advice that I gave to you was good," said he.

"Your advice was that I should make no move whatever," said she. "That could not be hard advice to take, if he were disposed to make any move in my direction. But, as I told you, he only called once, and then we were out. Have you learned anything?"

"I have learned that whomsoever she marries, she will never marry Harold Wynne," said Edmund.

"Great heavens! You have found this out? Are you certain? Men are so apt to rush at conclusions."

"Yes; some men are. I have always preferred the crawling process, though it is the slower."

"That is a confession—crawling! But how have you found out that she will not marry him?"

"He has treated her very badly."

"That has got nothing whatever to do with the question. Heavens! If women declined to marry the men that treat them badly, the statistics of spinsterhood would be far more alarming than they are at present."

"She will not marry him."

"Will she marry you?"

Miss Craven had sprung to her feet. She was in a nervous condition, and it was intensified by his irritating reiteration of the one statement.

"Will she marry you?" she cried, in a voice that had a strident ring about it. "Will she marry you?"

"I think it highly probable," said he.

She looked at him in silence for a long time.

"Let us return to the room," said she.

They went through the Moorish arch back to the drawing-room.

CHAPTER LIV
ON THE DECAY OF THE PAT AS A POWER

IT was a few days after Edmund Airey had made his revelation—if it was a revelation—to Helen Craven, that Harold received a visitor in the person of Archie Brown. The second week in January had now come. The season of German Opera was over, and Parliament was about to assemble; but neither of these matters was engrossing the attention of Archie. That he was in a state of excitement anyone could see, and before he had even asked after Harold's health, he cried, "I've fired out the lot of them, Harry; that's the sort of new potatoes I am."

"The lot of what?" asked Harold.

"Don't you know? Why, the lot of Legitimists," said Archie.

"The Legitimists? My dear Archie, you don't surely expect me to believe that you possess sufficient political power to influence the fortunes of a French dynasty."

"French dynasty be grilled. I said the Legitimists—the actors, the carpenters, the gasmen, the firemen, the check-takers, Shakespeare, and Mrs. Mowbray of the Legitimate Theatre. I've fired out the lot of them, and be hanged to them!"

"Oh, I see; you've fired out Shakespeare?"

"He's eternally fired out, so far as I'm concerned. Why should I end my days in a workhouse because a chap wrote plays a couple of hundred years ago—may be more?"

"Why, indeed? And so you fired him out?"

"I've made things hum at the Legitimate this morning"—Archie had once spent three months in the United States—"and now I've made the lot of them git. I've made W. S. git."

"And Mrs. Mowbray?"

"She gits too."

"She'll do it gracefully. Archie, my man, you're not wanting in courage."

"What courage was there needed for that?"—Archie had picked up a quill pen and was trying, but with indifferent success, to balance it on the toe of his boot, as he leant back in a chair. "What courage is needed to tell a chap that's got hold of your watch chain that the time has come for him to drop it? Great Godfrey! wasn't I the master of the lot of them? Do you fancy that the manager was my master? Do you fancy that Mrs. Mowbray was my—I mean, do you think that I'm quite an ass?"

"Well, no," said Harold—"not quite."

"Do you suppose that my good old dad had any Scruples about firing out a crowd of navvies when he found that they didn't pay? Not he. And do you suppose that I haven't inherited some of his good qualities?"

"And when does the Legitimate close its doors?"

"This day week. Those doors have been open too long already. Seventy-five pounds for the Widow's champagne for the Christmas week—think of that, Harry. Mrs. Mowbray's friends drink nothing but Clicquot. She expects me to pay for her entertainments, and calls it Shakespeare. If you grabbed a chap picking your pocket, and he explained to the tarty chips at Bow Street that his initials were W. S. would he get off? Don't you believe it, Harry."

"Nothing shall induce me."

"The manager's only claim to have earned his salary is that he has been at every theatre in London, and has so got the biggest list of people to send orders to, so as to fill the house nightly. It seems that the most valuable manager is the one who has the longest list of people who will accept orders. That's theatrical enterprise nowadays. They say it's the bicycle that has brought it about."

"Anyhow you've quarrelled with Mrs. Mowbray? Give me your hand; Archie. You're a man."

"Quarrelled with Mrs. Mowbray? It was about time. She went to pat my head again to-day, when there was a buzz in the manager's office. She didn't pat my head, Harry—the day is past for pats, and so I told her. The day is past when she could butter me with her pats. She gave me a look when I said that—if she could give such looks on the stage she'd crowd the house—and then she cried, 'Nothing on earth shall induce me ever to speak to you again.' 'I ask nothing better,' said I. After that she skipped. I promised Norah that I'd do it, and I have done it."

"You promised whom?"

"Norah. Great Godfrey! you don't mean to say that you haven't heard that Norah Innisfail and I are to be married?"

"Norah—Innisfail—and—you—you?"

Harold lay back in his chair and laughed. The idea of the straightlaced Miss Innisfail marrying Archie Brown seemed very comical to him.

"What are you laughing about?" said Archie. "You shouldn't laugh, considering that it was you that brought it about."

"I? I wish that I had no more to reproach myself with; but I can't for the life of me see how—"

"Didn't you get Mrs. Lampson to invite me to Abbeylands, and didn't I meet Norah there, bless her! At first, do you know, I fancied that I was getting fond of her mother?"

"Oh, yes; I can understand that," said Harold, who was fully acquainted with the systems which Lady Innisfail worked with such success.

"But, bless your heart! it was all motherly kindness on Lady Innisfail's part—so she explained when—ah—later on. Then I went with her to Lord Innisfail's place at Netherford and—well, there's no explaining these things. Norah is the girl for me! I've felt a better man for knowing her, Harry. It's not every girl that a chap can say that of—mostly the other way. Lord Innisfail heard something about the Legitimate business, and he said that it was about time I gave it up; I agreed with him, and I've given it up."

"Archie," said Harold, "you've done a good morning's work. I was going to advise you never to see Mrs. Mowbray again—never to grant her an interview—she's an edged tool—but after what you've done, I feel that it would be a great piece of presumption on my part to offer you any advice."

"Do you know what it is?" said Archie, in a low and very confidential voice: "I'm not quite so sure of her character as I used to be. I know you always stood up for her."

"I still believe that she never had more than one lover at a time," said Harold.

"Was that seventy-five pound's worth of the Widow swallowed by one lover in a week?" asked Archie. "Oh, I'm sick of the whole concern. Don't you mention Shakespeare to me again."

"I won't," said Harold. "But it strikes me that Shakespeare is like Madame Roland's Liberty."

"Whose Liberty?"

"Madame Roland's."

"Oh, she's a dressmaker of Bond Street, I suppose. They're all Madames there. I dare say I've got a bill from her to pay with the rest of them. Mrs. Mowbray has dealt with them all. Now I'm off. I thought I'd drop in and tell you all that happened, as you're accountable for my meeting Norah."

"You will give her my best regards and warmest congratulations," said Harold. "Accept the same yourself."

"You had a good time at their Irish place yourself, hadn't you?" said Archie. "How was it that you didn't fall in love with Norah when you were there? That's what has puzzled me. How is it that every tarty chip didn't want to marry her? Oh, I forgot that you—well, wasn't there a girl with lovely eyes in Ireland?"

"You have heard of Irish girls and their eyes," said Harold.

"She had wonderful gray eyes," said Archie. Harold became grave. "Oh, yes, Norah has a pair of eyes too, and she keeps them wide open. She told me a good deal about their party in Ireland. She took it for granted that you—"

"Archie," said Harold, "like a good chap don't you ever talk about that to me again."

"All right, I'll not," said Archie. "Only, you see, I thought that you wouldn't mind now, as everyone says that she's going to marry Airey, the M.P. for some place or other. I knew that you'd be glad to hear that I'd fired out the Legitimate."

"So I am—very glad."

Archie was off, having abandoned as futile his well-meant attempts to balance the quill on the toe first of one boot, then of the other.

He was off, and Harold was standing at the window, watching him gathering up his reins and sending his horses at a pretty fair pace into the square.

It had fallen—the blow had fallen. She was going to marry Edmund Airey.

Could he blame her?

He felt that he had treated her with a baseness that deserved the severest punishment—such punishment as was now in her power to inflict. She had trusted him with all her heart—all her soul. She had given herself up to him freely, and he had made her the victim of a fraud. That was how he had repaid her for her trustfulness.

He did not stir from the window for hours. He thought of her without any bitterness—all his bitterness was divided between the thoughts of his own cruelty and the thoughts of Edmund Airey's cleverness. He did not know which was the more contemptible; but the conclusion to which he came, after devoting some time to the consideration of the question of the relative contemptibility of the two, was that, on the whole, Edmund Airey's cleverness was the more abhorrent.

But Archie Brown, after leaving St. James's, drove with his customary rapidity to Connaught Square, to tell of his achievement to Norah.

Miss Innisfail, while fully recognizing the personal obligations of Archie to the Shakesperian drama, had agreed with her father that this devotion should not be an absorbing one. She had had a hint or two that it absorbed a good deal of money, and though she had been assured by Archie that no one could say a word against Mrs. Mowbray's character, yet, like Harold—perhaps even better than Harold—she knew that Mrs. Mowbray was an extremely well-dressed woman. She listened with interest to Archie's account of how he had accomplished that process of "firing out" in regard to the Legitimate artists; and when he had told her all, she could not help wondering if Mrs. Mowbray would be quite as well dressed in the future as she had been in the past.

Archie then went on to tell her how he had called upon Harold, and how Harold had congratulated him.

"You didn't forget to tell him that people are saying that Mr. Airey is going to marry Miss Avon?" said Norah.

"Have I ever forgotten to carry out one of your commissions?" he asked.

"Good gracious! You didn't suggest that you were commissioned by me to tell him that?"

"Not likely. That's not the sort of new potatoes I am. I was on the cautious side, and I didn't even mention the name of the girl." He did not think it necessary to say that the reason for his adoption of this prudent course was that he had forgotten the name of the girl. "No, but when I told him that Airey was going to marry her, he gave me a look."

"A look? What sort of a look?"

"I don't know. The sort of a look a chap would give to a surgeon who had just snipped off his leg. Poor old Harry looked a bit cut up. Then he turned to me and said as gravely as a parson—a bit graver than some parsons—that he'd feel obliged to me if I'd never mention her name again."

"But you hadn't mentioned her name, you said."

"Neither I had. He didn't mention it either. I can only give you an idea of what he said, I won't take my oath about the exact words. But I'll take my oath that he was more knocked down than any chap I ever came across."

"I knew it," said Norah. "He's in love with her still. Mamma says he's not; but I know perfectly well that he is. She doesn't care a scrap for Mr. Airey."

"How do you know that?"

"I know it."

"Oh."

CHAPTER LV
ON SHAKESPEARE AND ARCHIE BROWN

IT was early on the same afternoon that Beatrice Avon received intimation of a visitor—a lady, the butler said, who gave the name of Mrs. Mowbray.

"I do not know any Mrs. Mowbray, but, of course, I'll see her," was the reply that Beatrice gave to the inquiry if she were at home.

"Was it possible," she thought, "that her visitor was the Mrs. Mowbray whose portraits in the character of Cymbeline were in all the illustrated papers?"

Before Beatrice, under the impulse of this thought, had glanced at herself in a mirror—for a girl does not like to appear before a woman of the highest reputation (for beauty) with hair more awry than is consistent with tradition—her mind was set at rest. There may have been many Mrs. Mowbrays in London, but there was only one woman with such a figure, and such a face.

She looked at Beatrice with undisguised interest, but without speaking for some moments. Equally frank was the interest that was apparent on the face of Beatrice, as she went forward to meet and to greet her visitor.

She had heard that Mrs. Mowbray's set of sables had cost someone— perhaps even Mrs. Mowbray herself—seven hundred guineas.

"Thank you, I will not sit down," said Mrs. Mowbray. "I feel that I must apologize for this call."

"Oh, no," said Beatrice.

"Oh, yes; I should," said Mrs. Mowbray. "I will do better, however, for I will make my visit a short one. The fact is, Miss Avon, I have heard so much about you during the past few months from—from—several people, I could not help being interested in you—greatly interested indeed."

"That was very kind of you," said Beatrice, wondering what further revelation was coming.

"I was so interested in you that I felt I must call upon you. I used to know Lady Innisfail long ago."

"Was it Lady Innisfail who caused you to be interested in me?" asked Beatrice.

"Well, not exactly," said Mrs. Mowbray; "but it was some of Lady Innisfail's guests—some who were entertained at the Irish Castle. I used also to know Mrs. Lampson—Lord Fotheringay's daughter. How terrible the blow of his death must have been to her and her brother."

"I have not seen Mrs. Lampson since," said Beatrice, "but—"

"You have seen the present Lord Fotheringay? Will you let me say that I hope you have seen him—that you still see him? Do not think me a gossiping, prying old woman—I suppose I am old enough to be your mother—for expressing the hope that you will see him, Miss Avon. He is the best man on earth."

Beatrice had flushed the first moment that her visitor had alluded to Harold. Her flush had not decreased.

"I must decline to speak with you on the subject of Lord Fotheringay, Mrs. Mowbray," said Beatrice, somewhat unequally.

"Do not say that," said Mrs. Mowbray, in the most musical of pleading tones. "Do not say that. You would make me feel how very gross has been my effrontery in coming to you."

"No, no; please do not think that," cried Beatrice, yielding, as every human being could not but yield, to the lovely voice and the gracious manner of Mrs. Mowbray. What would be resented as a gross piece of insolence on the part of anyone else, seemed delicately gracious coming from Mrs. Mowbray. Her insolence was more acceptable than another woman's compliment. She knew to what extent she could draw upon her resources, both as regards men and women. It was only in the case of a young cub such as Archie that she now and again overrated her powers of fascination. She knew that she would never pat Archie's red head again.

"Yes, you will let me speak to you, or I shall feel that you regard my visit as an insolent intrusion."

Beatrice felt for the first time in her life that she could fully appreciate the fable of the Sirens. She felt herself hypnotized by that mellifluous voice—by the steady sympathetic gaze of the lovely eyes that were resting upon her face.

"He is so fond of you," Mrs. Mowbray went on. "There is no lover's quarrel that will not vanish if looked at straight in the face. Let me look at yours, my dear child, and I will show you how that demon of distrust can be exorcised." Beatrice had become pale. The word *distrust* had broken the spell of the Siren.

"Mrs. Mowbray," said she, "I must tell you again that on no consideration—on no pretence whatever shall I discuss Lord Fotheringay with you."

"Why not with me, my child?" said Mrs. Mowbray. "Because I distrust you—no I don't mean that. I only mean that—that you have given me no reason to trust you. Why have you come to me in this way, may I ask you? It is not possible that you came here on the suggestion of Lord Fotheringay."

"No; I only came to see what sort of girl it is that Mr. Airey is going to marry," said Mrs. Mowbray, with a wicked little smile.

Beatrice was no longer pale. She stood with clenched hands before Mrs. Mowbray, with her eyes fixed upon her face.

Then she took a step toward the bell rope. "One moment," said Mrs. Mowbray. "Do you expect to marry Edmund Airey?"

Beatrice turned, and looked again at her visitor. If the girl had been less feminine she would have gone on to the bell rope, and have pulled it gently. She did nothing of the sort. She gave a laugh, and said, "I shall marry him if I please."

She was feminine.

So was Mrs. Mowbray.

"Will you?" she said. "Do you fancy for a moment—are you so infatuated that you can actually fancy that I—I—Gwendoline Mowbray, will allow you—you—to take Edmund Airey away from me? Oh, the child is mad—mad!"

"Do you mean to tell me," said Beatrice, coming close to her, "that Edmund Airey is—is—a lover of yours?"

"Ah," said Mrs. Mowbray, smiling, "you do not live in our world, my child."

"No, I do not," said Beatrice. "I now see why you have come to me to-day."

"I told you why."

"Yes; you told me. Edmund Airey has been your lover."

"*Has been?* My child, it is only when I please that a lover of mine becomes associated with a past tense. I have not yet allowed Edmund Airey to associate with my 'have beens.' It was from him that I learned all about you. He alluded to you in his letters to me from Ireland merely as 'a gray eye or so.' You still mean to marry him?"

"I still mean to do what I please," said Beatrice. She had now reached the bell rope and she pulled it very gently.

"You are an extremely beautiful young person," said Mrs. Mowbray. "But you have not been able to keep close to you a man like Harold Wynne—a man with a perfect genius for fidelity. And yet you expect—"

Here the door was opened by the butler. Mrs. Mowbray allowed her sentence to dwindle away into the conventionalities of leave-taking with a stranger.

Beatrice found herself standing with flushed cheeks and throbbing heart at the door through which her visitor had passed.

It was somewhat remarkable that the most vivid impression which she retained of the rather exciting series of scenes in which she had participated, was that Mrs. Mowbray's sables were incomparably the finest that she had ever seen.

Mrs. Mowbray could scarcely have driven round the great square before the butler inquired if Miss Avon was at home to Miss Innisfail. In another minute Norah Innisfail was embracing her with the warmth of a true-hearted girl who comes to tell another of her engagement to marry an eligible man, or a handsome man, let him be eligible or otherwise.

"I want to be the first to give you the news, my dearest Beatrice," said Norah. "That is why I came alone. I know you have not heard the news."

"I hear no news, except about things that do not interest me in the least," said Beatrice.

"My news concerns myself," said Norah.

"Then it's sure to interest me," cried Beatrice.

"It's so funny! But yet it's very serious," said Norah. "The fact is that I'm going to marry Archie Brown."

"Archie Brown?" said Beatrice. "I hope he is the best man in the world— he should be, to deserve you, my dear Norah."

"I thought perhaps you might have known him," said Norah. "I find that there are a good many people still who do not know Archie Brown, in spite of the Legitimate Theatre and all that he has done for Shakespeare."

"The Legitimate Theatre. Is that where Mrs. Mowbray acts?"

"Only for another week. Oh, yes, Archie takes a great interest in Shakespeare. He meant the Legitimate Theatre to be a monument to the interest he takes in Shakespeare, and so it would have been, if the people had only attended properly, as they should have done. Archie is very much disappointed, of course; but he says, very rightly, that the Lord Chamberlain isn't nearly particular enough in the plays that he allows to be represented, and so the public have lost confidence in the theatres—they are never sure that something objectionable will not be played—and go to the Music Halls, which can always be trusted. Archie says he'll turn the Legitimate into a Music Hall—that is, if he can't sell the lease."

"Whether he does so or not, I congratulate you with all my heart, my dearest Norah."

"If you had come down to Abbeylands in time—before that awful thing happened—you would have met Archie. We met him there. Mamma took a great fancy to him at once, and I think that I must have done the same. At any rate I did when he came to stay with us. He's such a good fellow, with red hair—not the sort that the old Venetian painters liked, but another sort. Strictly speaking some of his features—his mouth, for instance—are too large, but if you look at him in one position, when he has his face turned away from you, he's quite—quite—ah—quite curious—almost nice. You'll like him, I know."

"I'm sure of it," said Beatrice.

"Yes; and he's such a friend of Harold Wynne's," continued the artful Norah. "Why, what's the matter with you, Beatrice? You are as pale—dearest Beatrice, you and I were always good friends. You know that I always liked Harold."

"Do not talk about him, Norah."

"Why should I not talk about him? Tell me that."

"He is gone—gone away."

"Not he. He's too wretched to go away anywhere. Archie was with him to-day, and when he heard that—well, the way some people are talking about you and Mr. Airey, he had not a word to throw to a dog—Archie told me so."

"Oh, do not talk of him, Norah."

"Why should I not?"

"Because—ah, because he's the only one worth talking about, and now he's gone from me, and I'll never see him again—never, never again!" Before she had come to the end of her sentence, Beatrice was lying sobbing on the unsympathetic cushion of the sofa—the same cushion that had absorbed her tears when she had told Harold to leave her.

"My dearest Beatrice," whispered Norah, kneeling beside her, with her face also down a spare corner of the cushion, "I have known how you were moping here alone. I've come to take you away. You'll come down with us to our place at Netherford. There's a lake with ice on it, and there's Archie, and many other pretty things. Oh, yes, you'll come, and we'll all be happy."

"Norah," cried Beatrice, starting up almost wildly, "Mr. Airey will be here in half an hour to ask me to marry him. He wrote to say that he would be here, and I know what he means." Mr. Airey did call in half an hour, and he found Beatrice—as he felt certain she should—waiting to receive him, wearing a frock that he admired, and lace that he approved of.

But in the meantime Beatrice and Norah had had a few words together beyond those just recorded.

CHAPTER LVI
ON THE BITTER CRY

EDMUND AIREY drank his cup of tea which Beatrice poured out for him, and while doing so, he told her of the progress that was being made by the agitation of the Opposition and the counter agitation of the Government. There was no disguising the fact that the country—like the fool that it was—had been caught by the bitter cry from Siberia. There was nothing like a bitter cry, Edmund said, for catching hold of the country. If any cry was only bitter enough it would succeed. Fortunately, however, the Government, in its appeal against the Atheism of the Continent, had also struck a chord that vibrated through the length and breadth of England and Scotland. The Government orators were nightly explaining that no really sincere national effort had ever been made to convert the Jews. To be sure, some endeavours had been made from time to time to effect this great object—in the days of Isaac of York the gridiron and forceps had been the auxiliaries of the Church to bring about the conversion of the Hebrew race; and, more recently, the potent agency of drawing-room meetings and a house-to-house collection had been resorted to; but the results had been disappointing. Statistics were forthcoming—nothing impresses the people of Great Britain more than a long array of figures, Edmund Airey explained—to show that, whereas, on any part of the West coast of Africa where rum was not prohibited, for one pound sterling 348 negroes could be converted—the rate was 0.01 where rum was prohibited—yet for a subscription of five pounds, one could only depend on 0.31 of the Jewish race—something less than half an adult Hebrew—being converted. The Government orators were asking how long so scandalous a condition of affairs was to be allowed to continue, and so forth.

Oh, yes, he explained, things were going on merrily. In three days Parliament would meet, and the Opposition had drafted their Amendment to the Address, "That in the opinion of this House no programme of legislation can be considered satisfactory that does not include a protest against the horrors daily enacted in Siberia."

If this Amendment were carried it would, of course, be equivalent to a Vote of Censure upon the Government, and the Ministers would be compelled to resign, Edmund explained to Beatrice.

She was very attentive, and when he had completed a clever account of the political machinery by which the operations of the Nonconformist Conscience are controlled, she said quietly, "My sympathies are certainly with Siberia. I hope you will vote for that Amendment."

He laughed in his superior way.

"That is so like a girl," said he. "You are carried away by your sympathies of the moment. You do not wait to reason out any question."

"I dare say you are right," said she, smiling. "Our conscience is not susceptible of those political influences to which you referred just now."

"'They are dangerous guides—the feelings'," said he, "at least from a standpoint of politics."

"But there are, thank God, other standpoints in the world from which humanity may be viewed," said she.

"There are," said he. "And I also join with you in saying, 'thank God!' Do you fancy that I am here to-day—that I have been here so frequently during the past two months, from a political motive, Beatrice?"

"I cannot tell," she replied. "Have you not just said that the feelings are dangerous guides?"

"They lead one into danger," said he. "There can be no doubt about that."

"Have you ever allowed them to lead you?" she asked, with another smile.

"Only once, and that is now," said he. "With you I have thrown away every guide but my feelings. A few months ago I could not have believed it possible that I should do so. But with God and Woman all things are possible. That is why I am here to-day to ask you if you think it possible that you could marry me."

She had risen to her feet, not by a sudden impulse, but slowly. She was not looking at him. Her eyes were fixed upon some imaginary point beyond him. She was plainly under the influence of some very strong feeling. A full minute had passed before she said, "You should not have come to me with that request, Mr. Airey.

"Why should I not? Do you think that I am here through any other impulse than that of my feelings?"

"How can I tell?" she said, and now she was looking at him. "How can I tell which you hold dearer—political advancement, or my love?"

"How can you doubt me for a moment, Beatrice?" he said reproachfully—almost mournfully. "Why am I waiting anxiously for your acceptance of my offer, if I do not hold your love more precious than all other considerations in the world?"

"Do you so hold it?"

"Indeed I do."

"Then I have told you that my sympathies are altogether with Siberia. Vote for the Amendment of the Opposition."

"What can you mean, Beatrice?"

"I mean that if you vote for the Amendment, you will have shown me that you are capable of rising above mere party considerations. I don't make this the price of my love, remember. I don't make any compact to marry you if you adopt the course that I suggest. I only say that you will have proved to me that your words are true—that you hold something higher than political expediency."

She looked at him.

He looked at her.

There was a long pause.

"You are unreasonable. I cannot do it," he said.

"Good-bye," said she.

He looked at the hand which she had thrust out to him, but he did not take it.

"You really mean me to vote against my party?" said he.

"What other way can you prove to me that you are superior to party considerations?" said she.

"It would mean self-effacement politically," said he. "Oh, you do not appreciate the gravity of the thing."

He turned abruptly away from her and strode across the room.

She remained silent where he had left her.

"I did not think you capable of so cruel a caprice as this," he continued, from the fireplace. "You do not understand the consequences of my voting against my party."

"Perhaps I do not," said she. "But I have given you to understand the consequences of not doing so."

"Then we must part," said he, approaching her. "Good-bye," said she, once more.

He took her hand this time. He held it for a moment irresolutely, then he dropped it.

"Are you really in earnest, Beatrice?" said he. "Do you really mean to put me to this test?"

"I never was more in earnest in my life," said she. "Think over the matter—let me entreat of you to think over it," he said, earnestly.

"And you will think over it also?"

"Yes, I will think over it. Oh, Beatrice, do not allow yourself to be carried away by this caprice. It is unworthy of you."

"Do not be too hard on me, I am only a woman," said she, very meekly.

She was only a woman. He felt that very strongly as he walked away.

And yet he had told Harold that he had great hope of Woman, by reason of her femininity.

And yet he had told Harold that he understood Woman and her motives.

"Papa," said Beatrice, from the door of the historian's study. "Papa, Mr. Edmund Airey has just been here to ask me to marry him."

"That's right, my dear," said the great historian. "Marry him, or anyone else you please, only run away and play with your dolls now. I'm very busy."

This was precisely the answer that Beatrice expected. It was precisely the answer that anyone might have expected from a man who permitted such a *ménage* as that which prevailed under his roof.

CHAPTER LVII
ON THE REJECTED ADDRESSES

THE next day Beatrice went with Norah Innisfail and her mother to their home in Nethershire. Two days afterwards the Legitimate Theatre closed its doors, and Parliament opened its doors. The Queen's Speech was read, and a member of the Opposition moved the Amendment relating to Siberia. The Debate on the Address began.

On the second night of the debate Edmund Airey called at the historian's house and, on asking for Miss Avon, learned that she was visiting Lady Innisfail in Nethershire. On the evening of the fourth day of the debate—the Division on the Amendment was to be taken that night—he drove in great haste to the same house, and learned that Miss Avon was still in Nethershire, but that she was expected home on the following day.

He partook of a hasty dinner at his club, and, writing out a telegram, gave it to a hall-porter to send to the nearest telegraph office.

The form was addressed to Miss Avon, in care of Lord Innisfail, Netherford Hall, Netherford, Nethershire, and it contained the following words, "*I will do it. Edmund.*"

He did it.

He made a brief speech amid the cheers of the Opposition and the howls of the Government party, acknowledging his deep sympathy with the unhappy wretches who were undergoing the unspeakable horrors of a Siberian exile, and thus, he said he felt compelled, on conscientious grounds (ironical cheers from the Government) to vote for the Amendment.

He went into the lobby with the Opposition.

It was an Irish member who yelled out "Judas!"

The Government was defeated by a majority of one vote, and there was a "scene" in the House.

Some time ago an enterprising person took up his abode in the midst of an African jungle, in order to study the methods by which baboons express themselves. He might have spared himself that trouble, if he had been present upon the occasion of a "scene" in the House of Commons. He would, from a commanding position in the Strangers' Gallery, have learned all that he had set his heart upon acquiring—and more.

It was while the "scene" was being enacted that Edmund Airey had put into his hand the telegraph form written out by himself in his club.

"*Telegraph Office at Netherford closes at 6 p.m.,*" were the words that the hall-porter had written on the back of the form.

The next day he drove to the historian's, and inquired if Miss Avon had returned.

She was in the drawing-room, the butler said.

With triumph—a sort of triumph—in his heart, and on his face, he ascended the staircase.

He thought that he had never before seen her look so beautiful. Surely there was triumph on her face as well! It was glowing, and her eyes were more lustrous even than usual. She had plainly just returned, for she had on a travelling dress.

"Beatrice, you saw the newspapers? You saw that I have done it?" he cried, exultantly.

"Done what?" she inquired. "I have seen no newspaper to-day."

"What? Is it possible that you have not heard that I voted last night for the Amendment?" he cried.

"I heard nothing," she replied.

"I wrote a telegram last evening, telling you that I meant to do it, but it appears that the office at Netherford closes at six, so it could not be sent. I did not know how much you were to me until yesterday, Beatrice."

"Stop," she said. "I was married to Harold Wynne an hour ago."

He looked at her for some moments, and then dropped into a chair.

"You have made a fool of me," he said.

"No," she said. "I could not do that. If I had got your telegram in time last evening I would have replied to it, telling you that, whatever step you took, it would not bring you any nearer to me. Harold Wynne, you see, came to me again. I had promised to marry him when we were together at that seal-hunt, but—well, something came between us."

"And you revenged yourself upon me? You made a fool of me!"

"If I had tried to do so, would it have been remarkable, Mr. Airey? Supposing that I had been made a fool of by the compact into which you entered with Miss Craven, who would have been to blame? Was there ever a more shameful compact entered into by a clever man and a clever woman to make a victim of a girl who believed that the world was overflowing with sincerity? I was made acquainted with the nature of that compact of yours, Mr. Airey, but I cannot say that I have yet learned what are the terms of your compact—or is it a contract?—with Mrs. Mowbray. Still, I know something. And yet you complain that I have made a fool of you."

He had completely recovered himself before she had got to the end of her little speech. He had wondered how on earth she had become acquainted with the terms of his compact with Helen. When, however, she referred to Mrs. Mowbray, he felt sure that it was Mrs. Mowbray who had betrayed him.

He was beginning to learn something of women and their motives.

"Nothing is likely to be gained by this sort of recrimination," said he, rising. "You have ruined my career."

She laughed, not bitterly but merrily, he knew all along that she had never fully appreciated the gravity of the step which she had compelled him—that was how he put it—to take. She had not even had the interest to glance at a newspaper to see how he had voted. But then she had not read the leading articles in the Government organs which were plentifully besprinkled with his name printed in small capitals. That was his one comforting thought.

She laughed.

"Oh, no, Mr. Airey," said she. "Your career is not ruined. Clever men are not so easily crushed, and you are a very clever man—so clever as to be able to make me clever, if that were possible."

"You have crushed me," he said. "Good-bye."

"If I wished to crush you I should have married you," said she. "No woman can crush a man unless she is married to him. Good-bye."

The butler opened the door. "Is my husband in yet?" she asked of the man.

"His lordship has not yet returned, my lady," said the butler, who had once lived in the best families—far removed from literature—and who was, consequently, able to roll off the titles with proper effect.

"Then you will not have an opportunity of seeing him, I'm afraid," she said, turning to Mr. Airey.

"I think I already said good-bye, Lady Fotheringay."

"I do believe that you did. If I did not, however, I say it now. Good-bye, Mr. Airey."

He got into a hansom and drove straight to Helen Craven's house. It was the most dismal drive he had ever had. He could almost fancy that the message boys in the streets were, in their accustomed high spirits, pointing to him with ridicule as the man who had turned his party out of office.

Helen Craven was in her boudoir. She liked receiving people in that apartment. She understood its lights.

He found that she had read the newspapers.

She stared at him as he entered, and gave him a limp hand.

"What on earth did you mean by voting—" she began.

"You may well ask," said he. "I was a fool. I was made a fool of by that girl. She made me vote against my party."

"And she refuses to marry you now?"

"She married Harold Wynne an hour ago."

Helen Craven did not fling herself about when she heard this piece of news. She only sat very rigid on her little sofa.

"Yes," resumed Edmund. "She is ill-treated by one man, but she marries him, and revenges herself upon another! Isn't that like a woman? She has ruined my career."

Then it was that Helen Craven burst into a long, loud, and very unmusical laugh—a laugh that had a suspicion of a shrill shriek about some of its tones. When she recovered, her eyes were full of the tears which that paroxysm of laughter had caused.

"You are a fool, indeed!" said she. "You are a fool if you cannot see that your career is just beginning. People are talking of you to-day as the Conscientious One—the One Man with a Conscience. Isn't the reputation for a Conscience the beginning of success in England?"

"Helen," he cried, "will you marry me? With our combined money we can make ourselves necessary to any party. Will you marry me?"

"I will," she said. "I will marry you with pleasure—now. I will marry anyone—now."

"Give me your hand, Helen," he cried. "We understand one another—that is enough to start with. And as for that other—oh, she is nothing but a woman after all!"

He never spoke truer words.

But sometimes when he is alone he thinks that she treated him badly.

Did she?